PHILIP JOSE FARMER

". . . has an imagination capable of being kindled by the ir-
redeemable mystery of the universe and of the soul, and in
turn able to kindle the imagination of others—readers who
for a couple of generations have been turning to science fiction to keep wonder and ecstasy alive. . . . It is the deepest
level of childhood response which Farmer has reached in
(the RIVERWORLD) novels. . . ."

Leslie A. Fielder
writing in *Los Angeles Times*

THE FABULOUS RIVERBOAT

PHILIP JOSÉ FARMER

A BERKLEY MEDALLION BOOK
PUBLISHED BY
BERKLEY PUBLISHING CORPORATION

For the unholy trinity of Bobs:
Bloch, Heinlein, and traurig—
may I meet them on
the banks of the River,
where we'll board the
fabulous Riverboat

"Resurrection, like politics, makes strange bedfellows," Sam Clemens said. "I can't say that the sleeping is very restful."

Telescope under one arm, he puffed on a long, green cigar while he paced back and forth on the poopdeck of the *Dreyrugr* (Bloodstained). Ari Grimolfsson, the helmsman, not understanding English, looked bleakly at Clemens. Clemens translated for him in wretched Old Norse. The helmsman still looked bleak.

Clemens loudly cursed him in English for a dunderheaded barbarian. For three years, Clemens had been practicing tenth-century Norse night and day. And he was still only half intelligible to most of the men and women aboard the *Dreyrugr*.

"A ninety-five-year-old Huck Finn, give or take a few thousand years," Clemens said, "I start out down The River on a raft. Now I'm on this idiot Viking ship, going upRiver. What next? When will I realize my dream?"

Keeping the upper part of his right arm close to his body so he would not drop the precious telescope, he pounded his right fist into his open left palm.

"*Iron!* I need iron! But where on this people-rich, metal-poor planet is iron? There has to be some! Otherwise, where did Erik's ax come from? And how much is there? Enough? Probably not. Probably there's just a very small meteorite. But maybe there's enough for what I want. But where? My God, The River may be twenty million miles long! The iron, if any, may be at the other end.

"No, that can't be! It has to be somewhere not too far away, within 100,000 miles of here. But we may be going in the wrong direction. Ignorance, the mother of hysteria, or is it vice versa?"

He looked through the telescope at the right bank and cursed again. Despite his pleas to bring the ship in so that he could scan the faces at a closer range, he had been refused. The king of the Norseman fleet, Erik Bloodaxe, said that this was hostile territory. Until the fleet was out of it, the fleet would stay close to the middle of The River.

The *Dreyrugr* was the flagship of three, all alike. It was eighty feet long, built largely of bamboo and resembled a Viking dragonboat. It had a long low hull, an oak figurehead carved into a dragon's head, and a curled-tail stern. But it also had a raised foredeck and poopdeck, the sides of both extending out over the water. The two bamboo masts were fore-and-aft rigged. The sails were a very thin but tough and flexible membrane made from the stomach of the deep-dwelling "riverdragon" fish. There was also a rudder controlled by a wheel on the poopdeck.

The round leather-and-oak shields of the crew hung over the sides; the great oars were piled on racks. The *Dreyrugr* was sailing against the wind, tacking back and forth, a maneuver unknown to the Norsemen when they had lived on Earth.

The men and women of the crew not handling the ropes sat on the oarsmen benches and talked and threw dice and played poker. From below the poopdeck came cries of exultation or curses and an occasional faint click. Bloodaxe and his bodyguard were shooting pool, and their doing so at this time made Clemens very nervous. Bloodaxe knew that enemy ships three miles up The River were putting out to intercept them, and ships from both banks behind them were putting out to trail them. Yet the king was pretending to be very cool. Maybe he was actually as undisturbed as Drake had supposedly been just before the battle of the Great Armada.

"But the conditions are different here," Clemens muttered. "There's not much room to maneuver on a river only a mile and a half wide. And no storm is going to help us out."

He swept the bank with the telescope as he had been doing ever since the fleet set out three years ago. He was of medium height and had a big head that made his none-too-broad shoulders look even more narrow. His eyes were blue; his eyebrows, shaggy; his nose, Roman. His

6

hair was long and reddish brown. His face was innocent of the mustache that had been so well known during his terrestrial life. (Men had been resurrected without face hair.) His chest was a sea of brown-red curly hair that lapped at the hollow of his throat. He wore only a knee-length white towel secured at the waist, a leather belt for holding weapons and the sheath for his telescope, and leather slippers. His skin was bronzed by the equatorial sun.

He removed the telescope from his eye to look at the enemy ships trailing by a mile. As he did so, he saw something flash in the sky. It was a curving sword of white, appearing suddenly as if unsheathed from the blue. It stabbed downward and then was gone behind the mountains.

Sam was startled. He had seen many small meteorites in the night sky but never a large one. Yet this daytime giant set his eyes afire and left an afterimage on his eyes for a second or two. Then the image faded, and Sam forgot about the falling star. He scanned the bank again with his telescope.

This part of The River had been typical. On each side of the mile-and-a-half-wide River was a mile-and-a-half-wide grass-grown plain. On each bank, huge mushroom-shaped stone structures, the grailstones, were spaced a mile apart. Trees were few on the plains, but the foothills were thick with pine, oak, yew and the irontree. This was a thousand-foot-high plant with gray bark, enormous elephant-ear leaves, hundreds of thick gnarly branches, roots so deep and wood so hard that the tree could not be cut, burned or dug out. Vines bearing large flowers of many bright colors grew over their branches.

There was a mile or two of foothills, and then the abruptness of smooth-sided mountains, towering from 20,000 to 30,000 feet, unscalable past the 10,000-foot mark.

The area through which the three Norse boats were sailing was inhabited largely by early nineteenth-century Germans. There was the usual ten percent population from another place and time of Earth. Here, the ten per-

7

cent was first-century Persians. And there was also the ubiquitous one percent of seemingly random choices from any time and any place.

The telescope swung past the bamboo huts on the plains and the faces of the people. The men were clad only in various towels; the women, in short towellike skirts and thin cloths around the breasts. There were many gathered on the bank, apparently to watch the battle. They carried flint-tipped spears and bows and arrows but were not in martial array.

Clemens grunted suddenly and held the telescope on the face of a man. At this distance and with the weak power of the instrument, he could not clearly see the man's features. But the wide-shouldered body and dark face suggested familiarity. Where had he seen that face before?

Then it struck him. The man looked remarkably like the photographs of the famous English explorer Sir Richard Burton that he'd seen on Earth. Rather, there was something suggestive of the man. Clemens sighed and turned the eyepiece to the other faces as the ship took him away. He would never know the true identity of the fellow.

He would have liked to put ashore and talk to him, find out if he really was Burton. In the twenty years of life on this river-planet, and the seeing of millions of faces, Clemens had not yet met one person he had known on Earth. He did not know Burton personally, but he was sure that Burton must have heard of him. This man—if he was Burton—would be a link, if thin, to the dead Earth.

And then, as a far-off blurred figure came within the round of the telescope, Clemens cried out incredulously.

"Livy! Oh, my God! Livy!"

There could be no doubt. Although the features could not be clearly distinguished, they formed an overwhelming, not-to-be-denied truth. The head, the hairdo, the figure and the unmistakable walk (as unique as a fingerprint) shouted out that here was his Earthly wife.

"Livy!" he sobbed. The ship heeled to tack, and he lost her. Frantically, he swung the end of the scope back and forth.

Eyes wide, he stomped with his foot on the deck, and he bellowed, "Bloodaxe! Bloodaxe! Up here! Hurry!"

He swung toward the helmsman and shouted that he should go back and direct the ship toward the bank. Grimolfsson was taken aback at first by Clemens' vehemence. Then he slitted his eyes, shook his head, and growled out a no.

"I order you to!" Clemens screamed, forgetting that the helmsman did not understand English. "That's my wife! Livy! My beautiful Livy, as she was when she was twenty-five! Brought back from the dead!"

Someone rumbled behind him, and Clemens whirled to see a blond head with a shorn-off left ear appear on the level of the deck. Then Erik Bloodaxe's broad shoulders, massive chest and huge biceps came into view, followed by pillarlike thighs as he came on up the ladder. He wore a green-and-black checked towel, a broad belt holding several chert knives and a holster for his ax. This was of steel, broadbladed and with an oak handle. It was, as far as Clemens knew, unique on this planet, where stone and wood were the only materials for weapons.

He frowned as he looked over the river. He turned to Clemens and said, "What is it, *sma-skitligr?* You made me miscue when you screamed like Thor's bride on her wedding night. I lost a cigar to Toki Njalsson."

He took the ax from its holster and swung it. The sun glinted off the blue steel. "You had better have a good reason for disturbing me. I have killed many men for far less."

Clemens' face was pale beneath the tan, but this time it was not caused by Erik's threat. He glared, the wind-ruffled hair, staring eyes and aquiline profile making him look like a kestrel falcon.

"To hell with you and your ax!" he shouted. "I just saw my wife, Livy, there on the right bank! I want . . . I demand . . . that you take me ashore so I can be with her again! Oh, God, after all these years, all this hopeless searching! It'll only take a minute! You can't deny me this; you'd be inhuman to do so!"

9

The ax whistled and sparkled. The Norseman grinned.

"All this fuss for a woman? What about *her?*" And he gestured at a small dark woman standing near the great pedestal and tube of the rocket-launcher.

Clemens became even paler. He said, "Temah is a fine girl! I'm very fond of her! But she's not Livy!"

"Enough of this," Bloodaxe said. "Do you take me to be as big a fool as you? If I put into shore, we'd be caught between the ground and river forces, ground like meal in Freyr's mill. Forget about her."

Clemens screamed like a falcon and launched himself, arms out and flapping, at the Viking. Erik brought the flat of the ax against Clemens' head and knocked him to the deck. For several minutes, Clemens lay on his back, eyes open and staring at the sun. Blood seeped from the roots of the hair falling down over his face. Then he got to all-fours and began to vomit.

Erik gave an impatient order. Temah, looking sidewise with fright at Erik, dipped a bucket at the end of a rope into The River. She threw the water over Clemens, who sat up and then wobbled to his feet. Temah drew another bucket and washed off the deck.

Clemens snarled at Erik. Erik laughed and said, "Little coward, you've been talking too big for too long! Now, you know what happens when you talk to Erik Bloodaxe as if he were a thrall. Consider yourself lucky that I did not kill you."

Clemens spun away from Erik, staggered to the railing, and began to climb upon it. "Livy!"

Swearing, Bloodaxe ran after him, seized him around the waist and dragged him back. Then he pushed Clemens so heavily that Clemens fell on the deck again.

"You're not deserting me at this time!" Erik said. "I need you to find that iron mine!"

"There isn . . ." Clemens said and then closed his mouth tightly. Let the Norseman find out that he did not know where the mine—if there was a mine—was located, and he would be killed on the spot.

"Moreover," Erik continued cheerfully, "after we find

the iron, I may need you to help us toward the Polar Tower, although I think I can get there just by following The River. But you have much knowledge that I need. And I can use that frost giant, Joe Miller."

"Joe!" Clemens said in a thick voice. He tried to get back onto his feet. "Joe Miller! Where's Joe? He'll kill you!"

The ax cut the air above Clemens' head. "You will tell Joe nothing of this, do you hear? I swear by Odin's blind socket, I will get to you and kill you before he can put a hand on me. Do you hear?"

Clemens got to his feet and swayed for a minute. Then he called, in a louder voice, "Joe! Joe Miller!"

A voice from below the poopdeck muttered. It was so deep that it made the hairs on the backs of men's necks rise even after hearing it for the thousandth time.

The stout bamboo ladder creaked beneath a weight, creaked so loudly it could be heard above the song of wind through leather ropes, flapping of membranous sails, grind of wooden joints, shouts of crew, hiss of water against the hull.

The head that rose above the edge of the deck was even more frightening than the inhumanly deep voice. It was as large as a half pony of beer and was all bars and arches and shelves and flying buttresses of bone beneath a pinkish and loose skin. Bone circled the eyes, small-seeming and dark blue. The nose was inappropriate to the rest of his features, since it should have been flat-bridged and flaring-nostriled. Instead, it was the monstrous and comical travesty of the human nose that the proboscis monkey shows to a laughing world. In its lengthy shadow was a long upper lip, like a chimpanzee's or comic-strip Irishman's. The lips were thin and protruded, shoved out by the convex jaws beneath.

His shoulders made Erik Bloodaxe's look like pretzels. Ahead of him he pushed a great paunch, a balloon trying to rise from the body to which it was anchored. His legs and arms seemed short, they were so out of proportion to the long trunk. The juncture of thigh and body was level with Sam Clemens' chin, and his arms, extended, could hold, and had held, Clemens out at arm's length in the air for an hour without a tremor.

He wore no clothes nor did he need them for modesty's sake, though he had not known modesty until taught by Homo sapiens. Long rusty-red hair, thicker than a man's, less dense than a chimpanzee's, was plastered to the body by his sweat. The skin beneath the hairs was the dirty-pink of a blond Nordic.

He ran a hand the size of an unabridged dictionary through the wavy, rusty-red hair that began an inch above the eyes and slanted back rapidly. He yawned and showed huge human-seeming teeth.

"I vath thleeping," he rumbled, "I vath dreaming of Earth, of *klravulthithmengbhabafving*—vhat you call mammothth. Thothe vere the good old dayth."

He shuffled forward, then stopped. "Tham! Vhat happened! You're bleeding! You look thick!"

Bellowing for his guards, Erik Bloodaxe stepped backwards from the titanthrop. "Your friend went mad! He thought he'd seen his wife—for the thousandth time—and he attacked me because I wouldn't take him in to the bank to her. Tyr's testicles, Joe! You know how many times he's thought he saw that woman, and how many times we stopped, and how many times it always turned out to be a woman who looked something like his woman but wasn't!

"This time, I said no! Even if it had been his woman, I would have said no! We'd be putting our heads in the wolf's mouth!"

Erik crouched, ax lifted, ready to swing at the giant. Shouts came from middeck, and a big redhead with a flint ax ran up the ladder. The helmsman gestured for him to leave. The redhead, seeing Joe Miller so belligerent, did not hesitate to retreat.

"Vhat you thay, Tham?" Miller said. "Thyould I tear him apart?"

Clemens held his head in both hands and said, "No. He's right, I suppose. I don't really know if she was Livy. Probably just a German hausfrau. I don't know!"

He groaned. "I don't know! Maybe it *was* her!"

Fishbone horns blared, and a huge drum on the middeck thundered. Sam Clemens said, "Forget about this, Joe, until we get through the straits—if we do get through! If we're to survive, we'll have to fight together. Later . . ."

"You alvayth thay *later*, Tham, but there never ith a later. Vhy?"

"If you can't figure that out, Joe, you're as dumb as you look!" Clemens snapped.

Tearshields glinted in Joe's eyes, and his bulging cheeks became wet.

"Every time you get thcared, you call me dumb," he said. "Vhy take it out on me? Vhy not on the people that thcare you the thyit outa you, vhy not on Bloodakthe?"

"I apologize, Joe," Clemens said. "Out of the mouths of babes and apemen. . . . You're not so dumb, you're pretty smart. Forget it, Joe. I'm sorry."

Bloodaxe swaggered up to them but kept out of Joe's reach. He grinned as he swung his ax. "There shall soon be a *meeting of the metal!*" And then he laughed and said, "What am I saying? Battle any more is the meeting of stone and wood, except for my star-ax, of course! But what does that matter? I have grown tired of these six months of peace. I need the cries of war, the whistling spear, the chunk of my sharp steel biting into flesh, the spurt of blood. I have become as impatient as a penned-up stallion who smells a mare in heat; I would mate with Death."

"Bull!" Joe Miller said. "You're jutht ath bad ath Tham in your vay. You're thcared, too, but you cover it up vith your big mouth."

"I do not understand your mangled speech," Bloodaxe said. "Apes should not attempt the tongue of man."

"You underthtand me all right," Joe said.

"Keep quiet, Joe," Clemens said. He looked upRiver. Two miles away, the plains on each side of The River dwindled away as the mountains curved inward to create straits not more than a quarter mile wide. The water boiled at the bottom of the cliffs, which were perhaps 3,000 feet high. On the cliff-tops, on both sides, unidentified objects glittered in the sun.

A half mile below the straits, thirty galleys had formed three crescents. And, aided by the swift current and sixty oars each, they were speeding toward the three intruders. Clemens viewed them through his telescope and then said, "Each has about forty warriors aboard and two rocket-launchers. We're in a hell of a trap. And our own rockets have been in storage so long, the powder's likely to

14

be crystallized. They'll go off in the tubes and blow us to kingdom come.

"And those things on top of the cliffs. Apparatus for projecting Greek fire?"

A man brought the king's armor: a triple-layered leather helmet with imitation leather wings and a nosepiece, a leather cuirass, leather breeches and a shield. Another man brought a bundle of spears: yew shafts and flint tips.

The rocket crew, all women, placed a projectile in the swivable launching tube. The rocket was six feet long, not counting the guide stick, built of bamboo, and looked exactly like a Fourth of July rocket. Its warhead contained twenty pounds of black gunpowder in which were many tiny chips of stone: shrapnel.

Joe Miller, the deck creaking beneath his 800 pounds, went below to get his armor and weapons. Clemens put on a helmet and slung a shield over his shoulder, but he would not use a cuirass or leggings. Although he feared wounds, he was even more frightened of drowning because of the heavy armor if he fell into The River.

Clemens thanked whatever gods there were that he had been lucky enough to fall in with Joe Miller. They were blood-brothers now—even if Clemens had fainted during the ceremony, which demanded mingling of blood and some even more painful and repulsive acts. Miller was to defend him, and Clemens was to defend Miller to the death. So far, the titanthrop had done all the battling. But then he was more than big enough for two.

Bloodaxe's dislike of Miller was caused by envy. Bloodaxe fancied himself as the world's greatest fighter and yet knew that Miller would have no more trouble dispatching him in combat than Miller would with a dog.

And with a small dog at that.

Erik Bloodaxe gave his battle orders, which were transmitted to the other two ships by flashes of sunlight off obsidian mirrors. The ships would keep sails up and try to steer between the galleys. This would be difficult because a ship might have to change course to avoid ramming and

15

so lose the wind. Also, each ship would thrice be subjected to crossfire.

"The wind's with them," Clemens said. "Their rockets will have more range until we're among them."

"Teach your grandmother to suck . . ." Bloodaxe said and stopped.

Some bright objects on the cliff-tops had left their positions and now were swooping through the air in a path that would bring them close above the Vikings. The Norsemen shouted with bewilderment and alarm, but Clemens recognized them as gliders. In as few words as possible, he explained to Bloodaxe. The king started to relay the information to the other Vikings but had to stop because the lead galleys fired off the first volley of rockets. Wobbling, trailing thick black smoke, ten rockets arced toward the three sailships. These changed course as quickly as possible, two almost colliding. Some of the rockets almost struck the masts or the hulls, but none hit and all splashed unexploded, falling into The River.

By then the first of the gliders made its pass. Slim-fuselaged, long-winged, with black Maltese crosses on the sides of its slim and silvery fuselage, it dived at a 45-degree angle toward the *Dreyrugr*. The Norsemen archers bent their yew bows and, at a command from the chief archer, loosed their shafts.

The glider swooped low over the water, several arrows sticking out of the fuselage, and it settled down for a landing on The River. It had failed to drop its bombs on the *Dreyrugr*. They were somewhere below the surface of The River.

But now other gliders were coming in at all three ships, and the enemy lead galleys had loosed another flight of rockets. Clemens glanced at their own rocket-launcher. The big blond crew-women were swiveling the tube under the command of small dark Temah, but she was not ready to touch the fuse. The *Dreyrugr* was not yet within range of the nearest galley.

For a second, everything was as if suspended in a photograph: the two gliders, their wingtips only two feet apart, pulling up out of the dive and the small black

16

bombs dropping toward the decks of their targets, the arrows halfway toward the gliders, the German rockets halfway toward the Viking ships, on the downcurve of their arcs.

Clemens felt the sudden push of wind behind him, a whistling, an explosion as the sails took the full impact of air and rolled the ship over sharply on its longitudinal axis. There was a tearing sound as if the fabric of the world were being ripped apart; a cracking as if great axes had slammed into the masts.

The bombs, the gliders, the rockets, the arrows were lifted upward and backwards, turned upside down. The sails and masts left the ship, as if they had been launched from tubes, and soared away. The ship, released from the push of sail, rolled back to horizontal from an almost 90-degree angle to The River. Clemens was saved from flying off the deck in the first slam of wind only because the titanthrop had seized the wheel with one hand and clutched him with the other. The helmsman had also clung to the wheel. The rocket crew, their shrieks carried upRiver by the wind, mouths open, hair whipping, flew like birds from the ship, soared and then splashed into The River. The rocket tube tore loose from its pedestal and followed them.

Bloodaxe had grabbed the railing with one hand and kept hold of his precious steel weapon with the other. While the ship rocked back and forth, he managed to stick the axhandle in the holster and then to cling to the railing with both hands. It was well for him that he did, because the wind, screaming like a woman falling off a cliff, became even more powerful and within a few seconds, a hot blast tore at the ship, and Clemens was as deafened and as seared as if he were standing near a rocket blast.

A great swell of Riverwater lifted the ship high. Clemens opened his eyes and then screamed but could not hear his own voice because of his stunned ears.

A wall of dirty brown water, at least fifty feet high, was racing around the curve of the valley between four and five miles away. He wanted to close his eyes again but could not. He continued to gaze with his lids rigid until the

17

elevated sea was a mile away. Then he could make out the individual trees, the giant pines, oaks, and yews scattered along the front of the wave, and, as it got closer, pieces of bamboo and pine houses, a roof somehow still intact, a shattered hull with a half mast, the sperm-whale-sized, dark-gray body of a Riverdragon fish, plucked from the five-hundred-feet depths of The River.

Terror numbed him. He wanted to die to escape this particular death. But he could not, and so he watched with frozen eyes and congealed mind as the ship, instead of being drowned and smashed beneath hundreds of thousands of gallons of water, rose up and up and up on the slope of the wave, up and up, the dirty brown wreckage-strewn cliff towering above, always threatening to avalanche down upon the ship, and the sky above, now turned from bright noon-blue to gray.

Then they were on the top, poised for a downward slide, rocked, dipped, and went down toward the trough. Smaller, but still huge waves fell over the boat. A body landed on the deck near Clemens, a body catapulted from the raging waters. Clemens stared at it with only a spark of comprehension. He was too iced with terror to feel anymore; he had reached the limits.

And so he stared at Livy's body, smashed on one side but untouched on the other side! It was Livy, his wife, whom he had seen on that Riverbank.

Another wave that almost tore him and the titanthrop loose struck the deck. The helmsman screamed as he lost his grip and followed the woman's corpse overboard.

The boat, sliding upward from the depths of the trough, turned to present its broadside to the wave. But the boat continued to soar upward, though it tilted so that Miller and Clemens were hanging from the stump of the wheel's base as if they were dangling from a tree trunk on the face of a mountain. Then the boat rolled back to horizontal position as it raced down the next valley. Bloodaxe had lost his grip and was shot across the deck and would have gone over the other side if the ship had not righted itself in time. Now he clung to the port railing.

On top of the third wave, the *Dreyrugr* sped slantwise

down the mountain of water. It struck the broken forepart of another vessel, shuddered, and Bloodaxe's grip was torn loose by the impact. He spun along the railing, hit the other railing on the edge of the poopdeck, shattered it, and went on over the edge and below to the middeck.

Not until morning of the next day did Sam Clemens thaw out of his shock. The *Dreyrugr* had somehow ridden out the great waves long enough to go slanting across the plains on the shallower but still rough waters. It had been shot past hills and through a narrow pass into a small canyon at the base of the mountain. And, as the waters subsided from beneath it, the boat had settled with a crash into the ground.

The crew lay in terror thick as cold mud while The River and the wind raged and the sky remained the color of chilling iron. Then the winds ceased. Rather, the downRiver winds stopped, and the normal soothing wind from upRiver resumed.

The five survivors on deck began to stir and to ask questions. Sam felt as if he could barely force the words out through a numbed mouth. Stammering, he told them of the flash he had seen in the sky fifteen minutes before the winds struck. Somewhere down the valley, maybe two hundred miles away, a giant meteorite had struck. The winds created by the heat of passage through the air and by the displacement of air by the meteorite had generated those giant waves. Terrible as they were, they must have been pygmies compared to those nearer the point of impact. Actually, the *Dreyrugr* was in the outer edge of the fury.

"It had quit being mad and was getting downright jovial when we met it," Sam said.

Some of the Norse got unsteadily to their feet and tottered across the deck. Some stuck their heads out of the hatches. Bloodaxe was hurting from his roll across the deck, but he managed to roar, "Everybody belowdecks! There will be many more great waves much worse than this one, there's no telling how many!"

Sam did not like Bloodaxe, to put it mildly, yet he had to admit that the Norwegian was bright enough when it came to the ways of water. He himself had supposed that the first waves would be the last.

The crew lay down in the hold wherever they could find space and something stable to hang onto, and they waited, but not for long. The earth rumbled and shook, and then The River struck the pass with a hiss like a fifty-foot-high cat, followed by a bellow. Borne upward by the flood pouring through the pass, the *Dreyrugr* rocked and spun around and around as it rocked. Sam turned cold. He was sure that if there had been daylight, he and the others would look as grayblue as corpses.

Up the boat went, occasionally scraping against the walls of the canyon. Just as Sam was about to swear that the *Dreyrugr* had reached the top of the canyon and was going to be carried over its front in a cataract, the boat dropped. It sank swiftly, or so it seemed, while the waters poured out through the pass almost as quickly as they had entered. There was a crash, followed by the heavy breathing of men and women, a groan here and there, the dripping of water, and the far-away roar of the receding river.

It was not over yet. There was more waiting in cold numb terror until the great mass of water would rush back to fill the spaces from which it had been displaced by the blazing many hundreds of thousands of tons mass of the meteorite. They shivered as if encased in ice, although the air was far warmer than it had even been at this time of night. And, for the first time in the twenty years on this planet, it did not rain at night.

Before the waters struck again, they felt the shake and grumble of earth. There was a vast hiss and a roar, and again the boat rose up, spun, bumped against the walls of the canyon and then sank. This time, the ship did not strike the ground so hard, probably, Sam thought, because the boat had hit a thick layer of mud.

"I don't believe in miracles," Sam whispered, "but this is one. We've no business being alive."

Joe Miller, who had recovered more swiftly than the rest, went out on a half-hour scouting trip. He returned with the naked body of a man. His burden was, however, alive. He had blond hair under the mud-streaks, a handsome face and blue-gray eyes. He said something in German to Clemens and then managed to smile after he had been deposited gently on the deck.

"I found him in hith glider," Joe said. "Vhat vath left of it, that ith. There'th a number of corptheth outthide thith canyon. Vhat you vant to do vith him?"

"Make friends with him," Clemens croaked. "His people are gone; this area is cleaned out."

He shuddered. The image of Livy's body placed on the deck like a mocking gift, the wet hair plastered over one side of her smashed face, the one dark eye staring darkly at him, was getting more vivid and more painful. He felt like sobbing but could not and was glad of it. Weeping would make him fall apart into a cone of ashes. Later, when he had the strength to stand it, he would weep. So near. . . .

The blond man sat up on the deck. He shivered uncontrollably and said, in British English, "I'm cold."

Miller went belowdecks and brought up dried fish, acorn bread, bamboo tips and cheese. The Vikings had stored food to eat when they were in hostile areas where they were forbidden to use their grails.

"That thtupid ath, Bloodakthe, ith thtill alive," Miller said. "He'th got thome broken ribth and he'th a meth of bruitheth and cutth. But hith big mouth ith in perfect vorking order. Vouldn't you know it?"

Clemens began crying. Joe Miller wept with him and blew his huge proboscis.

"There," he said, "I feel much better. I never been tho thcared in all my life. Vhen I thaw that vater, like all the mammothth in the vorld thtampeding towardth uth, I thought, Good-bye Joe. Good-bye, Tham. I'll vake up thomevhere along The River in a new body, but I'll never thee you again, Tham. Only I vath too terrified to feel thad about it. Yethuth, I vath thcared!"

The young stranger introduced himself. He was Lothar von Richthofen, glider pilot, captain of the Luftwaffe of his Imperial Majesty, Kaiser Alfred the First of New Prussia.

"We've passed a hundred New Prussias in the last ten thousand miles," Clemens said. "All so small you couldn't stand in the middle of one and heave a brick without it landing in the middle of the next. But most of them weren't as belligerent as yours. They'd let us land and charge our grails, especially after we'd shown them what we had to trade for use of the stones."

"Trade?"

"Yes. We didn't trade goods, of course, but all the freighters of old Earth couldn't carry enough to last out a fraction of The River. We traded ideas. For one thing, we show these people how to build pool tables and how to make a hair-setting spray from fish glue, deodorized."

The Kaiser of this area had been, on Earth, a Count von Waldersee, a German field marshal, born 1832, died 1904.

Clemens nodded, saying, "I remember reading about his death in the papers and having great satisfaction because I had outlived another contemporary. That was one of the few genuine and free pleasures of life. But, since you know how to fly, you must be a twentieth-century German, right?"

Lothar von Richthofen gave a brief summary of his life. He had flown a fighter plane for Germany in the Weltkrieg. His brother had been the greatest of aces on either side during that war.

"World War I or II?" Clemens said. He had met enough twentieth-centurians to know some facts—and fancies—about events after his death in 1910.

Von Richthofen added more details. He had been in World War I. He himself had fought under his brother and had accounted for forty Allied planes. In 1922, while flying an American film actress' and her manager from Hamburg to Berlin, the plane had crashed and he had died.

"The luck of Lothar von Richthofen deserted me," he said. "Or so I thought then."

23

He laughed.

"But here I am, twenty-five years old in body again, and I missed the sad things about growing old, when women no longer look at you, when wine makes you weep instead of laugh and makes your mouth sour with the taste of weakness and every day is one day nearer to death.

"And my luck held out again when that meteorite struck. My glider lost its wings at the first blow of wind, but instead of falling, I floated in my fuselage, turning over and over, dropping, rising again, falling, until I was deposited as lightly as a sheet of paper upon a hill. And when the backflood came, the fuselage was borne by the water and I was nuzzled gently against the foot of the mountain. A miracle!"

"A miracle: a chance distribution of events, occurring one time in a billion," Clemens said. "You think a giant meteor caused that flood?"

"I saw its flash, the trail of burning air. It must have crashed far away, fortunately for us."

They climbed down from the ship and slogged through the thick mud to the canyon entrance. Joe Miller heaved logs that a team of draft horses would have strained to pull. He shoved aside others, and the three went down through the foothills and to the plains. Others followed them.

They were silent now. The land had been scoured free of trees except for the great irontrees. So deeply rooted were these that most still stood upright. Moreover, where the mud had not settled, there was grass. It was a testimony to the toughness and steadfast-rootedness of the grass that the millions of tons of water had not been able to rip out the topsoil.

Here and there was the flotsam left by the backflood. Corpses of men and women, broken timber, towels, grails, a dugout, uprooted pines and oaks and yews.

The great mushroom-shaped grailstones, spaced a mile apart along the banks on both sides, were also unbroken and unbent, although many were almost buried in mud.

"The rains will eventually take care of the mud," Clemens said. "The land slopes toward The River." He avoided the corpses. They filled him with a prickly loathing. Besides, he was afraid that he might see Livy's body again. He did not think he could stand it; he would go mad.

"One thing sure," Clemens said. "There'll be nobody between us and the meteorite. We'll have first claim on it, and then it'll be up to us to defend all that treasure of iron from the wolves that will come loping on its scent.

"Would you like to join up? If you stick with me, you'll have an airplane some day, not just a glider."

Sam explained a little about his Dream. And he told a little about Joe Miller's story of the Misty Tower.

"It's only possible with a great deal of iron," he said. "And much hard work. These Vikings aren't capable of helping me build a steamboat. I need technical knowledge they don't have. But I was using them to get me to a possible source of iron. I had hoped that there might be enough ore from which Erik's ax was made for my purpose. I used their greed for the metal, and also Miller's story, to launch them on this expedition.

"Now, we don't have to search. We know where there must be more than enough. All we have to do is dig it up, melt it, refine it, shape it into the forms we need. And protect it. I won't string you along with a tale of easy accomplishment. It may take years before we can complete the boat, and it'll be damn hard work doing it."

Lothar's face blazed with a spark caught from Clemens' few words. "It's a noble, magnificent dream!" he said. "Yes, I'd like to join you, I'll pledge my honor to follow you until we storm Misty Tower! On my word as a gentleman and officer, on the blood of the barons of Richthofen!"

"Just give me your word as a man," Sam said dryly.

"What a strange—indeed, unthinkable—trio we make!" Lothar said. "A gigantic subhuman, who must have died at least 100,000 years before civilization. A twentieth-century Prussian baron and aviator. A great American humorist born in 1835. And our crew—" Clemens raised his thick eyebrows at the *our*—"tenth-century Vikings!"

"A sorry lot now," Sam said, watching Bloodaxe and the others plow through the mud. All were bruised from head to foot and many limped. "I don't feel so well myself. Have you ever watched a Japanese tenderize a dead octopus? I know how the octopus feels now. By the way, I was more than just a humorist, you know. I was a man of letters."

"Ah, forgive me!" Lothar said. "I've hurt your feelings! No offense! Let me salve your injuries, Mr. Clemens, by telling you that when I was a boy, I laughed many times reading your books. And I regard your *Huckleberry Finn* as a great book. Although I must admit I did not care for the way you ridiculed the aristocracy in your *Connecticut Yankee*. Still, they were English, and you are an American."

Erik Bloodaxe decided that they were too battered and weary to start the job of getting the ship down to The River that day. They would charge their grails at evening, eat, sleep, eat breakfast and then begin the backbreaking work.

They went back to the ship, took their grails from the hold and set them on the depressions on the flat top of a grailstone. As the sun touched the peaks of the mountains to the west, the men awaited the roar and the hot, blue flash from the stones. The electrical discharge would power the energy-matter converters within the false bottoms of the grail and, on opening the lids, the men would find cooked meats, vegetables, bread and butter, fruit, tobacco, dreamgum, liquor or mead.

But as darkness settled over the valley, the grailstones remained silent and cold. Across The River, fire sprang up momentarily from the grailstones there, and a faint roar reached them.

But the stones on the west bank, for the first time in the twenty years since the day of Resurrection, did not function.

26

The men and women felt as if God had failed them. The three-times-a-day offering of the stones had come to seem as natural as the rising of the sun. It was some time before they could ease the sickness in their stomachs to eat the last of the fish, sprouts, and cheese.

Clemens was in a blue funk for a while. But von Richthofen began talking of the necessity of ferrying the grails to the other side so they could eat in the morning. Presently Clemens got up and talked to Bloodaxe. The Norwegian was in a mood even fouler than usual, but he finally admitted that action must be taken. Joe Miller, the German, and a big redheaded Swede named Toke Kroksson trudged back up to the ship and then carried some oars back down. These three, with Clemens, took the grails across in the dugout; and Toke and Joe Miller paddled the dugout back. Miller, Clemens and von Richthofen settled down to sleep on top of a grailstone. It was clean, since the electrical discharge had burned off all the mud.

"We'll have to get under the stone when the rains come," Clemens said. He lay on his back, his hands under his head, and looked up at the night sky. It was no terrestrial sky, this blaze of twenty thousand stars greater than Venus in her glory and shimmering filaments tentacling out from glittering gas clouds. Some of the stars were so bright that they could be seen as pale phantoms even at noon.

"The meteorite must have smashed some of the grailstones on the west bank," Sam Clemens said. "And so it broke the circuit. My God, what a circuit! There must be at least twenty million stones hooked together, if the calculations of some are correct."

"There will be a terrible conflict raging up and down The River," Lothar said. "The west bankers will attack the east bankers so they can charge their grails. What a

27

war! There must be about thirty-five to thirty-seven billion people in this Rivervalley. All battling to the death for food."

"The hell of it ith," Joe Miller said, "that if half get kilt and tho there'th enough room on the grailstoneth, it von't do no good. Tventy-four hourth later, the dead vill all be alive again, and it'll all thtart over again."

Sam said, "I'm not so sure. I think it's been established that the stones have something to do with the resurrections. And if half of them are out of commission, there may be a considerable cut in production on the Lazarus line. This meteorite is a saboteur from the skies."

"I've thought for a long time that this world, and our resurrection, are not the work of supernatural beings," von Richthofen said. "Have you heard the wild tale that's been going up and down The River? There's a story that one man woke up before Resurrection Day and found himself in a very weird place. There were millions of bodies around him, floating in the air, nude men, women and children, their heads shaved, all slowly rotating under some invisible force. This man, an Englishman named Perkin, or Burton, some say, had died on Earth around 1890. He got loose but was intercepted by two beings—human—who put him back to sleep. Then he awoke, like the rest of us, on the banks of The River.

"Whoever is behind all this isn't infallible. They made a mistake with Burton. He got a glimpse into pre-Resurrection, a stage somewhere between our death on Earth and preparation for life on this world. It sounds fantastic, like a wish-fulfillment story. But then again. . . ."

"I've heard it," Sam Clemens said. He thought of telling about seeing Burton's face through the telescope just before he spotted Livy's. But the pain of thinking about her was too much for him.

He sat up and cursed and shook his fist at the stars and then began to weep. Joe Miller, squatting behind him, reached a gigantic hand out and touched him softly on the shoulder. Von Richthofen, embarrassed, looked the

28

other way. Presently, he said, "I'll be glad when our grails are charged. I'm itching for a smoke."

Clemens laughed and dried his tears and said, "I don't cry easily. But I've gotten over being ashamed about it when I do.

"It's a sad world, just as sad, in most ways, as the old Earth. Yet we have our youthful bodies again, we don't have to work for food or worry about paying bills, making our women pregnant, catching diseases. And if we're killed we rise up the following day, whole and hearty, although thousands of miles from where we died.

"But it's nothing like what the preachers said it would be. Which isn't, of course, surprising. And maybe it's just as well. Who'd want to fly around on aerodynamically unstable wings or stand around all day playing harps badly and screeching out hosannas?"

Lothar laughed and said, "Ask any Chinese or Indian coolie if this isn't a hell of a better world than the last world. It's just us spoiled modern Westerners who grumble and look for first and latest causes. We didn't know much about the operation of our Earthly cosmos, and we know less about this. But we're here, and we may eventually find out who put us here and why. Meanwhile, as long as there are beautiful and willing women—and there are—cigars, dreamgum, wine and a good fight, who cares? I'll enjoy this valley of bright shadows until the good things of life are once more taken from me. Lust to lust until it's dust to dust."

They were silent after a while, and Clemens could not get to sleep until just before the rains. He got down under the mushroom until the downpour ceased. Back on top of the stone, he shivered and turned for several hours, although he was covered with long heavy towels. Dawn came with Miller's ponderous hand shaking him. Hastily, he climbed down off the stone and got a safe distance from it. Five minutes later, the stone gave forth a blue flame that leaped thirty feet into the air and roared like a lion.

At the same time, the stones across the river bellowed.

29

Clemens looked at Lothar. "Somebody repaired the break."

Lothar said, "I've got goose pimples. *Who* is *somebody*?" He was silent for a while, but before they had reached the west bank, he was laughing and chattering like a guest at a cocktail party. Too cheerful, Clemens thought.

"*They*'ve never shown their hand before, that I know of," Sam said. "But this time I guess *they* had to."

The next five days were occupied in getting the ship down to the bank. Two weeks more were spent in repairing the *Dreyrugr*. All that time a watch was kept, but no one came into the area. When the ship was finally launched, still minus masts and sails, and was rowed down The River, there was not a live human in sight.

The crew, accustomed to seeing the plains thronged with men and women, were uneasy. The silence was unnerving. There were no animals on this world except for the fish in The River and earthworms in the soil, but the humans had always made enough noise.

"The hyenas'll be here soon enough," Clemens said to Bloodaxe. "That iron is far more precious than gold ever was on Earth. You want battle? You'll get enough down your throat to make you vomit."

The Norseman, swinging his ax, winced at the pain in his ribs. "Let them come! They'll know they've been in a fight to bring joy to the hearts of the Valkyrie!"

"Bull!" Joe Miller said. Sam smiled but walked to a position behind the titanthrop. Bloodaxe was afraid of only one being in the world, but he might lose his never easily controlled temper and go berserk. However, he needed Miller, who was worth twenty human warriors.

The ship traveled steadily for two days during the sunlit hours. At night, one man steered and the crew slept. Early in the evening of the third day, the titanthrop, Clemens and von Richthofen were sitting on the foredeck, smoking cigars and sipping at the whiskey their grails had given them at the last stop.

"Why do you call him Joe Miller?" Lothar asked.

"His real name is a rattling jawbreaker, longer than any technical term of a German philosopher," Clemens said. "I couldn't pronounce it when I first met him, I never did. After he learned enough English to tell me a joke—he was so eager he could hardly wait—I decided to call him Joe

Miller. He told me a tale so hoary I couldn't believe it. I knew it'd been around a long time; I first heard it, in a slightly different form, when I was a boy in Hannibal, Missouri. And I was still hearing it, much to my disgust, for the hundred thousandth time, when I was an old man. But to have to listen to that story from the lips of a man who'd died one hundred thousand years, maybe a million, before I was born!"

"And the story?"

"Well, there was this traveling hunter who'd been tracking a wounded deer all day. Night came and with it a violent storm. Seeing the light of a fire, the hunter stopped off at a cave. He asked the old medicine man who lived in it if he could spend the night there. And the old medicine man said, 'Sure, but we're pretty crowded here. You'll have to sleep with my daughter.' Need I go any further?"

"Tham didn't laugh," Joe rumbled. "Thometimeth I think he ain't got a thenthe of humor."

Clemens tweaked Joe's projectile-shaped nose affectionately. He said, "Thometimeth I think you're right. But actually I'm the most humorous man in the world because I'm the most sorrowful. Every laugh is rooted in pain."

He puffed on his cigar for a while and stared at the shore. Just before dusk, the ship had entered the area where the last of the intense heat from the meteorite had struck. Aside from the few irontrees, everything had been whistled off in a shock of searing flame. The irontrees had given up their huge leaves to the flames, and even the enormously resistant bark had burned off and the wood beneath, harder than granite, had become charred. Moreover, the blast had tilted or leveled many of these, snapping them off at the base. The grailstones had been blackened and were out of plumb but had retained their shape.

Finally, he said, "Lothar, now is as good a time as any for you to learn something of why we're on this quest. Joe can tell it in his way; I'll explain anything you don't understand. It's a strange tale, but no stranger, actually, than anything that's happened here since we all woke up from the dead."

32

"I'm thirthty," Joe said. "Let me get a drink firtht."

The dark-blue eyes, shadowed in the bone rings, focused upon the hollow of the cup. He seemed to peer therein as if he were trying to conjure up the scenes he was about to describe. Guttural, his tongue hitting certain consonants harder than others, thus giving his English a clanging quality, yet comical with its lisping, voice rising up from a chest deep and resonant as the well of the Delphian oracle, he told of the Misty Tower.

"Thomevhere upon The River, I avoke, naked ath I am now. I vath in a plathe that mutht be far north on thith planet, because it vath colder and the light vath not ath bright. There vere no humanth, yutht uth . . . uh, titantropth, ath Tham callth uth. Ve had grailth, only they vere much larcher than yourth, ath you can thee. And ve got no beer and vithkey. Ve had never known about alcohol, tho ve had none in our grailth. Ve drank The River vater.

"Ve thought ve vere in the plathe that you go to vhen you die, that the . . . uh . . . godth had given uth thith plathe and all ve needed. Ve vere happy, ve mated and ate and thlept and fought our enemieth. And I vould have been happy there if it had not been for the thyip."

"He means ship," Sam said.

"That'th vhat I thaid. Thyip. Pleathe don't interrupt, Tham. You've made me unhappy enough by telling me that there are no godth. Even if I've theen the godth."

Lothar said, "Seen the *gods?*"

"Not egthactly. I thaw vhere they live. I did thee their thyip."

Von Richthofen said, "What? What're you talking about?"

Clemens waved his cigar. "Later. Let him talk. If you interrupt him too much, he gets confused."

"Vhere I come from, you don't talk vhile another ith talking. Othervithe, you get punched in the nothe."

Sam said, "With a nose as big as yours, Joe, that must hurt."

Miller delicately stroked his proboscis.

"It ith the only vone I have, and I'm proud of it. Novhere in thith part of the valley hath any pigmy got a nothe like mine. Vhere I come from, your nothe indicateth the thithe of your—vhat'th your vord for it, Tham?"

Sam choked and took the cigar from his lips.

"You were telling us of the ship, Joe."

"Yeth. No! I vath not! I hadn't gotten to it yet. But ath I vath thaying, vun day I vath lying on the bank vatching the fith play. I vath thinking about getting up and making a hook and pole to catch thome. All of a thudden, I heard a thyout. I looked up. There, coming around the bend of The River vath thith terrible monthter.

"It vath awful. I jumped up, and I vath going to run avay vhen I thaw it had men on itth back. They looked like men, but vhen the monthter got clother, I thaw they were thpindly little runtth vith the mange and no notheth to thpeak of. I could have beat them all to death vith vone hand, and yet they were riding thith monthter Riverthnake like beeth on a bear'th back. Tho. . . ."

Clemens, listening, felt again as he had when he first heard the story. He felt as if he were standing by the side of this creature from the dawn of man. Despite the clanging and lisping and halting and slow groping after words, this Titan spoke impressively. Clemens could feel his panic and his wonder and almost overpowering urge to run away. Clemens could also feel the opposing urge, the primate's curiosity, the thing that made him, if not wholly a man, at least a near cousin. Behind the shelving brow lay the gray pulse that would not be content just to exist but must be fed on the shapes of unknown things, on patterns never before seen.

So Joe Miller stayed upon the bank, though his hand closed around the handle of the grail, ready to carry it with him if he had to flee.

The monster floated closer. Joe began to think that it might not be alive. But if it were not, why the great head poised at its front as if to strike? Yet it did not look alive. It gave a feeling of *deadness*. This did not mean much, of course. Joe had seen a wounded bear pretend death convincingly and then rise up and tear the arm off a fellow hunter.

Moreover, though he had seen the hunter die, he had also seen the hunter alive again, that day he awoke on the banks with others of his kind. And if he, and Joe, too, could come alive again, why couldn't this petrified snakelike head lose its dead woodenness and seize him in its teeth?

But he ignored his fears and, trembling, approached the monster. He was a Titan, older brother to man, fresh with the dawn and with the primate's have-to-know-what's-going-on.

A pygmy, mangy as the others but wearing on his brow a glass circlet with a stained-red flaming sun, beckoned to Joe Miller. The others upon the wooden beast stood behind the man with the glass circlet and held spears and strange devices that Joe learned later were bows and arrows. They did not seem frightened of the colossus, but that may have been because they were so tired from their seldom-ceasing rowing against the current that they did not care what happened.

It took a long time for the pygmy chief to get Joe aboard the ship. They came ashore to charge their grails while Joe backed away from them. They ate, and Joe ate also, but at a distance. His fellows had run for the hills, having been also panicked by the ship. Presently seeing that the Riversnake did not threaten Joe, they slowly approached it. The pygmies retreated to the ship.

And now the chief took a strange object from his grail and held a glowing wire to its tip, and smoke came from it and from the pygmy's mouth. Joe jumped at the first puff; his fellows scattered for the foothills again. Joe wondered if the noseless pygmies could be the brood of the dragon. Perhaps her children took this larval form, but, like their mother, they could breathe out fire and smoke?

"But I ain't a dummy," Joe said. "It didn't take me long to figure out that the thmoke came from the obchect, vhich in Englith ith a thigar. Their chief made it plain that if I'd get on the thyip, I could thmoke the thigar. Now, I muthl've been crathy to do tho, but I vanted to thmoke that thigar. Maybe I thought I'd impreth my tribe, I don't know."

He jumped on the ship, his weight causing it to tilt a little on the port. He swung his grail to show them that if they attacked him, he would bash their skulls in with it. They took the hint and did not come close. The chief gave Joe a cigar, and though Joe coughed a little and found the taste of tobacco strange, he liked it. Moreover, when he had drunk beer for the first time, he was entranced.

So Joe decided to go on the Riversnake's back up The River with the pygmies. He was put to work on a mighty sweep, and he was called Tehuti.

"Tehuti?" von Richthofen said.

"The Greek form is Thoth," Clemens said. "To the Egyptians, he looked something like the long-beaked ibis-god. I suppose he must also have reminded them of the baboon-god, Bast, but that tremendous nose outweighed that consideration. So, Thoth, or Tehuti, he became."

Days and nights flowed by like The River. Sometimes, Joe became tired and wished to be put ashore. By now, he could speak the pygmies' language, though haltingly. The chief would agree to do as Joe wished since it was obvious that any denial might result in the slaughter of his entire crew. But he would speak sadly of Tehuti's education ending there, just when he was doing so well. He had been a brute, though with the face of the god of wisdom, and soon he would be a man.

Brute? God? Man?

What were they?

The order was not quite right, the chief would say. The correct sequence, ever upward, was brute, man and god. Yet it was true you might see a god disguised as a beast, and man merged insensibly from animal into deity, balanced between the two, and now and then changed into one or the other.

That was beyond the breadloaf-shaped brain of Tehuti. He would squat and scowl at the nearing bank. There would be no more cigars or beer. The people on the bank were his kind, but they were also not his tribe, and they might kill him. Moreover, he was beginning for the first time to experience intellectual stimulation, and that would

36

cease once he was back among the titanthrops.

So he would look at the chief and blink, grin and shake his head and tell him he was going to stay on the ship. He took his turn at the sweep and resumed his study of the most marvelous of all things: a tongue that knew philosophy. He became fluent in their speech and began to grasp the wonderful things the leader told him, although sometimes it was as painful as grasping a handful of thorns. If this or that idea eluded him, he pursued it, caught it, swallowed it, perhaps vomited it up a score of times. Eventually, he digested it and got *some* nourishment from it.

The River flowed by. They rowed, always staying close to the shore, where the current was weakest. Days and nights, and now the sun did not climb so high in the heavens but was a little lower at its zenith than it had been the week before. And the air grew colder.

Sam said, "Joe and his party were getting close to the north pole. The inclination of this planet's equator to the plane of the ecliptic is zero. As you know, there are no seasons; day and night are equal in length. But Joe was approaching the point where he would see the sun always half below the horizon and half above. Or would have if it hadn't been for the mountains."

"Yeth. It vath alvayth tvilight. I got cold, though not ath cold ath the men. They vere thyivering their atheth off."

"His big bulk radiates heat slower than our puny bodies," Clemens said.

"Pleathe, pleathe! Thyould I talk or jutht keep my big mouth thyut?"

Lothar and Sam grinned at him.

He continued. The wind grew stronger, and the air became misty. He began to get uneasy. He wanted to turn back, but by now he did not want to lose the respect of the leader. He would go every inch of the way toward their unknown goal with them.

"You didn't know where they were going?" Lothar said.

"Not egthactly. They vanted to get to the headvaterth of

37

The River. They thought maybe the godth lived there, and there the godth vould admit them into the true aftervorld. They thaid that thith vorld vathn't the true vorld. It vath a thtage on the vay to the true vorld. Vhatever that ith."

One day, Joe heard a rumble that sounded as faintly but yet as near as gas moving within his bowels. After a while, as the noise became like thunder, he knew it was water falling from immense heights.

The ship swung into a bay protected by a finger of land. The grailstones no longer lined The River. The men would have to catch fish and dry them. There was also a store of bamboo tips on the ship; these had been collected in the sunlit region for just such an eventuality.

The leader and his men prayed, and the party began climbing a series of cataracts. Here the superhuman strength of Tehuti-Joe Miller helped them in overcoming obstacles. Other times, his great weight was a hindrance and a danger.

Upward they went, wet because of the everpresent spray. When they came to a cliff smooth as ice for a thousand feet up, they despaired. Reconnoitering, they found a rope dangling from the face of a cliff. It was formed to towels tied together. Joe tested its strength and climbed up, hand over hand, his feet braced against the cliff, until he reached the top. There he turned to watch the others follow him. The chief, first after Joe, tried much easier, and halfway up to the top he could go no farther. Joe pulled him and the extremely heavy weight of the rope to the top. He did the same for each man in the party.

"Where in hell did the rope come from?" von Richthofen said.

"Someone had prepared the way for them," Clemens said. "Given the primitive technology of this planet, no one could have found a way to get that rope up to the rock around which one end of the rope was tied. Maybe a balloon might have lifted a man up there. You could make a balloon of Riverdragonskin or human skins, you know. You could make hydrogen by passing steam over highly heated charcoal in the presence of a suitable catalyst. But in this world of scarce metal, where's the catalyst?

"Hydrogen could be made without a catalyst but at an enormous cost in fuel. But there was no evidence of the furnaces needed to make the hydrogen. Besides, why would the towels be left behind, when they'd be needed again? No, some unknown person, let's call him The Mysterious Stranger, put that rope there for Joe and party. Or for whoever might come along. Don't ask me who he was or how he did it. Listen. There's more."

The party, carrying the rope, walked for several miles in the mist-ridden twilight on a plateau. They came to another cliff where The River broadened out above them into a cataract. It was so wide, it seemed to Joe that there was enough water to float the moon of Earth upon it. He would not have been surprised to see that great silver-and-black orb appear on the brink of the cataract far above and hurtle down that thunder of waters and be smashed to pieces on the rocks in the maelstrom foot.

The wind became stronger and louder; the mist, thicker. Drops of water condensed on the towels they had now fastened around themselves from head to foot. The cliff before them was as mirror-smooth and perpendicular as the one just ascended. Its top was lost in the fog; it could be only fifty feet high or could be ten thousand. They searched along the foot, hoping for some kind of fissure. And they found one. It was like a small door at the juncture of plateau and cliff. It was so low, it forced them to get down on hands and knees and crawl. Joe's shoulders rubbed against the sides of the rock. But the rock was smooth, as if the hole had been made by man and rubbed until all roughness was gone.

The tunnel led at a slightly less than 45-degree angle upward and through the mountain. There was no estimating its distance. When Joe came out at the other end, however, his shoulders and hands and knees were rubbed raw and bleeding even with the protection of towels.

"I don't understand," von Richthofen said. "It seems to me that the mountains were shaped there to prevent men from getting to the end of The River. Why was this tunnel bored through solid rock to give intruders passage? And why wasn't a tunnel placed in the first cliff?"

"A tunnel in the first cliff might have been visible to whatever sentinels or patrols there are in that area," Clemens said. "But the second cliff was hidden in mist."

"That chain of white towels would be even more outstanding," the German said.

"Maybe it was placed there not too long before Joe got there," Clemens said.

Von Richthofen shivered.

"For Heaven'th thaketh, let me tell thith! After all, it ith my tale."

"And a big one, too," Clemens said, looking at Joe's huge buttocks.

"Thtickth and thotneth may break my boneth."

The party pushed on over another tableland for about ten miles. They slept or tried to, ate, and began climbing. Now, though the mountains were very steep and rough, they were scalable. Their chief enemy was lack of oxygen. They gasped for breath and had to halt often to rest.

By now Joe's feet were hurting him, and he was limping. He did not ask if he could rest. As long as the others walked, so would he.

"Joe can't stay on his feet as long as a human," Clemens said. "All of his species suffer from flat feet. Their weight is just too much for a biped that size. I wouldn't be surprised if his kind became extinct on Earth because of broken arches."

"I know one thpetthimen of Homo thapienth who'th going to suffer from a broken nothe if he don't keep hith nothe out of my buthineth, vhich ith telling thith thtory," Joe said.

They climbed until The River, broad as it was, was only a thread below them. Much of the time they could not see even that thread because of the clouds. Snow and ice made climbing even more dangerous. Then they found a way downward to another plateau and groped through the fog against a wind that howled and beat at them.

They found themselves beside a tremendous hole in the mountains. Out of the hole rushed The River, and on every side except Riverward the mountain rose straight and smooth. The hole was the only way to go. Out of it blasted a roar so loud they could not hear each other, the voice of a god who spoke as loud as death.

Joe Miller found a narrow ledge entering the cave high above the waters. Joe noticed that the leader had now dropped back behind him. After a while, the titanthrop became aware that all of the pygmies were looking to him as their guide and helper. When they shouted to make themselves heard above the bellow, they called him

Tehuti. There was nothing unusual in that, but before this he had detected overtones of jesting in their use of the name. No more. Now he was truly their Tehuti.

Clemens interrupted again. "It was as if we called the village idiot Jehovah or something like that. When men have no need of gods, they mock them. But, when afraid, they treat them with respect. Now, you might say, Thoth was leading them into the opening into the Underworld.

"Of course, I'm only indulging in mankind's vice of trying to make a symbol out of coincidence. If you scratch any dog, you'll scare out a flea."

Joe Miller was breathing heavily through his grotesque nose, and the vast chest rose and fell like a bellows. Clearly, the reliving of that experience had aroused the old terror in him.

The ledge was not like the tunnel in the mountain. It had not been prepared. It was rough, and there were gaps in it, and sometimes it ran so high that Joe had to crawl to squeeze between the ledge and the roof of the cavern. The darkness blinded him as if his eyes had been plucked out. His sense of hearing did not help him; the bellow filled his ears. Only his touch was left to guide him, and he was so agitated that he sometimes wondered if that were betraying him. He would have quit except that, if he did, the men behind him would not have been able to go on.

"Ve thtopped tvithe to eat and voneth to thleep," Joe said. "Jutht vhen I vath beginning to think ve might crawl until ve ran out of food, I thaw a grayneth ahead. It vathn't a light. Jutht a leththening of the darkneth."

They were out of the cave, in the open air, on the side of the mountain. Several thousand feet below them was a sea of clouds. The sun was hidden behind the mountains, but the sky above was not yet dark. The narrow ledge continued, and they crawled on their bloodied hands and knees downward now, since the ledge had narrowed to nothing.

Trembling, they clung to the tiniest of fingerholes. A man slipped and fell and clutched another man. Screaming, both disappeared into the clouds.

The air became warmer.

"The River was giving up its heat," Clemens said. "It not only originates at the north pole, it also empties there after picking up heat in its serpentine wanderings over the entire planet. The air at the north pole is cold but not nearly as cold as that on Earth. This is all speculation, of course."

The party came to another shelf on which they could stand, facing the mountain, and proceed sidewise, like crabs. The shelf curved around the mountainside. Joe halted. The narrow valley had widened into a great plain. He could hear, far below, the dash of surf against rock.

Through the twilight, Joe could see the mountains ringing the sea of the north pole. The cloud-covered waters formed a body about sixty miles in diameter. The clouds were thicker at the opposite end of the sea. He didn't know why then, but Sam had explained that the clouds hid the mouth of The River, where the warm waters came into contact with the cold air.

Joe took a few more steps around the curve of the ledge.

And he saw the gray metal cylinder sitting on the path before him.

For a moment, he did not understand what it was, it looked so alien. It was so unexpected. Then it flowed into familiar lines, and he knew it was a grail left by a man who had come before him on this dangerous path. Some unknown pilgrim had survived the same perils as he. Up to that point, that is. He had put the grail down to eat. The lid was open, and there was the stinking remnant of fish and moldy bread within it. The pilgrim had used the grail as a pack, perhaps hoping he might come across a grailstone and recharge it.

Something had happened to him. He would not have left the grail there unless he had been killed or had been so frightened he had run away without it.

At this thought, Joe's skin chilled.

He went around the outcropping that was sitting at a point where the ledge went around a shoulder of granite. For a moment, his view of the sea was blocked.

He went around the outcropping—and he cried out.

The men called and asked what troubled him.

He could not tell them because the shock had taken away his newly learned speech, and he spoke in his native tongue.

The clouds in the middle of the sea had roiled away for a few seconds. The top of a structure projected from the clouds. It was cylindrical and gray, like the top of a monster grail.

Mists rose and fell around it, now revealing, now veiling.

Somewhere in the mountains ringing the polar sea, a break existed. At that moment, the low sun must have passed this notch in the range. A ray of light fell through the notch and struck the top of the tower.

Joe squinted his eyes and tried to see into the brightness of the reflection.

Something round had appeared just above the top of the tower and was settling down toward it. It was egg-shaped and white, and it was from this that the sun was sparkling.

The next instant, as the sun passed by the notch, the sparkle died. The tower and the object above it faded into darkness and mist. Joe, crying out at the sight of the flying object, stepped back. His leg struck the grail left by the unknown pilgrim.

He swung his arms to regain his balance, but not even his apelike agility could save him. He toppled backward, bellowing horror as he turned over and over. Once he glimpsed the faces of his companions, a row of dark brown objects with the darker O's of mouths, watching his descent to the clouds and waters beneath.

"I don't remember hitting the vater," Joe said. "I avoke tranthlated about twenty mileth from where Tham Clementh vath. Thith vath a plathe vhere Northmen of the tenth thentury A.D. lived. I had to thtart learning a new language all over again. The little notheleththth people vere thcared of me, but they vanted me to fight for them. Then I met Tham, and ve became buddieth."

They were silent for a while. Joe lifted his glass to his thin and chimpanzee-flexible lips and poured out the rest

44

of the liquor. Somber, the other two watched him. The only sign of brightness about them was the glow of their cigar ends.

Von Richthofen said, "This man who wore a glass circlet with a sunburst. What did you say his name was?"

"I didn't."

"Well, then, what was it?"

"Ikhnaton. Tham knowth more about him than I do, and I lived for four yearth with him. At leatht, that'th vhat Tham thayth. But—" here Joe looked smug—"I know the *man* and all Tham knowth ith a few hithtorical factth, tho-called."

Von Richthofen said good night and went belowdecks. Sam paced back and forth, stopping once to light a cigarette for the helmsman. He wanted to sleep but could not. Insomnia had been skewering him for years; it drove through the middle of his brain, which spun on it like a wild gear, disengaged from his body's need for rest.

Joe Miller sat hunched against the railing and waited for his friend—the only man he trusted and loved—to go belowdecks. Presently his head drooped, the bludgeon-nose describing a weary arc, and he snored. The noise was like that of trees being felled in the distance. Sequoias split, screeched, cracked. Vast sighings and bubblings alternated with the woodchoppers' activities.

"Thleep vell, little chum," Sam said, knowing that Joe dreamed of that forever-lost Earth where mammoths and giant bears and lions roamed and where beautiful—to him—females of his own species lusted after him. Once he groaned and then whimpered, and Sam knew that he was dreaming again of being seized by a bear which was chomping on his feet. Joe's feet hurt day and night. Like all of his kind, he was too huge and heavy for bipedal locomotion. Nature had experimented with a truly giant subhuman species and then she had dismissed them as failures.

"*The Rise and Fall of the Flatfeet,*" Sam said. "An article I shall never write."

Sam gave a groan, a weak echo of Joe's. He saw Livy's half smashed body, given him briefly by the waves, then taken away. Or had she really been Livy? Had he not seen her at least a dozen times before while staring through the telescope at the multitudes on the banks? Yet, when he had been able to talk Bloodaxe into putting ashore just to see if the face was Livy's, he had always been disappointed. Now there was no reason to believe the corpse had been his wife's.

He groaned again. How cruel if it had been Livy! How like life! To have been so close and then to have her taken away a few minutes before he would have been reunited with her. And to have her cast upon the decks as if God—or whatever sneering forces ran the universe—were to laugh and to say, "See how close you came! Suffer, you miserable conglomeration of atoms! Be in pain, wretch! You must pay with tears and agony!"

"Pay for what?" Sam muttered, biting on his cigar. "Pay for what crimes? Haven't I suffered enough on Earth, suffered for what I did do and even more for what I didn't do?"

Death had come to him on Earth, and he had been glad because it meant the end forever to all sorrow. He would no longer have to weep because of the sickness and deaths of his beloved wife and daughters nor gloom because he felt responsible for the death of his only son, the death caused by his negligence. Or was it carelessness that had made his son catch the disease that killed him? Hadn't his unconscious mind permitted the robe to slip from little Langdon, while taking him for a carriage ride that cold winter day?"

"No!" Sam said so loudly that Joe stirred and the helmsman growled something in Norse.

He smacked his fist against his open palm, and Joe muttered again.

"God, why do I have to ache now with guilt for *any-thing* I've done?" Sam cried. "It doesn't *matter* now! It's all been wiped out; we've started with clean souls."

But it did matter. It made no difference that all the dead were once more alive and the sick were healthy and the bad deeds were so remote in time and space that they should be forgiven and forgotten. What a man had been and had thought on Earth, he still was and thought here.

Suddenly, he wished he had a stick of dreamgum. That might remove the clenching remorse and make him wildly happy.

But then it might intensify the anguish. You never knew if a horror so terrifying would come that you wanted to

47

die. The last time he had taken the gum, he had been so menaced by monsters that he had not dared try the gum again. But maybe this time . . . no!

Little Langdon! He would never see him again, never! His son had been only twenty-eight months old when he had died, and this meant that he had not been resurrected in the Rivervalley. No children who had died on Earth before the age of five had been raised again. At least, not here. It was to be presumed that they were alive somewhere, probably on another planet. But for some reason, whoever was responsible for this had chosen not to place the infant dead here. And so Sam would never find him and make amends.

Nor would he ever find Livy or his daughters, Sarah, Jean, and Clara. Not on a River said to be possibly twenty million miles long with possibly thirty-seven billion people on its banks. Even if a man started at one end and walked up one bank and looked at every person on that side and then, on reaching the end, walked back down the other side and did not miss a person, he would take—how long? A square mile a day would mean a round trip of, say 365 into 40,000,000,—what was that? He wasn't any good at doing sums in his head, but it must be over 109,000 years.

And even if a man could do this, could walk all those weary miles and make sure he never missed a face, at the end of over 100,000 years he still might not find the face. The longed-for person might have died somewhere ahead of the searcher and been translated back down The River, behind the searcher. Or the searchee may have passd by the searcher during the night, perhaps while the searchee was looking for the searcher.

Yet there might be another way to do this. The beings responsible for this Rivervalley and the resurrection might have the power to locate anybody they wished to. They must have a central file or some means of ascertaining the identity and location of the valley dwellers.

Or, if they did not, they could at least be made to pay for what they had done.

Joe Miller's story was no fantasy. It had some very puzzling aspects, but these hinted at something comforting. That was, that some nameless person—or being—wanted the valley dwellers to know about the tower in the mists of the north polar sea. Why? Sam did not know, and he could not guess. But that hole had been bored through the cliff to enable human beings to find out about the tower. And in that tower must be the light to scatter the darkness of ignorance. Of that Sam was sure. And then there was the widespread story of the Englishman, Burton or Perkin, probably Burton, who had awakened prematurely in the preresurrection phase. Was the awakening any more of an accident than the hole bored through the polar cliff?

And so Samuel Clemens had had his first dream, had nourished it until it had become The Great Dream. To make it real, he needed iron, much iron. It was this that had caused him to talk Erik Bloodaxe into launching the expedition in search of the source of the steel ax. Sam had not really expected that there would be enough of the metal to build the giant boat, but at least the Norse were taking him upRiver, closer to the polar sea.

Now, with a luck that he did not deserve—he really felt he deserved nothing good—he was within reach of more iron than he could possibly have hoped for. Not that that had kept him from hoping.

He needed men with knowledge. Engineers who would know how to treat the meteorite iron, get it out, melt it down, reshape it. And engineers and technicians for the hundred other things needed.

He toed Joe Miller's ribs and said, "Get up, Joe. It'll be raining soon."

The titanthrop grunted and rose like a tower out of a fog and stretched. Starlight glinted on his teeth. He followed Sam across the deck, the bamboo planks creaking under the eight hundred pounds. From below, somebody cursed in Norse.

The mountains on both sides were covered with clouds now, and the darkness was spreading over the valley and shutting off the insane glitter of twenty thousand giant

49

stars and glowing gas sheets. Soon it would rain hard for half an hour, and then the clouds would disappear.

Lightning streaked on the eastern bank; thunder bellowed. Sam stopped. Lightning always made him afraid, or, rather, the child in him afraid. Lightning streaked through him and showed him the haunted and haunting faces of those he had injured or insulted or dishonored and behind them were blurred faces reproaching him for nameless crimes. Lightning twisted through him; then he believed in an avenging God out to burn him alive, to drown him in searing pain. Somewhere in the clouds was the Wrathful Retributor, and He was looking for Sam Clemens.

Joe said. "There'th thunder thomevhere farther down The River. No! It ain't thunder! Lithen! Can't you hear it! It'th thomething funny, like thunder but different."

Sam listened while his skin prickled with cold. There was a very faint rumble downRiver. He got even colder as he heard a louder rumble from upRiver.

"What the hell is it?"

"Don't get thcared, Tham," Joe said. "I'm vith you."

But he was shivering, too.

Lightning spread a filamented whiteness on the east bank.

Sam jumped and said, "Jesus! I saw something flicker!"

Joe moved next to him and said, "I thaw it! It'th the thyip! You know, the vun I thaw above the tower. But it'th gone!"

Joe and Sam stood silent, peering into the darkness. Lightning exploded again, and this time there was no white eggshape high above The River.

"It flickered out of nothing and went back to nothing. Like a mirage," Sam said. "If you hadn't seen it, too, I'd have thought it was an illusion."

Sam awoke on the deck. He was stiff, cold and confused. He rolled over and squinted his eyes at the sun just clearing the eastern range.

Joe was on his back beside him, and the helmsman was sleeping beside the wheel.

But it was not this that brought him to his feet. The gold of the sun had faded out as he brought his gaze down; green was everywhere. The muddied plains and mountains, with straws and stubs of debris, were gone. There was short grass on the plains, tall grass and bamboo on the hill, and the giant pine, oak, yew and irontree everywhere on the hills.

"Business as usual," Sam muttered, wisecracking, though unconsciously, even in his shock. Something had put all aboard the *Dreyrugr* asleep, and while they were unconscious, the incredible work of clearing off the mud and replanting the vegetation had been done. This section of The River was reborn!

He felt insignificant, as weak and helpless as a puppy. What could he, or any human, do to combat beings with powers so vast they could perform this miracle?

Yet there had to be an explanation, a physical explanation. Science and the easy control of vast forces had done this; there was nothing supernatural about it.

There was one comforting hope. One of the unknown beings might be on the side of mankind. Why? *In what mystical battle?*

By then the entire ship was aroused. Bloodaxe and von Richthofen came up on deck at the same time. Bloodaxe frowned at seeing the German there because he had not authorized him to be on the poopdeck. But the sight of the vegetation shook him so much that he forgot to order him off.

The sun's rays struck down upon the gray mushroom shapes of the grailstones. They sparkled upon hundreds of little exhalations, mounds of seeming fog, that had suddenly appeared on the grass near the stones. The mounds shimmered like heat waves and abruptly coalesced into solidity. Hundreds of men and women lay upon the grass. They were naked, and near each was a pile of towels and a grail.

"It's a wholesale translation," Sam murmured to the German. "Those who died as a result of the western grails being shut off. People from everywhere. One good thing, it'll be some time before they can get organized, and they won't know there's a source of iron under their feet."

Lothar von Richthofen said, "How will we find the meteorite? All traces of it must be covered up."

"If it's still there," Sam said. He cursed. "Anybody who can do this overnight shouldn't have any trouble removing a meteorite, even of that size."

He groaned and said, "Or maybe it struck in the middle of The River and is now drowned under a thousand feet of water!"

"You look depressed, my friend," Lothar said. "Don't. In the first place, the meteorite may not have been removed. In the second place, what if it is? You can't be worse off than you were before. And there are still wine, women, song."

"I can't be satisfied with that," Sam said. "Moreover, I cannot conceive that we were raised from the dead so that we might enjoy ourselves for eternity. There's no sense to a belief like that."

"Why not?" Lothar said, grinning. "You don't know what motives these mysterious beings have for creating all this and placing us here. Maybe they feed upon feelings."

Sam was interested. He felt some of his depression lift. A new idea, even though it was in itself depressing, ex-hilarated him.

"You mean we might be emotional cattle? That our herders might dine upon large juicy steaks of love, ribs of hope, livers of despair, briskets of laughter, hearts of hate, sweetbreads of orgasm?"

"It's only theory," Lothar said. "But it's as good as any I've heard and better than most. I don't mind them feeding off me. In fact, I may be one of their prize bulls, in a manner of speaking. Speaking of which, look at that beauty there. Let me at her!"

Briefly illuminated, Sam now plunged back into the dark shadows. Perhaps the German was right. In which case, a human being had as much chance against the unknown as a prize cow had in outwitting her masters. Still, a bull could gore, could kill before he met inevitable defeat.

He explained the situation to Bloodaxe. The Norwegian looked doubtful. "How can we find this fallen star? We can't dig up the ground everywhere looking for it. You know how tough the grass is. It takes days to dig even a small hole with stone tools. And the grass soon grows to fill up the hole."

"There must be a way," Sam said. "If only we had a lodestone or some kind of metal detector. But we don't."

Lothar had been busy waving at the statuesque blonde on the shore, but he had been listening to Sam. He turned and said, "Things look different from the air. Forty generations of peasants can plow land over an ancient building and never know it. But an airman can fly over that land and see at once that something lies buried there. There is a difference in coloration, of vegetation sometimes, though that wouldn't apply here. But the earth reveals subterranean things to him who flies high. The soil is at a different level over the ruins."

Sam became excited. "You mean that if we could build a glider for you, you might be able to detect the site?"

"That would be very nice," Lothar said. "We can do that some day. But it won't be necessary to fly. All we have to do is climb high enough on the mountains to get a good view of the valley."

Sam swore joyfully. "It was a stroke of luck, picking you up! I never would have known about that!"

He frowned. "But we may not be able to climb high enough. Look at those mountains. They go straight up, smooth as a politician denying he ever made a campaign promise."

Bloodaxe asked impatiently what they were talking about. Sam replied. Bloodaxe said, "This fellow may be of some use after all. There is no great problem, no unsurmountable one, anyway, if we can find enough flint. We can chop steps up for a thousand feet. It will take much time, but it will be worth it."

"And if there is no flint?" Sam said.

"We could blast our way up," Bloodaxe said. "Make gunpowder."

"For that we need human excrement, of which there is no dearth," Sam said. "And the bamboo and pine can give us charcoal. But what about sulphur? There may be none within a thousand miles or more."

"We know there's plenty about seven hundred miles downRiver," Bloodaxe said. "But first things first. One, we have to locate the meteorite. Two, having done that, we must put off any digging for it until we have established a fort to hold it. I tell you, we may be the first to it, but we won't be the only ones. The wolves will be coming from upRiver and downRiver now, sniffing for it. There will be

54

many, and we will have to fight to hold the iron. So—first we locate the star, then we dig in to keep it."

Sam swore again. "We might be going right past it right now!" he said.

"Then we'll put in here," Bloodaxe said. "It's as good a place as any to start. Besides, we have to have breakfast."

Three days later, the crew of the *Dreyrugr* had determined that there was no flint or chert in the immediate area. Any that might have been there before must have been burned away by the impact of the meteorite. And when the new soil and vegetation had been laid down, it had contained no stone.

Sometimes rock useful for making tools and weapons could be found in the foothills, at the base of the mountains. Or, if the mountains were broken at the base, as they sometimes were, they yielded workable rock. This area was barren.

"We're out of luck," Sam moaned one night while talking to von Richthofen. "We haven't any way to find the meteorite. And even if we did, we would have no means for digging down to it. And if we could do that, how would we mine it? Nickel-iron is a very dense and hard material."

"You were the world's greatest humorist," Lothar said. "Have you changed a great deal since you were resurrected?"

"What's that got to do with it?" Sam said. "A humorist is a man whose soul is black, black, but who turns his curdles of darkness into explosions of light. But when the light dies out, the black returns."

Sam stared into the bamboo fire for a while. There were faces in there, compact, squeezed down, then elongating, spreading out, soaring upward—as the sparks fly—and thinning out until the night and the stars absorbed them. Livy, mournful, spiraled up. His daughter Jean, her face as still and cold as when she lay in the casket, on fire but icy, her lids shut, wavered and passed up with the smoke. His father in his casket. His brother Henry, his features burned and blistered by the steam boiler explosion. And

55

then a smiling grinning face, that of Tom Blankenship, the boy who was the model for Huckleberry Finn.

There had always been in Sam the child who wanted to float forever on a raft down the Mississippi, having many adventures but no responsibilities. Now he had the chance to drift forever on a raft. He could have uncounted numbers of thrilling experiences, could meet enough dukes and counts and kings to satisfy the most eager. He could be lazy, could fish, could talk night and day, wouldn't ever have to work for a living, could drift for a thousand years doing exactly as he pleased.

The trouble was that he could not do exactly as he wanted. There were too many areas where grail-slavery was practiced. Evil men took captives and deprived their prisoners of the luxuries given by their grails: the cigars, liquor, dreamgum. They kept the prisoner half starved, just alive enough so his grail could be used. They tied the slaves' hands and feet together, like chickens on the way to market, so they could not kill themselves. And if a man did succeed in committing suicide, then he was translated someplace else thousands of miles away and like as not would find himself in the hands of grail-slavers again.

Moreover, he was a grown man and just would not be as happy as a boy on a raft. No, if he went journeying on The River, he needed protection, comfort and, undeniable desire, authority. Also, there was his other great ambition to be pilot of a Riverboat. He had attained that for a while on Earth. Now, he would be a captain of a Riverboat, the largest, fastest, most powerful Riverboat that had ever existed, on the longest River in the world, a River that made the Missouri-Mississippi and all its tributaries, and the Nile, the Amazon, the Congo, the Ob, the Yellow River, all strung together, look like a little Ozark creek. His boat would be six decks high above the waterline, would have two tremendous sidewheels, luxurious cabins for the many passengers and crew, all of whom would be men and women famous in their time. And he, Samuel Langhorne Clemens, Mark Twain, would be the captain. And the boat would never stop until it reached the headwaters of The River, where the expedition would be launched against the monsters who had created this place and roused all of mankind again to its pain and disappointments and frustrations and sorrows.

The voyage might take a hundred years, maybe two or three centuries, but that was all right. This world did not have much, but it had more than enough time.

Sam warmed himself in the glow of his images, the mighty Riverboat, himself as captain in the wheelhouse, his first mate perhaps Mr. Christopher Columbus or Mr. Francis Drake, his Captain of Marines—no, not Captain, Major, since there would be only one aboard with the title of Captain—Sam Clemens, himself—his Major would perhaps be Alexander the Great or Julius Caesar or Ulysses S. Grant.

A pinprick of a thought pierced the glorious balloon sailing along in the wind of his dream. Those two ancient bastards, Alexander and Caesar, would never submit long to a subordinate position. They would plot from the very beginning to seize the captainship of the paddle-wheeler. And would that great man, U. S. Grant, take orders from him, Sam Clemens, a mere humorist, a man of letters in a world where letters did not exist?

The luminescent hydrogen of his images whistled out. He sagged. He thought of Livy again, so near but snatched away by the very thing that had made his other dream possible. She had been shown to him briefly, as if by a cruel god, and then taken away again. And was that other dream possible? He could not even find the vast store of iron that must be somewhere around here.

"You look tired and pale, Sam," Lothar said.

Sam stood up and said, "I'm going to bed."

"What, and disappoint that seventeenth-century Venetian beauty who's been making eyes at you all evening?" Lothar said.

"You take care of her," Sam said. He walked away. There had been some moments during the past few hours when he had been tempted to take her off to his hut, especially when the whiskey from the grail had first warmed him. Now he felt listless. Moreover, he knew that his guilt would return if he did take Angela Sangeotti to bed. He had suffered recurrent pangs during the twenty years here with the ten women who had been his mates. And now, strangely enough, he would feel guilt not only because of Livy but because of Temah, his Indonesian companion for the last five years.

"Ridiculous!" he had said to himself many times. "There is no rational reason why I should feel guilty about Livy. We've been separated for so long that we would be strangers. Too much has happened to both of us since Resurrection Day."

His logic made no difference. He suffered. And why not? Rationality had nothing to do with true logic; man was an irrational animal, acting strictly in accordance with his natal temperament and the stimuli to which he was peculiarly sensitive.

So why do I torture myself with things that cannot be my fault because I cannot help my responses?

Because it is my nature to torture myself for things that are not my fault. I am doubly damned. The first atom to move on primeval Earth and to knock against another atom started the chain of events that have led, inevitably, mechanically, to my being here and walking through the dark on a strange planet through a crowd of aged youths from everywhere and everytime to a bamboo hut where loneliness and guilt and self-recriminations, all rationally unnecessary but nevertheless unavoidable, await me.

I could kill myself, but suicide is useless here. You wake up twenty-four hours later, in a different place but still the same man who jumped into The River. Knowing that another jump won't solve a thing and probably will make you even more unhappy.

"Stone-hearted relentless bastards!" he said and shook his fist. Then he laughed sorrowfully and said, "But They can't help their hard hearts and cruelty any more than I can help what I am. We're all in it together."

This thought did not, however, make him wish any the less to get his revenge. He would bite the hand that had given him eternal life.

His bamboo hut was in the foothills under a large irontree. Although only a shack, it represented genuine luxury in this area, where stone tools to build houses were a rarity. The translatees had had to settle for makeshift housing, bamboo plants bent and tied together with grass ropes at the top and sides and covered with huge elephant-ear leaves from the irontrees. Of the five hundred varieties of bamboo in the valley, some could be split and made into knives, which, however, easily lost their edge.

Sam entered his hut, lay down on the cot, and covered himself with several big towels. The faint sound of distant revelry disturbed him. After tossing for a while, he gave in to the temptation to chew a piece of dreamgum. There was no predicting what its effect might be: ecstasy, bright manycolored shifting shapes, a feeling that all was right with the world, a desire to make love, or abysmal gloom with monsters springing out of the darkness at him, re-criminating ghosts from dead Earth, burning in the flames of hell while faceless devils laughed at his screams.

He chewed and swallowed his saliva and knew at once that he had made a mistake. It was too late then. He continued to chew while he saw before him that time when he was a boy and had drowned, or at least was close to it, and would have drowned if he had not been dragged from the waters. That was the first time I died, he thought, and then, no, I died when I was born. That's strange, my mother never told me about that.

He could see his mother lying on the bed, hair tangled, skin pale, eyelids half-opened, jaw dropped. The doctor was working on the baby—himself, Sam—while he smoked a cigar. He was saying out of the corner of his mouth to Sam's father, "Hardly seems worth saving."

His father said, "You had a choice between saving *that* and saving Jane?"

The doctor had a shock of bright red hair, a thick drooping red moustache, and pale blue eyes. His face was strange and brutal. He said, "I bury my mistakes. You worry too much. I'll salvage this bit of flesh, though it's really not worth doing, and save her, too."

The doctor wrapped him up and put him on the bed, and then the doctor sat down and began writing in a little black book. Sam's father said, "Must you write at a time like this?"

The doctor said, "I must write, though I'd get more writing done if I didn't talk so much. This is a log I keep on all the souls I bring into the world. I intend some day to write a big case history of the infants, find out if any ever amounted to anything. If I can bring *one* genius, *one*, into this vale of heavy tears, I will think my life worthwhile. Otherwise, I've been wasting my time bringing thousands of idiots, hypocrites, dogs in the mangers, *etc.* into this sad place."

Little Sam wailed, and the doctor said, "Sounds as if he's a lost soul before he's dead, don't he? As if he's bearing the blame for all the sins of the world on his tiny shoulders."

His father said, "You're a strange man. Evil, I think. Certainly not God-fearing."

"I pay tribute to the Prince of Darkness, yes," the doctor said.

The room was filled with the odor of blood, the doctor's boozy breath and cigar and sweat.

"What're you going to call him? Samuel? That's my name, too! It means 'name of God.' That's a joke. Two Samuels, heh? Sickly little devil, I don't think he'll live. If he does, he'll wish he hadn't."

His father roared, "Get out of my house, you devil's spawn! What kind of a man are you? Get out! I'll call in another doctor! I won't even let it be known that you attended my wife or had anything to do with this or was even in this house. I'll rid this house of your evil odor."

The doctor, swaying, threw his dirty instruments into the bag and snapped it shut.

"Very well. But you have delayed my passage through this miserable village of asses. I'm on my way to bigger and better things, my provincial friend. It was only out of the kindness of my heart that I took pity upon you because the quacks that serve this mudhole were out of town. I left the comforts of the tavern to come here and save an infant who would be better off dead, infinitely better. Which reminds me, though I don't know why, that you must pay my fee."

"I should throw you out of the house and pay you with nothing but curses!" Sam's father said. "But a man has to pay his debts no matter what the circumstances. Here's your thirty pieces of silver."

"Looks more like paper to me," the doctor said. "Well you can call in your dispenser of pills, folly and death, but just remember that it was Doctor Ecks that dragged your wife and baby from the jaws of death. Ecks, the unknown quantity, the eternal passer-through, the mysterious stranger, the devil dedicated to keeping other poor devils alive, also dedicated to the demon whiskey, since I can't abide rum."

"Out! Out!" Sam's father shouted. "Out before I kill you!"

"There's no gratitude in this world," Doctor Ecks mumbled. "Out of nothing I come, through a world populated by asses I pass, and into nothing I go. Ecks equals nothing."

Sweating, eyes open and rigid as those of a stone Apollo, Sam watched the drama. The scene and the actors were enclosed in a ball of pale yellow light through which veins of red shot like lightning and then faded out. The doctor turned his face once before he walked through the door of the house in Florida, Missouri, on November 30, 1835. He took the cigar from his mouth and grinned mockingly, revealing long yellow teeth with two abnormally white, abnormally long canines.

As if the scene were a film being shut off, it blinked out. Through the door which had been in Sam's birthplace and now was the door of the bamboo hut, another figure entered. It was momentarily silhouetted by the bright starlight, then slid into the shadows. Sam closed his eyes and steeled himself for another frightening experience. He groaned and wished he had not taken the dreamgum. Yet he knew that under the terror was a thread of delight. He hated and enjoyed this. The birth-drama was a fantasy, created by him to explain why he was the kind of man he was. But what was this shadowy figure moving silently and intently as death? From what deep cavern in his mind came this creature?

A baritone voice spoke. "Sam Clemens! Do not be alarmed! I am not here to harm you! I come to help you!"

"And what do you want in repayment for your help?" Sam said.

The man chuckled and said, "You're the kind of human being I like. I chose well."

"You mean I chose you to choose me," Sam replied.

There was a pause of several seconds, and then the man said, "I see. You think I'm another fantasy inspired by the gum. I'm not. Touch me."

"What for?" Sam said. "As a gum-inspired fantasy, you should know that you can be felt as well as seen and heard. State your business."

"Entirely? That would take too long. And I don't dare take much time with you. There are others in this area who might notice. That would be too bad for me, since they are very suspicious. They know there is a traitor among them, but they don't have the slightest idea who it could be."

"Others? They?" Sam answered.

"They—we Ethicals—are doing field work in this area

now," the figure said. "This is a unique situation, the first time that a completely unhomogenized assortment of humans has been thrown together. It presents a rare chance for study, and we are recording everything. I'm here as chief administrator, since I'm one of The Twelve."

"I'll have to figure you out after I wake up," Sam replied.

"You are awake, and I exist. I have objective reality. And, I repeat, I don't have much time."

Sam started to sit up but was pushed back by a hand which somehow communicated a sense of great power, muscular and mental. Sam shivered upon feeling it.

"You're one of Them," he whispered. "One of Them!"

He gave up his idea of seizing the man and calling for help.

"*Of* them, but not *with* them," the man said. "I'm with you human beings, and I intend to see that my people do not complete their filthy project. I have a plan, but a plan that will take much time, much patience, a slow and careful, devious development. I have contacted three humans now; you are the fourth. They are aware of parts of the plan but not all of it. If any one of them should be revealed and interrogated, he could tell the Ethicals only a little. The plan must unfold slowly and everything must appear accidental.

"Just as the meteorite must appear accidental."

Sam did start to sit up then but caught himself before the hand touched him.

"It was no accident?"

"No. I have known for some time of your dream of building a Riverboat and going to the end of The River. It would be impossible without iron. So I deflected the meteorite to bring its orbit within this planet's grip and cause it to crash near you. Not too near you, of course, otherwise you would have died and have been translated far from this area. There are safeguards to prevent such spatial matter from falling on the valley, but I managed to trip them out just long enough for the meteor to get through. Unfortunately, the guardians almost got to the

63

repulsion system in time. When the system went back into action, its effect caused the meteorite to go off the course I'd planned. As a result, we—I mean you—almost got killed. It was just luck that you weren't. But then I've found out that what you call luck is on my side."

"Then the falling star. . . ?"

"Is a deliberately felled star, yes."

Sam thought, if he knows so much about me, he must be one of the crew of the *Dreyrugr*. Unless he's able to make himself invisible. That isn't impossible. That egg-shaped ship I saw in the air was invisible; I only saw it because it was for some reason made visible very briefly. Maybe the lightning interfered with the apparatus that makes the ship invisible.

Then, What am I thinking? This is just another dreamgum fantasy.

The man said, "One of their agents is nearby! Listen carefully! The meteorite wasn't removed because we didn't have time. At least, that was *my* decision. It's buried under the plains and foothills ten miles from here. Go ten grailstones downRiver.

"You'll be on the perimeter of the original crater, where several large masses and many small pieces are buried. Start digging. The rest is up to you. I'll help you when I can, but I can't do anything obvious."

Sam's heart was beating so hard his own voice sounded muted.

"Why do you want me to build a boat?"

"You'll find out in time. For the present, be happy that you've been given what you need. Listen! There's a huge deposit of bauxite only five miles farther up, under the surface of the mountains, near the base. And near it is a small lode of platinum and two miles up from it, cinnabar."

"Bauxite? Platinum?"

"You fool!"

There was the sound of hard breathing. Sam could almost hear the man's internal struggle to control his disgust and fury. Then, calmly, "You'll need bauxite for aluminum and platinum for a catalyst for the many things you'll have in your boat. I haven't got time to explain. There are several engineers in this area who'll tell you what to do with the minerals. I must go. *He's* getting closer! Just do what I say. And, oh, yes, there's flint thirty miles upRiver!"

"But . . ." Sam said. The man was silhouetted briefly and was gone. Sam rose unsteadily and went to the door. Fires were still blazing on the banks, and small figures were capering in front of them. The stranger was gone. Sam went around to the back of the hut but there was no one there. He looked up at the sky, pale with great gas sheets and bright knots of white, blue, red and yellow stars. He had hopes he might catch a glimpse of a vehicle winking from visibility to invisibility. But there was nothing.

10

On returning to the hut, he was startled by a huge figure standing dark and immobile before his door. His heart hammering, he said, "Joe?"

"Yeah," answered the bass drum voice. Joe advanced to him and said, "There'th been thomone not human here. I can thmell him. He got a funny thtink, different than you humanth got. You know, it remindth me . . ."

He was silent for a while. Sam waited, knowing that the ponderous stone wheels were grinding out the flour of thought. Then Joe said, "Vell, I'll be damned!"

"What is it, Joe?"

"It'th been tho long ago, it happened on Earth, you know, thometime before I got killed there. No, it couldn't be. Jethuth Chritht, if vhat you thay ith true about how long ago I lived, it mutht've been maybe a hundred thouthand yearth ago!"

"Come on, Joe, don't leave me hanging up in the air."

"Vell, you ain't going to believe thith. But you got to remember that my nothe hath a memory, too."

"It ought to, it's bigger than your brain," Sam said. "Out with it, or are you trying to kill me with frustrated curiosity?"

"All right, Tham. I vath on the track of a *vifthangkruilth* tribethman, they lived about ten mileth from uth on the other thide of a big hill that looked like . . ."

"Never mind the details, Joe," Sam snapped.

"Vell, it vath late in the day and I knew I vath getting clothe to my enemy becauthe hith printth were tho frethh. And then I heard a noithe that made me think maybe the guy I vath following had backtracked on me and I vath going to get hith club thyoved all the vay up instead of vithevertha. Tho I dropped to the ground and crawled tvardth the noithe. And gueth vhat I thaw? Great Thcott, vhy didn't I ever tell you thith before? Vat a dummy I am!"

"I'll go along with that. So. . . ?"

"Vell, the guy I vath trailing had gotten vind of me, hough I don't know how, thinthe I'm ath thilent ath a veathel thneaking up on a bird, big ath I am. Anyvay, he had backtracked and might've come up behind me, maybe. But he vath lying on the ground, out cold ath a cavedigger'th ath. And there vere two humanth thtanding by him. Now, I'm ath brave ath the nektht guy and maybe braver, but thith vath the firtht time I ever thaw humanth, and it vath poththible I vath thcared. Cauthyiouth, anyvay.

"They vere dreththed up in clotheth, vat you've dethcribed to me ath clotheth. They had thome funny looking thingth in their handth, about a foot long, thick black thtickth that veren't vood, looked more like the thteel that Bloodakth'th akthe ith made of.

"I vath vell hidden but thothe bathtardth had thome vay of knowing I vath there. One of them pointed the thtick at me, and I became unconthious. Paththed out. Vhen I came to, the two humanth and the *vif* vere gone. I got to hell out of there, but I never forgot that thmell."

Sam said, "That's the whole story?"

Joe nodded. Sam said, "I'll be damned! Does that mean that these . . . these people . . . have been keeping an eye on us for half a million years? Or more? Or are they the same people?"

"Vhat do you mean?"

Sam told Joe that he must never tell anybody else what he was going to hear. He knew that the titanthrop could be trusted, yet when he explained he felt misgivings. X had required him not to utter a word to anybody else.

Joe nodded so much that the silhouette of his nose was like a log rising and falling in a heavy sea. "It all tieth in. It'th quite a cointhidenthe, ain't it? Me theeing them on Earth, then being taken along on Ikhnaton'th ekthpedithion and theeing the tower and airthyip, and now you being picked by thith Ekth to build the thteamboat. How about that, huh?"

Sam was so excited that he could not fall asleep until shortly before dawn. He managed to rouse himself for breakfast, though he would have preferred to stay in bed. While the Vikings, the German, Joe, and he were eating the contents of their grails, he told them a heavily censored version of his experience. But he told it as if it had been a dream. If he had not had Joe's olfactory backing for the mysterious stranger's presence, he would have thought it *was* a dream.

Von Richthofen, of course, pooh-poohed it, but the Norsemen believed in revelation via dream. Rather, most of them did. Among the inevitable sceptics, unfortunately, was Erik Bloodaxe.

"You want us to go traipsing ten miles and dig just because you had a wild nightmare?" he bellowed. "I've always thought you had a mind as weak as your courage, Clemens, and now I know it! Forget about it!"

Sam had been sitting down while eating. He rose to his feet and, glaring beneath the heavy brows, said, "Joe and I will go our own way then. We'll organize the locals to help us dig, and when we find the iron—as we surely will—you won't be able to buy your way into the organization for love or money. The first of which, by the way, you've never had on Earth or here, and the second of which just doesn't exist."

Bloodaxe, bread and steak spewing from his mouth, shouted and swung his ax. "No miserable thrall speaks to me like that! You'll dig nothing but your grave, wretch!"

Joe, who had already risen to stand by Clemens, growled and pulled his huge stone ax from his belt sheath. The Vikings stopped eating and walked away to arrange themselves a little behind their chief. Von Richtofen had been grinning while Clemens was describing his dream. The grin remained frozen, and he was quivering. The shaking was not from fright. Now he arose and without a word stood by Clemens' right side.

He said to Bloodaxe, "You have sneered at the fighting ability and courage of Germans, my Norse friend. Now you will have that sneer shoved down your throat."

Bloodaxe laughed loudly. "Two gamecocks and an ape!

68

You won't die easy deaths; I'll see that it takes you days to find the joy of death! Before I'm done, you'll be begging me to end your pain!"

"Joe!" Clemens said. "Make sure you kill Bloodaxe first. Then you can get up a little sweat knocking off the rest."

Joe raised the 50-pound weight of the flint head above his shoulder and rotated it through a 45-degree arc, back and forth, as easily as if it weighed an ounce. He said, "I can break hith breathtbone vith one throw and probably knock down theveral behind him."

The Norsemen knew that he was not bragging; they had seen him smash too many skulls. He was capable of killing half of them before they killed him, maybe of smashing all of them and still be standing. But they had sworn to defend Bloodaxe to the death and, much as many of them disliked him, they would not break their oath.

There should have been no cowards in the Rivervalley; courage should have become universal. Death was not permanent; a man was killed only to rise again. But those who had been brave on Earth were usually brave here, and those cowardly on Earth were cowardly here. The mind might know that death lasted only a day, but the cells of the body, the unconscious, the configurations of emotion, or whatever it was that made up a man's character, these did not recognize the fact. Sam Clemens dodged violence and the resultant pain—which he feared more than violent death—as long as he could. He had fought with the Vikings, swung an ax, wielded a spear, wounded and been wounded and once even killed a man, though it had been more by accident than skill. But he was an ineffectual warrior. In battle the valves of his heart were turned full open, and his strength poured out.

Sam knew this well, but about this he had no self-reproach or shame.

Erik Bloodaxe was furious and not at all afraid. But if he died, and he probably would, he would never be able to take part in Clemens' dream of the great riverboat or storm the citadels of the north pole. And, though he had scoffed at the dream, he still believed in a part of him that dreams could be revelations sent by the gods. Perhaps he was robbing himself of a glorious future.

Sam Clemens knew his man and was betting that his ambitions would overcome his anger. So they did. The king lowered the ax and forced a smile.

"It is not good to question what the gods send until you look into it," he said. "I have known priests who were given the truth in dreams by Odin and Heimdall, yet they had no hearts for battle and spoke lies except when they spoke for the gods. So we will dig for the iron. If there is iron, good. If not . . . then we will take up the matter where we left off."

Sam sighed with relief and wished he could quit shaking. His bladder and bowels pained him with their urgency to evacuate, but he did not dare to excuse himself at that moment. He had to play the role of the man who had the upper hand. Ten minutes later, unable to bear it any longer, he walked off toward his hut.

X, the Mysterious Stranger, had said that digging could take place anywhere near the tenth grailstone upRiver from their present position. However, the would-be diggers first had to straighten out the locals on who was running things. A Chicago gangster of the 20's and 30's, Alfonso Gilbretti, had allied himself with a Belgian coalmine and steel-mill magnate of the late nineteenth century and a Turkish sultan of the mid-eighteenth. This triumvirate had followed the by-now classical pattern of organizing a nuclear gang from those who had been merciless exploiters of their fellow men in crime, business, and other terrestrial activities. Those who objected to the newly self-constituted rulers had been disposed of the day before, and the gang had determined what share of the grails' output each "citizen" would pay for "protection." Gilbretti had picked out a harem of five women, of whom two were willing and one had died already because she had tried to break his head with a grail when he entered her hut the night before.

Clemens knew all this because of the grapevine. He

realized that the Vikings would be faced with two hundred toughs and at least a thousand of the so-called militia. Against them would be forty men and twenty women. But the locals were armed only with bamboo spears with fire-hardened tips while the invaders had Riverdragon-armor, flint axes and flint-tipped spears and arrows. And there was Joe Miller.

Bloodaxe announced from the ship what the Norsemen intended to do. If the locals wanted to participate, they could do so under the rulership of the Norsemen. However, no one would have to "contribute" any of his grail output and no woman would be taken by force.

Gilbretti hurled a spear and a Sicilian oath at Erik. The Norsemen escaped the effects of both and threw his ax. Its edge buried itself in Gilbretti's chest, and Bloodaxe was down off the ship and on the land and racing after his precious iron weapon, a flint-studded club in hand, before anybody could move. After him came Joe Miller and thirty men. The women shot arrows while a crew launched the last rocket into the toughs. It struck exactly on target, near the rear ranks of the closely arranged Gilbrettians. About forty were either killed, wounded or stunned.

Within seventy seconds, the Belgian magnate and the Turk were dead, their heads pulped by Joe's ax, and the others were either casualties or running for their lives.

None got away. The militia saw their chance to get revenge and either beat or stabbed most of them to death. The ten left alive were spreadeagled, and burning bamboo splints were thrust into them. Sam Clemens stood the screaming as long as he was able. He did not want to make himself unpopular by cutting the fun too short and so he tried to ignore the spectacle. Lothar von Richthofen said that he certainly understood the desire to hurt by those who had been hurt. But he would not put up with this barbarity a moment longer. He strode up to the nearest sufferer and silenced him with a single chop of his axe. He then ordered the others done away with immediately. Erik Bloodaxe might have interfered with this order, since he thought it proper that one's enemies should be put through some torture to teach them and others a lesson. But he had

71

been stunned by a piece of the rock-shrapnel thrown by the rocket explosion and was out of the picture for a while.

Reluctantly, the militia obeyed, although in their own fashion. They threw the nine survivors into The River, where the fire was certainly put out but not the pain of the splinters themselves. Some thrashed around for several minutes before drowning. And this was strange, since they could have killed the agony in their bowels by killing themselves, knowing they would be alive again and whole again in a short time. Such was the drive of their instincts for survival, they fought to keep their heads above water as long as possible.

11

Digging did not begin at once. First the locals had to be organized and definite administrative, judicial and legislative lines laid down and the military formed. The area constituting the new state had to be defined. Clemens and Bloodaxe argued about this for a while before deciding that three miles each way up and down The River from the site of the digging would make a manageable area. A sort of Maginot line was built on the borders; this consisted of a twenty-foot-wide strip of two-foot-long bamboo stakes, pointing at various angles, protruding from the ground. The line ran from the base of the mountains down to the bank of The River. Huts were built by the chevaux-de-frise, and spearmen and women lived in these as the garrisons.

A third cheval-de-frise was built on the banks. When this was finished, the dragonship was dispatched to the point upRiver where there was a flint mine, if the Mysterious Stranger was to be believed. Bloodaxe stayed behind with about fifteen of his men. He put his lieutenant, Snorri Ragnarsson, in charge of the expedition. Snorri was to bargain with the locals for flint by promising them a share of the iron when it was dug up. If the locals refused to part with the flint, then he was to threaten them. Bloodaxe thought that Joe Miller should go with the ship because the titanthrop's huge size and grotesque features would awe the locals.

Sam Clemens agreed with the Norseman's logic on this point but he did not like the idea of being separated from Joe. Yet he did not want to go on the ship with Joe, because of what Bloodaxe might do in his absence. The king was bad-tempered and arrogant. If he affronted the newly conquered people, he might cause a revolution which could overwhelm the small number of Vikings.

Sam strode back and forth in front of his hut, while he smoked and thought furiously. There was iron under the grass, more than enough to realize The Dream, yet he could not even start to dig for it until a multitude of preparations were made. And every step he thought to take was balked because a dozen other problems came up. He was so frustrated, he almost bit through his cigar. The people who were sitting on the flint mine needed something like the sight of Joe to be softened up for cooperation. But if Joe were absent, Bloodaxe might take advantage of this to kill Sam. He would not do it openly, because he feared Joe, but he could easily arrange an *accident*.

Sam cursed and sweated. "If I die, I'll be resurrected somewhere else, so far from this place it might take a thousand years to get back on a canoe. Meanwhile, other men will mine the iron and build *my* Riverboat. Mine! Mine! Not theirs! Mine!"

At this moment, Lothar von Richthofen ran up to him. "I've located two of the kind of men you're looking for. Only one isn't a man! Imagine that, a female engineer!"

The man, John Wesley O'Brien, was a mid-twentieth-century metallurgical engineer. The woman was half Mongolian, half Russian, and had spent most of her life in mining communities in Siberia.

Sam Clemens shook hands with them and told them briefly what he had to do now and what he expected to do later.

O'Brien said, "If there is a big bauxite deposit near here, then we can probably build the kind of ship you want."

He was very excited, as any man would be who had given up any hope of carrying on his Terrestrial profession here. There were many like him, men and women who wanted to work if for no other reason than to kill time. There were doctors who had nothing to do but set an occasional broken bone, printers who had no type to set or paper to use, mailmen with no mail to deliver, smiths with no horses to shoe, farmers with no crops to grow, housewives with no children to raise, the food already cooked, housecleaning done in fifteen minutes and no marketing to do, salesmen with nothing to sell, preachers whose religion was thoroughly discredited by the existence of this world, bootleggers with no means of making grain alcohol, buttonmakers with no buttons, pimps and whores whose professions were ruined by an excess of amateurs, mechanics with no autos, admen with no ads, carpet-makers with only grass and bamboo fibers to work with, cowboys without horses or cattle, painters with no paint or canvas, pianists without pianos, railroad men with no iron, stockbrokers with no stocks to deal in, and so on.

O'Brien continued, "However, you want a steamboat, and that's not very realistic. You'd have to stop at least once a day to chop wood for fuel, which would mean a long delay even if the locals permitted you to take their limited supply of bamboo and pine trees. Moreover, your axes, the boilers and other parts would wear out long before you reached the end of your journey, and you wouldn't have enough space to carry enough iron for replacements parts. No, what you need are electric motors.

"Now, there's a man in this area I met shortly after translation here. I don't know where he is just now but he must be somewhere close. I'll find him for you. He's an electrical wizard, a late twentieth-century engineer who knows how to build the type of motors you'll need."

"Hold your horses!" Sam said. "Where would you get all the tremendous amounts of electrical power you'd need? Would we have to build our own Niagara Falls to carry along with us?"

O'Brien was a short, slight youth with a plume of almost orange hair and a face with features so delicate he looked effeminate. He had a crooked smile which managed nevertheless to be charming. He said, "It's available everywhere up and down The River."

He pointed at the mushroom shape of the nearest grailstone. "Three times a day, those stones output an enormous electrical power. What's to prevent us from hooking up power lines to a number of them and storing the discharges to run the boat's motors?"

Sam goggled for a moment, then said, "Strike me dumb! No, that's a redundant phrase. I am dumb! Right before my eyes, and I never thought of it! Of course!"

Then he slitted his eyes and lowered his thick tangled eyebrows. "How in hell could you store all that energy? I don't know much about electricity, but I do know that you'd need a storage battery taller than the Eiffel Tower or a capacitor the size of Pike's Peak."

O'Brien shook his head. "I thought so, too, but this fellow, he's a mulatto, half Afrikaans, half Zulu, Lobengula Van Boom, he said that if he had the materials, he could build a storage device—a batacitor, he called it—a ten-meter cube, that could hold ten megakilowatts and feed it out a tenth of a volt per second or all at once.

"Now, if we can mine the bauxite and make aluminum wire, and there are many problems in doing even that, we can use the aluminum in circuits and electrical motors. Aluminum isn't as efficient as copper, but we don't have copper, and aluminum will do the job."

Sam's fury and frustration disappeared. He grinned, snapped his fingers, and made a little leap into the air. "Find van Boom! I want to talk to him!"

He puffed away, the end of his cigar as glowing as the images in his mind. Already, the great white paddle-wheeler was steaming (no, electrificating?) up The River with Sam Clemens in the pilothouse, Sam Clemens wearing a Riverboat captain's cap of Riverdragon leather on his head, Sam Clemens, captain of the fabulous, the unique paddle-wheeler, the great vessel churning on the start of its million mile-plus journey. Never such a boat, never such a River, never such a trip! Whistles blowing, bells clanging, the crew made up of the great and near-great men and women of all time. From mammoth sub-human Joe Miller of 1,000,000 B.C. to the delicate-bodied but vast-brained scientist of the late twentieth-century.

Von Richthofen brought him back to the immediate reality.

"I'm ready to start digging for the iron. But what do you intend to do about Joe?"

Sam groaned and said, "I can't make up my mind what to do. I'm as tense as a diamond cutter before he makes the first tap. One wrong thing, and the Kohinoor shatters. Okay, okay! I'll send Joe. I have to take a chance. But being without him makes me feel as helpless as a honeydipper without a bucket, a banker on Black Friday. I'll tell Bloodaxe and Joe, and you can start your crew. Only we ought to have a ceremony. We'll all have a snort, and I'll dig the first shovelful."

A few minutes later, his stomach warmed by a big shot of Bourbon, cigar in mouth, his speech finished, Sam started to dig. The bamboo shovel had a sharp edge, but the grass was so tough and thick that it was necessary to use the shovel as a machete. Sweating, swearing, declaring that he had always hated physical exertion and was not cut out to be a ditch-digger, Sam chopped away the grass. On driving the now-dulled shovel into the earth, Sam found he could not bring up even a half shovelful. It would be necessary to hack away at the grass and the dirt between.

"By the great horn spoon!" he said, flinging the shovel down on the ground. "Let some peasant who's cut out for this drudgery do it! I'm a brain-worker!"

The crowd laughed and set to work with flint and bamboo knives and flint axes. Sam said, "If that iron is ten feet down, it'll take us ten years to find it. Joe, you'd better bring back plenty of flint, otherwise we're done for."

"Do I have to go?" Joe Miller said. "I'll mithth you, Tham."

"You gotta go, as all men do," Sam said. "Don't worry about me."

12

During the next three days, a hole ten feet across and one foot deep was made. Von Richthofen organized the teams so that a new one replaced the previous crew every fifteen minutes. There was no lack of fresh and strong diggers, but delays were caused by the flaking of new flint tools and the making of new bamboo tools. Bloodaxe growled about the damage to the axes and knives, saying that if they were to be attacked, the stone weapons could not cut through the skin of a baby. Clemens begged him for the dozenth time to be allowed to use the steel ax, and Bloodaxe refused.

"If Joe were here, I'd have him take the ax away from him," Clemens said to Lothar. "And where is Joe, anyway? He should be back by now, empty-handed or bearing gifts."

"I think we ought to send somebody in a dugout to find out," von Richthofen said. "I'd go myself, but I think you still need me around to protect you from Bloodaxe."

"If something's happened to Joe, we'll both need protection," Sam said. "All right, that Pathan, Abdul, can be our spy. He could wriggle unnoticed through a basket of rattlesnakes."

At dawn, two days later, Abdul paddled in. He woke Sam and Lothar, who were sleeping in the same hut for mutual protection. In broken English, he explained that Joe Miller was tied up in a strongly built bamboo cage. Abdul had tried to get a chance to free Joe, but the cage had an around-the-clock guard.

The Vikings had been greeted with friendliness and sympathy. The chief of the region had seemed surprised that his flint for their iron would be a very good trade. He had held a big party to celebrate the agreement and had given his guests as much liquor and dreamgum as they wished. The Norse had been overcome while they snored drunkenly. Joe was asleep but had awakened while being tied up. With bare hands only, he had killed twenty men and injured fifteen before the chief had half stunned him with a club against the back of his neck. The blow would have broken anybody else's neck; it just reduced his fighting ability enough to permit men to swarm over him and restrain him while the chief hit him twice over the head.

"The chief knows Joe is a mighty warrior," Abdul said. "Greater than Rustam himself. I overheard some men talking, and they said their chief plans to use Joe as a hostage. He wants to become partners in the iron mine. If refused, he will not kill Joe but will make a slave out of him, although I doubt he can do that. He'll attack us, kill us, get the iron for himself.

"He can do it. He's building a huge fleet, many small ships carrying forty men each, hastily put together but serviceable to transport his army. He'll make an all-out attack with warriors armed with flint weapons, bows and arrows and heavy war-boomerangs."

"And who is this would-be Napoleon?" Sam said.

"His men called him King John. They say that he ruled over England when men wore armor and fought with swords. In the time of Saladin. His brother was a very famous warrior, Richard the Lion-Hearted."

Sam cursed and said, "John Lackland! The blackhearted pussyfooting Prince John! So rotten that the English swore never again to have a king named John! I'd sooner have a scoundrel like Leopold of Belgium or Jim Fiske after my hide!"

Thirty minutes later, Sam was shoved into an even deeper gloom. This time, the message came by word-of-mouth grapevine. Thirty miles downRiver, a huge fleet was sailing toward them. This consisted of sixty large single-masters, each carrying forty warriors. The leader of the armada was a king of an area which had been just outside the destruction caused by the meteorite. His name was Joseph Maria von Radowitz.

"I read about him in school!" von Richthofen said. "Let's see. He was born in 1797, died about 1853, I believe. He was an artillery expert and a good friend of

Fredrick Wilhelm IV of Prussia. He was called 'The Warlike Monk' because he was a general who also had strict religious views. He died when he was about fifty years old, a disappointed man because he had been dropped from favor. So now he's alive again, young, and no doubt trying to impose his Puritanism upon others, and killing those who don't agree with him."

An hour later, he got word that King John's fleet had set sail.

"John's force will get here first," he told Bloodaxe. "They'll be faster because the wind and current will be helping them."

"Teach your grandmother to suck eggs," Bloodaxe snorted.

"So what do you plan to do?"

"Smash the Englishman first and then destroy the German later," Bloodaxe replied. He swung his ax and said, "By the shattered hymen of Thor's bride! My ribs still hurt, but I will ignore the pain!"

Sam did not argue. When he was alone with Lothar, he said, "Fighting against hopeless odds until you die is all very admirable. But it doesn't pay off in preferred stock. Now, I know you're going to think I'm as spineless as a cockroach, Lothar, but I have a dream, a great dream, and it transcends all ordinary ideas of faithfulness and morality. I want that boat, Lothar, and I want to pilot it to the end of The River, no matter what!

"If we had a fighting chance, I wouldn't suggest this. But we don't. We're outnumbered and have inferior weapons. So I'm going to suggest that we make a deal."

"With whom?" von Richthofen said. He was grim and pale.

"With John. He may be the most treacherous king in the world, although the competition is fierce, but he's the one most likely to throw in with us. Radowitz's fleet is bigger than his, and even if John somehow managed to defeat it, he'd be so weakened we could take him. But if we ganged up with John, we could give Radowitz such a beating he'd take off like a hound dog, tail closed down like a latch."

80

Von Richthofen laughed and said, "For a moment I thought you were going to propose that we hide in the mountains and then come out to offer our services to the victor. I could not stand the idea of playing coward, of leaving these people to fight alone."

"I'll be frank," Clemens said, "even if I am Sam. I'd do that if I thought it was the only way. No, what I'm suggesting is that we get rid, somehow, of Bloodaxe. He'll never go along with taking John in as a partner."

"You'll have to watch John as if he were a poisonous snake," the German said. "But I see no other way out. Nor do I think it's treachery to kill Bloodaxe. It's just insurance. He'll get rid of you the first chance he gets."

"And we'll not really be killing him," Sam said. "Just removing him from the picture."

Clemens wanted to talk more about what they should do, but von Richthofen said that there had been enough talk. Sam was putting off the taking of action—as usual. Things had to be done right now.

Sam gave a sigh and said, "I suppose so."

"What's the matter?" Lothar said.

"I'm suffering from guilt before I've even incurred it," Sam replied. "I feel like a yellow dog, although there's no reason I should. None at all! But I was born to feel guilty about everything, even about being born."

Lothar threw his hands up in disgust and strode off, saying over his shoulder, "Follow me or hang back. But you can't expect me to think of you as the captain of our boat. Captains don't drag their feet."

Sam grimaced but went after him. Lothar talked to twelve men he thought trustworthy enough for what he proposed. The sun began to climb down from the zenith while the details were arranged and then the men went to arm themselves. They came back from their huts with bamboo spears and knives. One had a bamboo bow with six arrows, effective only at close range.

Lothar von Richthofen and Sam Clemens leading, the group strode up to the Norse king's hut. Six Vikings stood guard outside.

"We want to talk to Bloodaxe," Sam said, trying to keep his voice from quavering.

"He's in there with a woman," Ve Grimarsson said.

Sam raised his hand. Lothar ran past him and clubbed Grimarsson over the head. An arrow whistled past Sam's shoulder and stopped in the throat of a guard. Within ten seconds, the others had been killed or wounded too severely to continue fighting. There were shouts from a distance as a dozen other Vikings came running to protect their chief. Bloodaxe, naked, bellowing, his steel ax held high, rushed through the doorway. Von Richthofen lunged with his spear and impaled the Norseman on it. Bloodaxe dropped the ax and staggered back, driven by the German's weight on the spear, until he slammed into the bamboo wall of the hut. He stared; his mouth worked; blood ran from a corner of his lips; his skin was blue-gray.

The German then yanked the spear out of the Norseman's belly, and Bloodaxe crumpled.

There was a fight afterward with six of Clemens' men killed and four wounded. The Vikings did not give up until all were silenced and as dead as their king.

Sam Clemens, panting hoarsely, splashed with blood from others and bleeding from a gash on his shoulder, leaned on his spear. He had killed one man, Gunnlaugr Thorrfinnsson, puncturing his kidney from behind while the Viking was thrusting at von Richthofen. Too bad about Gunnlaugr. Of all the Norsemen, he enjoyed Sam's jokes the most. Now he was stabbed in the back by a good friend.

I've fought in 38 battles, Sam thought, and I've slain only two men. The other was a severely wounded Turk struggling to get to his feet. Sam Clemens, the mighty warrior, great-hearted hero. Thinking thus, he gazed with the horror and fascination that corpses had always had for him and would have if he lived 10,000 years.

And then he squawked with fright and yanked his left ankle away in a frantic effort to escape the hand gripping it. Unable to do so, he lifted his spear to drive it into the man who held him. He looked down into the pale blue eyes of Erik Bloodaxe. Life had surged up in Bloodaxe for a moment. The glaze was gone from his eyes and the skin was not so gray-blue. His voice was weak but strong enough for Sam, and others nearby, to hear him.

"*Bikkja!* Droppings of Ratatosk! Listen! I will not let you go until I have spoken! The gods have given me the powers of a *voluspa*. They want revenge for your treachery. Listen! I know there is iron beneath this blood-soaked grass. I feel the iron flowing in my veins. Its grayness turns my blood thick and cold. There is iron enough and more than enough for your great white boat. You will dig up this iron, and you will build a boat to rival *Skithblathnir*.

"You will be captain of it, Bitch Clemens, and your boat will sail up The River for more miles than *Sleipnir*'s eight legs could cover in a day. You will go back and forth, north and south, east and west, as the Rivervalley takes you. You will go around the world many times.

"But the building of the boat and the sailing thereof will be bitter and full of grief. And after years, two generations as known on Earth, after great sufferings, and some joys, when you think you are at long last near the end of the long long journey, then you will find me!

"Rather, I will find you! I will be waiting on a distant boat and I will kill you. And you will never get to the end of The River nor storm the gates of Valhalla!"

Sam became cold and brittle. Even when he felt the hand slacken its grip on his ankle, he did not move. He heard the death rattle and did not move or look down.

Faintly, Bloodaxe spoke again. "I wait!"

There was another rattle, more drawn out, and the hand fell away. Sam forced himself to step away, not sure that he would not break into a dozen pieces. He looked at von Richthofen and said, "Superstition! A man can't look into the future!"

Von Richthofen said, "I don't think so. But if things are as you believe, Sam, mechanical, automatic, then the future is predetermined. If things are ready-made, why can't the future open up for a minute, lights blaze in the tunnel of time, and a man see down the track?"

Sam did not answer. Von Richthofen laughed to show that he was joking and clapped Sam on the shoulder.

Sam said, "I need a drink. Badly." Then he said, "I don't take any stock in that superstitious rot."

But he believed that those dying eyes had seen into the years ahead, and he was thereafter to believe.

13

An hour before dusk, King John's fleet arrived. Sam Clemens sent a man out to tell John that he wanted to discuss a possible partnership. John, ever willing to talk to you before knifing you, agreed to a powwow. Sam stood on the edge of the bank while John Lackland leaned on the railing of his galley. Sam, his terror unfrozen by a dozen whiskeys, described the situation and spoke glowingly of the great boat to be built.

John was a short, dark man with very broad shoulders, tawny hair and blue eyes. He smiled frequently and spoke in an English not so heavily accented it could not be easily understood. Before coming to this area, he had lived for ten years among late-eighteenth-century Virginians. A fluent linguist, he had disburdened himself of much of the speech patterns of his twelfth-century English and Norman French.

He understood well why it would pay him to team up with Clemens against von Radowitz. No doubt he had mental reservations about what he would do after von Radowitz was disposed of, but he came ashore to swear eternal friendship and partnership. The details of the pact were arranged over drinks, and then King John had Joe Miller released from his cage on the flagship.

Sam did not shed tears easily, but several trickled down his cheeks on seeing the titanthrop. Joe wept like a perambulating Niagara Falls and almost broke Sam's ribs in his embrace.

Von Richthofen, however, told Clemens later, "At least, with Bloodaxe, you knew fairly well where you stood. You've made a bad trade."

"I'm from Missouri," Sam replied, "but I never was much of a mule trader. However, if you're running for your life, a pack of wolves snapping at your heels, you'll trade a foundered plug for a wild mustang, as long as he'll carry you out of danger. You worry later about how to get down off of him without breaking your neck."

The battle, which started at dawn the next day, was long. Several times, disaster came close for Clemens and King John. The Englishman's fleet had hidden near the east bank in the early morning fog and then had come up behind the German fleet. Flaming pine torches thrown by John's sailors started fires on many of von Radowitz's boats. But the invaders spoke a common language, were well disciplined, had soldiered together a long time, and were far better armed.

Their rockets sank many of John's boats and blasted holes in the cheval-de-frise along the bank. The Germans then stormed ashore under cover of a hail of arrows. During the landing, a rocket exploded in the hole dug to get to the iron. Sam was knocked over by the blast. Half stunned, he rose. And he became aware of a man he had never seen before standing by him. Sam was sure that the man had not been in this area until this moment.

The stranger was about five feet seven inches tall and was stockily, even massively, built. Like an old red ram, Sam thought, though the stranger looked, of course, as if he were twenty-five years old. His curly auburn hair hung down his back to his waist. His black eyebrows were as thick as Sam's. His eyes were large, dark brown with chips of pale green. His face was aquiline and jutting-chinned. His ears were large and stood out at almost right angles from his head.

The body of an old red ram, Sam thought, with the head of a great horned owl.

His bow was made of a material that Sam had seen before, though it was rare. It was made from two of the curved horns that ring a Riverdragon-fish's mouth. The two were joined together to make one double recurved bow. This type was by far the most powerful and durable bow in the valley but had one disadvantage. It took extremely powerful arms to bend it.

The stranger's leather quiver held twenty arrows, flint-tipped, the shafts carved laboriously from the fin bones of the Riverdragon and feathered with carved pieces of bone so thin that the sun shone through them.

He spoke in a German with a thick, non-Germanic, unidentifiable accent. "You look like Sam Clemens."

"I am," Clemens replied. "What's left of me. But how did you. . . ?"

"You were described to me by—" the stranger paused—"one of Them."

Sam did not understand for a moment. The part-deafness caused by the explosion, the yells of men killing each other only twenty yards away, other, more distant rocket explosions, and the sudden appearance of this man gave everything an unreal quality.

He said, "He sent . . . the Mysterious Stranger . . . he sent you! You're one of the twelve!"

"He? Not he! *She* sent me!"

Sam did not have time to question him about this. He checked the impulse to ask the man if he was any good with the bow. He looked as if he could wrest from the bow the last atom of potentiality. Instead, Sam climbed to the top of the pile of dirt by the hole and pointed at the nearest enemy ship, its prow against the bank. A man standing on its poopdeck was bellowing orders.

"Von Radowitz, the leader of the enemy," Sam said. "He's out of range of our feeble bows."

Smoothly, swiftly, pausing only to aim briefly, not bothering to gauge the wind which blew always at this time of day at a steady six miles an hour, the bowman loosed his black arrow. Its trajectory ended in the solar plexus of von Radowitz. The German staggered backward under the impact, whirled to reveal the bloody tip sticking from his back, and fell backward over the railing and into the waters between boat and bank.

The second-in-command rallied his men, and the bowman drove a shaft through him. Joe Miller, clad in Riverdragon-leather armor, swinging his huge oaken club, ravaged among the Germans in the center of the line of battle. He was like an 800-pound lion with a human brain. Death and panic went with him. He smashed twenty skulls by the minute and occasionally picked up a man with his free hand and threw him to knock down a half dozen or so.

At different times, five men managed to slip behind Joe, but the black bone arrows of the newcomer always intercepted them.

The invaders broke and tried to get back to their boats. Von Richthofen, naked, bloody, grinning, danced before Sam. "We've won! We've won!"

"You'll get your flying machine yet," Sam said. He turned to the archer. "What is your name?"

"I have had many names, but when my grandfather first held me in his arms he called me Odysseus."

All Sam could think of to say was, "We've got a lot to talk about."

Could this be the man of whom Homer sang? The real Ulysses, that is, the historical Ulysses, who *did* fight before the walls of Troy and about whom legends and fairy tales were later collected? Why not? The shadowy man who had talked in Sam's hut had said he had picked twelve men out of the billions available. What his means were for choosing, Sam did not know, but he presumed the reasons were good. And the Mysterious Stranger had told him of one choice: Richard Francis Burton. Was there some kind of aura about the twelve that enabled the renegade to know the man who could do the job? Some tiger color of the soul?

Late that night, Sam, Joe, Lothar and the Achaean, Odysseus, walked to their huts after the victory celebration. Sam's throat was dry from all the talking. He had tried to squeeze out of the Achaean all he knew about the siege of Troy and his wanderings afterward. He had been told enough to confuse, not enlighten, him.

The Troy that Odysseus knew was not the city near the Hellespont, the ruins that Terrestrial archeologists called Troy VIIa. The Troy that Odysseus, Agamemnon and Diomedes besieged was farther south, opposite the island of Lesbos but inland and north of the Kaikos River. It had been inhabited by people related to the Etruscans, who lived at that time in Asia Minor and later emigrated to Italy because of the Hellenic invaders. Odysseus knew of the city which later generations had thought was Troy.

Dardanians, barbarophones, lived there; they were related to the true Trojans. Their city had fallen five years before the Trojan war to other barbarians from the north.

Three years after the siege of the real Troy, which had lasted for only two years, Odysseus had gone on the great sea-raid of the Danaans, or Achaeans, against the Egypt of Rameses III. The raid had ended in disaster. Odysseus had fled for his life by sea and had indeed gone unwillingly on a journey that took three years and resulted in his visiting Malta, Sicily and parts of Italy, lands unknown then to the Greeks. There had been no Laestrygonians, Aeolus, Calypso, Circe, Polyphemus. His wife was named Penelope, but there were no suitors for him to kill.

As for Achilles and Hector, Odysseus knew of them only as the principals in a song. He supposed both of them to have been Pelasgians, the people who lived in the Hellenic peninsula before the Achaeans came down out of the north to conquer it. The Achaeans had adapted the Pelasgian song to suit their own purposes, and later bards must have incorporated it in the *Iliad*. Odysseus knew *The Iliad* and *The Odyssey*, because he had met a scholar who could recite both epics from memory.

"What about the Wooden Horse?" Sam said, fully expecting to draw a blank with his question. To his surprise, Odysseus not only knew of it but said that he had indeed been responsible for it. It was a deception conceived in desperation by madness and should have failed.

And this, to Sam, was the most startling of all. The scholars had united in denying any reality to this story, saying that it was patently impossible. They should have been correct, since the idea did seem fantastic, nor was it likely that the Achaeans would be stupid enough to build the horse or the Trojans stupid enough to fall for it. But the wooden horse had existed, and the Achaeans had gotten into the city by hiding inside the horse.

Von Richthofen and Joe listened to the two talk. Sam had decided that, despite the Ethical's warning to tell no one about him, Joe and Lothar should know of him. Otherwise, Sam would be doing so many things that would be inexplicable to anyone closely associated with him. Besides, Sam felt that his taking others into the secret would show the Ethical that Sam was really running things. It was a childish gesture, but Sam made it.

Sam said good night to all but Joe and lay down on the cot. Although very tired, he could not get to sleep. The snores issuing from Joe like a maelstrom through a keyhole did not help soothe his insomnia. Also, his excitement over tomorrow's doings made his nerves ripple and brain pulse. Tomorrow would be a historic day, if this world was to have a history. Eventually, there would be paper, ink, pencils, even a printing press. The great Riverboat would have a weekly journal. There would be a book which would tell of how the hole was deepened by exploding rockets captured from von Radowitz's ships. Perhaps the iron would be exposed tomorrow; it surely must.

And there was in addition his worries about King John, the jesting slyboots. God knew what that insidious mind was planning. It was doubtful that John would do anything treacherous until the boat was built, and that would be years from now. There was no need to worry yet, none at all. Despite which, Sam worried.

14

Sam awoke with a start, his heart beating as if some monster of his nightmares had kicked it. Wet air was blowing in through the interstices of the bamboo walls and the mat hanging over the entranceway. Rain crashed against the leaf-covered roof, and thunder boomed from the mountains. Joe was still snoring his private thunder.

Sam stretched, and then he cried out and sat up. His hand had touched flesh. Lightning from far away paled the darkness by two shades and gave vague shape to someone squatting by the cot.

A familiar baritone spoke. "You needn't look for the titanthrop to come to your aid. I've ensured that he'll not wake until dawn."

By this, Sam knew that the Ethical could see where no light was. Sam picked up a cigar from the little folding table and said, "Mind if I smoke?"

The Mysterious Stranger took so long replying that Sam wondered. The glow from the hot wire in Sam's lighter would not be bright enough to reveal the man's features, and probably he was wearing a mask or some device over his face. Did he dislike the odor of cigars, perhaps of tobacco in any form? Yet he hesitated to say so because this characteristic might identify him? Identify whom? The other Ethicals who knew that they had a renegade among them? There were twelve, or so the Stranger had said. If they ever learned that he, Sam Clemens, had been contacted by an Ethical, and learned of the Ethical's dislike of tobacco, would They know at once the renegade's identity?

Sam did not voice his suspicions. He would keep this to himself for possible later use.

"Smoke," the Stranger said. Although Sam could not see him or hear him move, he got the impression that he backed off a little.

"What's the occasion for this unexpected visit?" Sam said.

"To tell you I won't be able to see you again for a long time. I didn't want you to think I'd deserted you. I'm being called away on business you wouldn't understand even if I were to explain it. You're on your own now for a long time. If things should go badly for you, I won't be able to interfere even in a subtle way.

"However, you have all you need at present to occupy you for a decade. You'll have to use your own ingenuity to solve the many technical problems that will arise. I can't supply you with any more metals or materials you might need or extricate you from difficulties with invaders. I took enough chances in getting the meteorite down to you and in telling you where the bauxite and platinum are.

"There will be other Ethicals—not the Twelve, but second-order—to watch you, but they won't interfere. They won't think the boat any danger to The Plan. They'd rather you didn't have the iron and they'll be upset when you 'discover' the platinum and bauxite. They want you Terrestrials to be occupied with psychic development, not technological. But they won't stick their noses in."

Sam felt a little panic. For the first time, he realized that, though he hated the Ethical, he had come to depend strongly on him for moral and material support.

"I hope nothing goes wrong," Sam said. "I almost lost my chance at the iron today. If it hadn't been for Joe and that fellow, Odysseus. . . ."

Then he said, "Hold it! Odysseus told me that the Ethical who talked to him was a woman!"

The darkness chuckled. "What does that mean?"

"Either you're not the only renegade or else you can change your voice. Or maybe, maybe you're not telling me the truth at all! Maybe you're *all* in on this and feeding out fine lies for some plan of your own! We're tools in your hands!"

"I'm not lying! And I can't tell you about your other guesses. If you, or the others I've chosen, are detected and questioned, their stories will confuse my colleagues."

There was a rustle. "I must go now. You're on your own. Good luck."

"Wait! What if I fail?"

"Somebody else will build the boat, but I have good reasons for wanting you to do it."

"So I am just a tool. If the tool breaks, throw it away, get another."

"I can't assure your success. I'm not a god."

"Damn you and all your kind!" Sam shouted. "Why couldn't you have let things be as they were on Earth? We had the peace of death forever. No more pain and grief. No more never-ceasing toil and heartache. All that was behind us. We were free, free of the chains of flesh. But you gave us the chains again and fixed it so we couldn't even kill ourselves. You set death beyond our reach. It's as if you put us in hell forever!"

"It's not that bad," the Ethical said. "Most of you are better off than you ever were. Or at least as well off. The crippled, the blind, the grotesque, the diseased, the starved are healthy and young. You don't have to sweat for or worry about your daily bread, and most of you are eating better by far than you did on Earth. However, I agree with you in the larger sense. It was a crime, the greatest crime of all, to resurrect you. So . . ."

"I want my Livy back!" Sam cried. "And I want my daughters! They might as well be dead as separated from me, I mean from each other, forever! I'd rather they were dead! At least, I wouldn't be in agony all the time because they might be suffering, but in some terrible plight! How do I know they're not being raped, beaten, tortured? There's so much evil on this planet! There *should* be, since it has the original population of Earth!"

"I could help you," the Ethical said. "But it might take years for me to locate them. I won't explain the means because they're too complicated and I have to leave before the rain is over."

Sam rose and walked forward, his hands out.

The Ethical said, "Stop! You touched me once!"

Sam halted. "Could you find Livy for me? My girls?"

"I'll do it. You have my word. Only . . . only what if it does take years? Suppose you have the boat built by then—in fact, are already a million miles up The River. And then I tell you I've found your wife, but she's three million miles downRiver? I can notify you of her location, but I positively cannot bring her to you. You'll have to get her yourself. What will you do then? Will you turn back and spend twenty years backtracking? Would your crew permit you to do so? I doubt it. Moreover, even if you did this, there's no certainty that your woman would still be in the original location. She may have been killed and translated elsewhere, even farther out of reach."

"Damn you!" Sam yelled.

"And, of course," the Ethical said, "people change. You may like her when you find her."

"I'll kill you!" Sam Clemens yelled. "So help me. . . !"

The bamboo mat was lifted. The Stranger was silhouetted briefly, a batlike, cloaked shape with a dome covering for the head. Sam clenched his fists and forced himself to stand like a block of ice, waiting for his anger to melt away. Then he began pacing back and forth until finally he threw his cigar away. It had turned bitter; even the air he breathed was harsh.

"Damn them! Damn *him!* I'll build the boat and I'll get to the north pole and I'll find out what's going on! And I'll kill him! Kill them!"

The rains stopped. There were shouts from a distance. Sam went outside, alarmed because the Stranger might have been caught, although it did not seem likely. And he knew then that his boat meant more than anything else, that he did not want anything to happen to interfere with its building, even if he could take immediate revenge on the Ethical. That would have to come later.

Torches were coming across the plain. Presently, the bearers were close enough for Sam to make out the faces of some guards and that of von Richthofen. There were three unknowns with them.

An arrangement of large towels, held together by magnetic clasps, fell shapelessly about their bodies. A hood shadowed the face of the smallest stranger. The tallest was a man with a long, lean, dark face and a huge hooked nose.

"You're runner-up in the contest," Sam said. "There's

someone in my hut who has a nose that beats yours all hollow."

"Nom d'un con! Va te fair foutre!" the tall man said. "Must I always be insulted, no matter where I go? Is this the hospitality you give strangers? Did I travel ten thousand leagues under incredibly harsh conditions to find the man who can put good steel in my hand once more, only to have him verbally tweak my nose? Know, ignorant insolent lout, that Savinien de Cyrano II de Bergerac does not turn the other cheek. Unless you apologize, immediately, most sincerely, plead with the tongue of an angel, I will stab you through with this nose that you so mock!"

Sam apologized abjectly, saying that his nerves had been frayed by the battle. He looked in wonder at the legendary figure, and he wondered if he could be one of the chosen twelve.

The second man, a blond-haired and blue-eyed youth, introduced himself as Herrman Göring. A spiral bone, taken from one of the Riverfishes, hung from a cord around his neck, and by this Sam knew that he was a member of the Church of Second Chance. This meant trouble, because the Second Chancers preached absolute pacifism.

The third stranger threw the hood back and revealed a pretty face with long black hair done in a Psyche knot.

Sam staggered and almost fainted. "Livy!"

The woman started. She stepped closer to him and, silently, pale in the torchlight, looked at him. She was weaving back and forth, as shocked as he.

"Sam," she said weakly.

He took a step toward her, but she turned and clung to de Bergerac for support. The Frenchman put his arm around her and glared at Sam Clemens. "Courage, my little lamb! He will not harm you while I am here! What does he *mean* to you?"

She looked up at him with an expression that Sam could not mistake. He howled and shook his fist at the stars, just coming out from the clouds.

15

The Riverboat moved through his dream like a glittering, twenty-million-carat diamond.

There had never been a boat like it nor would there ever be another.

It would be named the *Not For Hire*. No one would ever be able to take it away from him, it would be so strongly armored and weaponed. Nor would anyone be able to buy or rent it from him.

The name glowed in great black letters against the white hull. *NOT FOR HIRE*.

The fabulous Riverboat would have four decks: the boiler deck, the main deck, the hurricane deck and the landing deck for the aerial machine. Its overall length would be four hundred and forty feet and six inches. The beam over the paddle-wheel guards would be ninety-three feet. Mean draft, loaded, twelve feet. The hull would be made of magnalium or, perhaps, plastic. The great stacks would spout smoke now and then, because there was a steam boiler aboard. But this was only to propel the big plastic bullets for the steam machine guns. The giant paddle-wheels on the sides of the Riverboat would be turned by enormous electrical motors.

The *Not For Hire* would be the only metal boat on The River, the only boat not propelled by oars or wind, and it would make anybody sit up and stare, whether he was born in 2,000,000 B.C. or in A.D. 2000.

And he, Sam Clemens, would be The Captain, capital T, capital C, because, aboard this vessel, carrying a crew of one hundred and twenty, there would be only one Captain.

King John of England could call himself Admiral if he wished, though if Sam Clemens had anything to do with it, he'd be First Mate, not Admiral. And if Sam Clemens *really* had anything to do with it, King John—John Lackland, Rotten John, Dirty John, Lecher John, Pigsty John—would not even be allowed on the boat. Sam

Clemens, smoking a big green cigar, wearing a white cap, dressed in a white kilt with a white towel over his shoulders for a cape, would lean out of the starboard port of the great pilothouse and yell, *Avast there, you lubbers! Grab hold of that putrescent mass of immortality and treachery and toss him off the gangplank. I don't care if he lands in The River or on the bank! Get rid of that human garbage!*

Over the railing of the boiler deck Prince John would sail. Slyboots John, screaming, cursing in his French-accented Middle English or in Anglo-Norman French or in Esperanto. Then the gangplank would be drawn up, bells would ring, whistles would blow, and Sam Clemens, standing behind the pilot, would give the order to begin the voyage.

The voyage! Up a River for maybe ten million miles or maybe twenty million miles, for maybe forty years or a hundred years. Such a Riverboat, such a River, such a voyage had never been dreamed of on Earth, long dead Earth! Up The River, the only one on this world, on the only boat like this, with Sam Clemens as *La Sipestro,* The Captain, and also addressed as *La Estro,* The Boss.

He was so happy!

And then, as they headed out toward the middle of The River, just to test the current, which was strongest in the center of the mighty stream, as the thousands along the bank waved and cheered or wept after the boat, after him, Samuel Langhorne Clemens, alias Mark Twain—The Captain, The Boss—he saw a man with long yellow hair and broad shoulders pushing through the crowd.

The man wore a towellike cloth, secured by magnetic tabs under the material, as a kilt. His leather sandals were made of the hide of the whale-sized Riverdragon-fish. Around his thickly muscled neck he wore a string of brilliantly colored hornfish vertebrae. In his huge powerful hand he gripped the wooden shaft of a large war ax of iron. His pale-blue eyes were fixed on Samuel Clemens and that broad hawk-nosed face was grim.

Sam Clemens screamed to the pilot, *"Faster! Faster! Full speed ahead!"*

The great paddle-wheels began to dip into the water more swiftly—*Chunk—chunk*. Even through the fiberglass-insulated deck the vibrations made the deck quiver. Suddenly the blond man, Erik Bloodaxe, tenth-century Viking King, was in the pilothouse.

He shouted at Sam Clemens in Old Norse. *Traitor! Droppings of Ratatosk! I told you I would wait along the banks of The River! You betrayed me so you could get the iron from the fallen star and build your great Riverboat!*

Sam fled the pilot house and down the ladders from deck to deck and down into the dark bowels of the hold, but Erik Bloodaxe was always two steps behind.

Past the colossal rotating electric motors Sam Clemens ran, and then he was in the chemistry room, where the engineers were making potassium nitrate from human excrement and mixing it with sulfur and charcoal to make gunpowder. Sam grabbed hold of a lighter and a resin torch, pressed the slide, and a white-hot glowing wire slid out of the case.

Stop, or I'll blow up the whole boat! Sam screamed.

Erik had stopped, but he was swinging the big ax around and around over his head. He grinned and said, *Go ahead! You haven't got the guts! You love the Riverboat more than you love anything, even your faithless but precious Livy! You wouldn't blow her up! So I'm going to split you down the middle with my ax and then take the Riverboat for myself!*

No! No! Sam screamed. *You wouldn't dare! You can't! You can't! This is my dream, my love, my passion, my life, my world! You can't!*

The Norseman stepped closer to him; the ax whistled over his head.

I can't? Just stand there and see!

Over his shoulder Sam saw a shadow. It moved forward and became a tall, faceless figure. It was X, the Mysterious Stranger, the renegade Ethical who had sent the meteorite crashing into the Rivervalley so that Sam could have the iron and nickel to build his Riverboat on this mineral-poor planet. And so he could sail up The River to the North Polar Sea where the Misty Tower, the

Big Grail, call it what you would, was hidden in the cold fog. And there Sam, with the eleven men chosen by X for his as-yet-unrevealed plan, would storm the Tower and find—find what? Whatever was there.

Stranger! Sam called. *Save me! Save me!*

The laughter was like a wind from the polar sea, turning his guts to crystal.

Save yourself, Sam!

No! No! You promised! Sam yelled. And then his eyes were open and the last of his groans died away. Or had he dreamed that he was groaning?

He sat up. His bed was made of bamboo. The mattress was a bamboo fiber cloth stuffed with giant leaves of the irontree. The blanket was made up of five towels secured together by magnetic tabs. The bed was against the wall of a room twenty feet square. It held a desk and a round table and about a dozen chairs, all of bamboo or pine, and a fired-clay chamber pot. There were also a bamboo bucket half full of water, a tall broad case with many pigeonholes for rolls of paper, a rack with bamboo and pine spears with flint and iron tips, yew bows and arrows, a war ax of nickel-iron and four long steel knives. On the wall were a number of pegs from which white towels hung. On one hatstand was a naval cap, an officer's, made of leather covered with a thin white cloth.

On the table was his grail, a gray metallic cylinder with a metal handle.

On the desk were glass bottles containing a soot-black ink, a number of bone pens, and one nickel-iron pen. The papers on the desk were of bamboo, though there were a few sheets of vellum from the inner lining of the stomach of the hornfish.

Glass windows (or ports, as he called them) looked out all around the room. As far as Sam Clemens knew, this was the only house with glass windows in the entire river-valley. Certainly, it was the only one for 10,000 miles either way from this area.

The sole light came from the sky. Though it was not yet dawn, the light was a trifle brighter than that cast by the full moon on Earth. Giant stars of many colors, some so big they looked like chipped-off pieces of the moon, jam-packed the heavens. Bright sheets and streamers hung between the stars, behind them, and even, seemingly, in front of some of the brightest. These were cosmic gas clouds, glories that never ceased to thrill the more sensitive of humanity along The River.

Sam Clemens, smacking his lips at the sour taste of the liquor he had drunk that evening and the even sourer taste of the dream, stumbled across the floor. He opened his eyes completely when he reached the desk, picked up a lighter, and applied the extended hot wire to a fish-oil lamp in a stone bracket.

He opened a port and looked out toward The River. A year ago he would have seen only a flat plain about a mile and a half wide and covered with short, tough, bright-green grass. Now it was a hideous mass of piled-up earth, deep pits and many buildings of bamboo and pine containing brick furnaces. These were his steel mills (so-called), his glass factory, his smelters, his cement mills, his forges, his blacksmith shops, his armories, his laboratories, and his nitric- and sulfuric-acid factories. A half a mile away was a high wall of pine logs enclosing the first metal boat he would build.

Torches flared to his left. Even at night the men were digging out the siderite chunks, hauling up pieces of the nickel-iron.

Behind him had been a forest of thousand-foot-high irontrees, red pine, lodgepole pine, black oak, white oak, yew trees and thick stands of bamboo. These had stood on the foothills; the hills were mostly still there but the trees, except for the irontrees, were all gone, along with the bamboo. Only the huge irontrees had withstood the steel axes of Clemens' people. The tall grasses had been cut down and their fibers chemically treated to make ropes and paper, but their roots were so tough and so tangled that there had not been enough reason to chop them out. The labor and the materials used in chopping through the roots of the short grass of the plains to get to the metal there had been very expensive. Not in terms of money, because that did not exist, but in terms of sweat, worn-out stone and dulled steel.

Where this area had been beautiful with its many trees and bright grass and the colored blooms of the vines that covered the trees, it was now like a battlefield. It had been necessary to create ugliness to build a beautiful boat.

Sam shivered at the wet and chilly wind which always came late at night from upRiver. He shivered also at the thought of the desolation. He loved beauty and nature's order and he loved the parklike arrangement of the valley, whatever else he thought about this world. Now he had made it hideous because he had a dream. And he would have to extend that hideousness, because his mills and factories needed more wood for fuel, for paper, for charcoal. All that his state possessed was used up and he had about used up all that Cernskujo to the immediate north and Publiujo to the immediate south would trade him. If he wanted more he would have to war on his closest neighbors or make arrangements for trading with the more distant states or those just across The River. Or else conquer them and take their wood away from them. He did not want to do that; he abhorred war in principle and could barely stand it in practice.

But if he was to have his Riverboat he had to have wood as fuel for his factories.

He also had to have bauxite and cryolite and platinum if he was to have aluminum generators and motors.

The nearest source of all three was in Soul City, that nation twenty-six miles downRiver dominated by Elwood Hacking, who hated whites.

So far, Sam had been able to trade iron weapons for bauxite, cryolite, cinnabar and platinum. Sam's own state, Parolando, needed the weapons badly. Adding one burden to the other, Hacking insisted that Parolando use its own men to mine and transport the ore.

Sam sighed deeply. Why in hell hadn't the Mysterious Stranger directed the meteorite to fall right by the bauxite deposits? Then, when Sam and Bloodaxe's Vikings had sailed into this area immediately after the meteorite had struck, they could have claimed the land that was now

101

Soul City for their own. When Hacking arrived, he would have been forced to join Clemens or to leave.

Still, even with the Stranger's powers, it could not be easy to deflect a hundred-thousand-ton iron-nickel siderite from its course and make it fall only twenty-six miles from the bauxite and other minerals. Actually the Stranger had supposed that he had hit the target on the bull's eye. He had told Sam, before he disappeared on some unknown mission, that the minerals were upRiver, all within a seven-mile range. But he had been mistaken. And that had made Sam both glad and angry. He was angry because the minerals were not all within his reach, but he was also happy that the Ethicals could make a mistake.

That fact did not help the humans imprisoned forever between sheer mountains 20,000 feet high in a valley about 9.9 miles wide on the average. They would be imprisoned for thousands of years, if not forever, unless Samuel Langhorne Clemens could build his Riverboat.

Sam went to the unpainted pine cabinet, opened a door and pulled out an opaque glass bottle. It held about twenty ounces of bourbon donated by people who did not drink. He downed about three ounces, winced, snorted, slapped his chest and put the bottle back. Hah! Nothing better to start off the day with, especially when you woke up from a nightmare that should have been rejected by the Great Censor of Dreams. If, that is, the Great Censor had any love and regard for one of his favorite dream-makers, Sam Clemens. Maybe the Great Censor did not love him after all. It seemed that very few *did* love Sam anymore. He had to do things he did not want to do in order to get the boat built.

And then there was Livy, his wife on Earth for thirty-four years.

He swore, caressed a nonexistent moustache, reached back into the cabinet, and pulled the bottle out again. Another snort. Tears came, but whether engendered by the bourbon or the thought of Livy, he did not know. Probably, in this world of complex forces and mysterious operations—and operators—the tears were caused by

102

both. Plus other things which his hindbrain did not care to let him peep into at this moment. His hindbrain would wait until his forebrain was bent over, tying its intellectual shoestrings, and would then boot the posterior of said forebrain.

He strode across the bamboo mats and looked through the port window. Down there, about two hundred yards away, under the branches of the irontree, was a round, conical-roofed, two-room hut. Inside the bedroom would be Olivia Langdon Clemens, his wife—his *ex*-wife—and the long, lanky, tremendously beaked, weak-chinned Savinien de Cyrano II de Bergerac, swordsman, libertine, and man-of-letters.

"Livy, how could you?" Sam said. "How could you break my heart, the heart of Your Youth?"

A year had passed since she had shown up with Cyrano de Bergerac. He had been shocked, more shocked than he had ever been in his seventy-four years on Earth and his twenty-one years on the Riverworld. But he had recovered from it. Or he would have recovered if he had not gotten another shock, though a lesser one. Nothing could exceed the impact of the first. After all, he could not expect Livy to go without a man for twenty-one years. Not when she was young and beautiful again and still passionate and had no reasonable hope of ever seeing him again. He had lived with a half dozen women himself, and he could not expect chastity or faithfulness from her. But he had expected that she would drop her mate as a monkey drops a heated penny when she found him again.

Not so. She loved de Bergerac.

He had seen her almost every day since the night she had first come out of the mists of The River. They spoke politely enough and sometimes they were able to crack their reserve and laugh and joke just as they had on Earth. Sometimes, briefly but undeniably, their eyes told each other that the old love was vibrating between them. Then, when he felt that he had broken out with longing, just like the hives, so he told himself later, laughing while he felt like crying, he had stepped toward her, despite himself, and she had stepped back to Cyrano's side if he happened

103

to be there or looked around for him if he wasn't.

Every night she was with that dirty, uncouth, big-nosed, weak-chinned, Adam's-appled, but colorful, strong-minded, witty, vigorous, talented, scary Frenchman. The virile frog, Sam muttered. He could imagine him leaping, croaking with lust, toward the white, blackly outlined, curving figure of Livy, leaping, croaking . . .

He shuddered. This was no good. Even when he brought women up here secretly—though he did not have to hide anything—he could not quite forget her. Even when he chewed dreamgum he could not forget her. If anything, she sailed into the drug-tossed sea of his mind more strongly, blown by the winds of desire. The good ship *Livy*, white sails bellying out, the trim cleancut curving hull . . .

And he heard her laughter, that lovely laughter. That was the hardest thing to endure.

He walked away and looked out through the fore ports. He stood by the oak pedestal and the big-spoked Riverboat's wheel he had carved. This room was his "pilothouse" and the two rooms behind made up the "texas." The whole building was on the side of the hill nearest to the plain. It was on thirty-foot stilts and could be entered through a staircase or ladder (to use a nautical term) on the starboard side or through a port directly from the hill behind the rear chamber of the texas. On top of the pilothouse was a large bell, the only metal bell in the world, as far as he knew. As soon as the waterclock in the corner struck six, he would clang the big bell. And the dark valley would slowly come to life.

Mists still overhung The River and the edge of the banks, but he could see the huge squat mushroom shape of the grailstone a mile and a half down the slope of the plain just by the water's edge. A moment later, he saw a boat, toy-size, emerge from the mists. Two figures jumped out and pulled the dugout onto the shore, then ran off to the right. The light from the skies was bright enough for Sam to see them, though he sometimes lost them when buildings intervened. After going around the two-story pottery factory, they cut straight into the hills. He lost them then, but it seemed that they were heading for John Plantagenet's log "palace."

So much for the sentinel system of Parolando. Every quarter mile on The River's front was guarded by a hut on thirty-foot stilts with four men on duty. If they saw anything suspicious, they were to beat on their drums, blow their bone horns and light their torches.

Two men slipping out of the fog to carry news to King John, ex-King John, of England?

Fifteen minutes later Sam saw a shadow running between shadows. The rope attached to the small bell just inside the entrance rang. He looked through the starboard port. A white face looked up at him. Sam's own spy, William Grevel, famous wool merchant, citizen of London, died in 1401 in the Year Of Our Lord. There were no sheep or, in fact, any mammals other than man along The River. But the ex-merchant had shown great aptitude for espionage, and he loved to stay up all night and skulk around.

Sam beckoned to him; Grevel ran up the "ladder" and entered after Sam had unbarred the thick oak door.

Sam said, in Esperanto, *"Saluton, leutenanto Grevel. Kio estas?"*

(Translation: "Hello, Lieutenant Grevel. What's the matter?")

Grevel said, *"Bonan matenon, Estro. Ciu grasa*

fripono, Rego Johano, estas jus akceptita duo spionoj."

(Translation: "Good morning, Boss. That fat rascal, King John, has just received two spies.")

Neither Sam nor Grevel could understand each other's English, but they got along very well in Esperanto, except now and then.

Sam grinned. Bill Grevel had let himself down from the limb of an irontree, passing directly over a sentry, and down a rope onto the edge of the roof of the two-story building. He had passed through the bedroom, where three women slept, and then crawled to the top of the staircase. John and his spies, a twentieth-century Italian and a sixth-century Hungarian, were at a table below Grevel. The two had reported the results of their trip upRiver. John was furious and justly so, from his viewpoint.

Sam, hearing Grevel's report, also became furious.

"He tried to assassinate Arthur of New Brittany? What is that man trying to do, ruin all of us?"

He paced back and forth, stopped, lit a big cigar and began pacing again. Once he stopped to invite Grevel to a bite of cheese and a glass of wine.

It was one of the ironics of Chance or, perhaps, of the Ethicals, for who knew what things they arranged, that King John of England and the nephew he had murdered most foully should have been located within thirty-two miles of each other. Arthur, Prince of Brittany of dead Earth, had organized the peoples among whom he found himself into a state he called New Brittany. There were very few old Bretons in the ten-mile-long territory he ruled, but that did not matter. New Brittany it was.

It had taken eight months before Arthur had discovered that his uncle was his neighbor. He had traveled incognito to Parolando to verify with his own eyes the identity of the uncle who had slit his throat and dropped his weighted body into the Seine. Arthur wanted to capture John and keep him alive for as long as possible under exquisite torture. Killing John would only bar him, possibly forever, from getting his revenge. John, murdered, would awake the next day someplace thousands of miles away on The River.

106

But Arthur had sent emissaries demanding that John be given up to him. These demands had been rejected, of course, though only Sam's sense of honor and his fear of John kept him from agreeing to Arthur's demands.

Now John had sent four men to assassinate Arthur. Two had been killed; the others had escaped with minor wounds. This would mean invasion. Arthur not only had wanted revenge on John, he would like to get possession of the meteorite iron.

Between Parolando and New Brittany, a fourteen-mile stretch of the right bank of The River was known as Chernsky's Land, or in Esperanto, *Cernskujo*. Chernsky, a sixteenth-century Ukrainian cavalry colonel, had refused an alliance with Arthur. But the nation immediately to New Brittany's north was governed by Iyeyasu. He was a powerful and ambitious person, the man who had established the Tokugawa Shogunate in 1600 with its capital at Yedo, later called Tokyo. Sam's spies said that the Japanese and the Breton had met six times in a war conference.

Moreover, just to the north of Iyeyasujo was Kleomanujo. This was governed by Cleomenes, a king of Sparta and half-brother to that Leonidas who held the pass at Thermoplyae. Cleomenes had met three times with Iyeyasu and Arthur.

Just south of Parolando was an eleven-mile stretch called Publia, after its king, Publius Crassus. Publius had been an officer in Caesar's cavalry during the Gallic campaigns. He was inclined to be friendly, although he extracted a big price for letting Sam cut down his timber.

South of Publia was Tifonujo, ruled by Tai Fung, one of Kublai Khan's captains, killed on Earth when he fell drunk off a horse.

And south of Tifonujo was Soul City, headed by Elwood Hacking and Milton Firebrass.

Sam stopped and glared from under bushy brows at Grevel. "The hell of it, Bill, is there isn't much I can do. If I tell John I know about his trying to murder Arthur, who may deserve murder, for all I know, then John knows that

107

I've got spies inside the house. And he'll just deny everything, ask that I bring his accusers forth—and you know what would happen to them, to *you*."

Grevel paled.

Sam said, "Start your blood running again, I won't do it. No. The only thing to do is to keep quiet and watch for developments. But I'm choking up to here with keeping quiet. That man is the most despicable I ever met—and if you knew my vast range of acquaintances, including publishers, you would feel the depth of my words."

"John could be a tax-collector," Grevel said, as if he had plumbed the depths of insult. And he had, for him.

"It was a bad day when I had to agree to take John on as a partner," Sam muttered, blowing out smoke as he turned toward Grevel. "But if I hadn't taken him in, I'd have been robbed of my chance at the iron."

He dismissed Grevel after thanking him. The skies just above the mountains across The River were red. Soon the entire vault would be rosy on the edges and blue above, but it would be some time before the sun cleared the mountain. Before then, the grailstones would be discharging

He washed his face in a basin, combed his thick bush of reddish hair straight back, applied the toothpaste with the tip of his finger to his teeth and gums, and spat. Then he fastened a belt with four sheaths and a bag dangling from a strap and put it around his waist. He placed a long towel around his shoulders as a cape, picked up a cane of oak shod with iron and, with the other hand, picked up the grail. He went down the stairs. The grass was still wet. It rained every night at three o'clock for a half hour, and the valley did not dry until after the sun came up. If it were not for the absence of disease germs and viruses, half the valley's humans would have died of pneumonia and flu long ago.

Sam was young and vigorous again, but he still did not like to exercise. As he walked, he thought of the little railway he would like to build from his house to the edge of The River. But that would be too restrictive. Why not build an automobile with a motor that burned wood alcohol?

People began joining him: he was kept busy with *"Saluton!"* and *"Bonan Matenon!"* At the end of his walk, he gave his grail to a man to put on a depression on the top of the gray granite mushroom-shaped rock. About six hundred of the gray cylinders were placed in the depression, and the crowd retreated to a respectful distance. Fifteen minutes later, the rock erupted with a roar. Blue flames soared twenty-five feet high and thunder echoed from the mountain. The appointed grail keepers for the day got onto the rock and passed the cylinders around. Sam took his back to the pilothouse, wondering on the way why he did not delegate someone to carry his grail down for him. The truth was, a man was so dependent on the grail, he just could not trust it out of his sight.

Back in the house, he opened the lid. In six containers in snapdown racks were breakfast and various goodies.

The grail had a false bottom in which was concealed an energy-matter converter and programmed menus. This morning he got bacon and eggs, toast with butter and jam, a glass of milk, a slice of cantaloupe, ten cigarettes, a marihuana stick, a cube of dreamgum, a cigar, and a cup of some delicious liqueur.

He settled down to eat with gusto and got, instead, a bad taste. Looking out through the starboard port (so he wouldn't see into Cyrano's door), he saw a youth on his knees before his hut. The fellow was praying, his eyes closed, his hands church-steepled. He wore only a kilt and a spiral bone from a Riverfish suspended by a leather string around his neck. His hair was dark blond, his face was broad, and his body was muscular. But his ribs were beginning to show.

The praying man was Hermann Göring.

Sam swore and reared up from his chair, knocking it backward, picked it up and moved his breakfast from his desk to the big round table in the center of the room. The fellow had spoiled his appetite more than once. If there was one thing Sam could not stand, it was an ex-sinner, and Hermann Göring had sinned more than most and was now, by way of compensation, holier than most. Or so it seemed to Sam, though Göring claimed that he was the lowliest of the low—in a sense.

Take your damned arrogant humility away, Sam had said. *Or at least take it downwind . . .*

If it had not been for the Magna Carta which Sam had drawn up (over King John's protests, thus repeating history), Sam would have kicked Göring and his followers out long ago. Well, at least a week ago. But the Carta, the constitution of the state of Parolando, the most democratic constitution in the history of mankind, gave total religious freedom and total freedom of speech. Almost total, anyway. There had to be some limitations.

But his own document forbade Sam to stop the missionaries of the Church of the Second Chances from preaching.

Yet if Göring continued to protest, to make speeches, to convert more to his doctrine of pacifist resistance, Sam Clemens would never get his Riverboat. Hermann Göring had made a symbol of the boat; he said that it represented man's vanity, greed, lust for violence, and disregard of the Creator's designs for the world of man.

Man should not build riverboats. He should build more stately mansions of the soul. All man needed now was a roof over his head to keep off the rain and thin walls for a little privacy now and then. Man no longer had to earn his bread by the sweat of his brow. His food and drink were given to him with nothing expected in return, not even gratitude. Man had time to determine his destiny. But man must not transgress on others, not rob them of their possessions, their love or their dignity. He must respect others and himself. But he could not do this through thievery, robbery, violence, contempt. He must . . .

Sam turned away. Göring had some fine sentiments to which Sam subscribed. But Göring was wrong if he thought that licking the boots of the people who had put them here was going to lead to any Utopia or salvation for their souls. Humanity had been tricked again; it was being used, misused and abused. Everything, the resurrection,

110

the rejuvenation, freedom from disease, free food and liquor and smokes, freedom from hard work or economic necessity, everything was an illusion, a candy bar to lead baby-mankind into some dark alley where . . . Where? Sam did not know. But the Mysterious Stranger had said that mankind was being tricked in the cruelest hoax of all, even crueler than the first hoax, that of life on Earth. Man had been resurrected and put on this planet as the subject of a tremendous scholarly study. That was all. And when the studies were completed, Man would go down into darkness and oblivion once more. Cheated again.

But what did the Stranger have to gain by telling this to certain selected men? Why had he chosen a small number to help him defeat his fellow Ethicals? What was the Stranger really after? Was he lying to Sam and Cyrano and Odysseus and the others whom Sam had not yet met?

Sam Clemens did not know. He was as much in The Great Dark as he had been on Earth. But he did know one thing for certain. He wanted that Riverboat.

The mists had cleared away; breakfast time was over. He checked the water clock and rang the big bell on the pilothouse. As soon as it had ceased tolling, the wooden whistles of the sergeants began shrilling. Up and down the ten-mile stretch of the Rivervalley known as Parolando the whistles shrilled. Then the drums began to beat, and Parolando went to work.

17

There were 1,000 people in Parolando, but the Riverboat would be taking only one hundred and twenty. Twenty of these already knew for sure they would be going.
Sam and Joe Miller, Lothar von Richthofen, Van Boom,
de Bergerac, Odysseus, three engineers, King John, and
their hutmates had been promised. The rest would know
whether or not they had worked for nothing a few days
before the boat sailed. At that time, the names would be
written on slips of paper and placed inside a big wire cage.
The cage would be whirled around and around, and then
Sam would stop it, and, blindfolded, would reach in and
pull out, one after the other, one hundred names. And
these lucky ones would be the crew of the *Not For Hire*.

The *Not For Hire* had about 5,000,000 miles to travel,
if the Stranger could be believed. Averaging about 335
miles every twenty-four hours, it would take over forty-
one years to reach the end of The River. But it would not
average that much, of course. The crew would have to put
into shore for extensive vacations on land and repairs
would have to be made. In fact, the Riverboat might wear
out, although Sam planned on taking many spare parts.
Once the boat was on its way it could not put back for
parts or pick them up anywhere else. There would be no
metal of any consequence from this place on.

It was strange to think that he would be about one hundred and forty years old when he got to the headwaters of
The River.

But what was that when he had thousands of years of
youth to go?

He looked through the bow ports. The plain was full of
people streaming down from the hills to the factories.
Behind him the hills would be alive with others on their
way to the factories in the hills. A small army would be
working on the big dam to the northwest, near the base of

the mountains. A concrete wall was being constructed between two steep hills to dam up the water flowing from a spring near the top of the mountain. When the lake behind the dam was full, its overflow would drive electrical generators to power the mills.

At present, the electrical energy needed came from a grailstone. A giant stepdown transformer of aluminum took the energy three times a day, sent it through brobdingnagian aluminum wires to a two-story device known as the batacitor. This was a late-twentieth-century electronic discovery that could accept hundreds of kilovolts in a hundredth of a microsecond and could discharge it at any rate from a tenth of a volt to one hundred kilovolts. It was the prototype of the batacitor that would be put on the Riverboat. At present the energy was chiefly used in a cutting device made by van Boom that sliced through the pieces of nickel-iron dug up on the plain. The energy could also be moderated to melt the metal. The aluminum for the wires and the batacitor had been laboriously and expensively made from aluminum silicate derived from the clay under the grass along the base of the mountains. But that supply had run out and now the only economically feasible source was in Soul City.

Sam sat down at his desk, pulled out a drawer and removed a tall book bound in fish-bladder leather and with pages of bamboo-fiber paper. It was his diary, *The Memoirs of a Lazarus*. For the time being he was using ink made of water and tannic acid from oak bark and of carbon from finely ground charcoal-in-suspension to write down day-by-day happenings and his reflections. When the technology of Parolando was improved enough, he would use the electronic recorder that van Boom had promised him.

He had no sooner started writing than the drums began beating. The big bass drums represented dashes; the small soprano drums, dots. The code was Morse; the language, Esperanto.

Von Richthofen would be landing in a few minutes.

Sam stood up to look out again. A half a mile away was the bamboo catamaran on which Lothar von Richthofen had sailed downRiver only ten days ago. Through the starboard ports Sam saw a squat figure with tawny hair coming out of the gateway of King John's log palace. Behind him came bodyguards and sycophants.

King John was making sure that von Richthofen did not give Sam Clemens any secret messages from Elwood Hacking.

The ex-monarch of England, present coruler of Parolando, wore a kilt with red and black checks, a poncholike arrangement of towels, and knee-length, red-leather Riverdragon boots. Around his thick waist was a wide belt with a number of sheaths containing steel daggers, a short sword, and a steel ax. One hand held a steel rod coronet, one of many sources of contention between Sam and King John. Sam did not want to waste metal on such useless anachronisms, but John had insisted and Sam had given in.

Sam found some satisfaction now in thinking about the name of his little nation. Parolando in Esperanto meant *pair land* and was so called because two men governed it. But Sam had not mentioned to John that another translation could be *Twain Land*.

John followed a hard-dirt path around a long, low factory building, and then he was at the foot of the staircase of Sam's quarters. His bodyguard, a big thug named Sharkey, pulled the bell rope and the little bell tinkled.

Sam stuck his head out and shouted, "Come aboard, John!"

John looked up at him from pale blue eyes and motioned to Sharkey to precede him. John was cautious about assassins, and he had reason to be. He was also resentful about having had to come to Sam, but he had known that von Richthofen would report to Sam first.

Sharkey entered, inspected Sam's pilothouse and looked through the three rooms of the texas. Sam heard a growl, as low and powerful as a lion's, from the rear bedroom. Sharkey came back swiftly and closed the door.

Sam smiled and said, "Joe Miller may be sick, but he

114

can still eat ten Polish prizefighters for breakfast and call for a second helping."

Sharkey did not reply. He signaled through the port that John could come up without fear of being ambushed.

The catamaran was beached now, and the tiny figure of von Richthofen was coming across the plain, holding his grail in one hand and the wooden winged ambassadorial staff in the other. Through the other port Sam could see the lanky figure of de Bergerac leading a platoon toward the south wall. Livy was not in sight.

John entered.

Sam said, *"Bonan matenon, Johano!"*

It galled John that Sam refused to address him as *Via Rega Moŝto*—Your Majesty—in private. *La Konsulo*—the Consul—was their correct title and even that came reluctantly from Sam's lips. Sam encouraged others to call him La Estro, The Boss, because that angered John even more.

John grunted and sat down at the round table. Another bodyguard, a big dark proto-Mongolian with massive bones and immensely powerful muscles, Zaksksromb, who presumably had died about 30,000 B.C., lit up a huge brown cigar for John. Zak, as he was known, was the strongest man in Parolando, with the exception of Joe Miller. And it could be argued that Joe Miller was not a man—or, at least, certainly not Homo sapiens.

Sam wished Joe would get out of bed. Zak made him nervous. But Joe was sedating himself with dreamgum. Two days ago a chunk of siderite had slipped from a crane's tongs as Joe was passing beneath it. The operator swore it had been an accident, but Sam had his suspicions.

Sam puffed on his cigar and said, "Hear anything about your nephew lately?"

John did not start, but his eyes did widen a trifle. He looked at Sam across the table.

"No, should I?"

"I just wondered. I've been thinking about asking Arthur down for a conference. There's no reason why you two should be trying to kill each other. This isn't Earth, you know. Why can't we call off old feuds? What if you did drop him off in a sack into the estuary? Let bygones be bygones. We could use his wood, and we need more limestone for calcium carbonate and magnesium. He's got plenty."

John glared, then hooded his eyes and smiled.

Tricky John, Sam thought. Smooth John. Despicable John.

"To get wood and limestone we'd have to pay with steel arms." John said. "I'm not about to permit my dear nephew to get his hands on more steel."

"Just thought I'd broach the subject to you," Sam said, "because at noon—"

John stiffened. "Yes?"

"Well, I thought I'd bring up the subject to the Council. We might have a vote on it."

John relaxed. "Oh?"

Sam thought, *You think you're safe. You've got Pedro Anséurez and Frederick Rolfe on your side and a five-to-three vote in the Council is a nay vote . . .*

Once again he contemplated suspending the Magna Carta so that things could be done that needed to be done. But that might mean civil war and that could mean the end of the dream.

He paced back and forth while John described in a loud voice and sickening detail his latest conquest of his latest blonde. Sam tried to ignore the words; he still got mad because the man boasted, although by now any woman who accepted John had only herself to blame.

The little bell tinkled. Lothar von Richtofen entered. He was now wearing his hair long and so, with his handsome, somewhat Slavic, features, he looked like a less stocky and better-looking Göring. The two had known each other well during World War I, since both had served under Baron Manfred von Richthofen, Lothar's older brother. Lothar was a wild, brash, and essentially likable person, but this morning his smiles and his debonair bearing were gone.

"What's the bad news?" Sam said.

116

Lothar took the cup of bourbon that Sam offered, downed it, and said, "Sinjoro Hacking has just about finished putting up fortifications. Soul City has walls twelve feet high and ten thick on all fronts. Hacking was nasty to me, very nasty. He called me an *ofejo* and a *honkio*, words new to me. I did not care to ask him for an explanation."

"*Ofejo* might be from the English *ofay*," Sam said, "but I never heard the other word. *Honkio*?"

"You'll hear those words a lot in the future," Lothar said, "if you deal with Hacking. And you will. Hacking finally got down to business after spewing out a torrent of abuse, mostly about my Nazi ancestors. I never heard of the Nazis on Earth, you know, since I died in a plane crash in 1922. He seemed to be angry about something—maybe his anger had nothing to do with me originally. But the essence of his speech was that he might cut off the bauxite and other minerals."

Sam leaned on the table until things came back into focus. Then he said, "I'll take a shot of Kentucky courage myself."

Von Richthofen continued, "It seems that Hacking isn't too happy with the makeup of his state. It's one-fourth Harlem blacks who died between 1960 and 1980, you know, and one-eighth eighteenth-century Dahomeyan blacks. But he has a one-fourth nonblack population of fourteenth-century Wahhabi Arabs, fanatics who still claim that Mohammed is their prophet and they're here just for a short trial period. Then there is the one-fourth composed of thirteenth-century, Asiatic-Indian, Dravidian, black-skinned Caucasians, and one-eighth of people from anywhere and anytime. A slight majority of the one-eighth is twentieth-century."

Sam nodded. Though resurrected humanity consisted of persons who lived from 2,000,000 B.C. to A.D. 2008, one-fourth had been born after A.D. 1899—if estimates were correct.

"Hacking wants his Soul City to be almost entirely black. He said that he had believed that integration was possible when he lived on Earth. The young whites of his day were free of the racial prejudices of their elders and he

117

had known hope. But there aren't too many of his former white contemporaries in his land. And the Wahhabi Arabs are driving him out of his mind. Hacking became a Moslem on Earth, did you know that? First, he was a Black Muslim, an American home-grown variety. Then he became a real Moslem, made a pilrimage to Mecca and was quite certain that the Arabs, even if they were white, were not racists.

"But the massacre of the Sudanese blacks by the Sudanese Arabs and the history of Arabic enslavement of blacks disturbed him. Anyway, these nineteenth-century Wahhabi are not racist—they're just religious fanatics and too much trouble. He didn't say so, but I was there ten days and I saw enough. The Wahhabis want to convert Soul City to their brand of Moslemism, and if they can't do it peacefully, they'll do it bloodily. Hacking wants to get rid of them and the Dravidians, who seem to regard themselves as superior to Africans of any color. Anyway, Hacking will continue to furnish us bauxite if we will send him all our black citizens in return for his Wahhabi and Dravidian citizens. Plus an increased amount of steel arms. Plus a larger share in the raw siderite."

Sam groaned. King John spat on the floor. Sam scowled and said, "*Merdo, Johano!* Not even a Plantagenet gobs on my floor! Use the spittoon or get out!"

He forced himself to push down his rage and frustration as King John bristled. Now was not a time to bring about a confrontation. The vainglorious ex-monarch would never back down on the spitting issue, which was, in reality, trifling.

Sam gestured self-deprecatingly and said, "Forget about it, John. Spit all you want to!" But he could not resist adding: "As long as I have the same privilege in your house, of course."

John growled and popped a chocolate into his mouth. He used the growling, grinding voice that indicated that he, too, was very angry but was imposing great self-control.

"This Saracen, Hacking, gets too much. I say we have

118

kissed his black hand long enough. His demands have slowed down the building of the ship—"

"Boat, John," Sam said. "It's a boat, not a ship."

"*Boato, smoato.* I say, let us conquer Soul City, put the citizens to the sword, and seize the minerals. Then we will be able to make aluminum on the spot. In fact, we could build the boat there. And, to make sure that we were not interfered with, we should conquer all the states between us and Soul City."

Powermad John.

Yet, Sam was inclined to think that he might, for once, be right. In a month or so Parolando would have the weapons that would enable it to do just what John was proposing. Except that Publia was friendly and its bills were not high, and Tifonujo, though it demanded much, had permitted itself to be stripped of trees. It was, however, possible that both states planned to use the nickel-iron they got for their wood to make weapons so that they could attack Parolando.

The savages across The River were probably planning the same thing.

"I'm not through," von Richthofen said. "Hacking made his demands about the trading of citizens on a one-to-one basis. But he won't come to any agreement unless we send a black to deal with him. He says he was insulted when you sent me, since I'm a Prussian and a Junkers to boot. But he'll overlook that, since we don't know any better, if we send him a member of the Council the next time. One who's black."

Sam's cigar almost fell out.

"We don't have a black Councilman!"

"Exactly. What Hacking is saying is that we had better elect one."

John passed both hands through his shoulder-length tawny hair and then stood up. His pale blue eyes were fiery under the lion-colored eyebrows.

"This Saracen thinks he can tell us how to conduct our internal affairs. I say, War!"

Sam said, "Now, just a minute, Your Majesty. You have good reason to be mad, as the old farmer said when

119

he fell in, but the truth is, we can defend ourselves quite well—but we cannot invade and occupy any large territory."

"Occupy?" John shouted. "We will slaughter half and chain the other half!"

"The world changed much after you died, John—uh, Your Majesty. Admittedly there are other forms of slavery than the outright form, but I don't want to get into an argument about definitions. There is no use making a fuss, as the fox said to the hens. We just appoint another Councilman, *pro tem*. And we send him to Hacking."

"There is no provision in the Magna Carta for a *pro tem* Councilman," Lothar said.

"We change the Carta," Sam said.

"That'll take a popular election."

John snorted disgust. He and Sam Clemens had gone through too many blazing arguments about the rights of the people.

"There's one other thing," Lothar said, still smiling but with an exasperated note in his voice. "Hacking asks that Firebrass be allowed to visit here for a tour of inspection. Firebrass is especially interested in seeing our airplane."

John sputtered. "He asks if we care if he sends a spy!"

"I don't know," Sam said. "Firebrass is Hacking's chief of staff. He might get a different idea of us. He's an engineer—I think he had a PhD, too, in physics. I've heard about him. What did you find out, Lothar?"

"He impressed me very much," von Richthofen said. "He was born in 1974 in Syracuse, New York. His father was black, and his mother was half Irish and half Iroquois Indian. He was in the second party to land on Mars and the first to orbit Jupiter—"

Sam was thinking, Men really did that! Landed on the Moon and then Mars. Right out of Jules Verne and Frank Reade, Jr. Fantastic, yet no more fantastic than this world. Or, indeed, than the mundane world of 1910. None of it could be explained in a manner to satisfy any reasonable man. It was all incredible.

"We'll put it up to the Council today, John," Sam said,

"if you have no objection. We'll have a general election on the *pro tem* Councilman. I personally favor Uzziah Cawber."

"Cawber was a slave, wasn't he?" Lothar said. "I don't know. Hacking said he didn't want any Uncle Toms."

Once a slave, always a slave, Sam thought. Even when a slave revolts, kills, and is killed as a protest against his slavery—resurrected, he still does not think of himself as a free man. He was born and raised in a world soaked with the rotten essence of slavedom and every thought he thinks, every move he makes is stained with slavery, subtly altered with slavery. Cawber was born in 1841 in Montgomery, Alabama, he was taught to read and write, he served in the house of his master as his secretary, he killed his master's son in 1863, escaped, and went West and became a cowboy, of all things, and then a miner. He was killed with a Sioux spear in 1876; the ex-slave killed by a man about to become a slave. Cawber is delighted with this world—or claims to be—because no man can enslave him here or keep him enslaved. But he is the slave of his own mind and of the reaction of his nerves. Even when he holds his head high, he will jump if somebody cracks a whip, and his head will bow before he can stop it . . .

Why, oh, why had man been brought back to life? Men and women were ruined by what had happened on Earth, and they would never be able to undo the damage. The Second Chancers claimed a man could change, entirely change. But the Second Chancers were a pack of dreamgummers.

"If Hacking calls Cawber an Uncle Tom, Cawber will kill him," Sam said. "I say, let's send him."

John's tawny eyebrows rose. Sam knew what he was thinking. Perhaps he could use Cawber, one way or another.

Sam looked at the waterclock. "Time for the inspection tour. Care to come along, John? I'll be with you in a minute," and he sat down at his desk to make a few more entries in his diary.

That gave John the chance to leave first, as befitted the

ex-King of England and of a good part of France. Sam thought it was ridiculous to worry about who preceded whom, yet he disliked John so much he could not bear to let him gain even this minor victory. Rather than argue about it, or just walk out ahead of him, and so cause John to throw a fit, he pretended he had work to do.

Sam caught up with the group, which included the six Councilmen, just outside the nitric-acid factory. They went through the factories swiftly. The stinks emanating from the nitric and sulfuric acids; from the destructive distillation of wood to make alcohol, acetone, creosote, turpentine and acetic acid; the formaldehyde vats and the treatment of human excrement and lichen scraped off the mountains to extract potassium nitrate—these, combined, were enough to make a hyena lose its breakfast. The Councillors were roasted and deafened in the steel mill and the grinding mills and the forges and blacksmith shops. They were covered with a white dust in the limestone mills and magnesium factory. In the aluminum factory they were again roasted, deafened, and stunk out.

The gunsmith shop up in the hills was not operating at the moment. Except for distant noises, it was quiet. But it was not beautiful. The earth had been dug up, the trees cut down, and smoke from the factories up The River was black and acrid along the mountains.

Van Boom, the late-twentieth-century, half Zulu, half Afrikaans, chief engineer, met them. He was a handsome man with a dark bronze skin and curly hair. He stood about six-three and weighed about two hundred and fifty. He had been born in a ditch during The Bloody Years.

He greeted them cordially enough (he liked Sam and tolerated John), but he did not smile as usual.

"It's ready," he said, "but I want my objections recorded. It's a nice toy and makes a lot of noise and looks impressive and will kill a man. But it's wasteful and inefficient."

"You make it sound like a Congressman," Sam said.

Van Boom led them into the high doorway of the bamboo building, where a steel handgun lay on a table. Van

Boom picked it up. Even in his big hand, the gun was huge. He strode past the others and out into the light of the sun. Sam was exasperated. He had held out his hand for the gun and the fellow had ignored him. If Van Boom intended to demonstrate it outside, why hadn't he said so in the first place?

"Engineers," Sam muttered. Then he shrugged. You might as well hit a Missouri mule between the eyes with your pinkie as try to change Van Boom's ways.

Van Boom held up the gun so that the sunshine twinkled against the silvery gray metal. "This is the Mark I pistol," he said. "Called so because The Boss invented it."

Sam's anger melted like ice in a Mississippi River thaw.

"It's a breech-loading, single-shot, flintlock hand weapon with a rifled barrel and a breakdown action."

He held the gun in his right hand and said, "You load it so. You press forward the lock switch on the left side of the barrel. This releases the breech lock. You then press down the barrel with the left hand. This action forces the trigger guard into the grip, where the guard acts as a lever to cock the hammer."

He reached into a bag strapped to his belt and removed a large brown hemispherical object. "This is a bakelite or phenol-formaldehyde-resin bullet, sixty caliber. You press the bullet, so, until it engages the lands of the barrel."

He removed from his bag a shiny package with black contents.

"This is a charge of black gunpowder wrapped in cellulose nitrate. Some time in the future, we'll have cordite instead of gunpowder. If we use this gun, that is. Now, I insert the load into the chamber with the primer end first. The primer is a twist of nitrate paper impregnated with gunpowder. Then I llft the barrel with my left hand, thus, locking it into place. The Mark I is now ready to fire. But, for emergency, if the primer does not ignite, you can pour priming powder into the touchhole just forward of the rear sight. In case of misfire, the gun may be cocked with the right thumb. Note that this flash vent on the right side of the action shield protects the shooter's face."

123

A man had brought out a large wooden target and had inserted it in a frame on four legs. The target was about twenty yards away. Van Boom turned toward it, held out the gun, clenched both hands and sighted along the front and rear sights.

"Get behind me, gentlemen," he said. "The heat of the passage through the air will burn off the surface of the bullet and leave a thin trail of smoke which you may be able to see. The plastic bullet has to be of such large caliber because of its light weight. But this increases the wind resistance. If we decide to use this gun—which I definitely am against—we might increase the caliber to seventy-five in the Mark II. The effective range is about fifty yards, but the accuracy is not good beyond thirty yards and nothing to brag about within that range."

The flint was in the hammer. When Van Boom would pull the trigger, the hammer would fall and scrape along the filelike surface of the frizzen. The frizzen covered the priming pan and should be knocked forward by the flint, uncovering the primer twist of the powder charge.

There was a click as the sear let the hammer go, a flash as the primer twist burned, and a booming. The click-flash-boom took up a time equal to saying click-flash-boom and Van Boom had had time between the click and the boom to bring the gun back into line after it had been jarred away by the impact of the heavy hammer and flint.

The bullet did leave a very faint trail of smoke, quickly dissipated by the fifteen-mile-an-hour wind. Sam, looking past Van Boom's arm, could see the bullet curve out and then back, carried by the wind. But Van Boom must have been practicing, because the bullet struck near the bull's eye. It went halfway into the soft pine, shattered and left a large hole in the wood.

"The bullet won't penetrate deeply into a man," Van Boom said, "but it will leave a large hole. And if it hits near bone, the fragments should break the bone."

The next hour was spent busily and happily with the Consuls and Councillors taking turns shooting. King John was especially delighted, though perhaps a little awed, be-

124

cause he had never seen a gun before. His first experience with gunpowder had come several years after he had been resurrected and he had seen only bombs and wooden rockets.

At last Van Boom said, "If you keep up, gentlemen, you will exhaust our supply of bullets—and it takes a lot of labor and materials to make these bullets. Which is one reason why I object to making any more. My other reasons are: one, the gun is accurate only at close range; two, it takes so long to load and shoot that a good bowman could drop three pistol handlers while they're loading and stay outside the effective range of the guns. Moreover, a plastic bullet isn't recoverable, whereas an arrow is."

Sam said, "That's a lot of nonsense! The mere fact that we would have these guns would demonstrate our technological and military superiority. We'd scare the enemy half to death before the battle started. Also, you forget that it takes a long time to train a good bowman, but anyone can shoot one of these after a relatively short lesson."

"True," Van Boom said. "But could they hit anyone? Besides, I was thinking of making steel crossbows. They can't be handled as fast as longbows, but they don't require any more training than guns do, and the bolts are recoverable. And they're a hell of a lot more deadly than these noisy, stinking gadgets."

"No, sir!" Sam said. "No, sir! I insist that we make at least two hundred of these. We'll outfit a new group, the Parolando Pistoleers. They'll be the terror of The River—you watch them! You'll see!"

18

For a change King John was on Sam's side. He insisted that the first two pistols should go to Sam and himself and the next dozen to their bodyguards. Then the new group could be organized and trained.

Sam was grateful for the backing, but he told himself to check on the men who formed the Pistoleers. He did not want it made up largely of men loyal to John.

Van Boom made no effort to hide his disgust. "I'll tell you what! I'll take a good yew bow and twelve arrows and stand fifty yards away. At a signal all eight of you can advance on me, firing at will with your Mark I's—and I'll drop all eight of you before you get close enough to hit me! Is it a deal? I'm willing to lay my life on the line!"

"Don't be childish," Sam said.

Van Boom rolled his eyes upward. "*I'm* childish? You're jeopardizing Parolando—*and* your boat—because you want *guns* to play with!"

"Just as soon as the guns are made you can start making all the bows you want," Sam said. "Look! We'll make armor, too, for the Pistoleers! That should dispose of your objections! Why didn't I think of that before? Why, our men will be dressed up in steel that'll repel the Stone Age weapons of the enemy as if they were straws. Let the enemy shoot his yew bows with his flint-tipped arrows. They'll bounce off the steel and the Pistoleers can take their time and blow the enemy into the next county!"

"You forget that we've had to barter our ore and even metal weapons for wood and other materials we need," Van Boom said. "The enemy will have arrows with steel tips that can drive through armor. Don't forget Grécy and Agincourt."

"There's just no dealing with you." Sam said. "You *must* be half Dutch—you're so stubborn."

"If your thinking is representative of the thinking of

white men, then I'm glad I'm half Zulu," Van Boom said.

"Don't get huffy," Sam replied. "And congratulations on the gun! Tell you what, we'll call it the Van Boom-Mark I. How's that?"

"I'd just as soon not have my name attached to it," the engineer said. "So be it. I'll make your two hundred guns. But I'd like to make an improved version, the Mark II we talked about."

"Let's make two hundred of these first, then we'll start on the Mark II," Sam said. "We don't want to mess around so long trying to get the perfect weapon that we suddenly find we don't have any at all. Still—"

He talked for a while about the Mark II. He had a passion for mechanical gadgets. On Earth he had invented a number of things, all of which were going to make him a fortune. And there was the Paige typesetting machine, into which he had sunk—and it *had* sunk—all the wealth he had made from his books.

Sam thought of the typesetting monster and how that wonderful contraption had bankrupted him. For a second, Paige and Van Boom were one and he felt guilty and a little panicky.

Van Boom next complained about the materials and the labor put into the AMP-1, their aerial machine prototype. Sam ignored him. He went with the others to the hangar, which was on the plains a mile north of Sam's quarters. The craft was only partly finished but would look almost as skeletal and frail when ready to fly as it did now.

"It's similar to some of the planes built in 1910," von Richthofen said. "I'll be exposed from my waist up when I sit in the cockpit. The whole machine looks more like a metal dragonfly than anything else. The main object is to test out the efficiency of the wood alcohol-burning motor and our materials."

Von Richthofen promised that the first flight would be made within three weeks. He showed Sam the plans for the rocket launchers which would be attached under the wings.

"The plane can carry about six small rockets, but it'll

127

mostly be good only for scouting. It won't go faster than forty miles an hour against the wind. But it'll be fun flying it."

Sam was disappointed that the plane wasn't a two-seater. He looked forward to flying for the first time in his life—his second life, that is. But von Richthofen said the next prototype would be a two-seater and Sam would be his first passenger.

"After you've tested it out," Sam said. He expected John to protest about this and to insist that he be taken up first. But evidently John was not too eager to leave the ground.

The last stop was at the boatyard, located halfway between the hangar and Sam's house. The craft within the pine-log enclosure would be completed within a week. The *Firedragon I* was the amphibious prototype of the boat that would be the launch for the big boat. It was a beautiful machine, made of thick magnalium, about thirty-two feet long, shaped like a U.S. Navy cruiser with wheels, with three turrets on its sleek top deck. It was powered by steam, burned wood alcohol, could operate in water or on land, carried a crew of eleven and was, so Sam declared, invincible.

He patted the cold gray hull and said, "Why should we worry about having bowmen? Or having anything but this? This juggernaut could crush a kingdom all by itself. It has a steam-powered cannon the like of which the world, Earth or this planet, has never seen. That is why it is steam-driven and why it has such a huge boiler."

All in all, the tour had made him happy. It was true that the plans for the great Riverboat had barely been started. But those took time. It was vital that the state be well protected at first, and just making the preparations was fun. He rubbed his hands and puffed on a new cigar, drawing the green smoke deeply into his lungs.

And then he saw Livy.

His beloved Livy, sick for so many years, and dead, finally, in Italy, in 1904.

Restored to life and youth and beauty, but not, alas, to him.

128

She was walking toward him, carrying her grail by its handle, wearing a white scarlet-edged kilt that came halfway down her thighs and a thin white scarf for a bra. She had a fine figure, good legs, handsome features. Her forehead was broad and satiny white. Her eyes were large and luminous. Her lips were full and shapely; her smile, attractive; her teeth, small and very white. She customarily wore her dark hair parted, combed down smooth in front but twisted into a figure eight in the back. Behind an ear she wore one of the giant crimson roselike blooms that grew from the vines on the irontrees. Her necklace was made of the convoluted red vertebrae of the hornfish.

Sam's heart felt as if it were being licked by a cat.

She swayed as she walked toward him, and her breasts bounced beneath the semiopaque fabric. Here was his Livy, who had always been so modest, had worn heavy clothes from the neck down to the ankle, and had never undressed before him in the light. Now she reminded him of the half-naked women of the Sandwich Islands. He felt uneasy, and he knew why. His queasiness among the natives had been as much due to their unwanted attraction for him as repulsion, each feeling dependent on the other and having nothing to do with the natives *per se*.

Livy had had a Puritanical upbringing, but she had not been ruined by it. On Earth she had learned to drink and to like beer, had even smoked a few times and had become an infidel or, at least, a great doubter. She had even tolerated his constant swearing and had let loose with a few blisterers herself if the girls were not around. The accusations that she had censored his books and thus emasculated them were off the target. He had done most of the censoring himself.

Yes, Livy had always shown adaptability.

Too much. Now, after twenty years of absence from him, she had fallen in love with Cyrano de Bergerac. And Sam had the uneasy feeling that that wild Frenchman had awakened in her something that Sam might have awakened if he had not been so inhibited himself. But after these years on The River and the chewing of a certain amount of dreamgum, he had lost many of his own inhibitions.

It was too late for him.

Unless Cyrano left the scene . . .

"Hello, Sam," she said in English. "How are you on this fine day?"

"Every day is fine here," he said. "You can't even talk about the weather, let alone do anything about it!"

She had a beautiful laugh. "Come along with me to the grailstone," she said. "It's almost time for lunch."

Every day he swore not to come near her because to do so hurt too much. And every day he took advantage of the smallest chance to get as close to her as he could.

"How's Cyrano?" he said.

"Oh, very happy because he's finally getting a rapier. Bildron, the swordsmith, promised that he'd have the first one—after yours and the other Councilmen's, of course. Cyrano had taken so long to reconcile himself to the fact that he would never hold a metal sword in his hand again. Then he heard about the meteorite and came here—and now the greatest swordsman in the world will have a chance to show everybody that his reputation wasn't a lie, which some liars say it was."

"Now, Livy," he said, "I didn't say people lied about his reputation. I said that maybe they exaggerated some. I still don't believe that story about his holding off two hundred swordsmen all by himself."

"The fight at the Porte de Nesle was authentic! And it wasn't two hundred! You're the one pumping it up, Sam, just as you always do. There was a crowd of hired thugs that could have been a hundred or might just as well have been. Even if there had been only twenty-five, the fact is that Cyrano attacked them all single-handed to save his friend, the Chevalier de Lignieres.

He killed two and wounded seven and ran the rest of them off. That is God's truth!"

"I don't want to get into an argument about the merits of your man," he said. "Or about anything. Let's just talk like we used to when we had so much fun—before you got sick."

She stopped. Her face set grimly.

"I always knew you resented my illness, Sam."

"No, that wasn't it," he said. "I think I felt guilty that you were sick, as if somehow I were to blame. But I never hated you for it. I hated myself if I hated anyone."

"I didn't say you hated me," she said. "I said you resented my illness and you showed it in many ways. Oh, you may have thought you were always noble and gentle and loving—and most of the time you were—you really were. But there were enough times when you looked, you spoke, you muttered, you gestured—how can I describe exactly how you were? I can't, but I knew you resented me, sometimes loathed me, because I was sick."

"I didn't!" he cried so loudly that a number of people stared.

"Why argue about it? Whether you did or not doesn't matter now. I loved you then and I still do, in a way. But not as I did."

He was silent during the rest of the walk across the plain to the big mushroom-shaped stone. The cigar tasted like burning skunk cabbage.

Cyrano was not present. He was superintending the building of a section of the wall which would eventually guard the shore of The River. Sam was glad. It was difficult enough for him to see Livy alone, but when she was with the Frenchman, he could not endure his thoughts.

In silence, he and Livy parted.

A beautiful woman with lovely, honey-colored hair approached him, and he was able to set aside his feelings about Livy for a while. The woman's name was Gwenafra. She had died at about the age of seven in a country that must have been Cornwall about the time the Phoenicians came there to exploit the tin mines. She had been resurrected among people of whom none spoke her ancient Celtic language and had been adopted by a group that spoke English. From her description, one of them had been that Sir Richard Francis Burton whom Sam had thought he'd seen on the shore just before the meteorite struck. Burton and his friends had built a small sailboat and set out for the headwaters of The River—as might have been expected of a man who had spent half his life exploring in the wildernesses of Africa and the other continents. On Earth Burton had sought the headwaters of the Nile and had found, instead, Lake Tanganyika. But on this world he had again been seeking the source of a river—the greatest River of them all—undaunted by the prospect that it might be ten million miles long or even twenty.

After little more than a year, his boat had been attacked by evil men, and one had stuck a stone knife into little Gwenafra and thrown her into The River, where she had drowned. She had awakened the next day on the banks somewhere far up in the northern hemisphere. The weather was colder, the sun weaker and the people there said that you did not have to go more than twenty thousand grailstones before you were in an area where the sun was always half above, half below the mountains. And there lived hairy, ape-faced men ten feet tall and weighing seven to eight hundred pounds.

(This was true, Joe Miller had been one of the titanthrops there.)

The people upRiver who adopted her spoke *Suomenkieltä,* which in English meant Finnish. DownRiver a little way were Swedes, twentieth-century people who lived a peaceful life. Gwenafra grew up relatively happy with her loving foster parents. She learned Finnish, Swedish, English, a Chinese dialect of the fourth century B.C., and Esperanto.

She drowned again by accident one day and woke up in this area. She still remembered Burton; she cherished a childhood crush she had had for him. But, being a realist, she was ready to love other men. And she had—and had just split with one, Sam had heard. She wanted a man who would be faithful to her, and these were not easy to find in this world.

Sam was very much attracted to her. The only thing that had kept him from asking her to move in with him had been the fear of angering Livy. That fear was ridiculous—she had no claim on him as long as she was living with Cyrano. And she had made it plain that she did not care what he did in his private life or his public life. Nevertheless, against all logic, he was afraid to take another woman as his hutmate. He did not want to snap the last thin link.

He chatted with Gwenafra awhile and confirmed that she was still unattached.

19

Lunch was upsetting. The "roulette wheel" concealed somewhere in the false bottom of the grail, the wild caster of dice, came up with a meal that only a Goshute Indian could have swallowed and even he might have gagged a little. Sam threw out all the food but was able to console himself with two cigars, cigarettes and six ounces of an unfamiliar but delicious liqueur. Just smelling it sent his taste buds into a dance.

The meeting with John and the Council took three hours. After much wrangling and a number of votes, it was decided to put to the people the question of amending the Carta so that a *pro tem* Councilman could be elected. John held up things for an hour, arguing that a vote wasn't needed. Why couldn't the Council simply say that the amendment was passed and that would be the end of it? No amount of explaining ever seemed to clarify such matters in John's head. It was not that he was unintelligent. It was just that he was not emotionally able to comprehend democracy.

The vote was unanimous to accept Firebrass as Hacking's official visiting fireman. But he would have a close eye kept on him.

After all this John rose and made a speech, occasionally lapsing from Esperanto into Norman French when he was overpowered by emotion. He thought that Parolando should invade Soul City before Soul City invaded Parolando. The invasion should be launched as soon as the handguns and the armored amphibian, *Firedragon I*, were ready. However, it might be best to test the mettle of their iron and the troops on New Brittany first. His spies were certain that Arthur planned to attack them soon.

John's two toadies backed him, but the others, including Sam, voted them down. John's face became red, and he swore and beat his fists on the oak table, but nobody decided to change his mind.

134

After supper the drums relayed a message from Hacking. Firebrass would be arriving tomorrow, some time before noon.

Sam retired to his office. By the light of lamps burning fish oil—soon they would have electricity—he and Van Boom and Tanya Velitsky and John Wesley O'Brien, the engineers, discussed their ideas about the Riverboat and drew rough sketches on paper. Paper was still scarce, but they would need enormous amounts for their blueprints. Van Boom said that they should wait until they were able to make a certain kind of plastic. Lines could be drawn on this with magnetized "pens" and corrections could easily be made by demagnetizing. Sam replied that that was fine. But he wanted to start building the Riverboat the moment the amphibian was completed. Van Boom said that he could not agree to that. Too many things were in the way.

Before the meeting broke up Van Boom pulled a Mark I gun out of a large bag. "We have ten of these now," he said. "This one is yours, compliments of Parolando's Engineering Corps. And here are twenty packages of powder and twenty plastic bullets. You can sleep with them under your pillow."

Sam thanked him, the engineers left and Sam barred the door. Then he went into the back room to talk to Joe Miller awhile. Joe was still awake, but he said he was taking no sedation that night. He would be getting up in the morning. Sam bade the giant good night and went into his bedroom, next to the pilothouse. He drank two shots of bourbon and lay down. After a while he managed to doze, though he was afraid that the three-o'clock rain would wake him as usual and he would have trouble getting back to sleep.

He awoke, but the rain was long past. Shouts came from somewhere and then an explosion that rattled the pilothouse. Sam leaped out of bed, wrapped a kilt around his waist, seized an ax and ran into the pilothouse. He suddenly remembered his pistol, but he decided he would go back for it when he found out what was going on.

The River was still smothered in fog, but hundreds of

135

dark figures were spilling out of it, and the tops of tall masts were sticking out above it. Torches were flaring all over the plains and in the hills. Drums were beating.

There was another explosion. A brightness in the night with bodies flying in all directions.

He looked through the starboard port. The gates of the log wall around King John's palace were open, and men were streaming out. Among them was the stocky figure of John.

By then more men had appeared out of the mists over the River. Bright starlight showed them lining up and moving out, rank after rank. The first of the invaders were by now in the great factories and advancing swiftly across the plain toward the foothills. Some explosions occurred inside factories as bombs were thrown to dislodge the defenders. And then a red tail flared out, disappeared, and something black shot toward him. Sam threw himself to the floor. A roar came beneath him, the floor heaved, and the glass ports blew in. A whiff of acrid smoke came to him and was gone.

He should get up and run, but he couldn't. He was deafened and frozen. Another rocket would be coming his way, and that one might be closer.

A giant hand gripped his shoulder and pulled him up. Another hand slid under his legs and he was being carried out. The arms and the chest of the giant were very hairy and as hard-muscled and as warm as a gorilla's. A voice as deep as if it were at the end of a railroad tunnel rumbled. "Take it eathy, Bothth."

"Put me down, Joe," Sam said. "I'm all right, except for my shame. And that's all right, too, I ought to feel ashamed."

His shock was fading, and a sense of relative calm flowed in to fill the vacuum. The appearance of the massive titanthrop had steadied him. Good old Joe—he might be a dumb subhuman and sick at the moment, but he was still worth a battalion.

Joe had put on his suit of leather armor. In one hand was the haft of an enormous double-headed ax of steel.

136

"Who are they?" he rumbled. "They from Thoul Thity?"

"I don't know," Sam said. "Do you feel up to fighting? How's the head?"

"It hurtth. Yeah, I can fight okay. Vere do ve go from here?"

Sam led him downhill toward the men collecting around John. He heard his name called and turned to see the tall lanky figure of de Bergerac, Livy by his side. She carried a small round shield of leather-covered oak and a steel-tipped spear. Cyrano held a long, dully shining blade. Sam's eyes widened. It was a rapier.

Cyrano said, *"Morbleu!"* He switched to Esperanto. "Your smith gave this to me just after supper—he said there was no sense in waiting."

Cyrano whipped the rapier, cutting the air with a sharp sound.

"I've come alive again. Steel—sharp steel!"

A nearby explosion made them all dive for the ground. Sam waited until he was sure that another rocket was not coming and then looked at his pilothouse. It had received a direct hit; its front was blown open; a fire was racing through it and would soon be in the texas. His diary was gone, but he could retrieve his grail later. It was indestructible.

In the next few minutes the wooden missiles, tails flaming, arched out, wobbling, from wooden bazookas held on the shoulders of the Parolandoj rocketeers. The missiles landed near and sometimes among the enemy and exploded with gouts of fire and much black smoke, quickly carried away by the wind.

Three runners reported. The attack had been launched from three places, all from The River. The main body was concentrated here, apparently to seize the Parolandoj leaders, the larger factories and the amphibian. The other two armies were about a mile away on each side. The invaders were composed of men from New Brittany and Kleomanujo and the Ulmaks from across The River. The

137

Ulmaks were savages who had lived in Siberia *circa* 30,000 B.C. and whose descendants had migrated across the Bering Straits to become Amerinds.

So much for King John's spy service, Sam thought. *Unless—unless he is in on the attack. But if he were he wouldn't be standing out here where he's likely to get killed any moment . . .*

Anyway, Arthur of New Brittany would never make a deal with the uncle who had murdered him.

The rockets continued to arc down from both sides, the five-pound warheads with their rock-fragment shrapnel taking a toll. The Parolandoj had the advantage; they could lie flat while their rockets exploded among upright targets. The invaders had to keep moving, otherwise they might just as well go home.

Nevertheless, it was frightening to lie on the ground and wait for the next noisy blast and hope that it would not come closer than the last one. There were screams from the wounded that were not, however, as heartrending as they would have been if Sam had not been so deafened that he could barely hear them and if he also had not been too worried about himself to think of others. Then, suddenly, the rockets had quit blowing up the world. A huge hand shook Sam's shoulder. He looked up to see that many around him were getting to their feet. The sergeants were yelling into the stunned ears of their men to form a battle array. The enemy was so close now that neither side was using the missiles or else they had all been launched.

Ahead was a dark body, a sea of screaming whooping fiends. They ran up the hill and the first, second and third ranks fell, pierced by arrows. But those behind did not break. They leaped over the fallen and kept on coming. Suddenly, the archers were being hammered down or thrust through or clubbed.

Sam kept close behind Joe Miller, who moved ahead slowly, his ax rising and falling. And then the giant was down, and the enemy were struggling on top of him like a pack of jackals on a lion, Sam tried to get to him; his ax smashed through a shield and a head and an uplifted arm

138

and then he felt a burning pain along his ribs. He was pushed back and back, while he slashed away with the ax and then it was gone, wedged in a skull. He stumbled over a pile of wood. Above him was the burning floor of his smashed house, still held up by three burning pylons.

He turned on his side, and there was the handgun, the Mark I, that he had left by his bedside. Near it lay three packages of powder with the nitrate-soaked twists and a number of the plastic bullets. The explosion had hurled them out of the house.

Two men whirled by him in a dance, their hands gripping each other, straining, grunting with the strain, glaring into each other's bloody faces. They stopped, and Sam recognized King John—his opponent was taller but not as thickly built. He had lost his helmet, and he, too, had tawny hair and eyes that were blue in the light of the flames overhead.

Sam broke open the pistol, put in the bullet and the charge as he had done that morning up in the hills, locked the barrel and rose to his feet. The two men still struggled, one slipping back a little, then the other, trying to throw each other. John held a steel knife in his right hand; the other man, a steel ax; each was grasping the weapon hand of the other.

Sam looked around. No one was coming at him. He stepped forward and extended the muzzle of the big pistol, holding it steady with both hands. He pulled the trigger, the click sounded, the gun was jarred to one side by the heavy hammer, there was a flash, he had the gun back in line, a boom, a cloud of smoke, and John's assailant fell to one side, the entire right side of his skull blown away.

John fell gasping onto the ground. Then he raised himself, looking at Sam, who was reloading the gun. "Many thanks, partner! That man was my nephew, Arthur!"

Sam did not reply. If he had been thinking more coolly he would have waited until Arthur had killed John and *then* blown Arthur's head off. It was ironic that he, Sam, who had much to gain by John's death, should be respon-

139

sible for saving him. Moreover, he could not expect gratitude from John. The man had no such thing in his soul.

Sam completed reloading the pistol and strode away, looking for Joe Miller. But he saw Livy reeling backward as a big Ulmak, whose left arm dangled bloodily, drove her back with blows of a stone ax on her shield. Her spear had been broken and in a few seconds he would have beaten her to her knees or shattered the shield. Sam reversed the pistol and broke the Ulmak's skull from behind with the butt of his gun. Livy fell exhausted and weeping on the ground. He would have gotten down to comfort her, but she seemed all right and he did not know where Joe Miller was. He plunged into the embattled mass and saw Joe on his feet again, demolishing heads, trunks and arms with sweeps of his great ax.

Sam stopped a few paces from a man who was coming up from behind Joe, a large ax in both hands. Sam fired, and the bullet took part of the man's chest off.

A minute later, the invaders were running for their lives. The sky was graying. By its light it was evident that Parolandoj were coming in from north and south. The other two columns had been shattered, and the reinforcements were outnumbering the invaders. Moreover, they brought rockets which blew up the boats and canoes waiting for the defeated.

Sam felt too exhilarated to be depressed by the losses and the damage. For the first time he came out of the blue funk that always seized him during a fight. He actually *enjoyed* the battle during the last ten minutes.

A moment later his pleasure was gone. A wild-eyed and naked Hermann Göring, his scalp caked with blood, appeared on the battleground. His arms were raised straight up, and he was shouting, "Oh, brothers and sisters! Shame! Shame! You have killed, you have hated, you have lusted for the blood and the ecstasy of murder! Why did you not throw down your arms and take in your enemies with love? Let them do with you what they would? You would have died and suffered but final victory would have

140

been yours! The enemy would have felt your love—and the next time he might have hesitated before again waging war. And the time after that and the next time he might have asked himself, 'What am I doing? Why am I doing this? What good is this? I have gained nothing—' and your love would have seeped through the stone over his heart and—"

John, coming up behind Göring, struck him on the back of the head with the hilt of his knife. Göring fell forward and lay on his face without moving.

"So much for traitors!" John shouted. He stared around wildly and then yelled, "Where are Trimalchio and Mordaunt, my ambassadors?"

Sam said, "They wouldn't be stupid enough to hang around here. You'll never catch them. They'll know you know they sold out to Arthur."

John's striking of Göring was illegal, since free speech was every one's right in Parolando. But Sam did not think that arresting John would be the right course at that moment. He, too, had felt like hitting Göring.

Livy, still weeping, staggered past. Sam followed her to where Cyrano sat on a pile of corpses. The Frenchman was wounded in a dozen places, though not seriously, and his rapier was bloody from tip to guard. He had given a splendid account of himself.

Livy threw herself on Cyrano. Sam turned away. She had not even thanked him for having saved her life.

There was a crash behind him. He turned. The rest of his house had fallen in, bringing the pylons with it.

He felt drained of strength, but there would be little rest for him today. The casualties and the damage had to be assessed. The dead had to be taken to the rendering factory up in the hills, since their fat was used to make glycerin. The practice was gruesome but necessary, and the owners of the bodies did not mind. Tomorrow they would be alive and well again somewhere far away along The River.

In addition, the entire population would have to be kept ready for a call to arms and the work of erecting the walls along the Riveredge would have to be speeded up. Scouts

141

and messengers would have to be sent out to determine just what the military situation was. The Ulmaks and the Kleomenujoj and the New Bretons might launch a full-scale attack.

A captain reported that Kleomenes, the leader of Kleomenujo, had been found dead near the Riveredge, where a piece of rock shrapnel had entered his skull. So ended the half-brother of the great Spartan, Leonidas, who defended the pass of Thermopylae. Or so he ended in this area, at least.

Sam appointed some men to leave by boat immediately for the two countries. They were to inform them that Parolando did not intend to take vengeance if the new leaders would guarantee friendship to Parolando. John complained that he should have been consulted, and there was a short but savage argument. Sam finally agreed that John was right in principle, but there was no time to discuss certain matters. John informed him that, under the law, Sam had to take the time. Any decision had to be agreed upon by both of them.

Sam hated to agree, but John was right. They couldn't be giving contradictory orders.

They went together to inspect the factories. These were not badly damaged. The invaders had not, of course, wanted to wreck them since they had intended to use them. The amphibian, the *Firedragon I*, was untouched. Sam shuddered when he thought of what might have happened if it had been completed and had fallen into the hands of the enemy. With it, they could have crushed the Parolandoj in the center and dug in to fight on the perimeter until reinforcements came. He would set up a large special guard around the vehicle.

He fell asleep after lunch in a Councilman's hut. It seemed that he had just closed his eyes when he was shaken awake. Joe was standing over him, breathing bourbon fumes from his tremendous proboscis.

"The delegathyon from Thoul Thity jutht landed."

"Firebrass!" Sam said, standing up from the chair. "I forgot all about him! What a time for him to show up!"

142

He walked down to The River, where a catamaran was beached near the grailstone. John was already there, greeting the delegation, which consisted of six blacks, two Arabs, and two Asiatic Indians. Firebrass was a short, bronze-skinned, curly-haired man with big brown eyes flecked with green. His huge forehead and shoulders and thickly muscled arms contrasted with his skinny legs, making him look all top. He spoke in Esperanto at first but later used English. It was a very strange English, full of terms and slang that Sam did not understand. But there was a warmth and openness about Firebrass that made Sam feel good just to have him around.

"We better go back to Esperanto," Sam said, smiling and pouring three more slugs of scotch into Firebrass' cup. "Is that spaceman's lingo or Soul City dialect?"

"Marsman's," Firebrass said. "Soul City English is pretty wild, but the official language, of course, is Esperanto, though Hacking was considering Arabic. But he isn't too happy about his Arabs anymore," he added in a lower voice, looking at Abd ar-Rahman and Ali Fazghuli, the Arab members of his delegation.

"As you can see," Sam said, "we are in no condition to have a long, leisurely conference. Not now. We have to clean up, get information about what's going on outside Parolando and set up our defenses. But you are welcome, of course, and we'll get around to business within a few days."

"I don't mind," Firebrass said. "I'd like to look around, if you don't mind."

"I don't, but my co-Consul has to give his consent, too."

John, smiling as if it hurt his teeth to be exposed to the air—and it probably did this time—said that Firebrass was welcome. But he would have to be accompanied by a guard of honor every time he left the quarters that would be assigned to him. Firebrass thanked him, but another delegate, Abdullah X, protested loudly and occasionally obscenely. Firebrass said nothing for a minute and then told Abdullah to be polite, since they were guests. Sam was grateful, though he wondered if the speech and Firebrass' command had not been prearranged.

It had not been easy to sit there and listen, though the vitriolics had been hurled at the white race in general and no one in particular. It troubled him, but Sam had to agree with Abdullah. He was right about conditions as they had been. But old Earth was dead; they were living in a new world.

Sam personally conducted the delegates to three huts, side by side, owned by men and women who had been killed last night. Then he moved into a hut near the delegation.

Drums boomed by the grailstone. After a minute, drums from across. The River thundered back an answer. The new chief of the Ulmaks wanted peace. The old chief, Shrubgrain, had been put to death, and his head would be delivered within the hour by canoe if peace could be arranged. Shrubgrain had failed his people by leading them to defeat.

Sam gave orders to transmit a request for a conference with the new chief, Threelburm.

Drums from Chernsky's Land said that Iyeyasu, who ruled a twelve-mile stretch of land between New Brittany and Kleomenujo, had invaded New Brittany. The news meant that the New Bretons would not be bothering Parolando, but it also worried Sam. Iyeyasu was a very ambitious man. Once he had consolidated his state with New Brittany he might decide he was strong enough to take Parolando.

More drums. Publius Crassus sent his congratulations and warmest regards, and he would be visiting tomorrow to see what he could do to aid Parolando.

And also to see how hard we've been hit and if we'd be easy pickings, Sam thought. So far, Publius had been cooperative, but a man who had served under Julius Caesar could have his own brand of Caesarism.

Göring, his head wrapped in a bloody towel, staggered by, supported by two of his followers. Sam hoped he would take the hint and leave Parolando, but he didn't have much faith in the German's perceptiveness.

He went to sleep that night while torches burned

144

everywhere over the land and guards peered into the shadows and the mists. His sleep was troubled, despite his intense fatigue. He tossed and rolled and once he awoke, his heart beating, his skin cold, certain that there was a third person in the hut. He fully expected to see the shadowy figure of the Mysterious Stranger crouched by his bed. But nobody was there except the monstrous form of Joe stretched out on the huge bamboo bed near him.

20

The next morning he arose unrefreshed in a refreshed world. The three-o'clock rain had washed away the blood and the stink of gunpowder. The bodies were gone, and the sky was clear and blue. Business as usual was resumed but without about four hundred and fifty men and women. Half of these were in the rendering factory; the rest, in the hospital. Those who wanted to be put out of their misery were given their wish. Time had been when an ax was the only euthanasiast but now, thanks to Parolando's technology, the work was done with a potassium cyanide pill.

Some decided to stick it out. In time their limbs or eyes would grow back in. Those who could not take the pain boarded The Suicide Express, and the bodies they left behind went to the rendering factory.

Sam's secretary had been killed. Sam asked Gwenafra if she would like to take Millie's place. Gwenafra seemed very pleased. The new position gave her a high status, and she had made no secret of the fact that she liked to be near Sam. Lothar von Richthofen, however, did not seem pleased.

"Why shouldn't she be my secretary, regardless of her relationship to you?" Sam said.

"There is no reason," Lothar said, "except that I might have a very good chance with her if she isn't around you much."

"Let the best man win."

"My sentiments, too, but I don't like your wasting her time or leading her on. You know that you won't take another hutmate as long as Livy is here."

"Livy has nothing to say about what I do," Sam said. "And don't forget that."

Lothar smiled slightly and said, "Sure, Sam."

Gwenafra tagged along with him, taking notes, sending messages, receiving them, arranging schedules and appointments. Though he was very busy, he found moments when he could talk and joke with her and he felt a warmth every time he looked at her. Gwenafra seemed to adore him.

Two days passed. The twenty-four-hour shift on the amphibian was showing results. The machine would be completed in another two days. The Soul City delegation strolled around with two of King John's men watching them. Joe Miller, who had gone back to his bed after the battle, said he was well again. Now Sam had both Gwenafra and the titanthrop with him, and his world seemed much more comfortable, though it was a long way from being Utopia. Word came via the drum telegraph that Odysseus had loaded his ships with flints and would be back in a month. He had gone as commander of a ten-boat fleet to barter with the chieftainess of Selinujo. On Earth she had been Countess Huntingdon, Selina Hastings, born 1707, died 1791. She was now a member of the Church of the Second Chance and traded her flint with Parolando only because Parolando permitted Göring's missionaries to preach at will in its territory. In return for the flint, she had been promised a small metal steamboat in which she proposed to go up and down The River and preach. Sam thought she was fooling herself. The first place she put into she was liable to have her throat cut for the sake of the boat. But that was her business.

The Councilmen met with the Soul City delegation at a round table in the largest room in John's palace. Sam would have liked to put it off, since John was in a mood even uglier than usual. One of his women had tried to kill him, or so he claimed. He had been stabbed in the side before he broke her jaw and knocked her head against the corner of a table. The woman had died an hour later still unconscious, and John's word that she had attacked him first had to be accepted. Sam would have liked to have collected some neutral eyewitness account, but that was impossible.

John was in pain from the stab wound, half drunk with bourbon as an anesthetic, and smarting because the woman had dared to defy him. He slumped in a large,

147

high-backed, ornately carved oak chair covered with red hornfish leather. One hand was around a clay vessel full of whiskey, a cigarette dangled from his lips, and he glowered at everybody.

Firebrass was talking.

"Hacking once believed in total segregation of whites and nonwhites. He believed, fiercely believed, that whites could never accept, not soul-accept, nonwhite peoples—that is, the blacks, Mongolians, Polynesians, and Amerindians. The only way nonwhites could live with dignity, feel beautiful, be a people with its own personality and pride, was to follow the way of segregation. Equal but separate.

"Then his leader, Malcolm X, quit the Black Muslims. Malcolm X saw that he was wrong. Not all whites were devils, racist fiends, any more than all blacks had flat noses. Hacking fled the states to live in Algeria and there he found that it was the attitude that made racism, not the color of the skin."

Hardly an original or surprising discovery, Sam thought. But he had told himself that he would not interrupt.

"And then the young whites of the Untied States, many of them, anyway, rejected their parents' prejudices, and they supported the blacks in their struggles. They got out on the streets and demonstrated, rioted, laid down their lives for the blacks. They genuinely seemed to like blacks, not because they thought they ought to, but because blacks were human beings and human beings can be liked or even loved.

"Hacking, however, wasn't ever really at ease with an American white, try though he did to think of them as human beings. He was ruined, just as most whites, most older whites, were ruined. But he tried to like those whites who were on his side and he respected those young whites that told their parents, their white racists society, to go to hell.

"Then he died, as everybody did, black or white. He found himself among ancient Chinese, and he wasn't very happy with them because they regarded all peoples except the Chinese as inferior."

148

Sam remembered the Chinese of Nevada and California in the early '60's, the hard-working, thrifty, quiet, meek, cheery little brown men and women. They had taken abuse that most people would not give a mule, been spat upon, cursed, tortured, stoned, robbed, raped, suffered about every indignity and crime that a people could suffer. They had had no rights whatsoever, no protector or protection. And they had never murmured, never revolted, they just endured. What thoughts had those masklike faces hidden? Had they, too, believed in the superiority of any Chinese to any white devil? If so, why had they not struck back, not once? They would have been massacred if they had, but they would have stood up like men for a few moments.

But the Chinese believed in time; time was the Chinese ally. If time did not raise a father to fortune, time would raise his son. Or his grandson.

Firebrass said, "So Hacking left in a dugout, floated downRiver, and after many thousands of miles settled down among some blacks of seventeenth-century A.D. Africa. Ancestors of the Zulus before they migrated to southern Africa. After a while he left them. Their customs were too repulsive, and they were too bloody-minded for him.

"Then he lived in an area where the people were a mixture of Dark Age Huns and dark whites of the New Stone Age. They accepted him well enough, but he missed his own people, the American blacks. So he took off again and was captured by ancient Moabites and enslaved, escaped, was captured by ancient Hebrews and put into grail slavery, escaped again, found a little community of blacks who'd been pre-Civil War slaves and was happy for a while. But their Uncle Tom attitudes and their superstitions got on his nerves and he took off, sailed downRiver, and lived with several other peoples. Then, one day, some big blond whites, Germans of some kind, raided the people he was with and he fought and was killed.

"He was resurrected here. Hacking became convinced that the only happy states on The River were going to be made up of people with similar colors, similar tastes, and

149

of the same terrestrial period. Anything else just won't work. People here aren't going to change. Back on Earth he could believe in progress, because the young were flexible-minded. The old ones would die off, and then the children of the young whites would be even more free of racial prejudice. But here that just isn't going to take place. Every man's set in his ways. So, unless Hacking just happened to find a community of late-twentieth-century whites, he would find no whites without racial hatreds or prejudices. Of course, the ancient whites didn't have any against blacks, but they're too strange for a civilized man."

Sam asked, "What's all this leading up to, Sinjoro Firebrass?"

"We want a homogeneous nation. We can't get all late-twentieth-century blacks, but we can get as black a nation as possible. Now, we know that you have approximately three thousand blacks in Parolando. We would like to exchange our Dravidians, Arabs, any nonblacks, for your blacks. Hacking is making similar proposals to your neighbors, but he doesn't have any lever with them."

King John sat up and said, loudly. "You mean he doesn't have anything they want?"

Firebrass looked coolly at John and said, "That's about it. But we'll have a lever some day."

"Do you mean when you have enough steel weapons?" Sam said.

Firebrass shrugged.

John crashed his empty cup down on the table. "Well, we don't want your Arabs or your Dravidians or any of your Soul City dregs!" he shouted. "But I'll tell you what we will do! For every ton of bauxite or cryolite or ounce of platinum, we will give you one of our black citizens! You can keep your Saracen infidels or send them packing downRiver or drown them for all we care."

"Wait a minute," Sam said. "We can't give our citizens away. If they want to volunteer, fine. But we don't just give anybody away. This is a democracy."

Firebrass' expression had darkened at John's outburst.

'I wasn't suggesting that you *give* anybody away," he said. 'We're not slave dealers, you know. What we want is a one-per-one voluntary exchange. The Wahhabi Arabs, whom ar-Rahman and Fazghuli represent, feel they're unwelcome at Soul City and they would like to go where they could congregate in their own community, form a sort of Kasbah, you might say."

Sam thought this sounded fishy. Why couldn't they do that just as well in Soul City? Or why didn't they just get up and leave? One of the beauties of this world was that ties or property or dependence on income did not exist. A man could carry everything he owned on his back—and building another house was easy in a world where new bamboo grew at a rate of two inches a day.

It was possible that Hacking wanted to get his people into Parolando so that they could spy or revolt when Hacking invaded.

Sam said, "We'll put your proposition about the exchange to each individual. That's all we can do. Now, does Sinjoro Hacking plan to keep on supplying us with the minerals and with wood?"

"As long as you keep on sending us raw ore and steel weapons," Firebrass said. "But Hacking is thinking of upping the price."

John's fist smashed into the tabletop again. "We will not be robbed!" he shouted. "We are paying too much now! Don't push us, Sinjoro Firebrass, or you may find yourselves with nothing! Nothing at all—not even your lives!"

"Take it easy, Your Majesty," Sam said quietly. To Firebrass he said, "John isn't feeling well. Please forgive him. However, he does have a point. We can be pushed only so far."

Abdullah X, a very big and very black man, jumped up and pointed a big finger at Sam. In English, he said, "You honkies had better quit badmouthing us. We won't take any crap from you, Mister Whitey! None! Especially from a man that wrote a book like you did about Nigger Jim! We don't like white racists and we only deal with them be-

151

cause there's nothing else we can do just now."

"Take it easy, Abdullah," Firebrass said. He wa smiling and Sam wondered if Abdullah's speech was th second part of a well-prepared program. Probably, Fire brass was similarly wondering if John's explosions ha been rehearsed. Actors didn't have to be politicians, bu politicians had to be actors.

Sam groaned and said, "Did you read *Huckleberry Finn*, Sinjoro X?"

Abdullah, sneering, said, "I don't read trash."

"Then you don't know what you're talking about, do you?"

Abdullah's face darkened. Firebrass grinned.

"I don't have to read that racist crap, man!" Abdullah shouted. "Hacking told me all about it and what he says is good enough for me!"

"You read it and then come back and we'll discuss it," Sam said.

"You crazy?" Abdullah said. "You know there aren't any books on this world."

"Then you lost out, didn't you?" Sam said. He was trembling a little; he wasn't used to being talked to like this by a black man. "Anyway," Sam said, "this isn't a literary tea-and-discussion group. Let's stick to the issue."

But Abdullah would not stop shouting about the books that Sam had written. And John, losing his temper, leaped up and screamed, *"Silentu, negraco!"*

John had taken the Esperanto word for "black" or "negro" and infixed the disparaging "-ac-" particle. He had gotten his point over quite well.

There was a moment of shock and silence. Abdullah X's mouth was open, then it closed, and he looked triumphant, almost happy. Firebrass bit his lip. John leaned on the table on his fists and scowled. Sam puffed on his cigar. He knew that John's contempt for all humanity had made him invent the term. John had no racial prejudice; he had never seen more than a half dozen blacks during his lifetime on Earth. But he certainly knew how to insult a person; the knowledge was second nature to him.

"I'm walking out!" Abdullah X said. "I may be going

152

home—and if I do you can bet your whiteass that you'll pay hell getting any more aluminum or platinum, Mister Charlie."

Sam rose to his feet and said, "Just a minute. If you want an apology, I extend it on behalf of all Parolando."

Abdullah looked at Firebrass, who looked away. Abdullah said, "I want an apology from him, now!"

He pointed at King John.

Sam leaned close to John and said softly, "There's too much at stake to play the proud monarch, Your Majesty! And you may be playing into their hands with your little fit. They are up to something, you can bet on that. Apologize."

John straightened up and said, "I apologize to no man, especially not to a commoner who is also an infidel dog!"

Sam snorted and gestured with his cigar. "Can't you get it through your thick Plantagenet head that there isn't any such thing as royal blood or divine right of kings anymore, that we're all commoners? Or all kings?"

John did not reply. He walked out. Abdullah looked at Firebrass, who nodded. Abdullah walked out.

Sam said. "Well, Sinjoro Firebrass, what next? Do you people go home?"

Firebrass shook his head, "No, I don't believe in hasty decisions. But the conference is suspended as far as the Soul City delegation is concerned. Until John Lackland apologizes, I'll give you until noon tomorrow to decide what to do."

Firebrass turned to leave. Sam said, "I'll talk to John, but he's as hardheaded as a Missouri mule."

"I'd hate to see our negotiations fold because one man can't keep his insults to himself," Firebrass said. "And I'd also hate to see our trade stop, because that would mean no Riverboat for you."

Sam said, "Don't get me wrong, Sinjoro Firebrass. I'm making no threats. But I won't be stopped. I'll get the aluminum if I have to kick John out of the country myself. Or, alternatively, if I have to go down to Soul City and get the aluminum myself."

153

"I understand you," Firebrass said. "But what you don't understand is that Hacking isn't out for power. He only wants to have a well-protected state so that his citizens can enjoy life. And they will enjoy their life because they'll all have similar tastes and similar goals. In other words, they'll all be black."

Sam grunted and then said, "Very well." He fell silent but just before Firebrass left he called, "One minute. Have you read *Huckleberry Finn*?"

Firebrass turned back. "Sure. I thought it was a great book when I was a kid. I read it again when I was in college, and I could see its flaws then, but I enjoyed it even more as an adult, despite its flaws."

"Were you disturbed because Jim was called Nigger Jim?"

"You have to remember that I was born in 1975 on a farm near Syracuse, New York. Things had changed a lot by then, and the farm had originally been owned by my great-great-great grandfather, who came up from Georgia to Canada via the underground railway and then purchased the farm after the Civil War. No, I wasn't offended by your use of the word. Negroes were called niggers openly in the time you wrote about and nobody thought anything of it. Sure, the word was an insult. But you were portraying people as they actually talked, and the ethical basis of your novel, the struggle between Huck's duty as a citizen and his feeling for Jim as a human being and the victory of the human feeling in Huck—I was moved. The whole book was an indictment of slavery, of the semi-feudal society of the Mississippi, of superstition—of everything stupid of that time. So why should I be offended by it?"

"Then why—"

"Abdullah—whose original name was George Robert Lee—was born in 1925 and Hacking was born in 1938. Blacks were niggers then to a lot of whites, though not to all. They found out the hard way that violence—or the threat of it, the same thing that the whites had used to keep them down—was the only way to get their rights as citizens of the United States. You died in 1910, right? But you must have been told by any number of people what happened after that?"

Sam nodded. "It's hard to believe. Not the violence of the riots. Plenty of that happened in my lifetime and nothing, I understand, ever equaled the Draft Act riots in New York City during the Civil War. I mean, what's hard to visualize is the licentiousness of the late twentieth century."

Firebrass laughed and said, "Yet you're living in a society that is far more free and licentious—from the viewpoint of the nineteenth century—than any society in the twentieth. You've adapted."

"I suppose so," Sam replied. "But the two weeks of absolute nudity during the first days after resurrection ensured that mankind would never again be the same. Not as regards nudity, anyway. And the undeniable fact of the resurrection shattered many fixed ideas and attitudes. Though the diehard is still with us, as witness your Wahhabi Moslem."

"Tell me, Sinjoro Clemens," Firebrass said. "You were an early liberal, far ahead of your times in many things. You spoke up against slavery and were for equality. And when you wrote the Magna Carta for Parolando you insisted that there should be political equality for all species, races and both sexes. I notice that a black man and a white woman live almost next door to you. Be honest, doesn't it disturb you to see that?"

Sam drew in smoke, blew it out and said, "To be honest, yes, it did disturb me. Well, to tell the truth, it almost killed me! What my mind told me and what my reflexes told me were two different things. I hated it. But I stuck to my guns, I said nothing, I became acquainted with that couple and I learned to like them. And now, after a year, it bothers me only a very little. And that will go away in time."

"The difference between you—representing the white liberal—and the youth of Hacking's day and mine was

155

that we were not bothered. We accepted it."

"Don't I get any credit for lifting myself by my mental bootstraps?" Sam asked.

"Yawblaw," Firebrass said, lapsing into English—of a sort. "Two degrees off is better than ninety. Pin it."

He went out. Sam was left alone. He sat for a long while, then stood up and went outside. The first person he saw was Hermann Göring. His head was still wrapped in a towel, but his skin was less pale, and his eyes did not look odd.

Sam said, "How's your head?"

"It still hurts. But I can walk without driving hot spikes in it every time I take a step."

"I don't like to see a man suffer," Sam said. "So I suggest that you could avoid more suffering, if not downright pain, by leaving Parolando."

"Are you threatening me?"

"Not with any action from me. But there are plenty who may get so riled up they'll run you out on a rail. Or take you down to The River and drown you. You're upsetting everybody with your preachings. This state was founded with one main goal, the building of the Riverboat. Now, a man may say anything he wants to and not run foul of the law here. But there are those who sometimes ignore the law, and I wouldn't want to have to punish them because you tempted them. I suggest that you do your Christian duty and remove yourself from the premises. That way, you won't be tempting good men and women to commit violence."

"I'm not a Christian," Göring said.

"I admire a man who can admit that. I don't think I ever met a preacher who came out and said so, in so many words."

"Sinjoro Clemens," Göring said, "I read your books when I was a young man in Germany, first in German and then in English. But levity or mild irony aren't going to get us any place. I am not a Christian, though I try to practice the better Christian virtues. I am a missionary for the Church of the Second Chance. All Terrestrial religions have been discredited, even if some won't admit it. The Church is the first religion to rise on the new world, the only one which has any chance to survive. It—"

"Spare me the lecture," Sam said. "I've heard enough from your predecessors and from you. What I'm saying, in utter friendliness and a desire to save you from harm and also, to be honest, to get you out of my craw, is that you should take off. Right now. Or you'll be killed."

"Then I'll rise at dawn tomorrow somewhere else and preach The Truth there, wherever I find myself. You see, here, as on Earth, the blood of the martyr is the seed of the Church. The man who kills one of us only ensures that The Truth, the chance for eternal salvation, will be heard by more people. Murder has spread our faith up and down The River far faster than any conventional means of travel."

"Congratulations," Sam said exasperatedly, dropping into English, as he often did when angry. "But tell me, doesn't the repeated killing of your missionaries bother you? Aren't you afraid of running out of body?"

"What do you mean?"

"Tenets, anyone?"

Sam got no reaction except a puzzled look. Sam resumed in Esperanto. "One of your major tenets, if I remember correctly, is that Man wasn't resurrected so he could enjoy life here forever. He is given only a limited time, though it may look like a long time to most, especially if they don't happen to be enjoying life here. You postulate something analogous to a soul, something you call a psychomorph, right? Or sometimes a *ka*. You have to, otherwise you can't claim a continuity of identity in a man. Without it a man who dies is dead, even if his body is reproduced exactly and made alive again. That second body is only a reproduction. The lazarus has the mind and the memories of the men who died, so he *thinks* he's the man who died. But he isn't. He's just a living duplicate. Death terminated the first man. He's through.

"But you solve this problem by postulating a soul—or a psychomorph or a *ka*—call it what you will. This is an entity which is born with the body, accompanies it, registers

157

and records everything the body does and, indeed, must be an incorporeal incorporation of the body, if you'll excuse that contradiction. So that, when the flesh dies, the *ka* still exists. It exists in some fourth dimension or in some polarization which protoplasmic eyes can't see or mechanical devices can't detect. Is that correct?"

"You're close enough," Göring said. "Crudely put but satisfactory."

"So far," Sam said, expelling a big cloud of green smoke, "we have—you have, not I—the postulated soul of the Christians and the Moslems and others *ad nauseam*. But you claim that the soul does not go to a hell or a heaven. It flits around in some sort of fourth-dimensional limbo. It would do so forever if it were not for the interference of other beings. These are extra-Terrestrials who came into existence long before humanity did. These superbeings came to Earth when mankind did not yet exist—in fact, they visited every planet in the universe that might have sentient life some day."

"You're not phrasing it exactly as we do," Göring said. "We maintain that every Galaxy has one—or perhaps many—ancient species inhabiting certain planets. These beings may have arisen in our Galaxy or they may have originated in an earlier, now dead, Galaxy or universe. In any event, they are wise and knew long ago that sentient life would arise on Earth, and they set up devices which started recording these sentients from the moment they appeared. These devices are undetectable by the sentients.

"At some time which these Ancients, as we call them, have determined, the recordings are sent to a special place. There the dead are fleshed out from the recordings by energy-matter converters, made whole and young again and then recordings are made of these bodies—which are destroyed and the dead are raised on a new world, such as this, again through e-m conversion.

"The psychomorphs, or *kas*, have an affinity to their protoplasmic twins. The moment a duplicate of the dead body is made, the *ka* attaches itself and begins recording.

158

So that, if the body is killed and duplicated a hundred times, the *ka* still retains the identity, the mind, and the memories of all the bodies. So that it is not just one duplicate after another being created. It is a matter of preservation of the pristine individual with a recording of everything that ever occurred in the immediate environment of all the protoplasmic bodies of the *ka*.

"But!" Sam said, waving his cigar and then stabbing its glowing end close to Göring's cheek. "But! You maintain that a man cannot be killed an indefinite number of times. You say that, after a couple of hundred times, death does have a final effect. Continued dying weakens the link between body and *ka* and eventually the duplication of the body does not cause the *ka* to merge with it. The *ka* wanders off, haunts the spooky corridors of the fourth dimension, or whatever. It becomes, in effect, a ghost, a lost soul. It is done for."

"That is the essence of our faith," Göring said. "Or I should say our knowledge, since we know this to be true."

Sam raised his bushy eyebrows. "Indeed? Know?"

"Yes. Our founder heard The Truth a year after Resurrection, a year to the day after all of humanity rose from the dead. A man came to him at night as he prayed for a revelation on a high ledge up in the mountains. This man told him certain things, showed him certain things, that no terrestrial mortal could tell or show. This man was an agent of The Ancients and he revealed The Truth, and he told our founder to go out and preach the doctrine of the Second Chance.

"Actually, the term Second Chance is a misnomer. It is really our First Chance, because we never had a chance for salvation and eternal life while we were on Earth. But life on Earth was a necessary prelude to this Riverworld. The Creator made the universe and then The Ancients preserved humankind—indeed, all sentients throughout the universe. They *preserved!* But *salvation* is up to mankind only!

"It is up to each man to save himself, now that he has been given the chance!"

159

"Through the Church of the Second Chance and that only, I suppose," Sam said. He did not want to sneer but he could not help himself.

"That is what we believe," Göring said.

"What were the credentials of this mysterious stranger?" Sam said. He thought of *his* Mysterious Stranger, and he felt panic. Could the two be the same? Or could both be from the same beings who called themselves the Ethicals? His Stranger, the man who sent the nickel-iron meteorite here and who had enabled Joe Miller to see the Tower in the far-off misty North Polar Sea, was a renegade of the Ethicals. If he were to be believed.

"Credentials?" Göring said. "Papers from God?"

He laughed.

"The founder knew that his visitor could not be just a man because he knew things that only a god, or a superior being, could know about him. And he showed him some things that he had to believe. And he told him how we were brought back to life and why. He did not tell him everything. Some things will be revealed later. Some things we must find out for ourselves."

"What is the name of this founder?" Sam said. "Or don't you know? Is that one of the hidden things?"

"No one knows," Göring said. "It is not necessary to know. What is a name? He only called himself Viro. That is, in Esperanto, a man. From the Latin *vir*. We call him La Fondinto, The Founder, or La Viro, The Man."

"Did you ever meet him?"

"No, but I have met two who knew him well. One was there when La Viro preached the first time, seven days after the Stranger had talked to him."

"La Viro is definitely male? Not a woman?"

"Oh, yes!"

Sam sighed deeply and said, "That's a great weight off my mind. If the founder had turned out to be Mary Baker Eddy, I would have curled up and died."

"What?"

"Never mind," Sam said, grinning. "I wrote a book about her once. I wouldn't want to meet her; she'd scalp me alive. But some of the wild mystical things you told me reminded me of her."

"Except for the *ka*, everything in our explanation is based on the physical. And the *ka* is physical, but at right angles, you might say, to our reality. We believe that it is science, the science of The Ancients, which has given us a physical resurrection. There's nothing supernatural about anything, except our belief in The Creator, of course. The rest is all science."

"Like Mary Baker Eddy's religion?" Sam asked.

"I do not know of her."

"So how do we attain this salvation?"

"By becoming love. And that implies, of course, that we do not offer violence, even in self-defence. We believe that we can become love only by attaining a certain transcendent state and that comes through self-knowledge. So far most of mankind has not learned how to use dreamgum; man has abused the drug, just as he abuses everything."

"And you think you have *become love*, whatever that phrase means?"

"Not yet. But I am on the way."

"Through dreamgum?"

"Not just with it. It helps. But you have to act, too, you have to preach and suffer for your belief. And learn not to hate. Learn to love."

"So that is why you oppose my Riverboat? You think that we are wasting our time by building it?"

"It's a goal that will bring no one any good. So far it has resulted in the devastation of the land, in greed and pain and bloodshed, in anxiety and treachery. In hate, hate, hate! And for what? So you can have what nobody else has, a giant boat of metal propelled by electricity, the apex of the technology this planet offers, a ship of fools. So you can journey to the headwaters of The River. When you get there, then what? You should be journeying to the headwaters of the soul!"

"There are some things you don't know," Sam said. His smugness was soured by a vision. There was a devil, crouching in the darkness, whispering in his ear. But someone had crouched in the darkness and whispered in

161

the ear of the founder of the Church, too. Was the Church's Stranger the devil? The being who had come to Samuel Clemens had said that the others were the devils and he wanted to save mankind.

The devil would say something like that, of course.

"Don't my words touch your heart at all?" Göring said.

Sam rapped his chest with his fist and said, "Yes, I do believe I have a touch of indigestion."

Göring made a fist and clamped his lips.

"Watch out, you'll lose your love," Sam said and walked away. But he did not feel particularly triumphant. It was a fact that he did have a little stomach upset. Invincible ignorance always upset him, even though he knew he should just laugh at it.

21

The afternoon of the next day arrived. Sam Clemens and John Lackland had been arguing all morning. Finally Sam, exasperated past caution and reasonableness, said, "We can't afford to have the bauxite cut off by Hacking! We can't afford anything that will put a stop to building the Riverboat! Maybe you're doing this to force a war between us and Soul City! It isn't going to work, Your Majesty!"

Sam had been walking back and forth, waving a panatela as he spoke. John sprawled before the oaken round table in Sam's pilothouse. Joe Miller sat in a corner on a big chair specially built for him. The massive paleolithic Mongolian, Zaksksromb, stood behind John.

Suddenly, Sam whirled and planked both fists on the table. Leaning on the table, his cigar in one corner of his mouth, the reddish tangle of his eyebrows drawn down, he snarled at John.

"You gave in once, at Runnymede, when you signed the Magna Carta. It was about the only decent thing you ever did during your reign—and there are some who say you had your fingers crossed then. Well, this is another showdown, John, Your Majesty. You apologize to Abdullah, who has a right to an apology—or I'll call a special session of the Council and we'll determine your fitness to continue as co-Consul!"

John glowered at him for a full minute at the least. Then he said, "Your threats don't scare me. But it's evident that you would sooner plunge our land into civil war than go to war with Soul City. I do not understand this madness, but then a rational man always has trouble understanding irrationality. So I will apologize. Why not? A king can afford to be gracious to a commoner. It costs him nothing and enhances his graciousness."

John rose and swaggered out, his huge bodyguard behind him.

Ten minutes later, Sam heard that John had appeared at the state guest house and offered his apology. Abdullah X accepted it, though sullenly. It was evident that he had been ordered to do so.

Just before the factory whistles announced the end of lunch hour, Cawber entered. He sat down without waiting for Sam to invite him. Sam raised his eyebrows, because this was the first time that this had happened. There was something indefinable in Cawber's attitude. Sam, watching him carefully, listening to every inflection of his voice, decided that his attitude was that of a slave who has decided to be a slave no more.

Cawber knew that he would be the emissary to Soul City. He sat leaning forward, huge black arms resting on the oak, his hands spread out. He spoke in Esperanto and, like many people, mostly in the present tense, using an adverb of time to indicate future or past if he wanted to clarify.

Cawber's team had talked to every one of the approximately three thousand undoubted Negroes (there was some confusion of classification about some of the prehistorics). A third of these was willing, though not eager, to go to Soul City in exchange for Hacking's unwanted citizens. Most were late-twentieth-century blacks. The others maintained that they had work that gave them prestige, that they like being on an equal footing with the whites, and that they did not want to give up their chance to be on the Riverboat.

The latter was probably the biggest determinant, Sam thought. He was not the only one who dreamed of the Riverboat. It drove through the minds of many during sleep, gleaming like a jewel with a firefly trapped inside it.

Firebrass and his people were requested to come to the conference room. Firebrass was late because he had been inspecting the airplane. He was laughing about its quaintness, fragility and slowness, and yet he was envious that von Richthofen would be the one to fly it.

"You'll certainly get a chance to fly it, too," Sam said. "Provided that you are still here, of course, when——"

164

Firebrass became serious. "What is your decision, gentlemen, regarding my government's proposal?"

Sam looked at John, who gestured that Sam had the floor. John intended that any possible ill feelings should first be directed at Sam.

"This is a democracy," Sam said. "And we can't tell our citizens to get out unless they've been guilty of illegal behavior. So, as I see it—as *we* see it—any citizen of Parolando may go to Soul City if he wishes. I think we actually reached basic agreement on this when we last met. It will be up to your government to negotiate with each citizen. As for taking in your Arabs and Dravidians and so forth—we'll give them a chance to come with us if they want to. But we reserve the right to get rid of them if they don't work out. Where they'll go then is up to them."

"Well," Firebrass said, "I don't suppose Hacking wants anybody who isn't willing to live in Soul City, no matter how black that person is."

"What about the shipments of minerals?" Sam said. "Will those be discontinued during the negotiations?"

"I really couldn't say," Firebrass replied. "I doubt it, but I'd have to confer with Hacking. Of course, you'll have to keep up your present rate of ore and weapons to us before the price is raised."

"I notice you said *is*, not *might be*," Sam said.

"Anything I say is subject to confirmation or negation from Soul City," Firebrass said, smiling.

It was then agreed that Cawber would go to Soul City as Parolando's ambassador of the Carta could be changed to arrange it. Everything else was still up in the air. Sam Clemens received the impression that Firebrass did not intend to speed things up. Quite the contrary. He was willing to let things drag on or even to put his own foot on the brake if things showed signs of accelerating. He wanted to remain in Parolando, and Sam could only think that he wished to do so in order to spy. Perhaps, he also wanted to stir up trouble.

Later, he discussed the meeting with John. John agreed that Firebrass was a spy, but he could not see why Firebrass would stir up trouble.

"He would want the boat to be built as swiftly as possible. The sooner it's completed, the sooner Hacking will try to seize it. Do you think for one moment that Hacking doesn't intend to get the boat? Do you think for one moment that we have a single neighbor who doesn't intend to try for the boat? Arthur made the abortive attempt to take us over because of his hatred for me. He should have waited until the boat was nearly completed and then, with Kleomenes and the Ulmaks, launched all the force they could mount in an all-out attack. As things worked out, he and Kleomenes were killed and Iyeyasu has invaded their countries while their successors are fighting among themselves."

"According to our spies, he's winning, too," Sam said.

"If he consolidates his state with the other two, then he'll be a very formidable enemy."

And so will you be John Lackland, Sam thought. *Of all the people I'll have to watch after the boat is built, you'll bear the closest watching . . .*

Firebrass announced that he and his delegation would remain as Soul City's embassy while the negotiations went on.

"It's nice to have you," Sam said. "But Soul City has its own industries. I know it's been using our ore to make weapons and several things our spies can't find out about."

Firebrass looked surprised and then he laughed uproariously. "You twist my stick, stymate!" he said in English. Then, in Esperanto, "Well, why shouldn't we be frank? I like that. Yes, we know you have spies among us—just as you know we have ours here. Who doesn't have his spies in his neighbors' lands? But what are you getting at?"

"You're the most technically trained man Hacking has. You're a PhD. You're in charge of the factories and of research and development. So why does Hacking send you here when he needs you there?"

"I've set everything up to run smoothly. Soul City

doesn't need me right now, and I was bored. I wanted to come here, where it's at."

"So you can see what we've got, like our Mark I handguns and our airplane and the amphibian and its steam cannon?"

Firebrass grinned and nodded. "Yes. Why not? If I don't see these things, someone else will."

Sam relaxed. He said, "Have a cigar. You can look all you want. We're not doing anything you wouldn't have figured out for yourself, except for the steam cannon maybe. That, by the way, is my invention. Come along with me. I'm very proud of it and want you to see it. It's almost finished."

Firedragon I rested inside its supporting framework of timbers. It was silvery gray and shaped like a flat-bottomed boat but had seven huge metal wheels with plastic tires on each side. Twin screws protected by a screen protruded from its rear. Its length was thirty feet, its beam was ten feet, and its height was twelve feet. Three turrets stuck out from the upper deck. One held the pilot, captain and radio operator, though at the moment Parolando had no radios. The center turret was higher than the others, and the barrel of a short stubby weapon encased in wood projected from it. The rear turret was designed for gunners who would be armed with Mark I handguns and perhaps rifles.

"The amphibian burns wood alcohol to generate steam," Sam said. "Let's go inside, through this hatch in the side here. You'll notice that the boiler takes up about a third of the interior. There's a good reason for that, as you'll see."

They climbed up a ladder into the interior of the center turret, which was lit by a single light bulb. Firebrass exclaimed at this. It was the only electric light bulb he had ever seen on The River. Sam explained that it was powered by a fuel cell.

"And here is the Superdooper Steam Machine Cannon," he said. He pointed at the cylinder sticking out of the gray bulkhead of the turret. Underneath it were a pistollike butt and a trigger. Firebrass got behind it, put his finger on the trigger and looked out through the opening above the barrel. He raised and lowered the weapon.

"There'll be a chair for the operator to sit in," Sam said. "He'll be able to rotate the turret any way he wants by pushing pedals. He can depress the gun about twenty degrees up or down. The steam from the boiler is the motive power for the eighty-caliber plastic bullets. The gun is fired from an open breech—that is, there's no bullet in the barrel when the trigger is pulled. Pulling the trigger releases a catch which permits the breech block to move forward, impelled by a spring. During its forward travel, the breech block picks up a plastic bullet from the clip and pushes it into the breech. Just before the block reaches the breech, the camming lugs on either side engage in their slots and turn the breech block a quarter turn to the right, thus locking the breech. You follow me?"

Firebrass nodded.

"Good. As soon as the quarter turn is completed, the inlet channel in the breech block comes into line with the feed channel from the high-pressure steam line. This allows hot, say approximately four-hundred-degree F., steam to enter the chamber in the breech block. The plastic cartridge is forced through the barrel by the expansion of steam. At the same time the steam pressure, acting against the rear of the chamber, begins to force the breech block back. Because of the greater weight of the block, however, the block doesn't begin to move until the bullet has already cleared the muzzle of the rifle.

"As the block begins to move backward, the camming lugs move in the camming slots and turn the bolt a quarter turn to the left, thus shutting off the steam. Then the breech block returns to its original position. If the trigger is still held back, the operation is repeated indefinitely."

Firebrass said, "I'm impressed. but won't the gun operate most efficiently if its temperature is the same as the incoming high-pressure steam? That way, less of the steam's energy would be used to heat the gun and this means more steam to propel the bullet. Ah, I see! You do have a hollow jacket around the barrel. The steam travels through that before it enters the weapon itself, right?"

"Yes. There's an insulating jacket of plaster encased in wood. Note that bleeder valve. It permits the gun to be heated up before use—a few seconds before it's fired. If that isn't done, the gun might jam. And since the gun's maximum temperature is the same as the steam in the boiler, there's no danger of burning up the barrel. You can use the gun like a fire hose. In fact, that'll be about the only way it'll be effective. The accuracy of a light plastic bullet with such comparatively low muzzle velocity isn't high."

Firebrass was far from being depressed because of the military superiority the amphibian would give Parolando. This probably was because he was planning on building one for Soul City. Or, if Parolando had one, then perhaps he might build two. In which case, Parolando would have to build three.

Soul City could not outbuild Parolando. But Parolando could not cut the supplies off, because then Soul City would cut off the bauxite, cryolite, platinum and iridium.

The exhilaration from showing off his deadly invention whistled out almost audibly from Sam. The only solution to the problem, if Soul City did start a weapons race, would be to smash Soul City and take direct control of the minerals. This meant putting off the building of the Riverboat. And it also meant offending the two states, Publiujo and Tifonujo, that lay between Parolando and Soul City. And if those two states got together, they would be formidable, what with the weapons that Parolando had to give them in exchange for their wood.

Sam had thought that that potentiality was bad enough. But a few days later Iyeyasu completed his conquest of his neighboring states and sent a mission to Parolando. He made no demands that could not be met. In fact, in one way his proposals were helpful. He said that his nation had lost enough trees, and he would like to give them a chance to grow again—but for an increase in the number of weapons from Parolando, he was willing to provide a large quantity of wood and of excrement for their gunpowder industry. He would invade the territories across The River and take their wood from them.

What it amounted to was that Parolando would be paying Iyeyasu to collect the wood forcibly from its neighbors. It would be cheaper and also a lot less painful for Parolandoj, who would not have to do their own killing, enslaving or raiding.

And Sam Clemens would have one more thing to rob him of sleep.

John Lackland thought the proposal excellent. "Our factories are turning out weapons efficiently," he said. "We can afford to export more. And we must build a fleet of *Firedragons* so that the swords we give these people will be easily overpowered by our machines."

"When are we going to start building the Riverboat?" Sam asked.

No one gave him an answer, but the next day Van Boom, Velitsky, and O'Brien, his chief engineers, brought him the first rough overall sketches. They were drawn in black on white plastic boards with a pencil connected to a fuel cell. The magnetic field at the tip of the pencil rearranged the loose and very thin covering of particles within its range. The lines remained polarized until a reverse field was passed over them. Thus, the demand for paper for drawings was greatly cut down, and the plans could be changed as desired.

Firebrass said he would like to help build the boat. Permission was given, though John objected at first. Sam replied that the more help they had, the faster the work would move. And he did not see how any amount of knowledge on Firebrass' part would enable him to steal the boat. Though Sam did not tell John, he had an idea about Firebrass. That was to get him so involved, so "het up" about the boat that he would take an offer of a berth on the vessel.

The machinery necessary to roll out the first plates for the hull was almost finished. The dam had been finished a week ago, and the water from the cataract was filling it up. The aluminum wires of the generators, which would be

170

turned by the waterfall from the dam, were being wound. The prototype batacitor, which would be four stories high, would be finished in a month, if enough materials were available.

Five hundred missionaries of the Church of the Second Chance asked for sanctuary in Parolando a few days later. Iyeyasu had kicked them out of his new state, promising various exquisite tortures if they tried to sneak back. Sam did not hear about them immediately because he was up at the dam.

The Chancers refused to go when John sent word to them to leave immediately. John Lackland, hearing this, smiled grimly, tugged at his lion-colored hair, and swore his favorite oath, "By the teeth of God!"

Sam was at the dam to supervise the installation of tons of dynamite inside the hollow walls. This was to be one more trick up his sleeve, a last-ditch operation—and perhaps a suicidal one—if ever an enemy were about to make a successful invasion.

Von Richthofen, red-faced and blowing hard from his run up the hill, told him of the arrival of the Chancers and their refusal to move. He did not mention John.

Sam told Lothar to tell the Chancers that he would be down in the evening. They could wait for him but were not to move outside a radius of twenty yards from the grailstone near which they had landed. For a moment, he considered ordering them to leave at once and telling the soldiers that they could pound them a little with the flats of their swords if they wished. He was hot and sweating and covered with cement dust, and he felt an especial animosity toward the Chancers. Here was a world blessed by the absence of flies and mosquitoes—and humans, the Chancers, were trying to fill the gap.

The rumbling and splash of giant mortars pouring out concrete, the yells of the straw bosses and the scraping of shovels and clatter of iron wooden-wheeled barrows kept Sam from hearing the explosions that came a half hour later. He knew nothing of what had happened until von Richthofen came running toward him again.

Sam felt as if he would come loose at the joints and

171

slump into a puddle. John had tested out the new guns on the Chancers. A hundred Mark I flintlocks had killed almost five hundred men and women in three minutes. John himself had fired and loaded ten times, using the last five bullets to finish off the wounded.

About thirty women, the most beautiful, had been spared. These had been taken to John's palace.

Long before he reached the water's edge, Sam saw the big crowd gathered around the grailstone. He sent Lothar ahead of him to clear the way. The crowd parted before them, like the Red Sea before Moses, he thought, but the Red Sea was before him after he got through the parting. The bodies were piled against each other, covered with blood, their flesh torn, bones shattered by the big-caliber bullets. In his ninety-seven years of life Sam had never grown accustomed to the silence of the dead. It seemed to hang over them like an invisible and chilling cloud. The mouth that would not speak again, the brain that could not think . . .

It did no good to remember that tomorrow these same people, in fresh and healthy bodies, would be up and doing somewhere along the banks. The effect of death could not be diluted with intellectualizing.

John was issuing orders about the disposal of the bodies to the soap and skin factories. He grinned at Sam like a bad boy caught pulling the cat's tail.

"This is a massacre!" Sam shouted. "A massacre! Unjustified! Unforgivable! There was no reason for it, you bloody-minded, killing beast! That's all you ever have been, you murdering dog, all you ever will be! Swine! Swine! Swine!"

John lost his smile and took a step back as Sam, his hands clenched, moved close to him. The huge massive-boned Zaksksromb, holding a big club of oak with steel spikes set in its end, started toward Sam.

Lothar von Richthofen shouted, "None of that—leave him alone or I call Joe Miller! And I'll shoot the first man who makes a move toward Sam."

Sam looked behind him. Lothar was holding a big pistol

172

in his hands, and it was pointed at John.

John's dark skin paled, and his eyes opened wide. Even the light-blue irises seemed to become paler.

Later Sam wished that he had told Lothar to fire. Even though the hundred pistoleers were John's men, they might have hesitated if John had been killed at the first shot. They were surrounded by armed men and women, most of whom were not fond of John and almost all of whom were shocked by the slaughter. They might have withheld their fire. Even if they had not, Sam could have thrown himself down to the ground and the first shots might have missed. After that, who knew what would have happened?

But it was no good fantasizing. He had not given the order.

Nevertheless, he had to take some strong and immediate action. If he let John get away with this, he would lose everybody's respect, not to mention his own. And he might as well resign his Consulship. In which case, he would lose the Riverboat.

He turned his head slightly, though not so much that he could not keep an eye on John. He saw Livy's white face and big dark eyes; she looked as if she were going to vomit. He ignored her and called to Cyrano de Bergerac, who was standing on the edge of the inner circle, his long rapier in his hand.

"Captain de Bergerac!" Sam pointed at John. "Arrest the co-Consul."

John was holding a pistol in one hand, but he did not bring up its muzzle.

He said in a mild voice, "I protest. I told them to get out at once and they refused to go. I warned them and they still refused—so I ordered them shot. What difference does it make, really? They will be alive tomorrow."

Cyrano marched straight to John, stopped, saluted, and said, "Your weapons, sire."

Zaksksromb growled and lifted his spiked club.

"No, Zak," John Lackland said. "According to the Carta, one Consul can arrest the other if he thinks the other is acting contrary to the Carta. I won't be under arrest long."

He handed Cyrano his gun, butt first, unbuckled his belt, and gave it to Cyrano. Its sheaths held a long knife and short sword.

"I will return to my palace while you and the Council decide my fate," he said. "According to the Carta, you must convene within an hour after the arrest and have a decision in two hours, as long as no national emergency interferes."

He walked away, Cyrano behind him. John's men hesitated a moment and then, at the thundered orders of Zaksksromb, followed John to the palace. Sam stared after them. He had expected more resistance. And then it occurred to him that John knew very well that Sam Clemens had to do just what he did or lose face. And John knew Sam well enough to know that Sam might want to avoid a decision that could lead to civil war, but he would not if he thought his Riverboat endangered.

So John had gone along with him. John did not want to force a showdown. Not now. He had satisfied his bloodlust for the moment. The Councilmen would meet and find that, legally, John was within his rights. Morally, he was not. But then his supporters would argue that even there he was justified. After all, the dead would be alive again and the lesson to the Second Chancers would be invaluable. They would steer clear of Parolando for a long time. And surely Sam Clemens would have to admit that this was desirable. If the Chancers continued to make converts, the Riverboat would never be built. Moreover, other states, less weakened with the Chancer philosophy, would invade Parolando.

And he, Sam Clemens, would say that next John's supporters would be claiming that it was all right to torture people. After all, the pain could last only so long, and any injury would be healed just by killing the victim. Then rape would be justified, because, after all, the woman wasn't going to be made pregnant or diseased—and if she got hurt, too bad. Kill her and she'd be all right in the morning. Never mind the mental damage. A little dreamgum would cure that.

No, Sam would say, it's a question, not of murder, but of rights. If you killed a man, you removed him without his consent to a place so far away he could walk a thousand years along the Riverbank and never get back. You took him away from his love, his friends, his home. Force was force and it was always . . .

Oh, oh! He'd better watch himself!

"Sam!" a lovely voice said.

He turned. Livy was still pale, but her eyes looked as if they were normal.

"Sam! What about the women he carried off?"

"Where's my head?" he said aloud. "Come on, Lothar!" Seeing the ten-foot-high Miller halfway across the plain, he waved at him and the titanthrop turned to intercept them. Lothar ordered a hundred archers who had just arrived to follow them.

Near the great log building, he slowed down. John knew that his co-Consul had forgotten about the abducted women, but that he would soon remember them. And John might be prepared to submit himself to the Council's judgment of the massacre, because, legally, he was within his rights. But surrendering the women to Sam might be just a little too much for John. His infamous temper might betray him, and then civil war would explode in Parolando.

22

Sam saw thirty or so women walking out through the open gates, and he knew that John had decided to rectify his mistake. Even so, he could be accused of kidnapping, a graver crime than murder in this topsyturvy world. But if the women were unharmed, it would be too much trouble to push the charge.

He stopped, and this time he thought his heart would stop. Gwenafra was with the women!

Lothar, crying her name, ran to her. She ran to him with her arms out, and they embraced.

After a minute of hugging, kissing and sobbing, she pulled herself away and went to Sam. He cursed himself because there was no one else he could reasonably blame. If he had shown that he wanted her when she had made it plain that he could have her, then she might not have turned to von Richthofen. Why hadn't he taken her, then? Why had he clung to the idea that Livy would eventually come back and that, if he took another woman now, Livy would resent it so much she would never have anything to do with him?

His thinking wasn't logical. But whatever the philosophers claimed, the main use of logic was to justify your emotions.

Gwenafra had kissed him while her tears ran down his bare chest. Now she left his arms and went back to Lothar, and Sam Clemens was left with the problem of what to do with—or to—John Lackland.

Hs trode through the gates with Joe Miller lumbering behind him. A moment later, von Richthofen had caught up with him. He was swearing and muttering in German, "I'll kill him!"

Sam stopped. "You get out of here! I'm mad enough, but I can control myself! You're in the lion's den now, and if you try anything, he can have you killed and claim self-defense. He'd love that. In fact, he may have done all this just to set up our murder."

Lothar said, "But you're here with only Joe!"

"I wouldn't ever call Joe an *only!* Anyway, if you hadn't been so busy mugging with Gwen, you would have heard me order the troops to storm the palace and kill everybody in it if I'm not out in fifteen minutes."

Lothar stared at Sam. "You've certainly gotten much more aggressive!"

"The more trouble I have and the longer the building of the Riverboat takes, the meaner I get," Sam said. There was no point in telling him that his anger at him and Gwenafra was turned onto John, who already had so much directed at him that he should have curled up and crisped away. And would have if there were any justice in the world.

He entered the largest building inside the stockade of tall lodgepole-pine logs and he brushed past Sharkey. The slope-shouldered thug started to block his way, but Sam did not break his stride. A cavernous growl came from the vast hairy figure behind Sam. Sharkey snarled soundlessly and made the mistake of not moving to one side far enough. A huge reddish-haired hip sent the two-hundred-and-thirty-pound man staggering back as if he were a hollow dummy.

"I'll kill you one of these days!" Sharkey said in English.

Joe turned his head slowly as if it were a turret on a battleship and the tremendous proboscis were a cannon. "Yeth? You and vhat army?"

"You're getting pretty snappy with the comeback, Joe," Sam muttered. "My influence, no doubt."

"I'm not ath dumb ath motht people think," Joe said.

"That wouldn't be possible."

His rage had become a dull red now. Even with Joe as his bodyguard, he was far from being safe. But he was banking that John would go only so far with him, because he wanted that boat, too.

John was sitting at the big round oaken table with a dozen of his thugs. The giant Zaksksromb was standing behind him. All held clay steins. The room reeked of tobacco and liquor. John's eyes were red, but then they usually were. Light came in through the windows but the direct sunlight was blocked off by the stockade poles. Some pine torches burned smokily.

Sam stopped, took a cigar out of the little box in the bag hanging from his belt and lit it. It angered him that his hand shook so much, and that increased his anger at John.

He said, "All right, *Your Majesty!* It was bad enough that you took those alien women for your own vile purposes! But to take Gwenafra? She's a citizen of this state! You really put your neck in the noose, John, and I'm not just using figurative language!"

John downed the whiskey in the stein and gently put it down on the table. Softly, he said, "I had those women removed for their own safety. The crowd was very ugly; they wanted to kill the missionaries. And Gwenafra was taken along through a mistake. I will ascertain who is responsible for that and punish him."

"John," Sam said, "I ought to arrest your assertions for vagrancy. They certainly are without any visible support. But I got to hand it to you. You just dispossessed the devil. You are now the father of lies and grand master, past, present and future, of deceit. If being barefaced is the criterion of the greatest liar, all other liars are whiskered like Santa Claus."

John's face turned red. Zaksksromb sneered and lifted his club chest-high. Joe growled.

John blew out a deep breath and said, smiling, "You are upset over a little blood. You will get over it. You cannot disprove anything I have said, isn't that right? By the way, have you called a meeting of the Council yet? The law of the land requires you to do so, you know."

The horrible thing was that John would get away with it. Everybody, including his supporters, would know he was lying. But there was nothing to do about it unless they wanted to start a civil war, and that would mean that the wolves—Iyeyasu, Hacking, maybe the supposed neutrals, Publius Crassus, Chernsky, Tai Fung, and the savages across The River—would invade.

Sam snorted and walked out. Two hours later, his expectations were realities. The Councilmen voted an official reprimand against John for his mishandling of the situation and his hastiness. He was directed to confer with his co-Consul in any such future situations.

No doubt John would laugh uproariously when he was told of the decision and he would call for more liquor, tobacco, marihuana and women to celebrate.

However, he did not have a complete victory. Every Parolando knew how Sam Clemens had stood up to John, stormed his palace with only one supporter, released the women and insulted John to his face. John knew that; his triumph was standing on shaky legs.

Sam asked the Council to exile every Second Chancer in Parolando for their own protection. But several Councillors pointed out that this would be illegal. The Carta would have to be changed. Besides, it was unlikely that John would take any more action against them after the warning he had received.

They knew as well as Sam why he was taking advantage of the emotional climate to oust the Second Chancers. But there were some stubborn men on the Council. Perhaps they felt angry because they had not been able to do anything about John, and at least they could make a stand for principle in this case.

Sam would have bet that the survivors of the massacre would want to leave immediately. But they insisted on staying. The slaughter had done nothing except to convince them that Parolando needed them very much. Göring was building several large huts for them. Sam sent word down that this should stop. Parolando was already short of wood. Göring sent word back that he and his male comrades would move out and sleep under the grailstones. Sam swore and blew smoke in the face of the Chancer messenger and said that it was too bad pneumonia did not exist. Afterward, he felt ashamed, but he did not relent. He wasn't going to scant his furnaces so that people he did not even want could sleep under a roof.

He felt upset enough, but that evening he got two messages which opened the earth under him. One was that Odysseus had disappeared at night from his boat while on the way back to Parolando. Nobody knew what had happened to him. He was just gone. The second message informed him that William Grevel, the man who'd been spying on John, had been found under a ledge at the base of the mountain, his skull smashed in.

Somehow, John had found him out and executed him. And John would be laughing because Sam could not prove that or, for that matter, even admit that Grevel had been working for him.

Sam called in von Richthofen and de Bergerac and others whom he considered to be his people. It was true that de Bergerac and he were hostile because of Livy, but de Bergerac preferred Clemens to John, with whom he had had some hot words.

"Maybe Odysseus' disappearance from the boat is only a coincidence," Sam said. "But that, plus Grevel's death, makes me wonder if John isn't striking at me through my friends. He may be planning on cutting you down, one by one, under circumstances where he can't be accused. He's crafty. He probably won't do anything now for some time. But Odysseus was gotten rid of in a place where an investigation will probably reveal nothing. And I can't accuse John about Grevel without exposing what I've been doing. So, watch out for situations where *accidents* could happen. And be careful when you are alone."

"*Morbleu!* de Bergerac said. "If it wasn't for this ridiculous law against dueling, I could challenge John and run him through. You, Sinjoro Clemens, were responsible for that law!"

"I was raised in a country where duels were common," Sam said. "The whole idea sickens me. If you'd seen the tragedies . . . well, never mind. I guess you did see, and it doesn't seem to have affected you. Anyway, do you think for one moment that John would ever let you live long enough to meet him for a duel? No, you'd disappear or have an accident, you can bet on that."

"Vhy can't Chohn have an acthident?" Joe Miller said.

"How would you get past the living wall of his bodyguards?" Sam said. "No, if John has an accident, it'll have to be a genuine one."

He dismissed them with the exception of de Bergerac and of Joe, who never left him unless he was sick or Sam wanted privacy.

"The Stranger said that he'd picked out twelve humans for the final onslaught against the Misty Tower," Sam said. "Joe, you, Richard Francis Burton, Odysseus and me make five. But none of us know who the other seven are. Now Odysseus is gone, and God knows if we'll ever see him again. The Stranger implied that all of the twelve would join the others on the Riverboat somewhere along the line. But if Odysseus was resurrected somewhere to the south, downRiver, so far away he can't get back up here before the Riverboat is built, then he is out of luck."

Cyrano shrugged and rubbed his long nose. "Why worry? Or is that your nature? For all we know, Odysseus is not dead. He may have been contacted by this Mysterious Stranger—who, by the way, Odysseus claims is a woman and so his Stranger is not the one that you and I met—*mordioux!*—I digress! As I said, Odysseus may have been called away suddenly by this so-mysterious person and we will find out in time what did happen! Let that shadowy angel—or fiend—take care of the matter. We must concentrate on getting this fabulous boat constructed and skewering anybody who gets in our way."

"That maketh thenthe," Joe said. "If Tham had a hair for every time he vorried, he'd look like a porcupine. Vhich, now that I come to think of it . . ."

"Out of the mouths of babes . . . and of tailless monkeys," Sam said. "Or is it the other end? Anyway, if everything goes well—and so far it hasn't—we'll start bonding the magnalium plates for the hull in thirty days. That'll be my happiest day, until we actually launch the boat. I'll be happier even than when Livy said yes . . ."

He could have cut himself off sooner, but he wanted to antagonize Cyrano. The Frenchman, however, did not react. Why should he? He had Livy; she was saying yes to him all the time.

"Me, I do not like the idea," Cyrano said, "since I am a peaceful man. I would like to have the leisure to indulge myself with the good things of life. I would like to have an

181

end to wars, and if there is to be any bloodshed, let it be between gentlemen who know how to wield their swords. But we cannot build the boat without interference, because those who do not have iron desire it and will not stop until they get it. So, me, I think that John Lackland may be right in one particular. Perhaps we should wage an all-out war as soon as we have enough weapons, and clear The River, on both sides, of all opposition for thirty miles both ways. We can then have unlimited access to the wood and the bauxite and platinum . . ."

"But if you did that, if you killed all the inhabitants, within a day your countries would be filled up," Sam said. "You know how resurrection works. Look at how swiftly this area was reinhabited after the meteorite had killed everybody in it."

Cyrano held up a long—and dirty—finger. Sam wondered if Livy was losing her battle to keep him clean.

"Ah!" Cyrano said. "But these people will remain unorganized, and we, being on the spot, will organize them, take them in as citizens of the expanded Parolando. We will include them in the lottery for the crew of the boat. In the long run, it would be faster to stop the boat building now and do as I suggest."

And I will send you forth in the lead, Sam thought. And it will be David and Bathsheba and Uriah all over again. Except that David probably didn't have a conscience, never lost a wink of sleep over what he'd done.

"I don't think so," Sam said. "In the first place, our citizens will fight like hell to defend themselves, because they're involved in the boat. But they're not going to engage in a war of conquest, especially after they figure out that bringing new citizens into the lottery is going to reduce their chances enormously. Besides, it isn't right."

De Bergerac stood up, his hand on the hilt of his rapier. "Perhaps you are right. But the day that you made an agreement with John Lackland and then murdered Erik Bloodaxe, that day was the day that you launched your boat on blood and treachery and cruelty. I do not reproach you, my friend. What you did was unavoidable, if you wanted the boat. But you cannot start thus and then shy away from similar, or even worse, acts. Not if you want your boat. Good night, my friend."

He bowed and left. Sam puffed on his cigar and then said, "I hate that man! He tells the truth!"

Joe stood up, and the floor creaked under his eight hundred pounds. "I'm going to bed. My head hurtth. Thith whole thing ith giving me a pain in my athth. Either you do or you don't. It'th that thimple."

"If I had my brainth in my athth, I'd thay the thame thing!" Sam snarled. "Joe, I love you! You're beautiful! The world is so uncomplex! Problems make you sleepy, and so you sleep! But I . . ."

"Good night, Tham!" Joe said and walked into the texas. Sam made sure that the door was barred and that the guards he'd posted around the building were alert. Then he went to bed, too.

He dreamed about Erik Bloodaxe, who chased him through the decks and into the hold of the Riverboat, and he awoke yelling. Joe was looming over him, shaking him. The rain was pounding the roof, and thunder was booming somewhere up along the face of the mountain.

Joe stayed awhile after making some coffee. He put a spoonful of dried crystals into cold water, and the coffee crystals heated the mixture in three seconds. They sipped their coffee and Sam smoked a cigarette while they talked about the days when they had voyaged down The River with Bloodaxe and his Vikings in search of iron.

"At leatht, ve uthed to have fun now and then," Joe said. "But not anymore. There'th too much vork to do and too many people out to thkin our hideth. And your voman *vould* thyow up vith that big-nothed Thyrano."

Sam chuckled and said, "Thanks for the first laugh I've had in days, Joe. Big-nosed! Ye Gods!"

"Thometimeth I'm too thubtle for even you, Tham," Joe said. He rose up from the table and walked back to his room.

There was little sleep thereafter. Sam had always liked to stay in bed even after a full night's sleep. Now he got less than five hours each night, though he did take a siesta sometimes. There always seemed to be someone who had to have a question answered or wanted to thrash out an issue. His chief engineers were far from agreeing on everything, and this alone disturbed Sam. He had thought engineering was a cut-and-dried thing. You had a problem, and you solved it the best way. But Van Boom, Velitsky and O'Brien seemed to be living in worlds that did not quite dovetail. Finally, to spare himself the aggravating and often wasted hours of wrangling, he delegated the final word to Van Boom. They were not to worry him about anything unless they needed his authorization.

It was amazing the number of things which he would have considered to be only in the engineering province which needed his authorization.

Iyeyasu conquered not only the Bushman-Hottentot area across The River from him but nine miles of the Ulmak territory. Then he sent a fleet down to the three-mile-long area below the Ulmaks, where seventeenth-century A.D. Sac and Fox Indians lived. This area was conquered with resultant slaughter of half the inhabitants. Iyeyasu then began dickering with Parolando for a higher price for his wood. Also, he wanted an amphibian just like the *Firedragon I.*

By then the second *Firedragon* was almost done.

At this time over five hundred blacks from Parolando had been exchanged for an equal number of Dravidians. Sam had steadfastly refused to accept the Wahhabi Arabs, or at least had insisted that the Asiatic Indians come first. Hacking apparently did not like this, but nothing had been said in the agreement about which group had priority.

Hacking, having heard from his spies about Iyeyasu's demands, sent a message. He wanted a *Firedragon*, too, and he was willing to exchange a great amount of minerals for it.

Publius Crassus and Tai Fung allied to invade the area across The River from them. This was occupied by Stone Age peoples from everywhere and every time and stretched for fourteen miles along the left bank. With their superior steel weapons and numbers, the invaders killed half the population and enslaved the rest. And they upped their price for the wood but kept it below Iyeyasu's.

Spies reported that Chernsky, who ruled the fourteen-mile-long nation just north of Parolando, had made a visit to Soul City. What happened there was anybody's guess, since Hacking had set up a security system that seemed to be one hundred percent effective. Sam had gotten in eight blacks to spy for him, and he knew that John had sent in at least a dozen. The heads of all were tossed from boats in the mists late at night onto the top of the wall along the bank of Parolando.

Van Boom came to Sam late one night and said that Firebrass had cautiously approached him.

"He offered me the position of chief engineer on the boat," Van Boom said.

"*He* offered it to you?" Sam said, his cigar almost dropping.

"Yes. He didn't say so in so many words, but I got the idea. The Riverboat will be taken over by the Soul Citizens, and I will be chief engineer."

"And what did you say about his fine offer? After all, you can't lose, either way."

"I told him not to etch a pseudocircuit. Come out and say it. He wouldn't, though he grinned, and I told him I hadn't sworn any oath of loyalty to you, but I had accepted your offer and that was as good. I wasn't going to betray you, and if Soul City invaded Parolando, I'd defend it to the death."

"That's fine, superb!" Sam said. "Here, have a snort of bourbon! And a cigar! I'm proud of you and proud of myself, to command such loyalty. But I wish . . . I wish . . ."

Van Boom looked over the cup. "Yes?"

"I wish you'd strung him along. We could have found out a lot with you feeding us information."

Van Boom put the cup down and stood up. His handsome brown features were ugly. "I am not a dirty spy!"

"Come back!" Sam said, but Van Boom ignored him. Sam buried his head in his arms for a minute and then picked up Van Boom's cup. Never let it be said that

Samuel Langhorne Clemens wasted good whiskey. Or even bad, for that matter. Although the grail never yielded any but the best.

The man's lack of realism irritated him. At the same time, he had a counterfeeling of warm pleasure. It was good to know that incorruptible men existed.

At least, Sam did not have to worry about Van Boom.

23

In the middle of the night, he awoke wondering if he did have to worry after all. What if Van Boom was not as upright as he said? What if the clever Firebrass had told Van Boom to go to Clemens with his story? What better way to put a man off his guard? But then it would have been better if Van Boom had pretended to Sam that he was pretending to go along with Firebrass.

"I'm beginning to think like King John!" Sam said aloud.

He finally decided that he had to trust Van Boom. He was stiff and sometimes a little strange, which was what you'd expect from an engineer, but he had a moral backbone as inflexible as a fossilized dinosaur's.

The work on the great Riverboat went on day and night. The plates of the hull were bonded, and the beams were welded on. The batacitor and the giant electric motors were built, and the work of the transportation system of the cranes and engines was ended. The cranes themselves were enormous structures on huge rails, powered by electricity from the prototype batacitor. People came from thousands of miles up and down The River, in catamarans, big galleys, dugouts and canoes, to see the fabulous works.

Sam and King John agreed that so many people wandering about would get in the way of the work and would enable spies to function more efficiently.

"Also, it'll put the temptation to steal before them, and we don't want to be responsible for tempting people. They have enough trouble as it is," Sam said.

John did not smile. He signed the order that expelled all noncitizens, except for ambassadors and messengers, and that kept any more from coming in. This still did not prevent many boats from sailing by while the occupants gawked. By then the dirt walls and stone walls along the bank were about finished. There were, however, many breaks through which the curious could stare. These were left for ingress of freight boats bringing in wood and ore and flints. Moreover, since the plain sloped up toward the hills, the tourists could see many of the factories and the cranes, and the great structure of the boatyard was visible for miles around.

After a while, the tourist trade petered off. Too many were getting picked up along the way by grail slavers. Word got around that it was getting dangerous to travel The River in that section. Six months passed. The wood supply in the area was cut off. Bamboo grew to full length in from three weeks to six weeks; the trees took six months to grow to full maturity. Every state for fifty miles both ways from Parolando had enough wood for their own uses only.

Parolando's representatives made treaties with more distant states, trading iron ore and weapons for wood. There was a very large supply of siderite masses left yet, so Sam was not worried about running out of it. But the mining of it took many men and materials and caused the central part of Parolando to look like a heavily shelled landscape. And the more wood that was brought in, the more men, materials, and machines had to be diverted from the boatbuilding to make weapons for trade. Moreover, the increase in shipping resulted in more demand for wood to build freighters. And more men had to be trained and shipped out as sailors and guards for the wood-carrying and ore-carrying fleets. It got to the point where boats had to be rented from neighboring states, and the rent, as always, was iron-nickel ore and finished weapons.

Sam wanted to be at the boatyard from dawn to dusk and even later, because he loved every minute of progress in the construction of the great boat. But he had so many administrative duties only indirectly or not at all connected with the boat that he could be in the boatyard only two to three hours—on a good day. He tried to get John to take over more of the administration, but John would accept only duties which gave him more power over the military forces or allowed him to exert pressure on those who opposed him.

The anticipated attempts at assassination of those close

to Sam did not occur. The bodyguards and the close watch at nights were continued, but Sam decided that John was going to lay low for a while. He had probably seen that it would be best for his purposes to wait until the boat was nearly finished.

Once, Joe Miller said, "Tham, don't you think maybe you're wrong about John? Maybe he'th going to be content vith being thecond-in-command of the boat?"

"Joe, would a sabertooth part with his canines?"

"Vhat?"

"John is rotten to the core. The old kings of England were never any great shakes, morally speaking. The only difference between them and Jack the Ripper was that they operated openly and with the sanction of Church and State. But John was such a wicked monarch that it became traditional to never name another English king John. And even the Church, which had a high tolerance for evil in high places, could not stomach John. The Pope slapped the Interdict on the entire nation and brought John crawling and begging to the feet of the Pope, like a whipped puppy. But I suppose that even when he was kissing the Pope's foot, he managed to suck a little blood from the big toe. And the Pope must have checked his pockets after he embraced John.

"What I'm trying to put across is that John couldn't reform even if he wanted to. He'll always be a human weasel, a hyena, a skunk."

Joe puffed on a cigar even longer than his nose and said, "Vell, I don't know. Humanth *can* change. Look at vhat the Church of the Thecond Chanthe hath done. Look at Göring. Look at you. You told me that in your time vomen vore clotheth which covered them from the neck to the ankleth, and you got ekthited if you thaw a good-looking ankle, and a thigh, oh my! Now you aren't too dithturbed if you thee . . ."

"I know! I know!" Sam said. "Old attitudes and what the psychologists call conditioned reflexes can be changed. That's why I say that anybody who still carries in him the racial and sexual prejudices he had on Earth is not taking

189

advantage of what The River offers. A man can change, but . . ."

"He can?" Joe said. "But you alvayth told me that everything in life, even the vay a man actth and thinkth, ith determined by vhat vent on long before he vath even born. Vhat ith it? Yeth, it'th a determinithtic philothophy, that'th vhat. Now, if you believe that everything ith fikthed in itth courthe, that humanth are mathyineth, tho to thpeak, then how can you believe that men can change themthelveth?"

"Well," Sam drawled, looking fierce, his excessively bushy eyebrows pulled down, his blue-green eyes bright above the falcon nose, "well, even my theories are mechanically determined and if they conflict, that can't be helped."

"Then, for heaven'th thaketh," Joe said, throwing up his football-sized hands, "vhat'th the uthe of talking about it? Or even doing anything? Vhy don't you jutht give up?"

"Because I can't help myself," Sam said. "Because, when the first atom in this universe bumped against the second atom, my fate was decreed, my very thought and action was fixed."

"Then you can't be, uh, rethponthible for vhat you do, right?"

"That's right," Sam said. He felt very uncomfortable.

"Then John can't help it that he'th a murdering treacherouth thoroughly dethpicable thvine?"

"No, but then I can't help it that I despise him for being a swine."

"And I thuppothe that if thomebody thmarter than I am came along and thyowed you, by thtrict undeniable logic, that you vere wrong in your philothophy, that you vould thay that he can't help thinking you're wrong? But he'th wrong, it'th jutht that he'th predetermined, mechanically, to think the vay he doeth."

"I'm right, and I know it," Sam said, puffing harder on his cigar. "This hypothetical man couldn't convince me because his own reasoning does not spring from a free will, which is like a vegetarian tiger—that is, it doesn't exist."

"But your own reathoning doethn't thpring from a free vill, either."

"True. We're all screwed. We believe what we have to."

"You laugh at thothe people who have vhat you call invinthible ignoranthe, Tham. Yet you're full of it, yourthelf."

"Lord deliver us from apes that think they're philosophers!"

"Thee! You fall back on inthultth vhen you can't think of anything elthe to thay! Admit it, Tham! You haven't got a lochical leg to thtand on!"

"You just aren't capable of seeing what I mean, because of the way you are," Sam said.

"You thyould talk to Thyrano de Bercherac more, Tham. He'th ath big a thynic ath you, although he doethn't go ath far ath you do vith determinithm."

"I'd think you two incapable of talking to each other. Don't you two resent each other, you look so much alike? How can you stand nose to nose, as it were, and not break up with laughter? It's like two anteaters . . ."

"Inthultth! Inthultth! Oh, vhat'th the uthe?"

"Exactly," Sam said. Joe did not say good night, and he did not call after him. He was nettled. Joe looked so dumb with that low forehead and the bone-ringed eyes and comical dill pickle nose and gorilla build and his hairiness. But behind those little blue eyes and the lisping was an undeniable intelligence.

What disturbed him most was Joe's comment that his deterministic belief was only a rationalization to excuse his guilt. Guilt for what? Guilt for just about everything bad that had happened to those whom he loved.

But it was a philosophic labyrinth which ended in a quagmire. Did he believe in mechanical determinism because he wanted to not feel guilty, or did he feel guilty, even though he should not, because the mechanical universe determined that he should feel guilty?

Joe was right. There was no use thinking about it. But if a man's thinking was set on its course by the collision of the first two atoms, then how could he keep from thinking about it if he were Samuel Langhorne Clemens, alias Mark Twain?

He sat up later than usual that night, but he was not working at his duties. He drank at least a fifth of ethyl alcohol mixed with fruit juice.

Two months before, Firebrass had said he could not understand the failure of Parolando to make ethyl alcohol. Sam had been upset. He had not known that grain alcohol could be made. He thought that the only supply of liquor would have to be the limited amounts that the grails yielded.

No, Firebrass had said. Hadn't any of his engineers told him? If the proper materials, such as acid, coal gas, or acetaldehyde and a proper catalyst were available, then wood cellulose could be converted into ethyl alcohol. That was common knowledge. But Parolando, until recently, was the only place on The River—he presumed—which had the materials to make grain alcohol.

Sam had called in Van Boom, who replied that he had enough to worry about without providing booze for people who drank too much as it was.

Sam had ordered materials and men diverted. For the first time in the history of The River, as far as anybody knew, potable alcohol was being made on a large scale. This resulted not only in happier citizens, except for the Second Chancers, but in a new industry for Parolando. They exported alcohol in exchange for wood and bauxite.

Sam fell into bed and the next morning, for the first time, refused to get up before dawn. But the next day he rose as usual.

Sam and John sent a message to Iyeyasu that they would regard it as a hostile act if he invaded the rest of the Ulmak territory or Chernsky's Land.

Iyeyasu replied that he had not intention of waging war on these lands, and he proved it by invading the state just north of his, Sheshshub's Land. Sheshshub, an Assyrian born in the seventh century B.C., had been a general of Sargon II, and so, like most powerful people on Earth, had become a leader on the Riverworld. He gave Iyeyasu a good fight, but the invaders were more numerous.

Iyeyasu was one worry. There were plenty of others to keep Sam going day and night. Hacking finally sent a message, through Firebrass, that Parolando should quit stalling. He wanted the amphibian promised so long ago. Sam had kept pleading technical difficulties, but Firebrass told him that was no longer acceptable. So the *Firedragon III* was reluctantly shipped off.

Sam made a visit to Chernsky to reassure him that Parolando would defend Cernskujo. Coming back, a half mile upwind of the factories, Sam almost gagged. He had been living so long in the acid-bath-cum-smoke atmosphere that he had gotten used to it, but any vacation from it cleansed his lungs. It was like stepping into a glue-and-sulphur factory. And, though the wind was a fifteen-mph breeze, it did not carry the smoke away swiftly enough. The air definitely was hazy. No wonder, he thought, that Publiujo, to the south, complained.

But the boat continued to grow. Standing before the front port of his pilothouse, Sam could look out every morning and be consoled for his toil and tiredness and for the hideousness and stench of the land. In another six months, the three decks would be completed, and the great paddle-wheels would be installed. Then a plastic coating would be put over that part of the hull which would come into contact with water. This plastic would not only prevent electrolysis of the magnalium, it would reduce the water turbulence, thus adding ten mph to the boat's speed.

During this time, Sam received some good news. Tungsten and iridium had been found in Selinujo, the country just south of Soul City. The report was brought by the prospector, who trusted no one else to transmit it. He also brought some bad news. Selina Hastings refused to let Parolando mine there. In fact, if she had known that a Parolandano was digging along her mountain, she would have thrown him out. She did not want to be unfriendly, indeed, she loved Sam Clemens, since he was a human being. But she did not approve of the Riverboat, and she would not permit anything to go out of her land that would help build the vessel.

Sam erupted, and, as Joe said, "Thyot blue thyit for mileth around." The tungsten was very much needed for hardening their machine tools but even more for the radios and, eventually, the closed-circuit TV sets. The iridium could be used to harden their platinum for various uses, for scientific instruments, surgical tools and for pen points.

The Mysterious Stranger had told Sam that he had set up the deposit of minerals here but that his fellow Ethicals did not know that he had done so. Along with the bauxite, cryolite, and platinum would be tungsten and iridium. But an error had been made, and the latter two metals had been deposited several miles south of the first three.

Sam did not tell John at once, because he needed time to think about the situation. John, of course, would want to demand that the metals be traded to Parolando or that war be declared.

While he was pacing back and forth in the pilothouse, clouding the room with green smoke, he heard drums. They were using a code which he did not know but recognized, after a minute, as that used by Soul City. A few minutes later, Firebrass was at the foot of the ladder.

"Sinjoro Hacking knows all about the discovery of tungsten and iridium in Selinujo. He says that if you can come to an agreement with Selina, fine. But don't invade her land. He'd regard that as a declaration of war on Soul City."

Sam looked out the starboard port past Firebrass. "Here comes John hot-footing it," he said. "He's heard the news, too. His spy system is almost as good as yours, a few minutes less good, I'd say. I don't know where the leaks in my system are, but they're so wide that I'd be sunk if I was a boat, and I may be anyway."

John, his eyes inflamed, his face red, and puffing and panting, entered. Since the introduction of grain alcohol, he had put on even more fat, and he seemed to be half drunk all the time and all drunk half the time.

Sam was angered, but at the same time, he was amused. John would have liked to summon him to his palace, in keeping with his dignity as ex-King of England. But he knew that Sam would not come for a long time, if at all, and meanwhile there was no telling how much hankypanky Firebrass and Sam would manufacture.

"What's going on?" John said, glaring.

"You tell me," Sam said. "You seem to know more about the shady side of affairs than I do."

"None of your wisecracks!" John said. Without being asked, he poured out a quart of purple passion into a stein. "I know what that message is about, even if I don't know the code!"

"I thought as much," Sam said. "For your information, in case you missed anything . . ." and he told him what Firebrass had said.

"The arrogance of you blacks is unendurable," John said. "You are telling Parolando, a sovereign state, how it must conduct itself in vital business. Well, I say you can't! We will get those metals, one way or the other! Selinujo doesn't need them; we do! It can't hurt Selinujo to give them up! We will give a fair trade!"

"In what?" Firebrass said. "Selinujo doesn't want weapons or alcohol. What can you trade?"

"Peace, freedom from war!"

Firebrass shrugged and grinned, thus incensing John even more.

"Sure," Firebrass said, "you can make your offer. But what Hacking says still goes."

"Hacking has no love for Selinujo," Sam said. "He kicked out all the Second Chancers, black or white."

"That's because they were preaching immediate pacifism. They also preach, and apparently practice, love for all, regardless of color, but Hacking says they're a danger to the state. The blacks have to protect themselves, otherwise they would be enslaved all over again."

"*The* blacks?" Sam said.

"*Us* blacks!" Firebrass replied, grinning.

This was not the first time Firebrass had given the impression that he was not so deeply concerned with skin color. His identification with blacks, as such, was weak. His life had not been untouched by racial prejudice, but it had not been much affected. And he said things now and then that indicated that he would like a berth on the boat.

All this, of course, could be a put-on.

"We'll negotiate with Sinjorino Hastings," Sam said. "It would be nice to have radios and TV for the boat, and the machine shops could use the tungsten. But we can get along without them."

He winked at John to indicate that he should take this line. But John was as stone-headed as usual.

"What we do with Selinujo is our problem, nobody else's!"

"I'll tell Hacking," Firebrass said. "But Hacking is a strong person. He won't take any crap from anybody, least of all white capitalist imperialists."

Sam choked, and John stared.

"That's what he regards you as!" Firebrass said. "And the way he defines those terms, you are what he says you are."

"Because I want this boat so badly!" Sam shouted. "Do you know what this boat is for, what its ultimate goal . . . ?"

He fought back his anger, sobbing with the effort. He felt dizzy. For a moment, he had almost told about the Stranger.

"What is it?" Firebrass said.

"Nothing," Sam replied. "Nothing. I just want to get to the headwaters of The River, that's all. Maybe the secret of this whole shebang is there? Who knows? But I certainly don't like criticism from someone who just wants to sit around on his dead black ass and collect soul brothers. If he wants to do that, more power to him, but I still hold to integration as the ideal. And I'm a Missouri white born in 1835! So how's that for going against your heritage and your environment? The point is, if I don't use the siderite metal to build a boat, which is designed for travel only, not for aggression, then someone else will. And that someone else may use it to conquer and to hold, instead of for tourist purposes.

"Now, we've gone along with Hacking's demands, paid his jacked-up prices for the ones when we could have gone down there and taken them from him. John's apologized for what he called you and Hacking, and if you think it's easy for a Plantagenet to do that, you don't know your history. It's too bad about the way Hacking feels. I don't know that I blame him. Of course, he hates whites. But this is not Earth! Conditions are radically different here!"

"But people bring their attitudes along with them," Firebrass said. "Their hates and loves, dislikes and likes, prejudices, reactions, everything."

"But they can change!"

Firebrass grinned. "Not according to your philosophy. Rather, not unless mechanical forces change them. So, Hacking isn't determined by anything to change his attitude. Why should he? He's experienced the same exploitation and contempt here as he did on Earth."

"I don't want to argue about that," Sam said. "I'll tell you what I think we should do!"

He stopped and stared out the port. The whitish-gray hull and upper works gleamed in the sun. How beautiful! And she was, in a sense, all his! She was worth everything he was being put through!

"I'll tell you what," he said more slowly. "Why doesn't Hacking come up here? Pay a little visit? He can look around, see for himself what we're doing. See our problems. Maybe he'll appreciate our problems, see we're not blue-eyed devils who want to enslave him. In fact, the more he helps us, the sooner he'll be rid of us."

"I'll give him your message," Firebrass said. "Maybe he'll want to do that."

"We'll greet him in style," Sam said. "A twenty-one gun salute, big reception, food, liquor, gifts. He'll see we aren't such bad fellows after all."

John spat. "Pah!" but he said no more. He knew that Sam's proposal was best.

Three days later, Firebrass brought a message. Hacking would come, after Parolando and Selinujo had agreed on the disposition of the metals.

Sam felt like a rusty old boiler in a Mississippi steamboat. A few more pounds of pressure, and he would blow sky-high.

"Sometimes, I think you're right!" he shouted at John.

"Maybe we should just take over these countries and get done with!"

"Of course," John said smoothly. "Now, it is obvious that that ex-Countess Huntingdon—she must be decended from my old enemy, the Earl of Huntingdon —is not going to give in. She is a religious fanatic, a nut, as you say. And Soul City will fight us if we invade Selinujo. Hacking can't go back on his word. And he's stronger now that we've given him the *Firedragon III*. But I say nothing about that; I do not reproach you. I have been thinking much about this mess."

Sam stopped pacing and looked at John. John had been thinking. Shadows would be moving inside shadows; daggers would be unsheathed; the air would get gray and chill with stealth and intrigue; blood would spurt. And the sleeping would do well to stir.

"I do not say that I have been in contact with Iyeyasu, our powerful neighbor to the north," John said. He was slumped down in the tall-backed red leather-covered chair and staring into the purple passion in the tilted stein.

"But I have information, or means of getting it. I am certain that Iyeyasu, who feels very strong indeed, would like to acquire even more territory. And he would like to do us a favor. In return for certain payments, of course. Say, an amphibian and a flying machine? He is wild to fly one of those himself, you know? Or didn't you?

"If he attacked Selinujo, Hacking could not blame us. And if Soul City and Iyeyasujo fought, and Soul City was destroyed and Iyeyasujo weakened, how could that fail to benefit us? Moreover, I happen to have learned that Chernsky has made a secret compact with Soul City and Tifonujo to fight if any of them are invaded by Iyeyasu. Certainly, the resultant carnage would find them weakened and us strengthened. We could then take them over or at least do what we wished without interference. In any case, we would ensure that we had uncontrolled access to the bauxite and the tungsten."

That skull under that mass of tawny hair must hold a thundermugful of worms. Worms that fed on corruption and intrigue and deviousness. He was so crooked, he was admirable.

"Did you ever meet yourself coming around a corner?" Sam said.

"What?" John said, looking up. "Is this another of your unintelligible insults?"

"Believe me, it's as close to a compliment as you'll ever get—from me. Of course, it's all hypothetical. But if Iyeyasu did attack Selinujo, what excuse would he have? They've never offended him, and they're sixty miles away from him on our side of The River."

"When did one nation ever need a reasonable excuse for invasion?" John said. "But the fact is that Selinujo keeps sending missionaries into Iyeyasujo, though he has kicked out all Chancers. Since Selinujo won't stop doing this, then . . ."

"Well," Sam said, "I couldn't let Parolando get involved in a deal like this. But if Iyeyasu decides on his own to fight, there's nothing we can do about it."

"And you call me dishonest!"

"There's nothing I could do about it!" Sam said, clamping down on his cigar. "Nothing! And if something develops that's good for the boat, then we'll take advantage of it."

"The shipments from Soul City would be held up while the fighting was going on," John said.

"We've got enough stock to keep going for a week. The big worry would be wood. Maybe Iyeyasu would be able to keep that coming even with a war going on, since the fighting will be south of us. We could handle the chopping and transportation ourselves. If he didn't intend to invade for a couple of weeks, we could lay in extra stocks of ore from Soul City by offering them increased payments. Maybe promise them an airplane, the APM-1. That's just a toy, now that we've almost got our first amphibian airplane finished. All this is hypothetical, you understand?"

"I understand," John said. He was not trying to mask his contempt.

Sam felt like shouting at him that he had no right to be contemptuous. Whose idea had it been, anyway?

It was the next day that the three chief engineers were killed.

Sam was there when it happened. He was standing on the scaffolding by the starboard side of the boat, looking down into the open hull. The colossal steam crane was lifting the immense electric motor which would be driving the port paddle-wheel. The motor had been moved during the night from the big building where it had been built. The moving had taken over eight hours and had been effected by the crane, which also had a gigantic winch. The winch, plus hundreds of men pulling on cables, had pulled the motor on its big car, which moved on steel rails.

Sam got up at dawn to watch the final work, the lifting and then the lowering of the motor into the hull and its attachment to the paddle-wheel axle. The three engineers were standing down in the bottom of the hull. Sam called down to them to get away, that they were too vulnerable if the motor should drop. But the engineers were stationed in three different places so that they could transmit signals to the men on the port scaffolding, who, in turn, were signaling the crane operator.

Van Boom turned to look up at Sam, and his teeth flashed whitely in his dark face. His skin looked purplish in the light of the big electric lamps.

And then it happened. A cable snapped, and another cable snapped, and the motor swung out to one side. The engineers froze for a second and then they ran, but they were too late. The motor fell to one side and crushed all three of them.

The impact shook the great hull and the vibrations made the scaffolding on which Sam stood quiver as if a quake were passing through the land.

Blood ran out from under the motor.

24

It took five hours to put in new cables on the crane, secure these to the motor and lift the motor. The bodies were removed, the hull washed out and then the motor was lowered again. A close inspection had determined that the damage to the motor casing would not affect the operation of the motor.

Sam was so depressed that he would have liked to have gone to bed and remained there for a week. But he could not do so. The work had to go on, and while there were good men who would see to it that it did go on, Sam did not want them to know how shaken he was.

Sam had many engineers, but Van Boom and Velitsky were the only ones from the twentieth century. Though he had advertised by word of mouth and through the drum systems for more, he had gotten none.

The third day, he asked Firebrass into his pilothouse for a private conference. After giving him a cigar and scotch, he asked him if he would be his chief engineer.

Firebrass' cigar almost dropped out of his mouth.

"Steer me, stymate! Do I read you unfrosted? You want me as your number one dillion?"

"Maybe we should talk in Esperanto," Sam said.

"Okay," Firebrass said. "I'll bring it down to dirt. Just what do you want?"

"I'd like you to get permission to work for me on a temporary basis, supposedly."

"Supposedly?"

"If you want it, the position is permanently yours. The day the boat sets out on the long journey, you can be its chief engineer."

Firebrass sat silent for a long time. Sam got up and paced back and forth. Occasionally, he looked out the ports. The crane had put in the starboard motor, and now it was lowering parts of the batacitor into the hull. This would be thirty-six feet high when all the parts were secured together. After it was installed, a trial run would check the operation of the batacitor and the motors. A double cable, six inches thick, would be run out for two hundred feet and its free end, attached to a large shallow hemisphere, would be slipped onto the top of the nearest grailstone. When the stone delivered its tremendous electrical energy, the energy would be transmitted by the cables into the batacitor, which would store it. And then the energy would be drawn out at a controlled rate to power the electrical motors.

Sam turned away from the port. "It's not as if I were asking you to betray your country," he said. "In the first place, all you have to do now is to request permission from Hacking to work for me on the building of the boat. Later, you can make up your mind about going with us. Which would you rather do? Stay in Soul City where there is actually little to do except indulge yourself? Or go with us on the greatest adventure of all?"

Firebrass said, slowly, "Now, if I accepted your offer, *if*, I say, I would not want to go as chief engineer. I would prefer to be the chief of your air force."

"That's not as important a position as chief engineer!"

"It's a lot more work and responsibility! Now, I like the idea of flying again, and . . ."

"You *can* fly! You *can* fly! But you'd have to serve under von Richthofen. You see, I promised him that he would be the chief of our air force, which, after all, will only consist of two planes. What do you care whether or not you're the chief, as long as you get to fly?"

"It's a matter of pride. I have thousands of hours more flying time than Richthofen, in planes far more complex and bigger and speedier. And I was an astronaut. I've been to the Moon and Mars and Ganymede and orbited Jupiter."

"That doesn't mean anything," Sam said. "The planes you'll be flying are very primitive. More like the World War I machines that Lothar flew."

"Why does a nigger always have to take second place?"

"That's unfair!" Sam said. "You could be chief

202

engineer! You'd have thirty-five people under your command! Listen, if I hadn't made Lothar that promise, you'd get the captaincy, believe me!"

Firebrass stood up. "I'll tell you what. I'll help you build the boat and set up the training of your engineer's department. But I get to fly during that time, too, and when the time comes we'll talk about who's going to be head of the air force."

"I won't break my promise to Lothar," Sam said.

"Yes, but many things may happen between now and then."

Sam was relieved in one way but disturbed in another. Hacking gave his permission, via drum, to use Firebrass. This suggested he wanted Firebrass to know the boat's operation because he would be serving Hacking as chief engineer some day. And even if this was not being considered by Firebrass, he might be planning to remove von Richthofen before the boat was ready for launching. Firebrass did not seem like a cold-blooded murderer but looks meant nothing, as anyone with intelligence finds out if he has lived a few years among the human race.

Hacking sent word a few days later that he would agree to an extra large shipment of minerals in Parolando in return for the AMP-1. Firebrass flew it the thirty-one miles to the northern limit of Soul City, where another flier, a black who had been a general in the U.S. Air Force, took it over. A few days later, Firebrass returned by sailboat.

The batacitor and the electric motors worked perfectly. The paddle-wheels turned over slowly in the air, then were speeded up, the vanes whistling they spun so swiftly.

When the time came, a canal would be dug from the water's edge to the great boat, and it would wheel out into The River under its own power.

Lothar von Richthofen and Gwenafra were not getting along at all. Lothar had always been a "lady killer," and he could not seem to help flirting. More often than not, he followed up the flirtation. Gwenafra had some definite ideas about fidelity with which Lothar agreed, in principle.

203

It was the practice that tripped him up.

Hacking sent word that he intended to visit Parolando himself in two days. He wanted to hold a series of conferences on their trade, to check on the well-being of Parolando's black citizens and to see the great Riverboat.

Sam sent word back that he would be happy to receive Hacking. He wasn't, but the essence of diplomacy was dissimulation. The preparations for housing Hacking and his large entourage and setting up the conferences occupied Sam so that he did not get much chance to supervise the work on the boat.

Also, special preparations had to be made for docking the large number of ore boats from Soul City. Hacking was sending three times as much as the normal shipment to show his sincerity of desire for peace and understanding. Sam would have preferred that the shipments be spaced out, but then it was desirable to get as much as possible in as short a time as possible. The spies said that Iyeyasu was collecting several large fleets and a great number of fighting men on both sides of The River. And he had sent more messages to Selinujo to stop trying to land their missionaries on his territory.

About an hour before noon, Hacking's boat docked. It was a large, two-masted, fore-and-aft rigged boat, about a hundred feet long. Hacking's bodyguard, all tall well-muscled blacks holding steel battle axes (but with Mark I pistols in big holsters) marched down the gangplank. Their kilts were pure black, and their leather helmets and cuirasses and boots were of black fishskin leather. They formed in ranks of six on each side of the gangplank, and then Hacking himself came down the gangplank.

He was a tall, well-built man with a dark-brown skin, somewhat slanting eyes, a broad pug nose, thick lips, and a prominent chin. His hair was in the style called "natural." Sam had not yet gotten used to this explosion of kinky hair on top of black men's heads. There was something indefinably indecent in it; a Negro's hair should be cut very close to the head. He still felt this way even after Firebrass had explained that the black American of the late-twentieth-century felt that "natural" hair was a symbol of his struggle for freedom. To them, close-cut hair symbolized castration of the black by the white.

Hacking wore a black towel as a cloak and a black kilt and leather sandals. His only weapon was a rapier in a sheath at his broad leather belt.

Sam gave the signal, and a cannon boomed twenty-one times. This was set on top of a hill at the edge of the plain. It was intended not only to honor Hacking but to impress him. Only Parolando had artillery, even if it consisted of only one .75 millimeter cannon.

The introductions took place. Hacking did not offer to shake hands nor did Sam and John. They had been warned by Firebrass that Hacking did not care to shake hands with a man unless he regarded him as a proven friend.

There was some small talk after that while the grails of Hacking's people were set on the nearest grailstone. After the discharge of energy at high noon, the grails were removed, and the chiefs of state, accompanied by their bodyguards and guards of honor, walked to John's palace. John had insisted that the first meeting be held in his place, doubtless to impress Hacking with John's primacy. Sam did not argue this time. Hacking probably knew, from Firebrass, just how things stood between Clemens and Lackland.

Later, Sam got some grim amusement from John's discomfiture at being bearded in his own house. During lunch, Hacking seized the floor and held it with a longwinded vitriolic speech about the evils the white man had inflicted on the black. The trouble was, Hacking's indictments were valid. Everything he said was true. Sam had to admit that. Hell, he had seen slavery and what it meant and had seen the aftermath of the Civil War. He had been born and raised in it. And that was long before Hacking was born. Hell, he had written *Huckleberry Finn* and *Pudd'nhead Wilson* and *A Connecticut Yankee*.

It did no good to try to tell Hacking that. Hacking paid him no attention.

That high-pitched voice went on and on, mixing

obscenities with facts, exaggerations with facts, lurid tales of miseries, beatings, murders, starvation, humiliations, and on and on.

Sam felt guilty and ashamed and, at the same time, angry. Why attack *him*? Why this blanket indictment?

"You are all guilty!" Hacking shouted. "Every white man is guilty!"

"I never saw more than a dozen blacks before I died," John said. "What can I have to do with your tale of injustices?"

"If you had been born five hundred years later, you would have been the biggest honky of them all!" Hacking said. "I know all about you, Your Majesty!"

Sam suddenly stood up and shouted, "Did you come here to tell us about what happened on Earth? We know that! But that is past! Earth is dead! It's what's taking place now that counts!"

"Yeah," Hacking said. "And what's taking place now is what took place on good old Earth! Things haven't changed one shitty little bit! I look around here, and who do I see is head of this country? Two honkies! Where's the black men! Your black population is about one-tenth of your population, and so you ought to have at least one black on a ten-man Council! Do I see one? Just one?"

"There's Cawber," Sam said.

"Yeah! A temporary member and he's only that because I demanded you send me a black ambassador!"

"The Arabs make up about a sixth of your state," Sam said, "and yet there isn't one Arab on your council."

"They're white, that's why! And I'm getting rid of them! Don't get me wrong! There's lots of Arabs that're good men, unprejudiced men! I met them when I was a fugitive in North Africa. But these Arabs here are religious fanatics, and they won't stop making trouble! So out they go! What we blacks want is a solid black country, where we're all soul brothers! Where we can live in peace and understanding! We'll have our own kind of world, and you honkies can have yours! Segregation with a capital S, Charlie! Here, a big S segregation can work, cause we don't have to depend on the white man for our jobs or

206

food or clothing or protection or justice or anything! We got it made, whitey! All we have to do is tell you to go to hell, keep away from us, and we got it made!"

Firebrass sat at the table with his dark-red kinky head bent over, looking down, and his bronzed hands placed over his face. Sam had the feeling that he was trying to keep from laughing. But whether he was laughing inside himself at Hacking or at the ones who were being berated, Sam could not guess. Perhaps he was laughing at both.

John kept drinking the bourbon. The redness of his face came from more than the liquor. He looked as if he could explode at any time. It was difficult to swallow insults about your injustice to blacks when you were innocent, but then John was guilty of so many hideous crimes that he should suffer for some, even if none were his. And, as Hacking said, John would have been guilty if he had been allowed a chance to be.

Just what did Hacking expect to gain by this? Certainly, if he wanted a closer relationship with Parolando, he was taking a peculiar approach to it.

Perhaps he felt that he had to put any white, no matter who, in his place. He wanted to make it clear that he, Elwood Hacking, a black, was not the inferior of any white.

Hacking had been ruined by the same system that had ruined almost all Americans, black, white, red or yellow, in one form or another, to a greater or lesser degree.

Would it always be this way? Forever twisted, hating, while they lived for who knew how many thousands upon thousands of years along The River?

At that moment, but for that moment only, Sam wondered if the Second Chancers were not right.

If they knew the way out from this imprisonment of hate, they should be the only ones to be listened to. Not Hacking or John Lackland or Sam Clemens or anybody who suffered from lack of peace and love should have a word to say. Let the Second Chancers . . .

But he did not believe them, he reminded himself. They were just like the other faith dispensers of Earth. Wellintentioned, some of them, no doubt of that. But without

207

the authority of truth, no matter how much they claimed it.

Hacking suddenly quit talking. Sam Clemens said, "Well, we didn't plan on any afterdinner speeches, Sinjoro Hacking, but I thank you for your volunteering; we all thank you as long as you don't charge us for it. Our exchequer is rather low at the moment."

Hacking said, "You have to make a joke out of it, don't you? Well, how about a tour? I'd love to see that big boat of yours."

The rest of the day was passed rather pleasantly. Sam forgot his anger and his resentments in conducting Hacking through the factories, the shops and, finally, through the boat. Even half finished, it was magnificent. The most beautiful sight he had ever seen. Even, he thought, even . . . yes, even more beautiful than Livy's face when she had first said she loved him.

Hacking did not become ecstatic, but he obviously was deeply impressed. He could not, however, refrain from commenting on the stench and the desolation.

Shortly before supper time, Sam was called away. A man who had landed from a small boat had demanded to see the ruler of the land. Since it was a Clemens man who took him in, Sam got the report. He went off at once in one of the two alcohol-burning "jeeps" that had been finished only a week before. The slender, good-looking blond youth at the guardhouse rose and introduced himself, in Esperanto, as Wolfgang Amadeus Mozart.

Sam questioned him in German, noting that, whatever the youth's identity, he did speak the soft Austrian version of High German. His vocabulary contained words which Sam did not understand, but whether this was because they were just Austrian vocabulary items or eighteenth-century items, he did not know.

The man calling himself Mozart said that he had been living about twenty thousand miles up The River. He heard about the boat, but what set him off on his journey was a tale that the boat would carry an orchestra to make music for the amusement of the passengers. Mozart had suffered for twenty-three years in this world of limited

208

materials, where the only musical instruments were drums, whistles, wooden flutes and pan pipes and a crude sort of harp made of bone and the guts of a Riverfish. Then he had heard about the mining of the siderite and the great Riverboat and its orchestra with piano, violin, flute, horns, and all the other beautiful instruments that he had known on Earth, plus others that had been invented since his death in 1791. And here he was. Was there a place for him in the music-making ranks of the boat?

Sam was an appreciator, though not a passionate lover, of some classical music. But he was thrilled at meeting the great Mozart face to face. That is, if this man was Mozart. There were so many phonies on The River, claiming to be everybody from the original one-and-only Jesus H. Christ down to P. T. Barnum, that he took no man's word for his identity. He had even met three men who claimed to be Mark Twain.

"It just so happens that the former archbishop of Salzburg is a citizen of Parolando," Sam said. "Even though you and he parted on bad terms, if I remember correctly, he'll be glad to see you."

Mozart did not turn pale or red. He said, "At last, somebody I knew during my lifetime! Would you believe . . ."

Sam would believe that Mozart had not met anybody he'd known on Earth. So far, he himself had met only three people he'd known, and his acquaintanceship had been extensive during his long life and worldwide travels. That his wife Livy was one of the three was a coincidence exceeding the bounds of probability. He suspected that the Mysterious Stranger had arranged that. But even Mozart's eagerness in seeing the archbishop did not confirm that he was indeed Mozart. In the first place, the impostors that Sam had met had frequently insisted that those who were supposed to be their old friends were either mistaken or else impostors themselves. They had more gall than France. In the second place, the archbishop of Salzburg did not live in Parolando. Sam had no idea where he was. He had sprung him just to test Mozart's reaction.

Sam agreed that Sinjoro Mozart could apply for citizenship. First, he straightened him out about the musical instruments. These had not been made yet. Nor would they be wood or brass. They would be electronic devices which could reproduce exactly the sounds of various instruments. But if Sinjoro Mozart was indeed the man he claimed to be, he had a good chance of being the conductor of the orchestra. And he could have all the time he wanted to compose new works.

Sam did not promise him that he would have the conductorship. He had learned his lesson about making promises.

A big party was held in John's palace in honor of Hacking, who seemed to have discharged his venom for the day at the first meeting. Sam talked with him for an hour and found that Hacking was very intelligent and literate, a self-educated man with a flair for the imaginative and the poetic.

That made his case even sadder, because such talent had been tragically wasted.

About midnight, Sam accompanied Hacking and party to the big thirty-room, second-story, stone-and-bamboo building set aside for state guests. This was halfway between his quarters and John's palace. Then he drove his jeep to his home, three hundred yards away. Joe sulked a little because he had wanted to drive, even though his legs were far too long for him to try this. They staggered up the ladder and barred the door. Joe went into the rear and flopped on his bed with a crash that shook the house on its stilts. Sam looked out the ports just in time to see Cyrano and Livy, their arms around each other, lurch into the door of their hut. To their left, set above them, was von Richthofen's hut, where he and Gwenafra had already gone to bed.

He muttered, "Good night!" not knowing just whom he was addressing, and fell into his own bed. It had been a long, hard and trying day, ending up with a huge party at which everybody had drunk stupendous quantities of purple passion or grain alcohol and water and chewed much dreamgum and smoked much tobacco and marihuana.

210

He awoke dreaming that he was caught in a California earthquake on the Fourth of July.

He leaped out of bed and ran on the trembling floor to the pilothouse. Even before he reached the ports, he knew that the explosions and the earth-shaking were caused by invaders. He never reached the ports, because a rocket, whistling, its tail flaming red, struck one of the stilts. The roar deafened him, smoke whirled in through the broken ports and he pitched forward. The house collapsed, and its front part fell down. History repeated itself.

25

He banged into the wood and broken glass and earth and lay with the wall under him while he tried to come up out of his stunned condition. A big hand picked him up. By the light of an explosion, he saw Joe's great-nosed face. Joe had climbed down from the open end of his room and thrown aside the lumber until he had found Sam. He held the handles of his grail and Sam's with his left hand.

"I don't know how, it's a miracle, but I'm not hurt bad," Sam said. "Just bruised and cut by glass."

"I didn't have time to put on my armor," Joe said. "But I got my akth. Here'th a thword for you and a pithtol and thome bulletth and powder chargeth."

"Who the hell can they be, Joe?" Sam said.

"I don't know. Thee! They're coming in through the holeth in the vallth vhere the dockth are."

The starlight was bright. The clouds that sent the rains down every night at three o'clock had not yet come, but the mists over The River were heavy. Out of these, men were still pouring to add to the masses spreading over the plains. Behind the walls, in the mists, must be a fleet.

The only fleet that could get close without causing an alarm would be the Soul City fleet. Anybody else arriving at this hour would have had to have been within view of the spies that Sam and John Lackland had set up along The River, even in hostile territory. It couldn't be Iyeyasu's fleet; that was still sitting in the docks as of the report received just before midnight.

Joe peered over a pile of wood and said, "There'th a hell of a battle around John'th palathe. And the guetht houthe, vhere Hacking and hith boyth vath, ith on fire."

The flames lit a number of bodies on the ground and showed the tiny figures struggling around the log stockade of John's palace. Then, the cannon and its caisson was pushed before the stockade.

"That's John's jeep!" Sam said, pointing at the vehicle which had just driven up behind the cannon.

"Yeah, and it'th our cannon!" Joe said. "But it'th Hacking'th men that're going to blatht John out of hith little love netht."

"Let's get to hell out of here!" Sam said, and he scrambled over the lumber and in the opposite direction. He could not understand why the invaders had not sent men to his house yet. The rocket that had hit had come from the plains. And if Hacking and his men had sneaked out of the guesthouse to launch a surprise attack in conjunction with an attack from the supposed ore boats, then Sam should have been a primary target along with John Lackland.

He'd find out later what it was all about—if there was a later.

That Hacking's men had gotten hold of the cannon was ill news for Parolando. Even as he thought this, he heard the big gun boom, one, two, three. He whirled in his flight and saw pieces of wood flying out from the smoke. John's walls were wide open, and the next few shells should reduce his log palace to rubble.

There was only one good thing about the invaders having their hands on the cannon. The supply of shells was limited to fifty. Even with the many tons of nickel-iron still in the ground, metal was not so common that it could be wasted to any extent on explosive shells.

Ahead was Cyrano and Livy's hut. The door was open, and the place was empty. He looked up the hill. Lothar von Richthofen, clad only in a kilt, carrying a rapier in one hand and a pistol in the other, was running toward him. A few paces behind was Gwenafra with a pistol and a bag of bullets and gunpowder packages.

There were other men and women coming toward him. Among them were a few crossbowmen.

He shouted at Lothar to organize them, and he turned to look down on the plains. The docks were still black with men. If only the cannon could have been turned to catch them packed together and unable to retreat. But the cannon had been wheeled around from John's palace, which

213

was flaming, and was being trained on Parolandanoj hurrying up the hill.

Then a big dark machine came through a wide breach in the wall. Sam cried out with dismay. It was the *Firedragon III* given to Hacking. But where were the three amphibians of Parolando?

Presently he saw two coming toward the hills. Of a sudden, the steam machine guns in the turrets began to stutter hissingly, and his men—*his* men!—were falling.

The Soul Citizens had captured the amphibians!

Everywhere he looked, he saw a battle raging. There were men fighting around the Riverboat. He cried out again, because he could not endure the thought of its being damaged. But no cannon shells were delivered near it. Apparently the enemy was as concerned about it as he was.

Rockets from the hills behind them were soaring over their heads and blowing up among the army below. Enemy rockets rose in reply; scores of red flames streaked above them; some came so close they could see the blur of the cylindrical body, the long bamboo stick protruding from the rear, and a whoosh as an exceptionally large one shot about ten feet above their heads. It just missed the top of the hill and blew up with a tremendous blast on the other side. Leaves from a nearby irontree fluttered down.

The next half hour—or was it two hours?—was a shrieking, yelling, shouting, gunpowder-stinking, blood-stinking, sweating, bowel-churning chaos. Time after time, the Soul Citizens charged up the hill, and time after time they were repelled by rockets, by sixty-nine-caliber plastic bullets, by crossbow bolts and longbow arrows. Then a charge carried them through to the defenders, and it was rapier, broadsword, ax, club, spear and dagger that drove them back.

Joe Miller, ten feet high, eight hundred pounds heavy, his hairy hide drenched with blood—his own and others—swung his ax with its eighty-pound nickel-steel head at the end of an oak shaft three inches thick and six feet long. It crashed through oak shield and leather armor, brushed aside rapiers and spears and axes, split breastbones, took off arms and necks, halved skulls. When

214

his enemies refused to come near him, he charged them. Time and again, he broke up charges that might otherwise have succeeded.

Many flintlock Mark I pistols were fired at him, but their shooters were so unnerved by him that they fired from too far away, and the big plastic bullets wobbled off to one side.

Then an arrow went through his left arm, and a man braver, or more foolhardy, than the rest stepped under his ax and thrust a rapier into his thigh. The butt end of the shaft came back and broke his jaw and then the reversed ax severed his head. Joe could still walk, but he was losing blood fast. Sam ordered him to retreat to the other side of the hill, where the badly wounded were being treated.

Joe said, "No! I ain't going!" and he fell to his knees with a groan.

"Get back there! That's an order!" Sam screamed, and he ducked, though it was too late, as a bullet whistled by his ear and smashed to bits against the side of an irontree. Some of the plastic must have ricocheted; he felt a stinging in his arm and calf.

Joe managed to heave himself up, like a sick elephant, and shambled off. Cyrano de Bergerac appeared from the darkness; he was covered with gunpowder smoke and streaked with blood. He held the basket hilt of a long, thin, bloody rapier in one hand and a pistol in the other. Behind him, equally dirty and bloody, her long dark hair loose behind her, was Livy. She carried a pistol and a bag of ammunition, and her function was to reload the pistols. Seeing Sam, she smiled, her teeth white in the powder-blackened face.

"My God, Sam! I thought you were dead! That rocket against your house. . . !"

"I wish you were behind *me* in this," he said.

That was all he had time to say, though he would not have said anything more, whatever the case. The enemy came back in another charge, slipping and sliding up over the piles of the fallen or leaping over them. The bowmen by then were out of ammunition, and the pistoleers had only a few more charges. But the enemy had about ex-

215

pended its powder too, though it had more arrows.

Joe Miller was gone, but Cyrano de Bergerac tried to make up for it and came close to doing so. The man was a demon, seemingly as thin and as flexible and as swift as the rapier he wielded. From time to time, he shot the pistol with his left hand into an opponent's face and then lunged with the rapier, thrusting into another. He would toss the gun behind him, and Livy would stoop and pick it up and reload. Sam thought, briefly, of what a change had come about in Livy. He had never suspected her potentiality for action under conditions like these. That frail, often sickly, violence-loathing woman was coolly performing duties that many men would have run from.

Among them me, he thought, if I had any time to think about it.

And especially now that Joe Miller was not by his side to protect him physically and to give him moral support, both of which he needed badly.

Cyrano thrust beneath a shield which a shrieking Wahhabi Arab lifted too high in his frenzy, and then Livy, seeing that she had to do it, that Cyrano could not, held the pistol in both hands and fired. The hammer made the barrel swerve, she brought it back into line, smoke and flame spurted out, and an Arab fell back with his shoulder torn off.

A massively built Negro leaped over the body with his ax raised in both hands and Cyrano, withdrawing the blade from the first man before he hit the ground, ran the axman through the adam's apple.

Then the enemy retreated down the hill again. But now they waited while the big dark-gray amphibian, like a *Merrimac* on wheels, huffed toward them. Lothar von Richthofen pushed against Sam who stepped aside when he saw the aluminum-alloy tube and the rocket with its ten-pound warhead. A man knelt while Lothar loaded the rocket into the bazooka and then aimed it. Lothar was very good at this, and the rocket sailed down, its fiery arc ending against the front of the amphibian, its bull's eye the single beam of light in its nose. Smoke covered it, and then the wind carried that away. The amphibian had stopped, but it came on now, its turrets turning and the steam guns lifting.

"Well, that was the last one," Lothar said. "We might as well get to hell out of here. We can't fight that. Who should know better than we, heh?"

The enemy was re-forming behind the armored vehicle. Many of them were uttering the ululating cries which the Ulmaks, the pre-Amerinds across The River, made during charges. Apparently, Hacking had enlisted those Ulmaks not yet conquered by Iyeyasu.

Suddenly, Sam could not see as well. Only the fires from the burning houses and from the open hearths and smelters, which were still operating, enabled him to see anything at all. The rain clouds had come as swiftly as they always did, like wolves chasing the stars, and within a few minutes it would rain savagely.

He looked around him. Every attack had thinned them out. He doubted that they could have withstood the next one, even if the amphibian had not come.

There was still fighting going on to the north and the south on the plains and the hills along the plains. But the shooting and the cries had lessened.

The plains seemed to be darker than ever with the enemy.

He wondered if Publiujo and Tifonujo had joined the invasion.

He took a last look at the giant hull of the Riverboat with its two paddle-wheels, half hidden beneath the scaffolding and behind the colossal cranes. Then he turned. He felt like weeping, but he was too numbed. It would be some time before the tears would come.

It was more likely that his blood would run out before then, after which there would be no tears. Not in this body, anyway.

Guided by the fires of a dozen scattered huts, he stumbled down the other side. Then the rains smashed down. And, at the same time, a tentacle of the enemy ran toward them from the left. Sam turned and pulled the trig-

217

ger of his flintlock, and the rain, of course, drowned out the spark. But the enemy's pistols were also rendered useless, except as clubs.

They came at the Parolandanoj with their swords and spears and axes. Joe Miller lunged forward, growling with a voice as deep as a cave bear's. Though wounded, he was still a formidable and terrifying fighter. By the flashes of lightning and the rumbling of thunder, his ax cut them down. The others jumped in to help him, and in a few seconds the Soul Citizen survivors decided they had had enough. They would run off and wait for reinforcements. Why get killed now when victory was theirs?

Sam climbed two more hills. The enemy attacked from the right. A wing had broken through and raced on ahead to cut down the men and take the women captive. Joe Miller and Cyrano met them, and the attackers ran away, slipping and sliding through the wet roots of the cutaway grass.

Sam counted the survivors. He was shaken. There were about fifteen. Where had they all gone? He would have sworn that at least a hundred had been with him when he ordered them to cut and run for it.

Livy was still close behind Cyrano. Since the guns were no good now, she kept at Cyrano's back and helped him with a spear thrust when she could.

Sam was cold and wet. And he was as miserable as Napoleon must have been on the retreat from Russia. All, all gone! His proud little nation and its nickel-iron mines and its factories and its invulnerable amphibians with their steam guns and its two airplanes and the fabulous Riverboat! All gone! The technological triumphs and marvels and the Magna Carta with the most democratic constitution any country had ever known and the goal of the greatest journey ever to be made! All gone!

And how? Through treachery, base treachery!

At least, King John had not been part of the betrayal. His palace had been demolished and he along with it, in all probability. The Great Betrayer had been betrayed.

Sam quit grieving then. He was still too frozen with the terror of battle to think much about anything except survival. When they got to the base of the mountain, he led them north along it until they were opposite the dam. A lake about a quarter of a mile long and a half a mile wide was before them. They cut down along it, coming after a while to a thick concrete wall across the top of which they walked. Then they were on top of the dam itself.

Sam walked back and forth a few paces until he found a sunken symbol, a diagonal cross, in the concrete. He called, "Here it is! Now, if only nobody squeals on us or some spy hasn't found out about it!"

He let himself down into the cold water while the lightning streaked and the thunder bellowed far away. He shivered but he kept on going down, and when the water was up to his armpits his foot struck the first rung. He took a deep breath, closed his eyes, and sank down, his hand running along the concrete until it encountered the first rung. After that he pulled himself down by other rungs and at the sixth knew that the entrance was a few inches below it. He went under it and then up, and his head popped up into air and light. A platform a few inches higher than the water was in front of him. Overhead was a dome the highest point of which was ten feet. Beyond the platform was an entrance. Six big electric light bulbs lit the chamber harshly.

Shivering, gasping, he climbed onto the platform and went to the entranceway. Joe followed him a moment later. He called weakly, and Sam had to turn back and help him crawl onto the platform. He was bleeding from a dozen places.

The others came after him, one by one. They helped him get the titanthrop through the entrance and down an incline into a large chamber. There were beds, towels, food, liquor, weapons and medicine. Sam had prepared this place for just such an emergency, but he had thought he was being foolishly cautious. Only the heads of the state and the workers who had built this place knew about it.

Another entrance, at the bottom of the dam, was hidden beneath the flow which powered the wheels connected to the generators. This led to a shaft up which a man could climb only to come to a seemingly blank wall. But the man who knew how could open that wall.

The whole project was, he knew, a product of the romantic foolishness of which he had not entirely rid himself. The idea of secret doors under a waterfall and under the lake and of hidden apartments where he could rest and plan his revenge while his enemies hunted in vain for him was irresistible. He had laughed at himself at times for having built the refuge. Now he was glad. Romanticism did have its uses.

Also hidden was a detonator. To set off the tons of dynamite inside the base of the dam he had only to connect two wires, and the dam would go up and the water of the lake would roar out and carry the central part of Parolando out into The River.

Sam Clemens and his Riverboat would also be destroyed, but that was the price to be paid.

The wounded were treated and put under the sedation of dreamgum or liquor. Sometimes, chewing the gum deadened the pain and other times it seemed to increase it. The only way to neutralize the pain-expanding effects then was to pour liquor down the patient.

They ate and slept while the guard watched at both entrances. Joe Miller was half unconscious most of the time, and Sam sat beside him and nursed him as best he could. Cyrano came back from his vigil at the door under the waterfall to report that it was night again outside. That was all he knew about the conditions outside. He had seen or heard no one through the waterfall.

Lothar and Sam were the least wounded. Sam decided that they should sneak out past the waterfall exit and spy. Cyrano protested that he should go, too, but Sam refused. Livy did not say anything, but she looked gratefully at Sam. He turned away; he did not want any thanks for sparing her mate.

He wondered if Gwenafra was dead or if she had been captured. Lothar said that she had disappeared during the last attack and that he had tried to get to her but had been driven back. He now felt ashamed of himself for not having done more, even though it had not been possible.

The two applied a dark stain all over their bodies and then went down the steel rungs of the shaft. The walls were damp here, and the rungs were slippery with moisture. Electric lights illuminated the shaft.

They went out behind the waterfall, which roared and splashed at them. The ledge curved around, following the lower half of the dam, until it ran out about twenty yards from the end. Here they climbed down steel rungs to the junction of the dam wall and the earth. From there, they walked cautiously along the channel which had been cut out of the earth. The roots of the grass still stuck out of the walls of the channel. The roots went deeper than any cuts made so far; it seemed impossible to kill the grass.

The sky was bright with the jampack of huge stars and the extensive glowing gas clouds. They were able to proceed swiftly in the pale darkness. After a half a mile, they went at right angles to the canal, heading toward John's ruined palace. Crouching in the shadows beneath the outflung branches of an irontree, they looked down on the plains below. There were men and women in the huts around them. The men were the victors, and the women were the victims. Sam quivered when he heard some of the screams and the calls for help, but he tried to push them out of his mind. To rush into any hut and try to rescue one women was to throw away their chances of doing any good for Parolando. And it would certainly result in their being captured or killed.

Yet, if he heard Gwenafra's voice, he knew that he would go to her rescue. Or would he?

The fires in the open hearths and the smelters were still blazing, and men and women were working in them. Evidently, Hacking had already put his slaves to work. Many guards stood around the buildings, but they were drinking liquor and ethyl alcohol.

The plains were well lit for as far as he could see with huge bonfires. Around them were many men and women, drinking and laughing. Occasionally a struggling and screaming woman was carried off into the shadows. Sometimes, she was not taken away.

Sam and Lothar walked down the hill as if they owned

it, but they did not go near the buildings or the fires.

Nobody had challenged them, though they had come within twenty yards of a number of patrols. Most of the enemy seemed to be celebrating the victory with purple passion or any other liquor they had been able to get from the supplies of their prisoners. The exceptions were the Wahhabi Arabs, whose religion forbade drinking alcohol. And there were a few blacks who were not on duty but who were abstemious. These were disciples of Hacking, who did not drink.

Whatever the laxity now, discipline had been maintained during the day. The corpses had been taken away, and a big stockade of poles removed from other buildings had been set up on the plain just beside the first of the hills. Though Sam could not see within it, he surmised from the guard towers around it that prisoners were within it.

The two strolled along, staggering now and then as if they were drunk. They passed within twenty feet of three short dark men who spoke a strange language. Sam could not identify it, though it sounded "African." He wondered if these were not eighteenth-century Dahomeyans.

They walked boldly between a nitric acid factory and an excrement-treatment building and out onto the plain. And they stopped. Twenty yards ahead, Firebrass was in a bamboo cage so narrow that he could not sit down in it. His hands were tied behind him.

On a big X-frame of wood, upside down, his legs tied to the upper part of the X and his arms to the lower members, was Göring.

Sam looked around. A number of men, talking and drinking, stood in the big doorway of the excrement plant. Sam decided not to go any closer or to try to talk to Firebrass. He longed to know why he was in the cage, but he did not dare to ask him. It was necessary to find out all he could and then get back to the hideout inside the dam. So far, the situation looked hopeless. It was best to sneak out during the rains and leave the country. He could blow up the dam and wash out everything, including the forces of Soul City, but he did not want to lose the boat. As long as he had a chance to get that back, he would let the dam alone.

They went on by Firebrass' cage, hoping he would not see them and call to them. But he stood bent over, leaning his head against the bamboo bars. Göring groaned once. They kept on going and soon were around the corner of the building.

Their slow and seemingly drunken wanderings took them near a big building that had been occupied by Fred Rolfe, King John's supporter on the Council. The number of armed men on guard around it convinced Sam that Hacking was inside it.

It was a one-story house of lodgepole-pine logs and bamboo. Its windows were unblinded, and the light from within showed people inside. Suddenly, Lothar gripped Sam's arm and said, "There she is! Gwenafra!"

The torch light shone on her long honey-colored hair and very white skin. She was standing by the window and talking to someone. After a minute, she moved away, and the bushy hair and black face of Elwood Hacking moved across the bright square. Sam felt sick. Hacking had taken her for his woman for the night.

Gwenafra had not looked frightened. She had seemed relaxed, but Gwenafra, though volatile and uninhibited most of the time, could be self-restrained when the occasion demanded.

He pulled Lothar away.

"There's nothing we can do now, and you'd be throwing away any chance she might have at all."

They drifted around for a while, observing the other factories and noting that the bonfires stretched both ways along the walls as far as their eye could detect. In addition to the Soul Citizens, there were the Ulmaks and a number of Orientals. Sam wondered if these could be the Burmese, Thai, and Ceylonese New Stone Age peoples living across The River from Selinujo.

To get out of Parolando, they would have to go over the wall. And they would have to steal several small boats if they were to get down The River to Selinujo. They had no idea about what had happened to Publiujo or Tifonujo, but they suspected that these countries would be next on Hacking's list. To escape just to the north to Chernsky's Land was foolish. Iyeyasu would be moving on that as soon as he found out about the invasion here, if he had not already done that.

It was ironic that they would flee to the very country the citizens of which had been forbidden entrance to Parolando.

They decided they would return to the dam now, tell what they had seen and make plans. The best chance to get away would be when it rained.

They rose and started to walk about, skirting the huts which housed the enemy and the captive women.

They had just passed into the shade of a gigantic iron-tree when Sam felt something tighten around his neck from behind. He tried to yell, to turn around, to struggle, but the big hand squeezed, and he became unconscious.

26

He awoke gasping and coughing, still under the irontree. He started to get up, but a deep voice growled, "None o' that! Sit still, or I'll split yer skull with this ax!"

Sam looked around. Lothar, his hands tied behind him and a gag in his mouth, was sitting propped up under a half-grown fir tree sixty feet away. The man who had spoken was a very big man with excessively broad shoulders, a deep chest and brawny arms. He wore a black kilt and black cape, and he held the handle of a medium-sized ax. Sheaths at his belt held a steel tomahawk and a steel knife, and a Mark I pistol was stuck in his belt.

He said, "You be Sam Clemens?"

"That's right," Sam said, his voice low, also. "What does this mean? Who are you?"

The big man jerked a head full of thick hair at Lothar. "I moved him away so he couldn't hear what we have to say. A man we both know sent me."

Sam was silent for a minute and then he said, "The Mysterious Stranger?"

The big man grunted. "Yes. That's what he said you called him. Stranger's good enough. I guess you know what it's all about, so there's not much use us jawing too long about it. You satisfied that I've talked with him?"

"I'd have to be," Sam said. "It's obvious that you've met him. You're one of the Twelve he's picked. It was a he, wasn't it?"

"I didn't jump him to find out," the man said. "I tell you, this child ain't ever run up against a human, red, black, or white, that ever threw a scare-fit into me. But that Stranger, he's the one that'd make a grizzly scoot just by looking at him. Not that I'm afraid of him, you understand, it's just that he makes me feel . . . strange. Like I was a feather-plucked bluejay."

"Enough of that. My handle's Johnston. Mought as well give you my history, since it'll save a lot of jawing later.

John Johnston. I was born in New Jersey about 1827, I reckon, and died in Los Angeles in the veterans' hospital in 1900. Between times, I was a trapper in the Rocky Mountains. Up to when I came to this River, I killed me hundreds of Injuns, but I ain't never had to kill a white man, not even a Frenchman. Not till I got here. Since then, well, I collected quite a few white scalps."

The man stood up and moved out into the starlight. His hair was dark but looked as if it would be a bright red in the noonday sun.

"I talk a hell of a lot more'n I used to," he said. "You can't get away from people in this valley. People give a child bad habits."

They walked over to Lothar. On the way, Sam said, "How'd you happen to get here? And at this time?"

"The Stranger told me where to find you, told me about you and your big boat, the Misty Tower, and all that. Why hash it all over? You know. I agreed to find you and go with you on your boat. Why not? I don't like being set down here. There ain't no elbow room; you can't turn around without knocking noses. I was about thirty thousand miles upRiver when I wake up one night, and there's that man sitting in the shadows. We had a long talk with him doing most of it. Then I got up and set out. I heard about some of what was going on here way up The River. I snuck into here while the fighting was still going on, and I been looking for you ever since. I listened to them blacks talking; they said they couldn't find your body. So I been skulking around, seeing what I could see. Once, I had to kill me one a those Ayrabs cause he stumbled across me. I was hungry, anyway."

They had reached Lothar, but Sam straightened up at the last words. "Hungry?" he said. "You mean. . . ?"

The man did not reply. Sam said, "Say, uh, you . . . you wouldn't be that Johnston called 'Liver Eating' Johnston, would you? The Crow Killer?"

The voice rumbled, "I made me peace with the Crows and became their brother. And I quit eating human liver some time after. But a man has to eat."

226

Sam shivered. He stooped down and untied Lothar's bonds and removed the gag. Lothar was furious, but he was also curious. And, like Sam, he seemed to find Johnston a little awing. The man exuded a peculiar savage force. Without even half trying, Sam thought. I'd hate to see him in action.

They walked back to the dam. Johnston did not say anything for a long time. Once, he disappeared, leaving Sam feeling strange and cold. Johnston was about six and a half feet tall and looked as if he weighed two hundred and eighty pounds, all bone and muscle. But he moved as silently as a tiger's shadow.

Sam jumped. Johnston was back. Sam said, "What happened?"

Johnston said, "Never mind. You say you didn't get around much. I been all over this place; I know the sitchyation passing well. Lots a your people to the north and the south got away over the walls. If they'd a stood up, they might've licked the blacks. But the blacks ain't won by a long shot. Iyeyasu is getting ready to move against them. I wouldn't be surprised none if he invades tonight. I scouted around his place some before I came here. He ain't going to put up with the blacks owning all this iron and the boat. He will take it away from them or know why."

Sam groaned. It made no difference whether Hacking or Iyeyasu had the boat, if he couldn't get it. But by the time they were inside the dam, he felt better. Maybe the two forces would destroy each other, and the Parolandanoj who'd fled could come back and take over. All wasn't lost yet.

Moreover, the appearance of the Herculean Liver Eating Johnston heartened him. The Mysterious Stranger had not entirely abandoned him. He was still planning, and he had sent a damn good man for fighting, if the stories about him could be believed. Johnston was the sixth man the Stranger had chosen. The other six would show up sometime. But then one had been lost. Odysseus had disappeared.

227

Still he could show up again. The River was a great place for bad pennies, if you could call the Twelve that. They were bad for *somebody*. For the Stranger's people, the Ethicals, Sam hoped.

In the dam, Johnston had to be introduced and the situation explained. Joe Miller, wrapped in towels, sat up and shook hands with Johnston. And Johnston, awe in his voice, said, "Night and day, this man-child seed many queer things. But I ain't never seed one like you. You didn't have to crush my hand, friend."

"I didn't try," Joe said. "You look pretty big and thtrong to me. Bethideth, I been thick."

About half an hour before the rains, they moved out. The land was relatively quiet by then. The celebrators had gone to bed, and everybody had cleared away from the fires in expectation of the rain. But the guard towers and the factories were full of enemy guards, and these had stopped drinking. Apparently, Hacking had called a halt to it.

Johnston, like a giant ghost, drifted away while they leaned against the side of the sulfuric acid factory. Ten minutes later, he was suddenly beside them.

"I been giving those blacks the ear," he said. "That Hacking is shore one smart nigger. All that drinking and whooping it up and staggering around, why, that's all put on! That's fer the benefit of spies from Iyeyasujo. Hacking knows the Jap is going to attack tonight, and he's making it look like it's gonna be easy. But his men are worried. They're short of gunpowder."

Sam was startled by the news. He asked Johnston if he had overheard anything else.

"Yeah, I heard a couple of them Citizens talking about why Hacking decided he had to attack us. He knew Iyeyasu was going to do it, so he decided he had to jump the gun. If he didn't, the Jap would have control of the metal and the amphibians and everything, and he'd just conquer Soul City next and then have everything. Them jackasses was laughing fit to kill. They said it was King John arranged with Hacking to take over. And then Hacking blew up King John in his own house because he didn't trust John. Said John was a traitor and even if he wasn't, he was a whitey and couldn't be trusted."

Sam said, "But why in hell would John do that to us? What did he have to gain?"

"Hacking and John was gonna conquer all the land for a hundred miles along The River and then split it. John was gonna rule the white half, and Hacking was gonna rule the black half. Half and half, with the two sharing everything equal. They was gonna build two boats, two of everything."

"What about Firebrass? Why's he in the cage?"

"Dunno, but somebody did call him a traitor. And that kraut, what's his name, Herring . . ."

"Göring."

"Yeah. Well, it wasn't Hacking was to blame for his being tortured. Some a them Wahhabi Ayrabs did it. They's got it in for the Second Chancers, you know, and they got him and tortured him, with the help a some a them African niggers, the Dahomeyans, who used to torture a dozen people before breakfast every day, according to what I heard. By the time Hacking heard of it and stopped it, Göring was dying. But he talked to Hacking, called him his soul brother and said he forgave him. Said he'd see him later along The River. Hacking was pretty shook up about it, from what his men said."

Sam digested the news, which set the teeth of his stomach even more on edge. He was so upset he couldn't even get any amusement from Hacking's double cross of the champion double-crosser, King John. He did have to admire Hacking's statesmanship and perception, however. Hacking had realized there was only one way to deal with John, and he had taken that way. But then Hacking did not have Sam Clemens' conscience.

The news changed everything. Apparently, Iyeyasu was on the way now, which meant that Sam's plans to sneak out during the rains would not work. The Soul Citizens were too alert.

"What's the matter, Sam?" Livy said. She was sitting

229

near him and looking sadly at him.

"I think it's all up with us."

"Oh, Sam!" she replied. "Where's your manhood? It *isn't* all up with us! You get depressed so easily if things don't go your way all the time! Why, this is the greatest opportunity you could ask for to get your boat back! Let Hacking and Iyeyasu destroy each other and then take over. Just sit back up in the hills until they have clawed each other to death and then jump on them while they're gasping out their last!"

Sam said angrily, "What are you talking about? Jump on them with fifteen men and women?"

"No, you stupe! You have at least five hundred prisoners in that stockade and God knows how many more in other stockades. And you have thousands who ran away to Cernskujo and Publiujo!"

"How can I get hold of them now?" Sam said. "It's too late! The attack will be launched in a few hours, you can bet on that! Besides, the refugees were probably put in stockades, too! For all I know, Chernsky and Publius Crassus may be in cahoots with Hacking!"

"You're still the same paralyzed pessimist I knew on Earth," she said. "Oh, Sam, I still love you, in a way, that is. I still like you as a friend, and . . ."

"Friend!" he said so loudly that the others jumped. Cyrano said, *"Morbleu!"* and Johnston hissed, "Shet up, you want them black Injuns to get us?"

"We were lovers for years," he said.

"Not always, by a long shot," she said. "But this is no place for a discussion of our failures. I don't intend to thrash those out, anyway. It's too late. The point is, do you or do you not want your boat?"

"Of course, I do," he said fiercely. "What do you think . . . ?"

"Then get off your dead ass, Sam!" she said.

From anybody else, the remark would have been unremarkable. But from her, his fragile, soft-voiced, clean-speeched Livy, it was unthinkable. But she had said it, and now that he thought back on it, there had been times on Earth, which he had suppressed in his memory, when . . .

"The lady makes a powerful lot a sense!" Johnston rumbled.

He had far more important things to think about. But the really important things were best recognized by the unconscious, and it must have been this that sent the thought. For the first time, he understood, really understood, with the cells of his body, from the brain on down, that Livy had changed. She was no longer *his* Livy. She had not been for a long time, perhaps had not been for some years on Earth before her death.

"What do you say, Mr. Clemens?" the mountain man rumbled.

Sam gave a deep sigh, as if he were breathing out the last fragments of Olivia Langdon Clemens de Bergerac, and said, "Here's what we do."

The rains lashed down; thunder and lightning made the skies and the land hideous for a half hour. Johnston appeared out of the rain with two bazookas and four rockets tied together on his broad back. Then he disappeared again and a half hour later was back with some throwing knives and tomahawks, all of steel, and some new blood, not his, splashed on his arms and chest.

The rain clouds went away. The land was brightly silver under the magnificent stars, as big as apples, as numerous as cherries on a tree in season, as luminous as jewels before electric lights. Then it got colder, and they shivered under the irontree. A thin mist formed over The River; within fifteen minutes, it was so thick that the waters and the grailstones and the high walls along the banks could not be seen. A half hour later, Iyeyasu struck. The big boats and the small boats, crammed with men and weapons, came from across The River, where the Sacs and Foxes had once ruled, from the northern part of the ex-Ulmak territory, from the land where the Hottentots and Bushmen had once lived in peace. And the main bulk came from the right bank of The River, from the three lands where Iyeyasu was now lord.

Iyeyasu attacked at ten points along the Riverfront walls. Mines blew up the walls, and men poured through the breaches. The number of rockets shot in the first ten minutes was awesome. Iyeyasu must have been saving them for a long time. The three amphibians of the defenders lumbered up, their steam machine guns chuffing and expelling the plastic bullets in garden hose fashion. The carnage they made was great, but Iyeyasu launched a surprise. Rockets with wooden warheads containing jellied alcohol (made from soap plus wood alcohol) struck all around the three armored vehicles and made direct hits on each at least twice. The crude napalm spread fierily over the vehicles, and if the burning stuff did not get inside the vehicles, it seared the lungs of the men inside.

Sam was shaken by the sight, but not so much that he did not tell Lothar to remind him of this when it was all over, if either of them was still around.

"They have to be made more airtight, and we'll have to install a closed-circuit air system, like Firebrass described," he said.

Johnston appeared as unexpectedly as if he had stepped out of a door in the night, and behind him was Firebrass. The man looked exhausted and as if he were in pain, but he still managed to grin at Sam. He was, however, trembling.

"Hacking was told that I was betraying him," Firebrass said. "And he believed his informant. Who was, by the way, our esteemed and always reliable King John. John told him that I was selling him down The River, that I had revealed everything to you so I could become chief of your air force. Hacking would not believe that I was dickering with you just to string you along. I can't blame him too much. I should have sent word through our spies what I was doing. That I didn't convince him that I wasn't double-crossing him didn't surprise me."

"Were you?" Sam said.

Firebrass grinned. "No, I wasn't, though I was mightily tempted. But why should I betray him when I'd been promised I could be head flier after Hacking took over the boat? The truth is, Hacking was eager to believe John.

232

He doesn't like me because I'm not his idea of what a soul brother should be. And I had too easy a life according to him. He resented it because I never lived in a ghetto and I had every advantage he didn't have."

"The job of chief engineer can still be yours," Sam said. "I'll admit that I'm relieved about not having to promise you the captaincy of the air force. But you can still fly, if you want to."

"That's the best offer I've had since I died," Firebrass said. "I'll take it."

He moved closer to Sam and whispered in his ear. "You would have had to take me along in some capacity anyway. I'm one of The Twelve!"

27

Sam felt as if a cold rod had been plunged through him from the top of his head down.

"The Ethical? The Stranger?"

"Yes. He said you called him the Mysterious Stranger."

"Then you *were* betraying Hacking?"

"That little speech I just made was for public consumption," Firebrass said. "Yes, I did betray Hacking, if you insist on using that word. But I regard myself as an espionage agent for a higher authority. I have no intention of worrying about all-black or all-white states on The River, when I can find out how and why we, the whole human race, were put here. I want answers to my questions, as Karamazov once said. All this white-black turmoil is trivial on this planet, no matter how important it was on Earth. Hacking must have sensed that I thought that, though I tried to conceal it."

Sam did not recover from the shock for some time. Meanwhile, the battle raged on the plain with the Soul Citizens getting the worst of it. Though they cost the invaders three men for one, they were pushed back within a half an hour. Sam decided that it was time for them to act, and they trotted off toward the stockade where the Parolando prisoners were kept. Lothar fired two rockets into the gates of the stockade, and before the smoke had cleared, the fifteen charged through the blasted gates. Cyrano and Johnston did most of the work in killing the fifteen guards. Cyrano was a demon with lightning for a sword, and Johnston downed four men with thrown tomahawks and three with thrown knives. He broke two legs and a chest with a foot like iron. The prisoners were directed to the armory, where bows and arrows and swords were still in supply.

Sam sent two men each to the north and the south to go over the walls and try to contact the Parolandanoj there.

Then he led the rest back up into the hills. They would camp by the dam until they saw how the battle was going. Sam did not have the slightest idea of what they should do. He told Cyrano he would have to play it by ear. He had to repress the impulse to remark that he was doing this even though Cyrano was tone deaf.

Afterward, Sam thanked whoever there was to thank that he had not camped on top of the dam itself. Instead, he had sat down on a knoll above and to the left side of the dam, facing outward. He had a better view of the hills and the plains, where the rockets were still exploding but were not as numerous as in the beginning. The starlight glimmered on the waters of the big lake behind the dam as if all was peace and quiet in the world.

Suddenly, Johnston leaped up and said, "Looky there! Yonder! Atop a the dam!"

Three dark figures had emerged from the water onto the dam. They ran toward the land. Sam told the others to withdraw behind the great trunk of the irontree. Joe Miller and Johnston seized the three as they raced up to the tree. One tried to stab Joe, and Joe squeezed the neck and the blood spurted out from broken veins and arteries. The others were knocked out. By the time they regained consciousness, they did not have to tell Sam what they had done. And he guessed that they had done so at the order of King John.

The earth shook under their feet, and the irontree leaves rattled like dishes in a pantry. The white wall of the dam flew outward with a gigantic cloud of smoke and a roar that pushed in on their eardrums. The enormous chunks of concrete flew through the smoke like white birds above a factory chimney. They tumbled over and over and struck the ground far ahead of the waters. The lake was no longer the peaceful and quiet glimmer of a wonderful world to come. It seemed to hurl itself forward. The roar as it raced down the canyon which Sam's men had dug with so much sweat and time deafened the watchers again.

The water, hundreds of thousands of tons, funneled by the canyon, rammed through the earthen walls, tearing out great chunks of it. The sudden withdrawal also removed a great amount of earth around the lake's shores, so much so that the watchers had to scramble for even higher ground. And the thousand-foot-high irontree, its two-hundred-feet-deep roots abruptly exposed, its foundation partly dug away, toppled over. It seemed to take a long time falling, and the explosions of enormous roots breaking and the whistling of air through the huge leaves and the vines covering it terrified the humans. They had thought they were far enough away, but even though the giant tree was falling away from them, they were threatened by eruptions of roots from the earth.

The tree struck with a crash on the other side of the lake and tore out the overhanging dirt and continued on down into the emptying lake. It slid out entirely from the root anchors on the bank and went on top first into the waters. These were whirling around and around, and, picking up the enormous tree as if it were a toothpick, the waters carried it down the canyon for a half a mile before it became wedged between the two walls of the canyon.

The waters roared out in a wall at least a hundred feet high by the time it had hit the plains. Its front must have borne a tangle of half-grown trees and bamboo plants, huts, people, and debris. It flashed across the mile and a half of plain, spreading out but channeled, for a few minutes, by the cyclopean secondary walls that Sam had built to defend the factories and the Riverboat, but which had proved useless in two attacks.

Everything was picked up and carried on out into The River. The factories crumbled as if they were made of cookies. The gigantic Riverboat was lifted up like a toy boat cast into the ocean surf. It rode out into The River, pitching, and then was sunk in darkness and turmoil. Sam threw himself on the ground and clawed at the grass. His boat was lost! Everything was lost, factories, mines, amphibians, airplanes, smithies, armories, and his crew. But worst of all, the Riverboat was lost. The dream was shattered, the great shining jewel of his dream had been smashed.

The grass was cold and wet in his face. His fingers felt

236

as if they were fastened in the flesh of the earth and would never come free again. But Joe's huge hand lifted him up and sat him down, as if he were a dummy. Joe's monstrous hairy body was pressed close to his, warming him. And Joe's grotesque face with the shelving brows and the absurdly long nose was by him.

"They're all gone!" Joe said. "Jethuth! Vhat a thight! There ain't nothing left, Tham!"

The plain was buried under a whirl and toss of waters, but in fifteen minutes the waters had drained off. The River had resumed its normal appearance along the shores of Parolando, though it must have been swollen downstream.

The great buildings and the boat in its scaffoldings were gone. The cyclopean walls on the sides, a mile apart, were gone. There were little lakes here and there where the mines and the basements of the factories had been. The vast weight of water had gouged out part of the plain where it had been dug up. But the roots of the grasses were so deep, so tough, and so thickly intertwined that even the scrape of hundreds of thousands of tons of water had not ripped the earth out. The stone and earth walls along the banks had been swept away as if they were sand.

The skies paled, and the starlit darkness became gray. The great fleet of the invaders was gone, somewhere far down The River, or under it, broken, smashed, fragments floating or half hulls upside down. The two armies on the plain and the sailors were all dead, crushed by the weight of the water, drowned, rubbed into nothing or squeezed out like toothpaste.

But Parolando extended for ten miles along The River, and the lake had, after all, only raged across a two-mile-broad area. Its main damage had been in the middle of Parolando, where it had carried everything out that stood within a half-mile-wide area. Those on the edges had been drowned and the buildings smashed or only submerged briefly.

Dawn brought with it a thousand men in boats or over the walls of Chernsky's Land from the north.

237

At their head was King John.

Sam drew up his men in battle formation with Joe Miller in the center, but King John limped forward, his hand held out in sign of peace. Sam went forward to talk to him. Even after John had explained what he had done, Sam expected to be killed. But later he realized that John needed him and Firebrass and others if he was going to get the boat rebuilt. Also, he would be taking a perverted pleasure in keeping Sam alive while Sam wondered when the dagger in the night would come.

As it turned out, not everything had to be started from scratch again. The boat, almost entirely undamaged, was found beached on a hill across The River a mile down. It had been deposited as gently as a cat's footstep by the withdrawing waters. The work of getting the great hull back was not easy; but it took much less time than making another one.

John explained more than once to Sam what he had done, but the deviousnesses and the two times two double crosses were so complicated that Sam could never see the picture as a whole. John had made a deal to betray Sam, knowing full well that Hacking would betray him also. John would have been disappointed if Hacking had not tried to stab him in the back. He would have lost all his faith in human nature.

John had made a deal with Iyeyasu to help him invade after Hacking's invasion. Iyeyasu liked the idea that Hacking would weaken his forces while taking Parolando. At the last moment, John had made a deal with Publius Crassus, Tai Fung and Chernsky that they would help him mop up on Iyeyasu's forces, which would be shattered by the waters released by the blown-up dam.

John had sent the three men to set off the explosives in the dam when the greatest number of invaders and defenders would be concentrated between the funneling secondary-defense walls. Beofre that happened, John had fled in his boat, hidden by the fog.

"Then you weren't in your palace when the cannons opened up on it?" Sam said.

"No," John replied, smiling his cat's smile. "I was miles to the north, traveling to meet Iyeyasu. You have never thought much of me, Samuel, but you should get down on your knees now and kiss my hand in gratitude. Without me, you would have lost all."

"If you had told me Hacking was going to invade, I could have kept everything," Sam said. "We could have ambushed Hacking."

The sun came up and struck the tawniness of John's hair and the peculiar gray-blue of his eyes. "Ah, yes, but Iyeyasu would still have been a formidable problem. Now he's gone, and there is little to keep us from ruling all the land we need, including the bauxite and platinum of Soul City and the iridium and tungsten of Selinujo. I presume you have no objections to conquering those two states?"

There was a bonanza in the aftermath. Hacking was taken prisoner, and Gwenafra was found alive. Both had been pushed during the fighting into the hills to the west. Hacking was getting ready to lead a charge back down the hills, when the edge of the waters deluged his part. Gwenafra escaped, though she almost drowned. Hacking had been hurled against a tree. Both his legs and one arm were broken, and he was bleeding internally.

Sam and John hastened to where Hacking lay under an irontree. Gwenafra cried when she saw them and embraced Sam and Lothar. She seemed to have given Sam a much longer embrace than she did Lothar, which was not entirely unexpected, since she and Lothar had been quarreling violently for the last few months.

John wanted to finish Hacking off with some refined tortures, preferably as soon after breakfast as possible. Sam objected strongly. He knew that John could have his way if he insisted, since his men outnumbered Sam's by fifty to one. But Sam was past being cautious, at that moment, anyway. And John backed away. He needed Sam and the men whose loyalty he commanded.

"You had a dream, White Sam," Hacking said in a weak voice. "Well, I had one, too. A land where brothers and sisters could loaf and invite their souls. Where we'd be

239

all black. You wouldn't know what that means. No white devils, no white eyes. Just black soul brothers. It would have been as near heaven as you can get in this hell of a world. Not that we wouldn't have had trouble, no place without trouble, man. But there wouldn't have been any white-man trouble. It'd be all ours. But that isn't to be."

"You could have had your dream," Sam said. "If you'd waited. After the boat was built, we'd have left the iron to whomever could take it. And then . . ."

Hacking grimaced. Sweat covered his black skin and his face was tight with pain. "Man, you must be out of your skull! You really think I believed that story about you sailing off on this quest for the Big Grail? I knew you was going to use that big boat to conquer us blacks and lock those chains around us again. An Old South whitey like you . . ."

He closed his eyes. Sam said, "You are wrong! If you knew me, if you'd taken the trouble to know me instead of stereotyping me . . ."

Hacking opened his eyes and said, "You'd lie to a nigger even when he was on his deathbed, wouldn't you? Listen! That Nazi, Göring, he really shook me up. I didn't tell them to torture him, just kill him, but those fanatical Arabs, you know them. Anyway, Göring gives me a message. *Hail and farewell, soul brother,* or something like that. *I forgive you, because you know not what you do.* Something like that. Ain't that a crock? A message of love from a damn Nazi! But you know, he had changed! And he could be right. Maybe all them Second Chancers are right. Who knows? Sure seems stupid to bring us up from the dead, give us our youth back, just so some can kick and some can hurt all over again. Stupid, isn't it?"

He stared up at Sam and then said, "Shoot me, will you? Put me out of my pain? I'm really suffering."

Lothar stepped up beside Sam and said, "After what you did to Gwenafra, I'll be glad to."

He pointed the muzzle of the big flintlock at Hacking's head.

Hacking grinned painfully and muttered, "Rape on principle, mother! I swore off that on Earth, but that

240

woman just brought out the devil in me! Besides, so what? What about all those black slave women you white mothers raped?"

As Sam walked away, the pistol boomed. He jumped, but he kept on walking. It was the kindest thing that Lothar could have done for Hacking. Tomorrow, he would be walking along the banks of The River somewhere far away. He and Sam might even see each other again, although Sam was not looking forward to that.

Lothar, stinking of gunpowder, caught up with him.

"I should have let him suffer. But old habits are hard to break. I wanted to kill him, so I did. That black devil just smiled at me. Then I spread his smile all over him."

"Don't say any more," Sam replied. "I'm sick enough. I'm about to chuck the whole thing and settle down with a steady job of missionarying. The only one whose suffering meant anything today were the Second Chancers."

"You'll get over that," Lothar said, and he was right. But it took three years.

The land was again like a shell-pocked battlefield, stinking with fumes and black with smoke. But the great Riverboat was completed. There was nothing to do to it now except to try it out. Even the last touch, the painting on the Riverboat's name in big black letters on the white hull, had been done. On both sides of the hull, ten feet above the water line, were the letters NOT FOR HIRE.

"What does that mean, Sam?" he had been asked by many.

"It means just what it says, contrary to most words in print or speech," Sam said. "The boat is no man's to hire. It's a free boat and its crew are free souls. No man's."

"And why is the boat's launch called *Post No Bills*?"

"That comes from a dream I had," Sam would say. "Somebody was trying to put up advertising on it, and I told him that the launch was built for no mercenary purpose. *What do you think I am, advance agent for P. T. Barnum?* I said."

There was more to the dream, but Sam told no one except Joe about this.

"But the man who was pasting up those garish posters, advertising the coming of the greatest Riverboat of them all and the greatest Riverboat show of them all was I!" Sam said. "I was both men in the dream!"

"I don't get it, Tham," Joe said.

Sam gave up on him.

28

The twenty-sixth anniversary of Resurrection Day was the day that the sidewheeler *Not for Hire* first turned its paddles. It was about an hour after the grailstones flamed to charge the breakfast grails. The cables and cap connected to the grailstone had been removed and the cables wound up within the hold through a port in the forward section on the starboard side. The grails had been removed from the stone a mile north and rushed to the big boat in the amphibious, armored, steam-driven launch, the *Post no Bills*. The fabulous Riverboat, gleaming white with red and black and green trimmings, moved out from the canal and into The River behind a huge breakwater on its starboard side. This deflected the current so that the boat would not be swung to the south as it emerged from the canal and so carried into the edge of the canal's mouth.

Whistles blowing, iron bells clanging, the passengers cheering as they leaned over the railings, the people on the banks shouting, the magnificent paddle-wheels churning, the *Not for Hire* moved with stately grace out into The River.

The Riverboat had an overall length of four hundred and forty feet and six inches. The beam over the paddle-wheel guards was ninety-three feet. The mean draft loaded was twelve feet. The giant electric motors driving the paddle-wheels delivered ten thousand shaft horsepower and enough power left over to take care of all the boat's electrical needs, which were many. Top speed, theoretically, was forty-five miles an hour in still water. Going upstream against the fifteen-mile-an-hour current, it would be thirty. Going downstream, it would be sixty. The boat would be going up The River most of the time and cruising at fifteen miles an hour relative to the ground.

There were four decks; the so-called boiler deck, the main deck, the hurricane deck and the landing deck. The pilothouse was at the fore edge of the hurricane deck, and the long texas, containing the captain's and chief officers' quarters, was behind the pilothouse. However, the pilothouse was itself double-decked. It was set forward of the two tall but thin smokestacks which rose thirty feet high. Firebrass had advised against the stacks, because the smoke from the big boilers (used only to heat water and to drive the machine guns) could be piped out on the side. But Sam had snorted and said, "What do I care about air resistance? I want beauty! And beauty is what we'll get! Whoever heard of a Riverboat without tall, graceful, impressive smokestacks! Have you no soul, brother?"

There were sixty-five cabins, each about twelve by twelve with snap-up beds and tables and folding chairs. Each cabin had a toilet and a washbasin with hot and cold running water, and there was a shower for every six cabins.

There were three big lounges, one in the texas, one on the hurricane deck and one on the main deck. These held pool tables, dart games, gymnastic equipment, card tables, a movie screen and a stage for dramas or musicals, and the main deck lounge held a podium for the orchestra.

The upper deck of the pilothouse was luxuriously furnished with carved oaken chairs and tables covered with red and white and black Riverdragon fish leather. The pilot sat in a large and comfortable swivel chair before the instrument board. On this was a bank of small closed-circuit TV screens, giving him views of the control centers of the boat. Before him was a microphone which enabled him to speak to anybody on the boat. He controlled the boat with two levers on a small movable board before him. The left stick controlled the port wheel; the right, the starboard. A screen before him was a radar indicator used at night. Another screen showed him the depth of the water from the bottom of the boat as measured by sonar. A toggle on the instrument board could switch the piloting to automatic, though the rule was that a pilot had to be on duty at all times.

Sam was dressed in bleached fish-leather sandals, a white kilt, a white cape and a white officer's cap of plastic and leather. He wore a bleached leather belt with a bleached holster containing a ponderous Mark II .69

four-shooter pistol and a bleached sheath with a ten-inch knife.

He paced back and forth, a big green cigar in his mouth, his hands held straight down except when he removed the cigar. He watched the pilot, Robert Styles, steering the boat for the first time. Styles was an old Mississippi pilot, a handsome youth, no liar, though given to inflating facts. When he had appeared about two years before, Sam had been overcome with joy. For one of the few times in his life, he had wept. He had known Rob Styles when they were both Mississippi pilots.

Styles was nervous, as anybody would be the first time, even the steel-nerved Captain Isaiah Sellers of ancient Mississippi fame. There was nothing to piloting the boat. A one-eyed Sunday school teacher with a hangover could do it, his six-year-old child could do it, once he got the hang of the two sticks. Push forward for increased speed, put in the middle position to stop the wheels, pull back to reverse the wheels. To steer the boat to port, pull back a little on the port stick and forward a little on the starboard stick. To steer to starboard, do the reverse.

But it took some practice before the proper coordination was achieved.

Luckily, there was no memory work involved in piloting a boat on this River. There were no islands, no sandbars, and there would be few logs with snags. If the boat got too close to shallow water, sonar activated an alarm bell. If a boat was ahead at night, or a log hidden in the water, the radar or sonar would indicate it and a red light would flash.

Sam watched Styles for half an hour while the banks floated by and the thousands of people on them waved and cheered. Or cursed, since many were disappointed because they had been eliminated from the crew by the lottery. But he couldn't hear the curses.

Then Sam took over the piloting, and, after another half hour, asked John if he would like to try. John was dressed entirely in black, as if he were determined to do just the opposite of whatever Sam did. But he took the sticks and did well for an ex-king who had never done a lick of work

245

in his life and had always let inferiors do whatever steering was necessary.

The boat sailed up past the dead Iyeyasu's kingdom, now split into three states again, and then Sam ordered the vessel turned back. Rob Styles got fancy and pivoted her "on a dime" as he said, demonstrating her maneuverability. While the port wheel backed, the starboard raced at full speed and the boat rotated as if stuck on a pin. Then she headed downstream. With the current and wind behind her, and the paddle-wheels turning at maximum speed, the *Not for Hire* raced along at sixty miles an hour. But not for too long. Sam had Styles bring her in close to the shore, where the sonar indicated about one foot of clearance between hull and bottom on the port side. Even above the slapping of the wheels and the splashing of water and the whistling and clanging of bells, they could hear the crowds. The faces whizzed by as if in a dream.

Sam opened the fore ports of the pilothouse so they could feel the wind and increase their impression of speed.

The *Not for Hire* raced all the way downstream to Selinujo, and then it turned again. Sam wished, almost, that there was another boat that he could race against. But it was being in heaven to have the only metal, electrically powered Riverboat in existence. A man couldn't have everything, not even in the after-Earthlife.

During the return trip, the huge hatch in the stern was lowered, and the launch slipped out through the entrance into The River. It cut back and forth at top speed and raced ahead of the mother boat. Its steam machine guns traced lines along the water, and the thirty steam guns on the *Not for Hire* shot back, though not at the launch.

The big three-place amphibian monoplane came out of the opening in the stern, too, and its wings were straightened out and locked, and then it took off. Firebrass was at the controls with his woman and Gwenafra as passengers.

A moment later, the tiny, one-seater, open-cockpit scout-fighter was shot off the top of the texas by a steam catapult. Lothar von Richthofen took it up, the wood-alcohol-burning motor buzzing, and raced ahead until he was out of sight. Then he returned, climbed and entertained with the first aerial acrobatics that the Riverworld had ever seen—to the best of Sam's knowledge.

Lothar concluded with a dive at the end of which he fired four rockets into the water and then the twin machine guns. These were .80 caliber and shot aluminum bullets from aluminum cartridges. There were one hundred thousand of these stored on the boat, and when they were all gone, they would not be replaced.

Lothar landed the tiny monoplane on the landing deck, the top of the texas, and the devices caught the hook trailed out by the plane. Even so, the whirling propeller stopped only ten feet from the smokestacks. Lothar took the plane up again and again landed. Then Firebrass returned in the amphibian, and he later took the wheeled plane up for one flight.

Sam looked down through the port front at the marines drilling on the fore part of the broad boiler deck. Under the midnoon sun, which heated the air to an estimated eighty degrees Fahrenheit, they marched back and forth and performed intricate maneuvers under Cyrano's orders. Their silvery duralumin plumed helmets were like those of the ancient Romans. They wore gray-and-red-striped chainmail shirts which fell halfway down their thighs. Their legs were cased in leather boots. They carried rapiers and long knives and the Mark II pistols. They were the pistoleers only, however. The main part of the marines were watching the show; these were the bowmen and the rocketeers.

Seeing Gwenafra's honey-colored head in the crowd on the main deck made him happy.

He saw Livy's dark head near her, and he was unhappy.

Gwenafra, after another six months of a jealousy-ridden life with von Richthofen, had accepted Sam's offer and moved in with him. But Sam still could not see Livy without some pain of loss.

If it were not for Livy, and for John's presence, he would have been as happy as he could be. But she would be with them throughout the possibly forty years of the

247

journey. And John, well, John made him uneasy and prowled through his nightmares.

John had been so willing to let Sam be the captain and so unhesitant about accepting the first mate's position that Sam knew he was up to no good. But when would The Mutiny, as Sam thought of it, take place? It was inevitable that John would try to take over the full command of the Riverboat, and any intelligent man, knowing this, would have dumped him, one way or the other.

But Sam had been too conscience-stricken by his killing of Bloodaxe. He could not commit another assassination, not even if he knew that John would not be permanently dead. A corpse was a corpse, and a double cross was a double cross.

The question was, when would John strike? At the beginning, or much later during the voyage, when Sam's suspicions had been lulled?

Actually, the situation was intolerable. But then it was surprising how much intolerableness a man could tolerate.

A yellow-haired, near-giant entered the pilothouse. His name was Augustus Strubewell, he was John's aide-de-camp, and he had been picked up by John during his sojourn in Iyeyasujo after Hacking's invasion. He had been born in 1971 in San Diego, California, had been an All-American fullback, a captain of the U.S. Marines, decorated for bravery in the Middle East and South America and had made a career in the movies and TV. He seemed a pleasant enough fellow, except that, like John, he bragged of his conquests among women. Sam did not trust him. Anybody who worked for John Lackland had to have something wrong with him.

Sam shrugged. He might as well enjoy himself for the moment. Why let anything rob him of the joy of the greatest day of his life?

He leaned out of the port and watched the marine drill team and the crowd. The sun sparkled on waves, and the breeze was cooling. If it became too warm, he could shut the ports and turn on the air conditioning. From the tall pole on the bow the flag of the *Not for Hire* flapped in the wind. It was square and bore a scarlet phoenix on a light-

248

blue field. The phoenix symbolized the rebirth of mankind.

He waved at the people massed along the bank and pressed a button which set off a series of steam whistles and clanging of bells.

He drew in smoke from his fine cigar and stuck his chest out and paraded back and forth. Strubewell handed John a glass full of bourbon, and then he offered Sam another. Everybody in the pilothouse—Styles, the six other pilots, Joe Miller, von Richthofen, Firebrass, Publius Crassus, Mozart, John Lackland, Strubewell, and three other of John's aides—took a glass.

"A toast, gentlemen," John said in Esperanto. "To a long and happy journey and may we all get what we deserve."

Joe Miller, standing near Sam, the top of his head almost touching the ceiling, held a glass containing about half a quart of bourbon. He sniffed at the amber liquor with his monstrous proboscis and then tasted it with the top of his tongue.

Sam was just about to toss the four-ounce drink down when he saw Joe's apish face grimace.

"What's the matter, Joe?" he said.

"Thith thtuff hath thomething in it!"

Sam sniffed and could detect nothing but the most excellent of Kentucky's best.

But when John and Strubewell and the others reached for their weapons, he threw the liquor in John's face. Yelling, "It's poison!" he dived for the floor.

Strubewell's Mark II pistol boomed. The plastic bullet shattered against the bulletproof plastic of the port above Sam's head.

Joe roared—he sounded like a lion suddenly released from its cage—and he threw his liquor into Strubewell's face.

The other aides fired once and then they fired again. The Mark II pistols were four-shot revolvers which electrically ignited the powder in the aluminum cartridges. They were even larger and heavier than the Mark I's, but they could be fired much more swiftly, and cordite, not black gunpowder, propelled the plastic bullets.

The pilothouse became a fury of booming, deafening explosives, the scream of shattered plastic richocheting, the shouts and screams of men and the bellowing of Joe.

Sam rolled over, reached up and flicked the automatic pilot switch. Rob Styles was on the floor, his arm almost torn off. One of John's aides was dying in front of him. Strubewell went flying over him and banged against the glass and then fell on him. John was gone, fled down the ladder.

Sam crawled out from under Strubewell. Four of his pilots were dead. All of the aides, except for Strubewell, who was only unconscious, were dead. Their necks had been broken or their jaws shattered by Joe. Mozart was crouched quivering in a corner. Firebrass was bleeding from the many plastic fragments, and Lothar was bleeding from a gash in his arm. One of the aides had struck him with a knife just before Joe twisted his head 180 degrees.

Sam arose shakily and looked out the port. The crowd watching the marines had dispersed, but not without leaving a dozen bodies behind. The Marines on the boiler deck were firing at men shooting at them from around the sides of the main deck. Some of the fire seemed to be coming from cabin ports in the main deck.

Cyrano stood with his rapidly dwindling crew of Marines, shouting orders. Then John's men charged, firing, and Cyrano went down. But he was up again, his sword silvery and then red. The enemy broke and ran away, and Cyrano ran after them. Sam shouted, "You fool! Go back!" but he was not heard, of course.

He tried to struggle up out of his shock. John had slipped something into their drinks, poison or a sedative, and only Joe's subhumanly sensitive nose had saved them from drinking and then keeling over and allowing John to take over the pilothouse with little trouble.

He looked out the starboard port. Only a half mile ahead was the huge breakwater behind which the boat was to anchor for the night. Tomorrow, the long journey would officially begin. *Would have begun,* he thought.

He flicked off the automatic pilot toggle switch and

took the control sticks in his hands.

"Joe," he said, "I'm going to run this right up alongside the bank. I may even ground us. Get out the bullhorn. I'll tell the people ashore what's happened, and we'll get help."

He pulled back on the starboard stick and advanced the port stick.

"What's wrong?" he yelled.

The boat was proceeding straight on its course up The River, holding to a distance of about a hundred yards off the shore.

He moved the sticks back and forth, frantically, but the boat did not deviate.

John's voice came from the intercom.

"It's no use, Samuel, Boss, Captain, swine! I have control of the boat. My engineer, the man who will be chief engineer, put in a duplicate set of controls . . . never mind where. I have cut off your controls, and the boat will go where I want it to. So you don't have any advantage at all. Now my men will storm the pilothouse and take you. But I would prefer that there be as little damage as possible. So, if you will just get off the boat, I will let you go unharmed. Provided, that is, that you can swim a hundred yards."

Sam raged and swore and pounded his fists on the instrument panel. But the boat continued on past the dock, while the crowds gathered there waved and cheered and wondered why the boat did not stop.

Lothar, looking out of the stern port, said, "They're trying to sneak up on us!" and he fired at a man who had appeared around the far end of the texas on the hurricane deck.

"We can't hold out long!" Firebrass said. "We don't have much ammunition!"

Sam looked at the fore ports. Some men and women had run out onto the boiler deck and then turned for a stand.

Livy was among them.

There was another charge. A man thrust at Cyrano, who was engaged in running his rapier through the man next to him. Livy tried to knock the blade aside with her

251

pistol, which must have been empty, but the sword went into her stomach. She fell backward with the sword still sticking out of her. The man who had killed her died a second later, when Cyrano's rapier went through his throat.

Sam cried, "Livy! Livy!" and he was out through the door of the pilothouse and running down the ladder. Bullets screamed by him and smashed against the bulkheads and the ladder. He felt a stinging and then heard a shouting behind him, but he did not stop. He was vaguely aware that Joe Miller and the others had run out after him. Perhaps they were trying to rescue him or perhaps they knew that they might as well get out now before they were overwhelmed in the trap of the pilothouse.

There were corpses and wounded everywhere. John's men had not been numerous; he had depended upon surprise, and it had not failed him. Dozens had been shot down in the first volleys, and dozens more had been shot during the panic. Many more had jumped into the water, seeing that there was no way to escape, no place to hide, and they were not armed.

Now the boat was turning into shore, its paddle-wheels operating at full speed, the water flying, the wheels chuff-chuffing, the deck trembling. John was turning the boat into shore, where a number of heavily armed men and women awaited him.

These would be the disaffected, the people who were angered because the lottery had cut them out of a place on the crew. Once they got aboard, they would sweep away the few left in Sam's party.

Sam had run along the hurricane deck after leaving the pilothouse ladder. He held a pistol with two shots left in it and his rapier in the other hand. He did not know how they had gotten into his hands; he had no memory of having removed them from his holster and sheath.

A face appeared at the edge of the deck on the ladder just ahead. He fired at it, and the face dropped back. He was on the edge of the deck then and shooting even as he leaned over to look down the ladder. The plastic bullet did

252

not miss this time. The man's chest erupted red, and he fell back down the ladder, taking two men with him. But others on the deck below raised their pistols, and he had to jump back. The volley missed him, though some bullets striking the edge blew apart and the fragments stung him on the legs.

Joe Miller, behind him, said, "Tham! Tham! There'th nothing to do but jump for it! They got uth thurrounded!"

Below, Cyrano, still wielding his rapier, holding off three men at one time, backed to the railing. Then his blade pierced a throat, the man fell, and Cyrano whirled and leaped over the railing. When he came up he began to swim strongly to get away from the starboard paddle-wheel thrashing toward him.

Bullets struck the sides of the cabins behind Sam, and Lothar cried, "Jump, Sam! Jump!"

But they could not jump yet. They could not have cleared the main deck below, let alone the boiler deck.

Joe had already turned and was running with his great ax toward the men firing from behind the rear of the cabins along the hurricane deck. The bullets streaked toward him, wobbling, leaving a thin trail of smoke, but he was too far away to worry about their accuracy. And he was depending upon his terrifying aspect and his prowess, which they well knew, to panic them.

The others ran behind him until they came to the great paddle-wheel housing. This was about ten feet from the edge of the hurricane deck, and if they stood up on the railing and leaped out, they could grab hold of the big iron eyes through which cables had been secured when the housing had been lifted and then placed over the wheel by the crane.

They jumped, one after the other, while bullets screamed by. They grabbed the eye, their bodies banging into the side of the hard metal housing. But they pulled themselves up and onto the top of the housing and crawled over, stood up and jumped out. The water was thirty feet below, a height which would have made Sam hesitate under different conditions. This time, he went out, fell straight, holding his nose, and plunged into the water feet first.

He came up in time to see Joe jump off, not from the housing but from the main deck. He had fought down the ladder and out across the deck, scattering the pygmies before him. Even so, his hairy skin was splotched with blood. He went over the side in a dive with pistols booming and arrows streaking after him.

Sam dived then, because several of the steam machine guns had been depressed and the .75 caliber bullets were probing for him.

The boat turned back about two minutes later. John must have discovered that his chief enemy had escaped. By then, Sam was ashore and running, though he thought his legs would fold under him. The firing was not renewed. Perhaps John had changed his mind about killing him. He would want Sam to suffer, and Sam would suffer most if he were still at the site of his defeat.

John's voice boomed out from a bullhorn. "Farewell, Samuel! You fool! Thanks for building the Riverboat for me! And I will change its name to one which will suit me better! I go now to enjoy the fruits of your labors! Think of me as much as you please! Farewell!"

His bullhorn-amplified laughter blasted Sam's ears.

Sam came out of his hiding place in a hut and climbed the wall on the edge of the water. The boat had stopped and let down a long gangplank on cables to permit the traitors to come aboard. He heard a voice below him and looked down. There was Joe, his reddish hairs black with water except where the blood was starting to appear again.

"Lothar and Firebrath and Thyrano and Johnthton made it," he said. "How you feel, Tham?"

Sam sat down on the hard-packed dirt and said, "If it would do any good, I'd kill myself. But this world is hell, Joe, genuine hell. You can't even commit a decent suicide. You wake up the next day, and there you are with your problems stuck on you with glue or stuck . . . well, never mind."

"Vhat do ve do now, Tham?"

254

Sam did not reply for a long time. If he couldn't have Livy, Cyrano could not have her, either. He could endure the thought of having lost her if she was not where he could see her.

Later, the shame at exulting in Cyrano's loss would come.

Not now. He was too stunned. The loss of the boat had been even a greater shock than seeing Livy killed.

After all these years of hard work, of grief, of betrayal, of planning, of hurting, of . . . of . . .

It was too much to bear.

Joe was grieved to see him cry, but he sat patiently by until Sam's tears had quit flowing. Then he said, "Do ve thtart building another boat, Tham?"

Sam Clemens rose to his feet. The gangplank was being drawn up by the electromechanical machinery of his fabulous Riverboat. Whistles were shrilling exultantly, and bells were clanging, John would still be laughing. He might even be watching Sam through a telescope.

Sam shook his fist, hoping that John was watching him.

"I'll get you yet, traitor John!" he howled. "I'll build another boat, and I'll catch up with you! I don't care what obstacles I encounter or who gets in my way! I'll run you down, John, and I'll blast your stolen boat out of The River with my boat! Nobody, absolutely nobody, the Stranger, the Devil, God, nobody, no matter what his powers, is going to stop me!

"Some day, John! Some day!"

EPILOGUE

Volume III of the Riverworld series will take Sam Clemens all the way up The River with Richard Francis Burton and the rest of The Twelve to the Misty Tower and the secret of the Ethicals.

Technological Note: Potassium nitrate is prepared on the Riverworld by feeding a certain type of earthworm human excrement. The end product of this diet is crystallized potassium nitrate, which, mixed with charcoal and sulfur, makes black gunpowder.

"We'll get better security, no matter what it takes."

Spoken like a true heir to power, Anne thought. "Thanks for bringing me home, Garrett, but it's late. I'm tired, and I want a hot bath...."

Garrett tipped his head to one side and looked interested. "Want me to stand guard?" All the comfortable feelings she'd been having about the way he was gently taking care of her vanished in a puff. "I meant, of course, that I would just make sure you didn't fall asleep in the tub and drown."

"I don't think that will be a problem, Garrett."

"It certainly wouldn't if I were there," he said cheerfully. "You know, McKenna, it's a darn shame you're so worried about office politics. We could have a lot of fun together."

Leigh Michaels had plans to be the world's best feature-writing newspaper reporter when she graduated at the top of her class from Drake University's School of Journalism. But other things intervened, and instead, she worked in radio, in public relations and as a reference librarian before starting to write romance novels.

But she doesn't see her career as a big change from her original plans. "I still investigate things and report them," she says. "I still dig into people and find out what makes them tick. And if one of my heroines turns out to be the editor of *Time* someday, I'll have all the fun of holding that job and none of the actual work!"

Books by Leigh Michaels

HARLEQUIN ROMANCE
3010—NO PLACE LIKE HOME
3023—LET ME COUNT THE WAYS
3070—A MATTER OF PRINCIPAL
3086—AN IMPERFECT LOVE
3119—AN UNCOMMON AFFAIR
3141—PROMISE ME TOMORROW

HARLEQUIN PRESENTS
1107—CLOSE COLLABORATION
1147—A NEW DESIRE
1245—ONCE AND FOR ALWAYS
1266—WITH NO RESERVATIONS

GARRETT'S BACK
IN TOWN
Leigh Michaels

Harlequin Books

TORONTO • NEW YORK • LONDON
AMSTERDAM • PARIS • SYDNEY • HAMBURG
STOCKHOLM • ATHENS • TOKYO • MILAN

ISBN 0-373-03171-8

Harlequin Romance first edition January 1992

GARRETT'S BACK IN TOWN

CHAPTER ONE

IT WAS ALMOST A MONTH now since the announcement that he was coming back to Lakemont, and ever since then Anne McKenna had seen Garrett's face no matter where she looked. At least it seemed that way, and it was certainly true his photograph had been plastered up in odd places all over the city for the past thirty days.

It was Garrett's face on the huge billboard that dominated the freeway exit to the university campus. It was Garrett's crooked smile on the back of the Metroliner bus that cut Anne off at a traffic light downtown and left her cursing—though she wasn't quite certain whether it was the bus or the smile that annoyed her more. It was Garrett's Roman nose and untidy, windblown hair plastered over every newsstand in the city. And every morning, when she picked up the *Chronicle* from her doormat, there was Garrett staring at her from the top of the front page, with that slightly quizzical twinkle in his eyes, and the tall red letters underneath that teased, *Garrett's Back in Town.*

Anyone who didn't know by now, she thought, must have been in a coma for the past month!

Of course, it would have been more accurate if the headline had said, *Garrett's Coming Back to Town at the End of the Month.* Anne had pointed out the fact to the managing editor the day after the slogan first appeared—but she was forced to agree with him that it didn't have the same sort of catchy rhythm. And she couldn't blame the management of the *Chronicle* for taking advantage of the opportunity to promote the newspaper. Garrett's views had appeared not only on the *Chronicle*'s editorial page five times a week for several years, but in a hundred other papers across the country as well, and for a prizewinning columnist to leave his base in Washington, D.C. to come back home to Lakemont, of course it was a feather in the newspaper's cap.

And the headline was true now, of course. It must be, she told herself, for the first opinion column of Garrett's triumphal return was supposed to be published in tomorrow's Sunday editions. It would be some sentimental pap about how touching it was to return to the old hometown after half a dozen years, Anne thought. Garrett was good at writing that sort of thing. Or perhaps it would be some equally sentimental claptrap about how impossible it was to truly go home at all....

Whichever, after tomorrow the hoopla would die down and the whole city could get back to normal. They could get Garrett off the billboards and the buses and back onto the editorial page where he belonged, where those not interested in his plentiful opinions about the human race could be free to ignore him.

Not that Anne would ignore him. In her position, it was scarcely wise to try. But Garrett's success set her social conscience on edge, just the same. *The whole thing is just one more example of the unfairness of life,* she told herself. *If his name wasn't Garrett, and if his daddy didn't own the newspaper, nobody would be hanging on his word, or giving adoring recognition to his offbeat view of the world. In fact, he'd probably be writing ads for a suburban shopping guide!*

The image tickled her fancy. Yes, Matthew James Garrett II would have been quite good at promoting the sale of used cars. He was certainly never at a loss for a pithy comment—at least in print.

She forced herself to relax. After all, Garrett wasn't worth her time to fret about, and besides, there were plenty of other things demanding her attention on this glorious September afternoon. Saturdays were typically slow days at the *Chronicle,* and the newsroom crew generally had an easy time of putting together the news sections for the Sunday morning edition. But the skeleton size of the work force meant that if anything important did break in the early-evening hours in Lakemont— if the mayor's car hit a tree, for instance, or one of Nicolet University's football players was busted for possession of drugs, or some nut decided to hold hostage a building full of people—then Anne McKenna's job as city editor, in charge of the evening shift, would suddenly get very exciting indeed.

That adrenaline high was one of the things she liked best about her job; the sheer challenge of reducing an unwieldy set of events to a clear, precise, readable front page, in the fewest possible ticks of the clock. Sometimes she even daydreamed about how she would handle a particular story. If the mayor's car *were* to hit a tree, for instance, and if one of the incredible number of gorgeous young women who worked in his office happened to be with him—

She pulled into the *Chronicle*'s parking garage, and the attendant barely glanced at the special sticker in the car window before waving her on and turning back to his radio. He was listening to the university football game, she deduced from the raucous cheering she heard as she pulled away from the tiny booth. Half of Lakemont must be out at the Nicolet stadium this afternoon; they certainly weren't downtown. It made her feel resentful for a moment. Goodness knew she liked football, too, but someone had to put the newspaper out.

She parked in her favorite out-of-the-way spot and paused, leaning against the concrete half wall at the very corner of the ramp, to enjoy a last breath of fresh air before going in. A few blocks to the east of the downtown skyscrapers, Lake Michigan gleamed, unruffled and impossibly blue under the crisp autumn sky. It was too cold now for swimming, but there were still people on the beach, walking, jogging—even a couple of hardy souls sunbathing. She watched the lake for a long, peaceful moment. There was certainly no comparable view from the newsroom, and there probably would not be much opportunity for contemplation, either. . . .

From the corner of her eye she glimpsed a hot-air balloon floating gently above the white sand beach, securely tethered and well away from the water, where it could be seen from all over the downtown area. The *Chronicle*'s balloon, Anne thought, or one just as huge and just as brilliant a shade of yellow gold. But why on earth was it tethered on the beach? Then the breeze caught the gas bag and turned it slightly, and she saw that the balloon had been recently repainted. Just above the newspaper's distinctive logo was a twelve-foot-high reproduction of Garrett's unmistakable face.

For one brief instant Anne wanted to find the nearest hunting rifle and start taking potshots at it.

Then she shook her head and smiled wryly and told herself to be patient; the manufactured excitement of Garrett's homecoming would soon be past, and Lakemont would be calm again.

THE MAYOR did not drive into a tree, but enough other things happened in the city that night to ensure that the newsroom was never quite calm, and it was nearly eight o'clock before everything was under control and Anne could take her dinner break. Even so, she decided to settle for the vending machines on the fifth floor instead of the restaurant in the main lobby—just in case.

The elevators were unusually slow, and she was looking at her watch and tapping her shoe against the black marble floor when one of the general-assignment reporters joined her. "I'm trying to decide whether a tuna fish sandwich from a machine is worth the wait," Anne joked.

The reporter was using the polished-brass elevator doors as a makeshift mirror, checking out the hem of her skirt. Anne thought it was a little strange; Holly Andrews was always neat, but she was no clotheshorse, certainly not when she worked the Saturday night shift.

Holly stopped inspecting her clothes and looked at Anne in surprise. "You aren't going upstairs, then?"

"Upstairs?" The only thing above the newsroom floor was the executive offices and conference rooms, and there was seldom any activity there during the evenings and weekends. "What do you mean, Holly?"

"Don't you ever read the bulletin board, dear girl? Oh, I forgot, you've had a couple of days off, haven't you? Jim Garrett is giving a cocktail party tonight—"

"For the prodigal son," Anne groaned. "Of course. He would."

"Well, why shouldn't he?" Holly asked practically. "It's probably the only chance we regular folks will ever get to meet him."

That, Anne thought, was true enough. The *Chronicle* had a sizable staff, and there was little personal contact between the general employees and top management. Anne knew Jim Garrett, of course, because as publisher he often sat in on the weekly sessions where the *Chronicle*'s news coverage was planned. But she doubted that he would remember her name if he met her outside the newsroom; she was only a second-level employee, after all. And as for his son, who would have even less reason to associate with the newsroom staff...well, Garrett would no doubt recognize her name. Unless, of course, he was so egotistically certain of his views that he paid no attention whatever to those who disagreed.

Relax, Anne, she told herself. *You might not run into Garrett for weeks, in the regular course of events. Maybe not at all.*

Perversely, the thought made her almost look forward to the party. "You're certain everyone is invited?" she asked.

Holly grimaced. "Invited? You know Jim Garrett. I'd say it's more like we're commanded to appear."

Anne smiled. "Oh, I see, it's fear of the boss that moves you. I thought at first that you were dying to meet the famous columnist, the one who thinks he can make or break reputations overnight."

Holly shivered, and with determination pushed the elevator button again. "Anne, I'd think you'd be a bit more careful, considering. You don't even know the man."

"Everybody who reads the *Chronicle* knows him. He makes no secret of his views, Holly."

The doors whooshed open and a blond vision in a floor-length bronze satin evening gown stepped out. Anne's mouth dropped open; it took a second for her even to recognize the *Chronicle*'s society editor. She was accustomed to seeing Dominique Delacourt in the elegant designer dresses she always sported at the office, but they hardly compared to this.

Dominique said briskly, "Don't bother to hold the elevator, girls. I'll catch the next one." She vanished into the newsroom without waiting for an answer.

Holly said under her breath, "I wonder what made her get dressed up like a tart at a circus?"

Then, almost in unison, they turned back to staring at their own reflections in the polished brass.

Anne straightened the cuff of her pine green dress—plain and practical, nicely tailored, but hardly the sort of thing she'd have chosen for a party—and tried to shake her blue black hair into smoothness. "She's got to be going somewhere else," she said, almost to herself. "That can't be required dress for a *Chronicle* party."

"I'm holding you responsible," Holly said drearily. "Because if you're wrong, we'll both be fodder for the famous columnist."

"Not a chance," Anne said stoutly. "We're not important enough."

The party filled the largest conference room and spilled over into the neighboring offices and even the elevator lobby. At least half the *Chronicle*'s staff was there, Anne concluded, and not one of them was wearing evening clothes. Two reporters were nose to nose in a corner, loudly disagreeing with the mayor's latest plan to cut crime, and Holly's ears perked. "I really want to hear that discussion," she said earnestly.

"Deserter," Anne accused good-naturedly.

She took a long, slow look around the room and didn't see Garrett anywhere. But the door of the publisher's office, in a corner overlooking the city's skyline, was open. *Perhaps,* she thought, *guests are being ushered in a few at a time for a sort of royal presentation!*

Across the room was a long table loaded with food, which struck her as much more appealing at the moment, anyway. The caterer's man at the portable bar in the corner gave her a tall glass of tonic water, and she drifted across the room to check out the food. The array would have put the average deli to shame, and she looked at it with a warm glow of well-being for a few seconds before reaching for a plate. Bless Holly, she thought as she picked up two slices of sourdough bread. No matter the occasion, this certainly beats the plastic and cardboard that comes out of the vending machines!

A couple of minutes later she looked up from her half-made sandwich just as a group of people came out of the publisher's private sanctum. It included most of the senior staff of the *Chronicle:* the managing editor, the head of the legal department, the directors of advertising and marketing and circulation, the publisher himself and—

Garrett looked younger than his photograph, Anne thought a bit bemusedly. It took her by surprise. If anything, she would have expected the opposite: that the photo he chose to use would be an attempt to hold on to lost youth. Not that the man was exactly old, if it came down to that, but he was in his middle thirties. What right did he have to walk around looking half a dozen years younger, as if he didn't have a care in the world—

Now you've got it, she told herself wryly. *It's because he doesn't have anything to worry about.*

She watched with interest as he broke away from the group outside the publisher's office and began to work the crowd, shaking a hand here and there, threading his way through the mob efficiently, without waste of time, but also without a hint of impatience.

I wonder why he hasn't gone into politics, she thought idly. He certainly had the gift of crowd control, and the right looks to impress the voters. He was tall and broad-shouldered, with a superb healthy-looking tan. He even had that slight intangible air of being a bad boy, which voters seemed to love. His thick honey-colored hair was just a little longer than that of the other men in the room, and his clothes—well, she'd bet that his tweed jacket hadn't come off the rack in any ordinary department store, but he wore it with a negligent air that said he'd owned it for a hundred-odd years.

Not politics, though, Anne thought. There was too much ironic humor in him, and too many impossible opinions. Perhaps he was holding out for a new variety of church, with himself as head prophet; he'd be good at that, too.

She smiled a little at the thought, and was startled to see an interested gleam spring into those impossibly dark brown eyes of his. Only then did she realize that he had not simply been greeting the crowd, but purposefully working his way closer to her.

Her tongue seemed to be stuck to the roof of her mouth. What on earth did Garrett have to say to her? And why was he coming straight to her side? He didn't— *couldn't*—know who she was, could he?

He veered slightly at the last moment, picked up a plate and began to pile it with potato salad.

Anne released the breath she hadn't realized she was holding, slowly, carefully and—she hoped—silently. She put a thick layer of turkey on her sandwich and moved casually on down the table, feeling like a battlefield coward who would cut and run if only there were a safe retreat.

Garrett was right behind her. They reached for the bowl of olives at the same time; Anne pulled back, and Garrett solicitously spooned several onto the edge of her plate and murmured, "I didn't expect to find someone like you at my party, you know."

The almost naive line took Anne off guard, and she looked up in surprise. He had sounded impressed, and admiring. It didn't ring true; she was attractive enough, if one happened to like small-boned women with dark blue eyes and heart-shaped faces, but she was hardly so drop-dead beautiful that men swarmed around her, and she had never been under any illusions about it.

"Silence?" he said huskily. "Not what I would have expected from you, Anne McKenna."

Only an intent listener would have wondered if there might be a challenge under the commonplace words. It was there, of course; Anne heard it, and a sort of breathless anticipation began to rise from her diaphragm. Crossing swords with Garrett was the most exciting thing likely to happen at any cocktail party this year, that was certain.

So he did know who she was; she wondered briefly if it had been coincidence that identified her, or if he had asked someone to point her out. Not that it mattered. The important thing was knowing that it had gotten under his skin, after all, that response she had written last month to a column of his she had disagreed with. And since he had gone out of his way to approach her, it must have stung him deeply.

"It was not only silence," she pointed out, "but shocked silence."

His eyebrows lifted. "At the compliment? Surely—"

"Not at all. I was just surprised that you couldn't come up with a better line than that. After all, you're the 'Man of the Moment—'" she added tomato and cheese to her sandwich and murmured with a frown "—a *brief* moment, one hopes, but at any rate..."

His eyes lighted with a golden glow of satisfaction. "So that vicious personal attack on me on the editorial page didn't vent all your fury, after all," he said. "Tell me, Miss McKenna, are you still holding that grudge about my name?"

"Of course I'm not holding a grudge, Garrett. You see, it isn't a grudge at all. It never was." She put up her chin and said firmly, "It's a moral conviction that if you'd been called Smith or Jensen or Dubrovnik instead of Matthew James Garrett II—do people ever call you Junior, by the way?"

"Not if they know what's good for them." He leaned against the corner of a nearby desk and began to eat his potato salad.

She was vaguely disappointed that he took it so calmly. "If it wasn't for your name, you wouldn't have a column at all, and you certainly wouldn't have your picture on buses and billboards and hot-air balloons." She took a long, thoughtful swallow of tonic water and added, "Though, when I think about it, I can't imagine a better forum for your work than a hot-air balloon."

Garrett laughed at that, a deep and genuine chuckle. He didn't seem to notice, or care, that they were drawing the attention of the surrounding crowd. "McKenna, haven't you ever heard it isn't wise to pick a fight with a man who buys ink by the barrel?"

"Figuratively speaking in this case, of course," Anne said sweetly, "since you don't even buy the ink yourself, actually. Your father does." She put a layer of roast beef on her sandwich and drizzled it with horseradish sauce. "And the same goes for your need for caution— I have access to a lot of ink myself."

He shook his head. "You disappoint me." He settled himself more carefully on the corner of the desk, as if he was prepared to sit through a lengthy discussion. "You're tripping yourself up in your own logic, you know. If you and everybody else at the *Chronicle* has the same freedom of the press, then it can't be my name that's the magic word."

"That is the most ridiculous excuse. Take your column for tomorrow's paper, for instance."

Garrett looked quizzical. "And how have you happened to read it already?" he asked gently. "I know, despite all the nasty things you say about me, you're really a fan."

"I was proofreading the page," she said, and then when he started to smile, regretted the attempt to defend herself. "As I was saying—"

Dominique Delacourt appeared beside Garrett, her bronze satin skirt swaying gently. She tipped up her face; Garrett kissed her cheek. "It's lovely to have you home, Matt," she said, slipping her arm through his. "But don't get bigheaded and think that I dressed up this way on your account. I have to make an appearance at the Carousel Ball after this—are you going? You should, you know."

Anne nodded politely to them both and moved to the far end of the table to add lettuce to her sandwich.

I should thank her for rescuing me before I made an even bigger fool of myself, Anne thought. *Whatever prompted me to start squabbling with him?* It was bad enough to do it in print, when she'd had a chance to think about what she was saying. But the man was impossible in person. He could change the subject in the middle of a word—

The small knot of people near the door of the publisher's office broke and shifted to new patterns, and two men wandered off together. One of them was Jim Garrett, his hands in the pockets of his trousers, his head bent. The other was the *Chronicle*'s senior corporate attorney, tall and rangy and somber, and looking very worried.

"He looks good, Jim," the attorney was saying. "He sounds good. But—"

"He's matured very well," Jim Garrett agreed.

It's not my fault, Anne told herself, *that my job has trained me to select a voice or two from a babble of sound, and ignore the rest. I'm not trying to eavesdrop. If Jim Garrett doesn't want to be overheard, then let him go into his office and shut the door.*

"This idea of putting him in charge—"

Jim Garrett shrugged. "Somebody's got to be in charge."

"But it's not as if you have to name your successor tonight, you know. You'll be in the hospital what, two or three days? Out of the office for a couple of weeks, perhaps? There's no reason to jump into anything. Why turn over the reins to an untried—"

"I'm not jumping into anything. But still, it's made me think about what will happen to the *Chronicle* in the long run. I'm not a young man anymore—"

Their voices faded into the background noise.

So that was the reason Garrett had come home, Anne thought. To follow in the tradition of his father, of his grandfather. To take his place, in turn, as the publisher of a proud and respected newspaper.

To step into a job that had been waiting for him since the day he was born. A job he was not trained for. A job for which his only real qualifications was his name.

It made her feel half-sick.

It wasn't that Garrett was completely untalented, she told herself; he could certainly write. But an unholy gift for alternately entertaining and infuriating an audience was hardly qualification enough for a job like this. A newspaper's publisher carried the weight of public responsibility.

And I'm not the only one who thinks he's lacking, Anne thought. The attorney had obviously shared her doubts; looking good and sounding good weren't enough, he'd implied, but Jim Garrett hadn't seemed to hear the protest. And Jim Garrett was very nearly all-powerful when it came to the *Chronicle,* so if he wanted to install his son in the publisher's chair, there was little anyone else could do to stop him. Matthew James Garrett II would sooner or later be the new boss.

And in five short minutes in his company, Anne had already managed to bring herself to his attention as a major troublemaker.

That's just great, McKenna, she told herself. *There are faster ways to commit professional suicide than to tell the new boss he's incompetent, but there aren't many surer ones!*

"Anne," said Holly, sounding a bit plaintive. "How in heaven's name are you planning to eat that thing?"

She looked down at her plate, where a skyscraper of a sandwich wobbled uncertainly. There were things on that plate she didn't even recognize, much less remember putting there. Her hands had stayed busy while her mind was preoccupied, that was certain.

She sighed. She certainly wasn't hungry anymore. "I'm going back to my desk," she said. "I've obviously been away from it too long as it is." She set down the plate and made her way to the door, hoping her departure looked like a calm retreat, and not the rout it was.

THE PRESSES had started to roll, and the final Sunday editions were being assembled and loaded onto the trucks. Now even a major disaster could not stop the process. No matter what the news, it would have to wait for tomorrow, when they would start from scratch again.

It was one of the things Anne liked best about newspapers; every day was a truly fresh start, a new challenge. That was also the discouraging part of the job, because no matter how good-looking today's paper was, how packed full of news, how crisply edited and elegantly displayed, it would not matter tomorrow. Of course, the occasional problems were soon forgotten, too.

But not anymore, she thought. Garrett had proved tonight that there was nothing wrong with his memory. She'd bet he could quote every line of that article she'd written.

She put on her gray tweed coat, slung her handbag over her shoulder and tucked a couple of books under her arm. Rather than wait for an elevator she walked down the three flights to the little bridge between the *Chronicle* building and the parking ramp. The pleasant warmth of the day had given way to one of the cold, crisp nights that Wisconsin was famous for in the fall. She clutched the collar of her coat close around her neck and wished she had parked a little closer to the door.

Well, there was no sense in trying to patch things up right now, that was certain. If she backed down on what she'd said, Garrett would only write her off as a hypocrite, and be even more inclined to rid himself of her. She was committed.

She was fumbling for her keys as she approached her car, and she didn't even hear the soft footsteps behind her until a hand seized her shoulder and spun her roughly around. "What the—" she began angrily, and bit her tongue as she stumbled heavily against the side of the car. She saw only a shadowy face, and thought, astonished, *My God, I'm being mugged!*

The straps of her handbag tightened around her arm like a tourniquet as her attacker seized the bag and pulled. Anne held on, almost convulsively, and kicked at him. Her toe connected with his shin, but at a cost—her pump flew off her foot and slid along the concrete, vanishing into the shadows.

The man swore and pushed her roughly, one hand against her breastbone, and she went down hard on the rough concrete floor and began to scream, too infuriated to think of giving up her stranglehold on the bag.

She could hear voices at the end of the walkway, and the knowledge gave additional power to her shrieks. It seemed forever before there was a masculine shout, followed by footsteps running toward her. Finally the excruciating tension on her arm relaxed as the mugger let go of the handbag and fled toward the corner of the ramp, leaping a low wall and plunging down the stairway that led into the dark night.

Her rescuer stopped at the top of the stairs, as if he couldn't decide whether to pursue the villain or aid the victim, then shook his head and came toward her. Anne tried to pull herself into a sitting position, but every muscle in her body was quivering, each to a separate rhythm, and she couldn't make them all cooperate.

He stood over her, hands on hips, and said, "McKenna, you damned fool—hasn't anyone ever told you not to resist when you're attacked?"

He sounds as if he could chew up the concrete, Anne thought. It was an interesting side of his character, but not surprising; of course, Garrett would turn his wrath on the victim!

"Don't you have any sense at all? People like that are dangerous!"

"Is that why you didn't chase him?" she asked nastily.

The man who had been with Garrett caught up with them. "Matt, don't lecture the poor girl," he said firmly. "She's hurt." He knelt beside Anne, his brow furrowed. "Miss . . . McKenna, isn't it?"

Garrett said, "Hurt? With the noise she was making, Dad? I doubt it. Lady, you've got a scream like a steam whistle."

"I could be mortally wounded and in shock, Garrett," Anne said thickly. Her throat was beginning to hurt, as if her vocal cords were swelling.

"And it's your own damn fault if you are, fighting like that. What's in the stupid purse that's so valuable, anyway?" But he dropped to one knee beside her and began to check for injuries.

She winced as he ran his hands over her shoulders, one of which had collided with the side of the car, but she could move her arm freely and after a minute he moved on to check the rest of her.

"Watch where you put your hands, Garrett," she recommended coolly, as his fingertips slid up her calf and over her knee.

He raised an eyebrow and muttered, "I'm watching, all right," but he didn't stop the gentle probing. He found the spot on her hip where she had bounced against the concrete, and Anne winced again.

"Shall I go and call an ambulance, do you think, Matt?" Jim Garrett asked quietly.

"I'm fine, really," Anne said. The blood was still pounding against her eardrums, but not as violently as before. "Just a little rough around the edges, that's all."

Garrett said, "It would be a lot more useful if you'd go down and ask the garage attendant if he saw the mugger, Dad." He helped her to stand up.

Anne was a little wobbly, and standing on one foot didn't help that. She tried to lean against the car without being obvious about it, but she bumped her hip again and had to bite her lip hard against the pain. That was probably why she said irritably, "Don't you think it's a little late to be going after him? He's long gone."

"What did you expect me to do, anyway?" Garrett said. "Fly off the edge of the ramp and catch him at the bottom? Sorry, but I left my Superman suit in the car."

"You're right, Matt," Jim Garrett interjected, "the attendant might have seen something. I'll go down and ask, but ..." He hesitated. "What about Miss McKenna?"

"I'll see that she gets home, Dad. See you later."

Anne didn't bother to quarrel with that; honesty said she wasn't capable of driving. She was still a little shakier than she liked to admit.

Garrett retrieved her keys, threw her handbag and the books into the back of the car and helped her into the passenger seat. Anne had to admit that sitting down was a relief, despite the tenderness in her hip.

He eyed her bare foot.

"Over there somewhere." She pointed. "I lost it when I kicked him in the shin."

He found her shoe in a dark corner and brought it back. "Next time, if you must fight, aim higher." He slid into the driver's seat, groaning as his thigh hit the turn-signal lever. "Where did you get this car, the toy store?" he growled, groping for the control to push back the seat. "And why did you park in such a godforsaken corner? It's no wonder the guy picked on you—you looked like an easy target."

"It's a brand-new car. I hate to let the doors get all battered up by careless drivers, so..." She was feeling very foolish.

"So you park where no one else does and get yourself battered up. Yes, I suppose there's a kind of convoluted, Anne-McKenna-style logic to that. Well, don't do it on the night shift anymore, all right?"

She sniffed. "I am so sorry to have disturbed your peaceful evening, Garrett." *You're only making things worse, Anne,* she told herself. *Have you lost your mind entirely?*

Once the first tear escaped and trickled hotly down her cheek, there was no stopping the rest from falling. The adrenaline rush had passed, and the genuine horror at what had happened, and at what could have happened if her attacker had been armed or if no one had been close at hand, was sinking into her soul. "Dammit, Garrett," she sobbed, "don't sneer at me! I don't know why I fought him. I hurt all over, and my dress is ruined, and I broke my fingernail, and—"

"You could have lost one hell of a lot more than a fingernail." It was gruff.

That nonreassuring thought made her cry even harder. "And I didn't even have any dinner, and—"

He turned toward her, and muttered something under his breath as his knee connected with the steering wheel.

"And don't tell me again that I'm a fool," she stumbled on irrationally. "I know I'm a fool, and I don't even want you to talk to me anymore—"

"All right," he said calmly. His arm went around her, gently, so as not to agitate her wounded shoulder, and his mouth came down on hers, so suddenly that she couldn't even blink in surprise.

His lips were hard, and the palm of his hand was cupping the back of her head slightly, so that she couldn't pull away. She couldn't seem to breathe, either, and her head was swimming and everything was starting to look blue by the time he let her go.

For almost ten full seconds after he released her, there was total silence. Then Anne finally gathered enough breath to gasp, "You sexist pig! I ought to—"

Garrett started the engine and said, sounding rather pleased with himself, "Do you honestly mean no one has ever done that before? I'll bet it's the only way guaranteed to shut you up. Arguing with you certainly doesn't do it. Now, first things first, what do you want to eat?"

CHAPTER TWO

"YOU DON'T have to feed me," Anne said, almost sullenly.

"I certainly shouldn't have to. You had a lovely sandwich at the party, and you didn't eat a bite of it. Is this a new form of dieting, construct a huge meal and then set it down and walk away?"

So he had seen that embarrassing gaffe. *Well,* she told herself stoically, *you didn't expect anything different, did you? He doesn't miss much.*

Garrett started to whistle, rather tunelessly. The sound rasped her nerves.

At the foot of the parking ramp the attendant came out of his little booth to peer into the car. Anne thought he looked livelier than she had seen him in all the months he'd been on the job, and slightly suspicious of the man behind the wheel, too. *Good instincts, Fred,* she thought. *Just a little late, though.*

"Miss McKenna," he said breathlessly. "You're all right, then? I didn't see anything at all, or I'd have called the police right away."

"Don't feel guilty," Garrett recommended. "He could have been lurking up there for hours."

Anne shuddered. "Thanks," she muttered. "That really makes me feel secure."

Garrett sent a crooked grin at her and a half salute, half wave at Fred, and gunned the motor. Anne would have protested at the less than gentle treatment of her car, except that she was still feeling rather shaky.

Three blocks down the street, Garrett pulled into a small parking lot. "Is Chinese food all right?" he said, looking doubtfully up at the garishly blinking red sign. "At least I assume that's what the Red Dragon sells—"

Anne was inspecting the damage to her clothes. One sleeve of her coat was half-ripped out, she saw with dismay. "You could just take me straight home," she said.

"Nope," Garrett said cheerfully. "I can't, because you haven't told me where you live. Sit still. I'll be right back."

The car door slammed, and the swirl of cold air it had admitted settled around her. She was relieved that he hadn't dragged her inside—ripped clothes, rumpled hair, torn stockings and all. She must look like a refugee. And yet the other half of her was annoyed because he so obviously didn't want to be seen with her in this condition, even in a place like the Red Dragon.

Idiot, she told herself. *The truth is you'd be irritated with him right now no matter what he did!*

It was only a few minutes before he was back. She looked at the size of the three bags he was juggling, and said, "How much food do you think I can eat?"

"Don't forget, I saw that sandwich. Besides, it isn't just you I'm worried about. Fighting off muggers gives me an appetite."

She swallowed a catty comment and tried to smother her sigh. She could hardly object if he invited himself to share, could she? After all, it was his food! "It's the Sherwood Forest town houses off Windsor Avenue."

"Nice," he said calmly. "New town house, new car— I had no idea that *Chronicle* city editors got paid so well."

There was not a hint of accusation about it, but Anne felt fury beginning to rise from the pit of her stomach. "I suppose the first thing you'll do is propose salary cuts," she said irritably. "Well, for your information, I rent the town house, and I've only got a new car because an elderly lady on her way to bridge club ran a red light and totaled my old one two months ago."

Garrett held up both hands in surrender. "Peace! I was only commenting on how well you must be doing—"

"And please put your hands back on the steering wheel," she recommended. "My insurance isn't as good as hers was, I'm afraid. The turn is up there."

He let the car idle down the slope from the avenue into the town house complex, and said, sounding very disappointed, "But it's so ordinary. From the name, I expected moats and drawbridges and towers and turrets—"

"Come on, Garrett. In a new development?"

"Well, if they're going to name it Sherwood Forest, they ought to plant trees at least," he said unrepentantly, as he pulled the car into the driveway she pointed out.

"There is a tree." She climbed out, trying to muffle a groan as her abused muscles protested, and started up the walk.

He looked at the single maple tree on the handkerchief-size front lawn and shook his head. "Quite a tree, too. It's no taller than I am." He began digging bags of Chinese food out of the back of the car.

"My keys, please?" Anne said crisply.

He tossed them to her. "Don't forget your purse. I'd hate for it to be stolen out of the car, after all the effort you went to tonight to protect it."

She wearily retraced her steps, and he gave her the handbag. He looked so innocent that she almost threw it at him.

Inside, he stood in the minuscule foyer, his arms full of bags, his head almost bumping the pewter chandelier, and said, "I take it all back—what I said about you doing so well. It's only a dollhouse!"

She had to admit the town house looked a lot smaller with him in it; somehow, despite his lean frame, Garrett seemed to take up a lot more room than any other six-foot male she'd ever known.

"Go get out of those clothes and check the damage while I make you some tea," he ordered. "Unless you'd rather have brandy?"

"You sound like my grandmother," she said grumpily.

"Are you complaining? I'll do my best to change, if you'll tell me who you'd rather I tried to sound like." Then he grinned and vanished around the corner, and as she dragged herself up the steps to her bedroom, she heard cabinet doors banging in the kitchen.

It took the last drops of energy she possessed to strip off her clothes. Her dress was ripped, her stockings were in shreds, one shoe was twisted completely out of shape. There was already an angry black bruise on her hip, and a nasty scratch down the side of her face. How in heaven's name had she gotten that?

She didn't bother to inspect the rest of her body. For one thing, she didn't particularly want to anticipate how many bits of her were apt to be purple and painful tomorrow; she'd find out soon enough. Besides, the sooner she got back downstairs, the sooner Garrett would finish his Chinese food and be gone, and she'd be free to sink into a tub of hot water and soak out her

aches. So she dragged out a faded gray sweatsuit embla-
zoned with the Nicolet University crest and managed to
crawl into it and back down the stairs.

The cartons of food were already laid out on the glass-
topped coffee table in the living room. The drapes had
been drawn, and Garrett was kneeling in front of the
fireplace, where he had coaxed a tiny blaze to life. Anne
thought he was certainly making himself at home.

She lowered herself into a chair with a sound that was
half sigh and half gasp of pain. Garrett sat back on his
heels and looked her over closely. Whatever he saw
seemed to satisfy him, though, for he turned back to the
fire. As soon as it was crackling greedily away at the first
small log, he pushed himself back on the hearth rug and
looked around. ''Is there anybody you'd like me to
call?''

She shook her head.

''You're all alone?'' It was gentle.

The question annoyed her, for some reason she
couldn't fathom, for it hadn't been insensitive. ''No, I'm
not, as a matter of fact. I have two brothers and a perfectly good set of parents in this town. I just don't see
any reason to call them in the middle of the night and
upset them, too.''

''Fair enough,'' he said calmly. ''I was actually more
concerned that someone might come bounding in from
an evening with the guys and misinterpret what he
found.''

She bit her tongue over that one. From around the
corner, the kettle started to whistle, and Garrett got up
to go and make her tea. It seemed to take an awfully long
time, and finally she followed him to the kitchen.

He was dunking a tea bag in a mug full of steaming
water. ''You aren't supposed to drown the poor thing,''

she said, trying to keep her voice light, and took over the job.

Garrett put one hand under her chin and turned her face to the light so he could study the scratch on her cheek. It seemed an unnecessarily long inspection, and finally she removed his hand from her chin and went to get out plates and flatware. "There's some beer in the refrigerator, and some soft drinks," she said. "Obviously tea isn't your thing, or you'd know how to make it."

He didn't argue with that. He followed her back to the living room with a bottle of imported beer. "Sure you wouldn't rather have one of these?" he asked.

She looked at the bottle with a jaundiced eye. "No, thanks, I've never liked the stuff."

The incongruity didn't seem to bother him. "Well, someone has good taste," he murmured.

Anne ignored him, sat down—carefully—on the couch and opened a carton. The savory smell of Mongolian beef wafted out, and she put a small spoonful on her plate.

Garrett poked at the fire and stopped to study the portrait that hung above the mantel. It was a huge photograph, soft and dreamy, of a very small girl with long black hair and chubby cheeks, wearing a blue velvet dress, with a huge book open on her lap and four boys, all older, gathered around her.

"You have two brothers, did you say?" he asked.

"Two here in Lakemont," Anne said shortly. "Two more who live elsewhere. If you'd like a full rundown, that's Patrick and Brendan at the top, Colin and Rowan—"

He turned to look at her in amazement. "With a set of names like that, how did you get to be just plain Anne?"

"Believe me," she said dryly, "I start every day with grateful thanks to my guardian angel for not letting them name me Bridget."

Garrett nodded understandingly. "It would have been a bit much for a byline, that's true."

She investigated another carton. It was chicken this time, rich with garlic and cashews. "Look, Garrett," she said. "If you're hinting that I should apologize for what I said in that article—"

He looked outraged. "Me? Hint? I wouldn't lower myself to that." He set down the beer bottle carefully on the coffee table. "But of course if you think you should..."

"I must warn you that I have no intention of doing that," Anne went on, as if he hadn't interrupted.

Garrett laughed and started to fill his plate. "You're feeling better," he said.

She nodded, half-surprised herself.

"You're not going to go into hysterics on me, after all?"

"Are you disappointed?"

"As a matter of fact, yes. I thought I'd have a chance to study a good clinical case."

But his tone was almost bantering, and Anne relaxed a little. She cleaned her plate almost absentmindedly, and curled up on the couch with her head on a needle-point pillow and stared at the flames. The log had caught nicely, and the soft hiss of the embers and the occasional crackle of sap were soothing, almost hypnotic.

"This is pleasant," he said. "Even though it's tiny. I suppose that means apartments are expensive around here."

"Relatively high, yes. Between the university and the growth in the hospital complex downtown, there aren't enough places for people to live. Why worry about it? You've just moved in with your father, haven't you?"

Garrett put another small log on the fire. "Only until he's recovered from his surgery, thank you very much. Then I'll be looking for a place of my own."

It didn't surprise her, exactly. She had a lovely, easy relationship with her own parents, but she still hadn't been able to wait to get out on her own. And for someone like Garrett, there was no doubt a woman, or an incessant, ever-changing stream of women, more likely! She had her doubts that Jim Garrett would exactly approve of that.

"I just heard about his surgery tonight," she said.

Garrett looked quizzical. "That's astounding. I told him that he couldn't hope to keep it secret, but perhaps he was right after all. What kind of a newspaper are you running down there, anyway?"

She ignored the jab. "It's nothing serious, I hope."

Garrett shrugged. "Serious enough. It's his coronary arteries."

"But I thought he said just a few days in the hospital—"

They've got some new techniques, so it isn't like open-heart surgery anymore. But it's not a day at the races, either. His doctor wanted to do it last month, said he could have a heart attack at any moment, but Dad insisted on waiting till I was home."

To run things at the newspaper, Anne finished in her mind, just in case it didn't go well, or he recovered more slowly than he expected. And, ultimately, to take over altogether. Well, it was apparent that Garrett knew what was expected of him, and approved. At least, he was obviously back in Lakemont to stay.

"So that's where you got it," she said.

"Got what?"

"That stubborn streak of yours."

Garrett grinned. "Me? My father is stubborn, yes. I'm just determined and persistent."

"You're obstinate and bullheaded," she said lazily, and looked up at him with a tiny frown. "You know, Garrett, I can't figure you out. You just don't fit any pattern at all. Every time I conclude that you're a flaming, bleeding-heart liberal, you endorse something that's so conservative it's reactionary."

"That's part of my charm," he agreed.

"What charm? Take that column of yours on the chances of another big earthquake in California—it's heartless to suggest that the government shouldn't help the victims when it hits."

"I didn't," he protested. "I only said that no one ordered them to build on top of a fault line. If they're dumb enough to do that and then not buy insurance, why should the taxpayers bail them out? Nobody would come to my financial aid if I drove my car a hundred miles an hour through a jungle and ruined it, and that's no more careless—"

"I'll bet you're even against Santa Claus and the Tooth Fairy."

"Santa Claus, yes," he said thoughtfully. "The old guy has gotten far too commercialized. The Tooth Fairy, well, I'll give her the benefit of the doubt for now. But I'll bet there's something crooked there somewhere."

Anne yawned. "Aren't you a bit young to be the morals guardian of the Western world?"

He looked very solemn. "Somebody's got to do it."

But his tone was mild, and so she laughed instead of getting irate all over again.

The fire was dying down by the time she finally, almost reluctantly, said, "We never did call the police, Garrett."

He poked at the log and settled back, cross-legged, on the hearth rug. "I'm sure Dad took care of it, and I suppose they'll want to talk to you tomorrow. Not that it will do much good, unless you think you can identify the guy."

She thought about it. "He was just a kid. No, I don't think I could. Not even hair color. It all happened so suddenly."

"And the only thing I saw was blue jeans and a black leather jacket, a description that must fit half the males in downtown Lakemont on any given night."

She yawned. "Well, I'd rather not have my mother reading about it in the *Chronicle*, I'll admit."

"Ah, now we're involved with the freedom of the press, and that's an entirely different matter. Haven't we had this argument before?"

She yawned again, hugely. "Are you referring to your contention that freedom of the press is only guaranteed to the man who owns one?"

"I didn't say it that way, you did. That's one thing about you, Just Plain Anne. You may be dead wrong in what you say, but you've got a knack for saying it well."

She didn't quite know how to answer that, so she said, "I don't suppose it will make any difference. The police are so understaffed as it is."

"And the ramp is private property, so there's a limit to what they can do, anyway. Don't worry about it. We'll get better security up there, no matter what it takes."

Spoken like a true heir to power, Anne thought. But she was far too weary to think about it anymore tonight; it was well into the wee hours of the morning. "Thanks for bringing me home, Garrett," she said. "But it's late, and I want a hot bath—"

He tipped his head to one side and looked interested. "Want me to stand guard?"

All the comfortable feelings she'd been having about the way he was so gently taking care of her vanished in a puff. "I think I can manage alone, thanks."

He added hastily, "I meant, of course, that I would just make sure you didn't fall asleep in the tub and drown."

"I don't think that will be a problem, Garrett."

"It certainly wouldn't if I were there," he said cheerfully. "You know, McKenna, it's a darned shame you have to be so politically shortsighted. We could have a lot of fun together."

She got him to the front door eventually, and locked the dead bolt when he left. And she didn't even ask how he planned to get home. That, she told herself tartly, was *his* problem.

"WHAT DO YOU MEAN, you were mugged?" Rudy Balfour sounded incredulous. He was standing with one hand braced on the trunk of the tiny maple tree, in the precise center of the patch of leaves Anne was trying to rake. "Anne, darling . . ."

Anne cursed her own runaway tongue for telling him what had happened. After all, no matter what happened to her, it wasn't Rudy's business anymore. But today the whole side of her face was faintly blue, and Rudy had spotted it right away and asked rather snidely if her latest date was responsible. After that accusation, anything but the truth would have made her look even more of a fool.

Dammit, she thought. She hadn't had a glimpse of the man in two solid weeks. Why did he have to come around today, anyway?

"You know, *mugged*," she said. "As in pushed around and knocked down and robbed."

"Knocked down?" He looked her over. "Well, at least you weren't hurt. That's one good thing."

The only good thing she could find about it, Anne thought bitterly, was that Rudy couldn't see the rest of the damage. The bruise on her hip was completely black now, and she could identify each separate muscle in her body, because every one of them ached. Raking leaves was sheer agony, and yet she thought that sitting still would, in the long run, be worse. "Would you mind moving a bit, Rudy?"

"What? Oh." He dodged her rake. "You know you shouldn't carry cash, Anne."

"I think I had all of ten dollars on me last night."

"Well, that's good. There's still the trouble of losing your credit cards and things like that, of course, but—"

She winced as an abused muscle in her leg protested, and didn't tell him that she hadn't lost her handbag after all. Garrett was right, she thought. No amount of money was worth this discomfort. No one with any sense resisted when attacked, not over a simple handbag!

Rudy hadn't missed the fleeting expression of pain, but he misunderstood its cause. "Don't tell me you've forgotten to cancel your credit cards. Anne, you fool—"

"Don't jump on me, Rudy. We're not engaged any-more. Besides, I've already been through it all with the police this morning, and frankly there is nothing you can add."

Rudy wasn't listening. He said a bit breathlessly, "Would you look at that?"

She had never heard quite that note of astonished ad-miration in Rudy's voice before, and so she turned around hastily, expecting a modern-day Lady Godiva at the very least.

But it was a car, pulling quietly up to the curb. Not just any car, either, but a huge, very old cream-colored convertible with the top down. It had running boards and a spare tire strapped to the side, a radiator grille that dominated the entire front end and a low sporty wind-shield. And getting out from behind the wheel, wearing dark glasses and a rust-colored sweater with the sleeves pushed up, his hair tousled by the wind—

"Hello, Garrett," she said with resignation, and kept raking.

"Garrett?" Rudy said. "That's Garrett? He looks like he's pretending to be the Great Gatsby."

She had to smile at that. Garrett must have heard it, she thought, but he didn't even twitch. Instead he came up the sidewalk slowly, and said, "Dad tried to call you to see how you were doing, Anne, and when he only got your machine he got concerned. I must admit, so did I." His voice was smooth and sultry. "I knew I should never have left you last night in your condition—"

"Did you think I'd drowned in the bathtub after all?"

Garrett's eyes lit, and he darted a glance at Rudy. But Rudy was still staring at the car. Garrett looked disap-pointed.

"But you seem to have turned out all right despite it all," he murmured. "In fact, you look quite good this morning. All things considered, of course."

She thought about hitting him with the rake. "That's easy to say. You haven't seen my bruises."

"I hope that's an invitation."

She smiled sweetly. "Not a chance."

"Pity." He took the rake out of her hands and began efficiently clearing the lawn. "It's a Pierce-Arrow," he said over his shoulder to Rudy, who was still staring at the car. "From the last model year, when they made just a few."

"I know," Rudy said reverently. "It was fifty years ahead of its time, wasn't it?"

Great, Anne thought. *Just what I need, a pair of old-car buffs swapping tales on my front lawn.* She gave in to the inevitable and introduced them. "Rudy teaches modern literature at Nicolet, Garrett. In fact, the university press has just published his first novel—"

"How nice for you," Garrett said without apparent interest. "Feel free to look the car over, if you like, Rudy. Anne—"

But the Pierce-Arrow was forgotten. "The book is getting wonderful reviews," Rudy said eagerly. "I've just brought Anne one of the first-run copies."

"How kind of you," Garrett murmured.

"I'd be happy to send you a review copy, Mr. Garrett."

Garrett took the garishly jacketed volume out of Rudy's hands, glanced at the title, fanned the pages and handed it back. Then he said, with charming frankness, "No, thank you. If you did, I'd feel obligated to review it, and our budding friendship might come to a screeching end."

Rudy drew himself up tightly, his arms folded, cradling the book against his chest as if to protect it. "Just as well," he said tightly. "You couldn't possibly understand it. It's apparent to everyone in town that you've never had a single thought that was too complicated to fit into a three-hundred-word column."

Anne winced and waited for Garrett's answer. She had no idea what it would be, but she knew it wouldn't take anywhere close to three hundred words for Garrett to devastate Rudy. And it was unfair, really. Rudy might have insulted Garrett, but that book was the child of his heart, and Garrett had insulted it first.

But Garrett only smiled at Rudy as if he were an annoying child, and turned to Anne. "My father wants you to come to dinner tonight—to check for himself that you're really all right, I suppose." He gestured toward a plastic bag that lay under the tree, and as Anne held it he started to fill it with leaves.

Dinner with the publisher. *Yesterday the man wasn't quite sure of my name,* Anne thought, *and today he's worried about me.* Maybe being mugged wasn't such a total loss after all. She nodded. "I'd be delighted."

Garrett didn't seem overwhelmed at her response. "Seven o'clock at the house. I've been delegated to pick you up. I was wrong about the tree," he mused as the last of the multitude of leaves went neatly into the bag. "It may be small, but it certainly takes itself seriously. See you tonight, then." He handed back the rake and sauntered off down the walk toward the Pierce-Arrow, carrying the bag of leaves out to the curb for the garbage collectors as he went.

"I was going to ask you to go to the coffeehouse poetry readings with me tonight," Rudy said reproachfully as the antique car purred off down the street.

And I would have refused, Anne thought. But she decided there was no point in making an issue of it. "Well, you can hardly expect me to turn down my boss because of a date that didn't even exist yet."

"I didn't have a chance to ask. Garrett just barged in out of nowhere as if he owned the place."

And so did you, Anne thought. After all, it was nearly two months now since she had given Rudy's ring back and canceled the tentative plans for the wedding next summer. If Rudy thought that bringing her a copy of his book gave him any rights where she was concerned, he was dead wrong.

But she kept her voice reasonable. "It's just as well. My mother might be at the coffeehouse tonight, and if she saw this scratch on my face..."

Rudy didn't seem to hear. "Why did he come back to Lakemont, anyway? Isn't Washington, D.C. where all the action is for columnists?"

Anne didn't feel obligated to tell him about the publisher's job. "Maybe he thought a little distance from the center of power might give him a valuable new perspective. Besides, a good column can be written from anywhere." *I don't believe it,* she thought. *Now I'm defending Garrett! My head aches....*

"So can a bad one," Rudy muttered. "Well, at least you'll appreciate the book."

It sounded like an order, Anne thought bemusedly. After he left, she put her rake away and retreated to her living room with an electric heating pad, a cup of hot chocolate and a book—not Rudy's—as a reward for a job well done.

She had to soothe her conscience a bit at the idea of rewarding herself for raking leaves when actually someone else had done most of the work. But after all, she reflected, she'd had to put up with both Garrett and Rudy—and that was no small job.

GARRETT WAS PROMPT, she had to say that for him. It had taken longer than she'd bargained for to cover the discolored scratch on the side of her face with makeup, and she was still fastening her earrings when he rang the bell. She hurried down the stairs with her shoes in her hand and flung open the door.

He didn't say anything for a long moment, and she almost shivered under his appraising gaze. She'd spent half the afternoon trying to decide on appropriate garb for dinner with the publisher; obviously she'd underestimated the occasion, because Garrett was wearing faultlessly tailored dinner clothes. Suddenly her simple, long-sleeved black dress seemed incredibly dowdy, and the heavy silver necklace with its sprinkling of charms became garish, if not actually tacky.

"Is this a new style?" he asked, gesturing at the black pumps that were still in her hand. "Carrying them like an evening bag?"

She didn't answer, just braced her hand against his arm and stepped into her shoes. His palm, warm and solid, came to rest over the back of her hand, trapping her just as she started to pull away. She shot a glance up at him and then looked away, and Garrett said quizzically, "Don't tell me you're going to be silent tonight, Anne."

She put her chin up. When one had an apology to make, her mother had always said, it was best to get it over with quickly. "I seem to remember saying a lot of things last night that should have been left unsaid."

Garrett gave her a long, thoughtful look and went straight to the point. "Before or after the mugging?"

She felt a delicate flush of color start at the base of her throat and climb to her hairline.

"I didn't know girls still blushed," he said, obviously delighted, and patted her hand gently. "What a charming bunch of contradictions you are, Just Plain Anne. A man could have a lot of fun unraveling you—"

"I don't think we should be late," she pointed out, and Garrett chuckled softly and helped her into her gray tweed coat.

He wasn't driving the Pierce-Arrow, and Anne sank into the front seat of a dark red sports car. Determined not to lose control of the situation again, she said, "I'm disappointed. I had so hoped to pretend I was Cinderella going to the ball in a pumpkin—I mean, in a grand old car—"

"You'd have frozen. I don't have the top fixed yet. But I'll take you for a ride someday. We'll take a picnic lunch and a blanket and lie under a tree somewhere—"

"Oh, that's all right," she said hastily. "I really don't—"

"And discuss society's woes," Garrett finished, and she felt like a fool. He gave her a quick, sideways glance. "Or would Rudy think I was trying to tread on his territory?"

As if I'd want to. Anne thought he might as well have said it; it was so very apparent.

"That was his imported beer I was drinking last night, wasn't it?"

"No," Anne said crisply. "It was mine."

"But you bought it for him. You're engaged to marry him, after all."

It startled her, and she answered without thinking. "Not anymore." Then she bit her tongue. "How did you know I ever was, anyway?"

"I was down at the *Chronicle* this afternoon using the morgue files, and I happened across the announcement of your engagement. Very bad picture of you, Anne." He was frowning. "What happened? Did he jilt you at the altar?"

"Nobody jilted anybody, and we never got close to the altar. Some relationships die with a bang, others with a whimper. Ours just sort of trailed off because I didn't like Rudy's temper, and he didn't like the hours I worked."

"He's got a temper that's worse than yours?" Garrett sounded intrigued. "No wonder he blew up when I turned down his precious book."

She sighed. "You could have been a bit more pleasant about it, Garrett. He's right, you know. It's gotten very good literary reviews."

He made a sound that was something like a snort. "That's even more reason to refuse to read it. Things that get good literary reviews these days generally give me a stomachache."

"I've got it. You always quarrel with the Establishment, just to be disagreeable!"

"No, only when the Establishment is wrong. As it generally is about literary novels. Do you know the definition of a literary novel?"

"The official one, or yours?" Anne asked with resignation.

"It's a book that a hundred people buy to put on the coffee table to impress their friends. Five of them actually try to read it, one comprehends part of it, and none of them enjoys it. But every one of the hundred says it is superb and profound, because they don't want to look stupid in front of their friends, who also bought the damned thing to put on the coffee table to impress—"

She applauded. "Is that a quotation from a column I missed, or did you make it up just for me on the spur of the moment?"

Garrett took his eyes off the street long enough to grin at her. "I knew you couldn't stay above a quarrel for long."

The early darkness had fallen over Lakemont like a blanket, and Anne had to admit she was grateful for the streams of warm air that poured through the sports car. It was a long way from the Sherwood Forest town houses on the west edge of the city to Pemberton Place, near the lakeshore, where the city's prominent families had clustered when Lakemont was new, and where the Garretts and a few other diehards had stubbornly remained when others fled to the suburbs.

The Garrett house was Tudor Revival, and it was one of the smaller houses on the block. Still, it was a sprawling mass of worn old paving brick and carved stone, with just a touch of stucco and half-timbering on the second story. Every leaded casement window in the front of the house was aglow, and each resembled an enormous diamond as it caught and fractured the light from within.

The carved double doors opened silently as they approached, and the white-haired butler at the door took Anne's coat as tenderly as if it were mink.

No wonder Garrett thinks my town house is tiny, she reflected as she looked around the entrance hall. It was sixteen feet up to the sculptured plaster ceilings. The walls were paneled in rich old walnut; there was a muted Persian rug on the floor and an equally muted oil painting glowing in the soft light.

Jim Garrett came across the hallway and took her hands. "Miss McKenna," he said. "I'm so glad to see you looking well after your awful experience. Come in and let me get you a drink. A glass of sherry, perhaps? Or something stronger?'' He drew her through a double doorway into a book-lined room where a fire blazed brightly. ''You know,'' he confided, ''Matt and I were talking it over earlier today. . . .''

Anne had never realized before how much alike Jim Garrett and his son looked, or how similar their behavior was, either, she told herself rather bemusedly as she found herself in a leather chair beside the fire, an unwanted glass of sherry in her hand.

''More security in the ramp, of course,'' Jim Garrett went on. ''There are guards on duty around the clock, starting today. But it would be so much safer if you would switch to working days, instead.''

She happened to be taking a sip of sherry at that moment, and she choked on it. It took her a moment to stop coughing and gain her breath, and that was a good thing, because by then she'd had time to reflect. Doubtless he meant well, she told herself, and simply hadn't considered the implications of what he had suggested.

She took a deep breath. ''Are you unhappy with the way I'm doing my job, Mr. Garrett?'' she asked.

He looked bemused. ''It isn't a matter of competence—''

''But that's the whole point, you see, Mr. Garrett.'' She set her sherry glass aside and clasped her hands tightly together. ''I was hired to do a job, and that job requires me to work in the evenings. To push me into a different job only because I'm a woman and supposedly too weak to defend myself, well, that would be blatant sexual discrimination, and it would be actionable under the law.''

There was sudden blank shock on Jim Garrett's face, and with a cold twinge down her spine Anne remembered the reason for the surgery he was to have in a matter of days. *He could have a heart attack at any time,* Garrett had told her.

"But my dear—" he said.

"Watch out, Dad." Garrett's voice was full of idle humor. "The next thing she's apt to say is that she's not *your dear,* and then she'll start beating on you with the heel of her shoe."

Anne glared at him and turned back to the publisher. "You can't have thought it through, sir," she began uncertainly.

A stir and a feminine voice at the front door drew Jim Garrett's attention away from her. He said something under his breath—Anne wasn't quite sure if it was apology or curse—and went out to greet another guest.

Garrett leaned against the mantel, his arms folded across his chest, and looked down at Anne. "That was not smooth," he said. "You've got a real knack for putting your foot in things, you know that, McKenna?"

The fact that he was right didn't make her feel any better. "*I've* got a knack?" she flared. "If you're asking me, I'd say your first management decision is a real dud, Garrett. Any kind of daytime job you could find for me would be a demotion. And trying to force a woman to take a lesser assignment just because she's a woman—"

"What in hell are you talking about?"

"I'm right, you know. I could sue the *Chronicle* and win a bundle."

"I wasn't asking about the discrimination bit." He sounded impatient. "I mean what you said about a management decision."

"Your father said he'd discussed it with you." She flung the accusation at him like a gauntlet. "Tell me, are you enjoying your interesting position as publisher-in-waiting?"

Those dark brown eyes flickered a little.

Anne raised her chin defiantly. "You're right, you know. The *Chronicle* does have a grapevine, and it's certainly no secret that that's why you've come back."

He was frowning a little.

Anne settled back in her chair. At least, she thought with satisfaction, Garrett wasn't going to get by with pulling strings behind the scenes and then pretending that he had nothing to do with it!

CHAPTER THREE

THE GUEST Jim Garrett had gone to greet turned out to be Dominique Delacourt. She swept into the library on a wave of perfume—Midnight Passion, Anne decided—and presented herself to Garrett to be kissed. There was obviously no doubt in her mind that he would want to oblige.

She's not all that old, really, Anne thought. *Thirty-five, perhaps, about the same age he is. It's that air of sophistication that makes her look older. And of course, Garrett's got just the opposite aura.* But there was one thing about Dominique, Anne told herself as she eyed the woman's spangled gold dinner dress. No one would ever dream of calling her Just Plain Dominique.

The last guests arrived a few minutes later, an older couple whom Jim Garrett introduced as Ted and Dorie Lehmann. "Ted's the president of Nicolet University," he said, "and Dorie is the one who keeps everything running smoothly on campus."

"That's more true than you know," Ted Lehmann said. "McKenna..." he added thoughtfully as he took Anne's hand. "We've got a professor named McKenna in the math department."

"My father," she said. "It was very fortunate for me. I got a first-quality education without having to pay tuition."

Ted Lehmann laughed. "I wish we could do that for everyone, right, Jim?"

Jim Garrett said with a smile, "But then Nicolet wouldn't have that exclusive reputation anymore, would it?" He poured drinks for the Lehmanns, and after a while he led the way into the huge dining room.

The crystal chandelier was turned down to a glow, casting striking shadows against the hand-painted mural on the walls. Anne was startled at first to see a round dining table in the center of the room; the casual shape seemed out of place in such a formal room. But of course, she thought, as Jim Garrett seated Dorie Lehmann at his right and Dominique at his left, it allowed a much more flexible seating arrangement than a more traditional oblong table would have done, in a household that didn't have a mistress to preside over the dining room.

What had happened to Garrett's mother, anyway? she wondered. Had she ever heard?

She had plenty of time to think about Garrett's mother and a whole lot of other questions, for while the round table encouraged general conversation, Dominique Delacourt seemed to have appointed herself as moderator. Certainly Jim Garrett made no effort to dislodge the woman and guide the talk himself; he merely sipped his sparkling water and made a careless comment now and then, as if his mind wasn't really on the conversation. It seemed to Anne that every time she glanced at him he was watching her, a frown cutting deeply between his brows.

It's accidental, she told herself. *He doesn't even know he's doing it. After all, it's a small table, so he could hardly help looking at you now and then. He's forgot-*

ten what I said earlier. He's probably just preoccupied with the surgery he's facing . . .

But she wasn't entirely successful at convincing herself.

Over the chocolate soufflé, Dorie Lehmann said, "Now I remember why your name sounded familiar, Anne, you're filling in over at the journalism school, aren't you? Teaching a class?"

Anne nodded. "Basic newswriting, on Tuesday and Thursday mornings. They're so short-staffed just now, and it's a chance to—"

Dominique interrupted. "You should get Matt to teach a class, Ted. He'd be wonderful."

"Yes," Garrett murmured, with an air of modesty that made Anne want to elbow him. "It's unfortunate that I haven't time to fit it into my schedule just now. But if you ever get into trouble and need expert advice, Anne, I'll be available."

Ted Lehmann laughed. "Careful, Matt, she may hold you to that promise. The one I'd like to get in the classroom is you, Jim. We could put together a seminar on media management. You can't tell me you wouldn't enjoy that."

Jim Garrett shook his head. "Oh, I would, but my doctor tells me I have to cut back as it is, not take on any new worries."

His gaze seemed to slide across Anne as he said it. *Does that include worries like discrimination lawsuits?* she wondered uneasily. *Should I apologize for what I said? It was true, and I meant it—but I certainly didn't intend to threaten him.*

There was no opportunity to tell him so, however. When they returned to the library for coffee, he and Ted Lehmann retired to a corner for what looked like a very serious conversation. Dominique linked her arm in Garrett's and drew him off beside the fire, and Anne toyed with her demitasse spoon and tried not to mind the fact that she felt very out of place.

Dorie Lehmann, sitting beside her on the deep leather couch, said, "We were interrupted at dinner when you were telling me why you're teaching. Please go on."

"It's a way to give something back to Nicolet, in appreciation for my education. I don't have a lot of cash, you see, so when the annual fund-raising drive comes along I'm not much help. But teaching a class—"

Dorie's slow smile could warm a room, Anne thought. It was like a huge, fluffy cloud of approval snuggling down around her.

"Tell me about it," Dorie said.

It was much later, and they'd had a long and cozy chat about a great many things, when Dorie glanced over to the corner with concern in her eyes. "I see I'll have to drag Ted away before he exhausts Jim completely," she said. "His surgery is on Tuesday, you know, and he must get his rest."

Even Dominique took the hint. She was standing even closer to Garrett by then, one hand raised to caress his lapel. "Matt, darling, you will take me home, won't you? I walked over because it's just a step, but it's so cold and dark now that I dread going out alone."

"Of course. You shouldn't go alone," Garrett said promptly. But Anne was startled when he went on, "You don't mind if Anne comes along, as well? I'll see you home first, of course."

It wasn't really a question, and there was some cynical satisfaction for Anne in knowing that Dominique minded very much indeed. It was almost amusing to watch her try to think of a way to object without looking rude. Before she succeeded, Garrett had excused himself and gone out to get his car.

The butler went down the front steps with them and opened the door of the sports car; Dominique stood aside, regal in her fur-trimmed cape, and gestured Anne in first.

Playing the great hostess, Anne thought ironically, as she fitted herself with difficulty into the infinitesimal rear seat of the car. Her abused hip protested.

It's a good thing I'm not tall, she told herself, *or overweight. And Dominique acts as if she's simply being gracious, allowing herself to freeze to death so I can get in out of the cold first.*

It was not just a step, as Dominique had said, but it was only half a block before they stopped in front of a white-brick replica of a château. *It figures,* Anne thought. *It certainly fits her image.*

Dominique waited patiently for Garrett to come around and open her door, and she laid her hand on his arm as if she were being escorted up a cathedral aisle and not an ordinary sidewalk on a brisk September night. At the front door, they stopped to chat.

It took rigid self-control for Anne to stay absolutely still until the pair were well up the sidewalk. Then she began to squirm, trying to find a more comfortable position. Something told her she might have a long wait; Dominique's attitude about the cold seemed to have changed abruptly. What on earth were they finding to talk about, anyway? Was she inviting him to return, after he'd dropped off the nuisance in the back seat?

"And if she is, what's it to you, McKenna?" Anne asked herself rudely.

She couldn't help but see when the two figures on the steps seemed to merge, and she turned her head quickly so she didn't have to watch. She hadn't felt this flustered since she was double-dating. No, she thought. It was worse than that. It reminded her of the time she'd sneaked into the movie theater to spy on her oldest brother and his date.

The car door opened. "Are you going to move to the front seat?" Garrett asked. "Or do you prefer to be chauffeured?"

"I don't think I *can* move," she said candidly.

He said something under his breath that she didn't quite catch, and reached into the car to haul her out.

Once settled in the front, with all her limbs in the right order, she murmured, "Now I understand how Picasso's models must have felt after a long day of posing. Like pretzels."

"Sorry. I'd forgotten that you aren't feeling especially gymnastic these days."

She didn't bother to answer that. Instead, she eyed the château as they drove away. "And you made catty remarks about my little town house," she mused, "and how I could possibly afford it all on my salary. Shame on you."

Garrett smiled, but he didn't answer. Strike one, Anne thought; he obviously didn't find the source of Dominique's money to be mysterious. Well, he'd probably known her all his life.

The late-night traffic was light, and from the freeway bridges she could look out over a golden web of streets. The car was quiet, its motion smooth, and she was lulled almost to the edge of sleep. She was startled when Garrett said suddenly, "Let's get one thing clear, by the way. Moving you to a daytime job was not my idea."

She opened her eyes and said equably, "All right, I believe you. Now that I think about it, why should you care whether I get mugged on a regular basis?"

She thought his jaw tightened a bit. "If my father had asked me what I thought of the idea, I'd have told him that you're too stubborn for your own good and not to bother about trying to help you out."

"Thank you," Anne said politely. "I appreciate your honest appraisal of me."

"Likewise." His voice was cool. "So I want to hear in detail just why you think I wouldn't make a decent publisher."

"I didn't say that, exactly," she said carefully.

"You certainly implied it. Go ahead and tell me. I won't hold it against you."

"That gives me such a confident feeling," she mocked.

"Would you rather I imagine what you think?"

"Well, as long as you put it that way—" She sat up. "I don't think the talent for the job is the sort of thing that comes down from generation to generation in the genetic code."

"And what on earth does that mean?"

"That it isn't automatic. Being a good publisher takes judgment and perception and understanding. Those things can't be conferred by someone saying, 'I dub thee Publisher!' The job requires the sort of seasoning that develops slowly from experience, from being under fire day after day."

"As you've learned it?" It was tart. "From the sample that I saw tonight when you threatened to sue the *Chronicle*—"

"At least I've been in the trenches," Anne said fiercely. "You didn't even see a problem! And that's only the beginning. When do you ever spend time in a newspaper office, anyway?''

"Five times a week when I deliver my column," Garrett said promptly.

Anne looked him over suspiciously, as best she could in the flicker of fast-passing streetlights; he wasn't ignorant, and he had to know how damning that sounded. Still, she suspected it was not far from the truth. "And you think that makes you an expert? As long as we're talking about your column," she added, "it's awfully easy to propose off-the-wall solutions when you're not the one who has to carry through with them and answer for the results. If all the outrageous things you suggest in that column of yours were taken seriously, half the country would be in a mess—"

"You're probably right," he said mildly. "Instead of which, the entire country is in a mess, and—"

"I shudder to think what the *Chronicle*'s editorial policy will be like with you in charge, knowing the kind of crazy things you believe in."

"You don't know me," he said. "Just the columnist."

She stared at him in disbelief. "You *are* the columnist, Garrett. You can't duck that one." She took a deep breath and went straight on. "The publisher's chair is a different thing altogether. The idea of you coming into the head office of the *Chronicle* and taking over the top job without any training—"

"I suppose I should be honored that you think I'm trainable at all." He sounded almost meek.

Anne hesitated, and then said, honestly, "Oh, I think you could learn, all right. But not if you think there's nothing you need to learn. And I also don't believe that your father has any sort of slow training program in mind. Of course, an apprenticeship period would be a nuisance for you—"

"It seems to me," Garrett said lazily, "that you know an awful lot about what my father thinks. Has he been calling you up to the executive floor to advise him, or have you been reading his thoughts in your crystal ball? Or have you, just possibly, been eavesdropping, Just Plain Anne?"

She bit her runaway tongue and finally said, "That was a cheap shot, Garrett."

"But you're not denying it's true, are you? All right, darling, who was he talking to?"

She said reluctantly, "The *Chronicle*'s head attorney. At the party last night."

"Yes," he mused, "that would explain why the whole plan is not a secret anymore." His good humor seemed to have returned, but she wondered uneasily if it was because he was planning to take the matter up with the unfortunate attorney.

The car slid smoothly to a halt in her driveway. Anne opened the door and said stiffly, "Thank you for bringing me home."

He opened his door. "I've never yet dropped a lady off without seeing her safely to her door."

"My door is all of fifteen feet away, Garrett."

But he was already out of the car by then, so she ceased what was obviously a useless protest. On the tiny front porch, he held out a proprietary hand for her key; Anne ignored him and put it into the lock herself. "Please thank your father, Garrett. I didn't have a chance—"

It was more a psychic sensation than any physical one; certainly he hadn't touched her, but she knew he intended to, and she ducked sideways just as he reached for her.

"Now what made you do that?" he asked, sounding more curious than offended.

"Oh, for heaven's sake," she muttered. "You're quite the efficient playboy, aren't you, Garrett? One trip, two goodnight kisses..."

He rubbed his forefinger across his chin thoughtfully. "Are you annoyed because I kissed Dominique?"

"Annoyed? Of course not. It's none of my business who you kiss, unless it's me, of course. I'm a bit disgusted, perhaps—"

"Why?"

She laughed harshly. "Don't you have any sensitivity at all, Garrett? Being an unwilling audience to that sort of thing is not—"

"But you didn't watch," he said. "Why didn't you?"

And how did he know that, she wondered. Not that it mattered. She tossed her head. "Because I am not a voyeur."

"Too bad. If you had, you'd have known that it wasn't 'that sort of thing' at all. It was this sort of thing."

She knew perfectly well what he intended to do, and she still couldn't sidestep him quickly enough. His mouth brushed hers, lips cool from the brisk wind. It was a light caress and so brief that she didn't even have time to think about stepping on his toes, or to consider any other sort of retaliation.

"Very charming," Anne drawled, when he raised his head. "I'm sure Dominique appreciated the demonstration just as much as I do. Now if it's all the same to you—"

"Nothing much to it, was there?" he whispered. "You see, I didn't kiss her like this—"

A half step brought him so close to her that the breath she was releasing seemed to be knocked from her body. One of his hands slid down over her spine, pressing her even more tightly against him, while the other caught her chin and turned her face up to his. She lay helpless against him, too far off balance to move, with both hands trapped against his chest, and little darts of fear— it *was* fear, wasn't it?—rushing through her veins, while he slowly and thoroughly kissed her, tasting and teasing and plundering by turns. He nibbled gently at her lower lip, and then his tongue began to tease deliciously against her teeth.

She whimpered, a little wordless protest, and his grip loosened until he was holding her a little way from him, his hands firm on her upper arms. She was glad of it; her knees didn't seem to want to work anymore.

"Now that was a kiss a voyeur could appreciate," Garrett said. If she hadn't known better, Anne would have said he sounded a little breathless. "You do understand the difference? 'Bye, Anne. See you around." He pushed the door open for her.

She went in, and slammed it. The wind that had swept in with her circled the tiny foyer and whipped back into her face, and she shivered.

Well, she thought philosophically, *at least now I know why Dominique didn't seem to mind standing on the château steps in the wind with him. As long as Garrett was around, one certainly didn't feel the cold.*

HE WAS at the regular news conference on Monday afternoon, sitting beside his father. That didn't surprise Anne at all, but the fact that he was silent throughout the

entire meeting did startle her. She had expected, somehow, that he would have all kinds of grand new ideas to
present. But perhaps her protest last night had done
some good after all. If he was at least willing to listen
and learn, instead of assuming that he already knew
everything...

Don't kid yourself, she thought. The fact that he
wasn't saying a word didn't mean he agreed with everything he heard; he might just be waiting patiently until
his position was a bit more solid. And then, when he did
get the chance to have his say, watch out. The thing
Garrett was best-known for across the nation was his
tendency to hold strong opinions. And the second thing
everyone knew about him was that he didn't hesitate to
express them.

Holly Andrews did not agree. "I don't think he'll
change anything much," she said over dinner on Monday evening at the restaurant next to the atrium lobby of
the *Chronicle* building. "After all, this is a very good
newspaper. We've had six Pulitzer nominations in the
past five years. What more could he want?"

"Seven."

"Well, that's not exactly a bad attitude, is it?" Holly
asked reasonably. "If he wants the prizes, at least he
won't be the sort who argues about the high costs of in-
vestigative reporting."

"I wouldn't bet on it." Anne succumbed to the temptation of the dessert cart and ordered a slice of chocolate cheesecake.

"Anne, you're hopeless." Holly drank her coffee
pensively, and finally said, "Do you know what your
problem is? You're seething with resentment."

"Go to the head of the class," Anne mocked. "I hate
the idea of this newspaper being taken over by a play-

boy whose inexperience is only matched by his arrogance."

Holly was shaking her head. "That's not it. Oh, you feel a bit protective of the *Chronicle,* I won't deny that. But your real resentment is entirely personal."

Anne stared at her, a bite of cheesecake suspended on her fork. "So I don't like Garrett," she conceded. "It's not—"

"No, it's not him, it's you. Bringing in an outsider to be the publisher means there won't be any promotions from inside. If the managing editor doesn't move up to the publisher's job, then he'll keep his present one. Which means that any promotion for you is still off in the far distant future. That's what is really annoying you."

"And I'm holding a grudge against Garrett because I want to be managing editor? Sure, I'd like the job someday, but I'm realistic about the odds, Holly. We can't all have the top job. Besides, I'm quite happy where I am."

"For how long?" Holly asked crisply. "And please don't tell me that working nights is your favorite pastime."

"I like the night side. It's where all the action is."

"And I suppose when you're married and have little kids you're still going to enjoy coming to work in the shank of the afternoon and staggering home at midnight?"

"I'll take care of that problem if it ever comes up. Which it isn't likely to anytime soon."

"You aren't still mourning for Rudy, are you?" Holly sounded incredulous.

"Of course not."

"Good. Because there's a new guy down in the circulation department. He's too short for me, but just right for—"

Anne cut her off. "Look, Holly, promotions may be slow around a newspaper, but I'm not crazy enough to think the fact that Garrett came back is going to keep me permanently shackled to the night city desk."

Oh, don't I? she thought a little hollowly. *I still half suspect that putting me back on days was his idea after all, and he was simply a little faster on his feet than his father was when it came to denying responsibility! And I also believe that it had nothing to do with the mugging incident; that was only an excuse to accomplish his own devious purpose: to get rid of any power I might have gathered.*

"To say nothing of the fact that you're not really being challenged anymore," Holly went on with determination. "I've never seen you reading so many magazines at your desk as you have lately."

"Keeping myself informed is part of my job."

"But you've been doing the same job for two years now. And you're ready for some new challenges."

Anne laughed. "All right. I still don't agree, but I know when to surrender. So what are we going to do about it, pal? Organize a coup to overthrow Garrett so I can have my promotion?"

Holly's smile flashed. "I don't make the news, dear. I get my kicks digging it out. I'll leave the office politics to you."

Anne stopped calculating the tip to consider that. Office politics: the managing and the finagling and the plotting and the scheming. Of course, she thought. That was what Garrett found so attractive about the *Chroni-*

cle, and the safe, secure, guaranteed-for-life office on the ninth floor.

SHE RAN into Rudy Balfour on Tuesday morning as she was leaving her classroom at Nicolet University, with a stack of her students' feature articles under her arm. "What brings you to this end of the campus?" she asked, too startled to be tactful.

"You, what else did you think? Do you have time for coffee?"

She hesitated and glanced at her watch, and then nodded. It was only a cup of coffee, after all. "But no more than that," she warned. "I have to be at work early."

He shrugged. "And I have a class at noon. We never could get our schedules coordinated, could we?"

The question was casual enough, but it still made her feel a little uneasy. She didn't want to review it all again.

The ice cream shop just across the street from the administration building was crowded, and they had to wait at the counter for their coffee. Finally they settled at a small table, with hardly enough room for two mugs and Anne's stack of papers.

"How was your business dinner?" Rudy asked, and answered his own question. "Boring, I suppose, like most of those things."

Anne made a noncommittal noise. Threatening to file a lawsuit against her employer, followed up by being quite lavishly kissed on her own doorstep as a lesson in voyeurism—yes, she thought, it had been just the ordinary dull evening!

"The coffeehouse got pretty exciting." Rudy stirred another packet of sugar into his coffee. "You'd have liked it." His gaze shifted away, almost shyly. "Have you read the book yet?"

It was a relief to find that it was only the book he had on his mind. *You idiot,* Anne thought, *for seeing something lurking in every shadow!* Reading his book was little enough to ask of her, after all. "Oh, Rudy, I'm sorry. I just haven't had time yet." Impulsively she put her hand over his. "I will, soon. I promise."

But the negative answer didn't seem to disturb him. He looked at her fingers, resting lightly on his, and his other hand came down over hers firmly, possessively. "Anne," he said, almost hoarsely. "You do still care, don't you? I knew that love couldn't vanish so quickly, without a trace."

She tried to pull away. "Rudy—" Her voice trembled a little.

"Please, darling, give me another chance. My damnable temper... but I've got control of it now. I simply never realized how terrible it was until I lost you over it."

"Rudy," she said unsteadily, "I just don't think—"

She stopped abruptly. *Surely,* she told herself, *I should be happy about this!* It hadn't been easy to break it off; she'd loved him, and it wasn't as if there had ever been violence, or any single incident that was unforgivable. It was just that anger of his, and the fact that she couldn't predict it, or control it, and so it frightened her. But if he really did see how destructive his temper could be, and if he really was working on it, then it was her obligation to give him a second chance.

Obligation? she asked herself harshly. Surely it shouldn't be an obligation but a joy.

He saw the uncertainty in her big blue eyes, and raised her fingers to his lips. "Thursday night," he said with sudden confidence. "Your next night off. We'll cele-

brate with dinner at the best place in town, the Lakemont Grand.''

"Not the engagement," she said a little desperately. "I
can't. I'm not ready for that."

"Yet," Rudy said firmly. He smiled at her. "Very
well. I understand that I'll have to prove myself. And I
will, darling. Believe me, I will."

Deep inside her, something seemed to shiver a little.
I'm glad, she told herself hollowly. *I'm very glad.*

CHAPTER FOUR

"I HAVE TO GO," she said, almost at random.

Rudy glanced at the neon-faced clock behind the soda fountain. "And I'm going to be late for my class," he said, and pushed his cup aside. "Till Thursday, then. I'll call you, darling." And he lingered in front of the ice cream parlor just long enough to kiss her goodbye.

Anne cringed a bit at the public nature of that kiss, but she submitted to the caress without a word of protest and stood there on the sidewalk, her arms full of papers, watching him dash across the street toward the liberal arts building and his waiting class.

I'm glad, she told herself. *I'm glad....*

The two words formed a sort of drumbeat rhythm in her brain, accompanying the soft click of her heels against the concrete walk. She had forgotten this morning that she would have papers to cope with, and it had been such a lovely day that she had walked the half mile to the campus. Now that same half mile back to her town house stretched out before her like a marathon run.

An hour ago, if someone had said she would give Rudy a second chance, that she would make a date with him for dinner and a discussion of their future, she would have been rolling on the sidewalk laughing at the idea that anything could change so much in so short a time. And yet... here she was, and she had done just that.

An hour ago she would have said earnestly that she regretted how things had turned out. She would have insisted she was sad that their plans had come to nothing. And she would have believed it. But presented with the opportunity to retrace their steps, to pick up again where they had parted, her first reaction had been panic. It was not fear of his temper that had made her hesitate in that first instant. It was the whole idea of committing herself to him. *Don't rush me,* she had wanted to scream at him.

Not ready? she asked herself in disbelief. *But you're twenty-seven years old, Anne! If you're not ready to make a commitment now, when on earth will you be? You don't have forever.*

Was this why she had found his anger so overwhelming, so frightening? Was it not Rudy after all, but her own fear that had driven her to end the engagement?

And if so, what on earth was making her so frightened? The idea of marriage itself? Of having babies? Of the responsibility of raising a family?

It was crazy to think of things like that, she thought. If she had suffered an unpleasant childhood herself, or a broken family, such fear might make sense. But there had never been a family more stable than the one she had grown up in, and she had always known that she wanted that same steadfast security for herself, when it was time. She had faith in her ability to raise children. She wanted several, and a solid, trusting home to raise them in. She wanted a husband who would also be a partner, and a friend....

And Rudy had fit into that pattern, or at least she'd thought he had. But then the unexpected explosions of anger had come, and Anne had begun to question. What if that anger was vented on a vulnerable child?

So why was she so hesitant to give him another chance? He wasn't asking her to rush into marriage with him to prove her faith, after all. If Rudy was truly making an effort to change, she should be eager for him to have the benefit of the doubt.

Had her concern about Rudy's temper been only a mask for the real problem? An excuse to wait for some impossibly perfect dream man to come along?

But I don't expect perfect agreement, she thought. *I'm certainly not used to it; Daddy's got a doctoral degree in math, and Mother simply will not learn to keep a checkbook balanced. Mother writes poetry and Daddy tries to help by rhyming 'nasal' with 'basil.'* That was far from perfection; half the time they drove each other mad, but they were still in love after forty years and heaven knew that deserved a medal.

"I want what my parents have," she muttered. "And I'm not willing to settle for less."

And that, she concluded, left her feeling completely lost, without a clue of what to do next about Rudy—or about herself.

THERE WAS A MEMO waiting in her computer terminal. It was addressed to all *Chronicle* employees and signed by the managing editor. "Jim Garrett's surgery was completed this morning with no complications," it said. "Though the next few hours are, of course, critical, his speedy recovery is expected."

She released a sigh of relief at the good news, and only then did she realize how much she had been thinking about Jim Garrett today. She had not had a chance to exchange a word with him since that aborted conversation in his library on Sunday evening, and the incident had been bothering her more than she had realized. It was almost as if he'd been avoiding her after that; he had not even broken away from Ted Lehmann to say goodbye when she left that night. And yesterday at the news conference he had stayed on the opposite side of the room, and ducked out the instant the meeting was over.

And aren't we feeling powerful today, she chided herself. *A city editor who can make the publisher so nervous that he can't stand being in the same room with her, much less take the chance of having a real conversation!*

The truth was that he'd probably forgotten all about it, she told herself. He was preoccupied with his own concerns on Sunday evening, and he left in such a hurry yesterday because he didn't want to hear twenty people's condolences on his illness and their reminiscences of when Great-Aunt Agnes had the same thing and died of it. Nevertheless . . .

Garrett was right, she told herself morosely. She'd put her mouth in gear before her better judgment had a chance to kick in, and she was going to regret it until she apologized. She could at least have let the man finish what he was saying before she made mincemeat of him. He might actually have been intending to offer her a promotion.

She turned that possibility over in her mind, and finally shook her head. Whatever Jim Garrett had intended, it could not have been a better job; there simply were no vacancies. Anne had reached the level of management where promotions were slow and limited, because senior people did not lightly leave a newspaper like the *Chronicle,* and most of them were years away from retirement. No, the very best Jim could have offered would have been a lateral move, the same job level on the day shift. And it probably would have been a step down, instead.

Still, Anne told herself, *you could have listened patiently and then said a polite "No, thank you," instead of acting like a card-carrying extremist.*

And there wouldn't be a chance to see him anytime soon, she reflected, so the image she had left with him was likely to be solidified into stone by the time she managed an apology.

You wanted him to remember your name, she told herself. *Well, you don't need to be concerned about that. He's going to remember you, for all the wrong reasons.*

At least she could try to minimize the damage, she thought, so she called the florist shop down the street and ordered a bouquet. "It's for Jim Garrett," she told the clerk. "At Nicolet University Hospital. I'm not sure which wing he's in, or pavilion, or whatever they're called now."

Holly Andrews leaned on the corner of Anne's desk and started to leaf through the stack of student papers in the In basket. "Apple-polisher," she accused under her breath.

Anne made a face at her.

"And his name isn't actually Jim, remember?" Holly added. "I happen to know they're awful sticklers over details like legal names at University Hospital."

Anne made the correction, and the clerk repeated it, in a long-suffering tone; Anne could almost hear the scratch of pen on paper as she made the change on her order form.

"Obviously, even more careful than editors are," Holly murmured sweetly.

Anne smiled. She'd discovered a glaring error in one of Holly's stories just last week, and taken her to task about the effect on the newspaper's credibility when its reporters seemed unaware of which streets intersected and which ones didn't. No wonder Holly was so delighted to have caught her.

By the time Anne put the telephone down, Holly had worked her way through most of the contents of the In basket. "Was there something you wanted?" Anne asked. "Or did you just come over to read my mail?"

"I'm only watching out for the kids who are going to be my competition in a few years." Holly looked over her shoulder; the newsroom was relatively quiet, and she leaned forward a little and lowered her voice. "What would you say if I told you our beloved mayor has been taking bribes and kickbacks for all the new construction in the city?"

Anne looked her over cautiously. "I'd say you'd better have ironclad proof."

"Darn," Holly said. "Everybody in town knows it, and nobody's got proof."

"Then talk to Garrett. He never seems to let the lack of facts stand in the way of a good column. And he's already taken a jab at the mayor."

Holly laughed. "Did you read his column today? I wonder how the mayor likes being called 'His Dishonor.' Well, if you won't let me write about corruption in city hall, can I go to that concert in Milwaukee next weekend?"

"Which concert?" Anne asked warily.

"The famous band from twenty years ago that's making its comeback tour. I think the *Chronicle* should cover it."

"And pay for your ticket?" Anne asked dryly.

"Yours, too, if you like. It's an important event in contemporary Wisconsin history. No? All right, then, what about the fall festival? We can both go on Thursday night and have a great time, too.''

It brought back the memory of Rudy with a crash. "I'm busy on Thursday. And if you come up with one more brilliant idea, Andrews, I'll assign you to cover the Junior League's charity tea tonight.''

"That's the society department's baby.''

"You can help. It's obvious you don't have enough to do.''

Holly looked injured. "But Anne,'' she said earnestly, "I'm only acting in the best tradition of workers everywhere. In fact, I'm just following your example.''

Anne glared at her. "And what example is that?''

"Buttering up the boss,'' Holly said wickedly, and vanished behind a partition before Anne could retaliate.

SHE WAS HALF-ASLEEP on the couch, a magazine open on her lap and a cup of hot chocolate growing cold on the table beside her, when the doorbell rang. She jerked upright to stare at the clock; it was almost midnight. Who on earth was coming to see her at this hour? Rudy, perhaps, to continue the morning's interrupted discussion? Oh, please heaven, she thought, anything but that!

She unearthed his book from under the morning's newspaper and left it prominently atop the coffee table, just in case, before she went to the door. But the obviously male silhouette on the little porch, his back to the door, couldn't be Rudy, who was not much taller than Anne herself. And this man's shoulders were hunched, too, which meant he was taller.

He turned as the door opened. "Hi, Anne. I thought you must still be up when I saw the lights.''

"Garrett,'' she said without enthusiasm.

He gestured at the security chain, which she had left fastened. "May I come in?"

"I'm not exactly dressed for visitors."

He peered through the small gap in the door at her quilted pink dressing gown. "Who's going to know?"

It was matter-of-fact and unanswerable.

"Besides, it's cold out here," he went on.

He was wearing a sweater over an open-necked shirt and a short leather jacket zipped only halfway up. His hands were in his trouser pockets; she would have bet he didn't have a pair of gloves. His head was bare as well, and the chilly breeze had ruffled the sun-streaked honey-colored hair.

"Of course it is when you're not prepared for it," she informed him. "That's what happens to people who leave Wisconsin for a few years, their blood gets thin. You could go home where it's warm."

He frowned, as if contemplating an insoluble problem in calculus.

Anne sighed. "Oh, all right, come in. But you'll have to remove your toes from the doorway first so I can take the chain off."

Garrett smiled. It was like the first sliver of sunshine cutting through a heavy mist. Anne reached for the chain and thought, *I should slam the door and lock the dead bolt and run. Who knows what he might want?*

He spotted her hot chocolate cup right away, and said hopefully, "That looks awfully good. I've been at the hospital all day."

"I thought you said once that you were above hinting," she said acidly, but she gave in and went to fix him a cup. He followed her to the kitchen like a new puppy on a leash, and she found herself nearly tripping over him as she moved around the small room. She tried to swallow her irritation—it wasn't his fault that her kitchen was so "efficient"—but it was hard to keep the annoyance out of her voice. "I suppose there's a reason why you're here," she said finally, as she piled whipped cream atop the hot liquid and sprinkled it with cinnamon.

"To thank you for the flowers, of course. It was very thoughtful of you." He was looking at the cup, rather than at her.

"It was nothing, really." But she was a bit confused. There had been a note in his voice, Anne thought, that she couldn't quite identify. Had he sounded slightly ironic, perhaps? Did he, like Holly, think that her only motivation had been to try to ingratiate herself with the boss?

Well, it's true, isn't it, McKenna? she asked herself. *That is why you sent the damned flowers!*

"I'll enjoy them." He picked up his cup and sniffed it appreciatively.

"What?" It was slightly shrill. "*You'll* enjoy them?"

"The bouquet was addressed to me." The whipped cream formed a tiny thin line along his upper lip. He took his time licking it off and added pleasantly, "Matthew James Garrett, the card said. And since I'm the only one of that name around at the moment—"

"But your father—"

"Is James Emerson Garrett."

She swallowed hard, and said rather wildly, "But he can't be. You've got a damned *number.*"

"Yes. I was named after my grandfather, who was the original Matthew James Garrett. That is why I am the second, and not Junior, as you so fondly believe I ought to be. I'm not wild about either idea, exactly, but then I wasn't consulted. Is it all clear now?" It was very kind.

She got me, Anne thought bitterly. *Damn Holly Andrews's black little soul; when she gets even, she really gets even!* "I should have known better than to trust a reporter for anything. Especially a legal name."

He grinned. "Yes. You should have. But that's generally the problem with editors."

"Drink your hot chocolate and get out, Garrett."

"Yes, ma'am. Mind if I drink sitting down? They don't seem to have chairs for visitors in the cardiac care division at University Hospital, so I've been on my feet all day."

"That's probably because they don't want visitors to sit down and stay." She led the way into the living room. At least it was closer to the front door.

"No doubt." He sounded as if he hadn't allowed the restriction to interfere with his actions in the least. "Please don't be upset about the mix-up, Anne. I think it's the very nicest bouquet I've ever been sent." He sat down on the couch and patted the seat beside him invitingly. "In fact, I think it's the only bouquet I've ever—"

She drew back her arm, as if aiming the hot chocolate. "You knew perfectly well who I intended the blasted flowers for, Garrett! And if you don't see that he gets them..."

Garrett eyed the threatening mug and said hastily, "He's got them. And he appreciates them very much, too. Even if you did give the *Chronicle*'s reputation for detail a black eye."

She dropped into the rocking chair by the empty fireplace, closed her eyes and put her head against the calico cushion tied to the chair back. "I suppose you took great pleasure in pointing out how incompetent I am."

"In this case," he mused, "I didn't have to. You'd already done it so very efficiently yourself."

She moaned a little. *That's just great, McKenna,* she thought. *You must be the only person in town who can turn a charitable gesture into a job crisis!*

She didn't see the momentary smile that quirked the corner of Garrett's mouth, but it would not have surprised her.

"That's part of my job, you know," she said gloomily. "Keeping track of details. I fired a reporter last month because he couldn't get his facts straight. His record was six different misspellings of the same name."

"Relax," Garrett said callously. "That means you've got five to go."

The telephone rang and she reached for it automatically. Most of her family knew that the easiest time to find her at home was midnight.

"Hello, darling," Rudy said. "I've got reservations for the Lakemont Grand for seven o'clock on Thursday."

"That's nice."

From the corner of her eye she watched as Garrett picked up Rudy's book from the coffee table and settled back with it on his knee. *Does he read minds?* she wondered. *Or is he just making a vague attempt to be polite and not listen to my phone call, and Rudy's book was the closest thing at hand?*

"Nice?" Rudy sounded almost hurt. "Is that all you can say?"

"Well, you did tell me that's where we were going."

"Oh, so I did. I just had to hear your voice tonight, to prove this morning wasn't my imagination. I can hardly believe this is real, you know."

That makes two of us, Anne thought.

"I really didn't intend to call you, though, in case you were reading." He sounded hopeful.

Garrett opened the book and spread one hand across the pages to hold it open. His other hand groped for his mug, as if he was too absorbed to take his eyes from the print.

"I haven't had a chance," Anne said carefully. "I'm saving it for the weekend when I haven't anything else to do."

Rudy laughed. "That leaves me with mixed feelings," he said cheerfully. "Should I let you read, or should we make other plans?"

"Let me read," Anne said rather desperately.

Garrett looked up at that, and then his eyes returned to the printed word as if drawn by a magnet.

Finally, she got Rudy off the telephone. Garrett said, "You still haven't put the poor boy out of his misery by reading his masterpiece?"

"I haven't had time."

"Make time. You shouldn't miss this." He turned a page.

"Garrett," she said with determination, "I've been thinking about that discussion we had Sunday. What was your father thinking about? The offer he made me, I mean? What sort of a day job did he have in mind?"

He shrugged. "How should I know?" He let the book close with his finger as a page marker.

"He said he'd talked to you," she reminded.

"Not about that. Why? Are you having second thoughts about the wisdom of telling him to go to hell?"

"I didn't tell him anything of the sort." Almost to herself, she mused, "There's nothing open that I know of, unless someone would want to swap shifts, and I doubt that's the case. And the only other option I can think of is reporting.''

"Some people don't think that's a step down.''

"Well, I do.''

"Why? Is that how you got started?''

"Yes.'' Anne grimaced at the memory. "Covering bridge clubs and tennis tournaments and fund-raising campaigns for a suburban paper in Chicago. I was lucky to get on at the *Chronicle* at all.''

"You had stiff competition?''

"Extremely. I was hired as a general-assignment reporter, so to move up to this job was a dream.''

"How far are you planning to go?''

"It depends. I don't get my jobs on the basis of who I know. I have to work for my promotions.''

"Oh, we're back to that again, are we?''

She rocked quietly for a moment and then said, "I'm sorry, Garrett. That was uncalled for.''

"Haven't you ever thought of going somewhere else?'' Garrett asked. "Being the editor in chief of *Time*, or something?''

The almost careless question sent a shiver through Anne's body, but she managed to keep her voice firm. "Are you suggesting that I might be wise to start looking for another job?''

He shrugged. "There are always options for someone who's ambitious.''

She said slowly, "I'd rather advance at a snail's pace in an excellent organization than very fast in a mediocre one. Unless—'' a note of challenge had crept into her voice "—unless what you're really saying is that I'm not going to be allowed to advance at all.''

Garrett shrugged. "That's not up to me to say.''

Yet, Anne thought. The single, all-important word was hanging in the air between them, as if he simply wasn't quite ready to say it.

His fingertips wandered across the glossy cover of Rudy's book. "Since you're not going to have time to read this, do you mind if I borrow it for a day or two?"

She thoughtfully twisted a lock of hair around her index finger, and said finally, "I don't think I want to lend it to you."

"Why not? I'll protect it with my life." He added earnestly, "But if you don't trust me not to lose it, I could just sit here and read it. I think there was a little hot chocolate left...."

Anne stood up. "Good night, Garrett. Enjoy the book. Don't be in any hurry about returning it."

He spun the book lightly into the air, and caught it between two fingers. "I'll get it back to you by the weekend, so you can keep your promise to Rudy."

She ushered him firmly to the front door and braced herself for a repetition of the night he had instructed her in the different styles of good-night kisses.

But tonight he only smiled at her. A smile that held, she thought, more than its share of mischief. He flicked her cheek with his fingertips, and was gone into the cold.

Damn, she thought helplessly. He was an expert at keeping people guessing; it was what made his readers turn to his column before even glancing at the front page, and the talent was obviously as effective in his personal life.

Unless, she thought somberly, that seemingly careless question about whether she'd ever considered moving on to another newspaper, another city, had been serious after all. If it had been a warning that she was finished at the *Chronicle* as soon as he took over, then it was no wonder that he hadn't pursued the casual flirtation he had so nonchalantly, and thoughtlessly, begun.

IT WAS a glorious day to be on the Nicolet campus, where the city seemed a thousand miles away. The last few leaves had given up their hold, and the trees were starkly bare and beautiful now under a sky that was deceptively calm and brilliantly blue.

Anne had overslept, and she'd been in a rush ever since, so it was with relief that she dismissed her class and started back to her car. There was not another thing demanding her attention and energy until evening, and she intended to enjoy this precious day of peace. Of course, the evening might be a different story, since it was tonight that Rudy was taking her to dinner.

"Anne!"

Damn, she thought. "This is getting to be a habit, Rudy."

"You're looking very pleased with yourself," he said. "Obviously you haven't heard."

He sounds grim, she thought. *He's had bad news—or he has very bad news to tell me.* "Heard what?" she said weakly.

He thrust a newspaper at her. "You must have missed this."

She scanned the front page, and he seized it from her hands and turned the section inside out with a snap. "Here. It's your precious Garrett. You lent him the book I gave you, didn't you?"

"Not really," she said automatically. "It was more like he hijacked it."

"But it was your copy, wasn't it? I should have known."

She scanned the column under the smiling photograph she had come to know so well, catching a phrase here and there. "'To preserve the right to free speech,'" she read aloud, "'a free society must put up with a lot of idiotic babble from time to time. Rudy Balfour's new novel is an excellent example....'"

I ought to have known the man was up to no good, she thought. *The past thirty-six hours have been far too peaceful to last.*

"Rudy, I'm sorry."

He was not mollified. "That's libel, and I ought to sue him for it!"

"Well, technically, it's only fair comment and criticism."

"That kind of insult is what you call *fair?*" Rudy howled. "What on earth made you give it to him?"

"I told you, I didn't have a lot of choice. Not that it makes much difference. He could have bought a copy—"

"At least then I'd have the satisfaction of knowing that he'd invested something in this attack! As it is, with you collaborating with him— Listen to this. 'Balfour's book does not deserve its certain fate, which is to lie unread on coffee tables across the nation—'"

"But that's a compliment, Rudy."

He raised his voice and went on. "'It has more value than that; as a sleeping aid it is unequaled by anything known to prescription medicine.'"

She bit her lip hard, but she couldn't swallow the smile altogether; the comment was so plain, so succinct and so clear that she could hear Garrett saying it, knowing perfectly well that he was waving a red flag at a bull and not giving a damn for the uproar that would result.

Rudy glared at her. "So you think that's funny, do you? Dammit, Anne—"

"It's vintage Garrett, you must admit," she said.

He flung the newspaper onto the sidewalk and stomped on it, grinding his heel into the print.

And this is the man who has control of his temper now, Anne thought, *and will never lose it again?*

"I don't think the Lakemont Grand would be a good idea at all, under the circumstances," he said brusquely, and walked away.

"I quite agree," she called after him.

At least that was over, she thought. All the mental anguish she had put herself through, trying to reason things out, when all the while her heart had known the truth, that Rudy couldn't change after all. What a waste of time it had been to worry about it!

But Rudy's bad behavior, embarrassing and unreasonable as it had been, did not excuse Garrett's. It had, after all, been an unprincipled attack. The farther she got from campus the more irritated she became. She didn't even know when she decided to confront him; perhaps it was not a conscious choice at all, but when she found herself within a couple of blocks of Pemberton Place she sought out the Garrett's Tudor Revival house.

The carriage house doors were open, and she could see Garrett, or part of him, at least, leaning over the engine of the Pierce-Arrow. He was clad in a heavy sweatshirt and a pair of faded jeans that fit like a second skin, and despite her annoyance with him she had to admit that he didn't look bad from this angle. The engine was running, and he appeared to be absorbed in his job. She deliberately softened her step, hoping that he might be startled enough by her sudden appearance to bump his head at least.

But he didn't even jump when she spoke beside him. He looked up briefly and reached for a screwdriver from the kit beside him. "Good. I've been trying to call you all morning."

"Oh? To warn me, no doubt."

"Warn you? Why?" His eyes were innocent. "Oh, did the column cause a storm?"

"You might say. I'd have my mail sniffed for explosives for a while, if I were you. I trust you're finished with my book."

"Oh, yes." He sounded quite content. "Hand me that wrench, would you?"

She thought about cracking him over the head with it. "You are a troublemaker, you know. You did that on purpose. You deliberately set out to pick a fight with poor Rudy."

"Did not. I never fight a battle of wits with an unarmed person. I said what I thought, that's all."

"Garrett, did you have to be so hateful about it?"

"If you had read the book, you'd have thought I was remarkably restrained." He handed back the wrench and looked up at her, eyes bright, resting his greasy hands on the spotless cream-colored paint. "I expected a little more detached approach from you, Anne. I didn't expect you would stand up for something you know nothing about. Or are you defending Rudy purely on principle?"

She bit her tongue. Defending Rudy was the last thing she wanted to do, principle or no.

"Are you on your way to work?"

She shook her head. "It's my day off."

"Tell you what," Garrett said. "I'll give you the book, and you go home and read it, and then we'll talk about it. If you still think I was unfair this morning, I'll write Rudy a letter of apology.''

"And publish it in your column?"

He didn't blink. "Absolutely."

"The book can't be that bad," she mused. "And you can't be that certain of yourself."

"How much are you willing to stake on it?"

"That column cost me dinner at the Lakemont Grand, and I won't settle for less."

"You drive a hard bargain, Just Plain Anne. Go see what my father has to say to you, and I'll get the book."

"Your father?" she asked weakly. "He's home?"

Garrett nodded. "He was released this morning."

"And he wants to talk to me?"

"Yes. It seems to be important, too. You don't think I've spent the better part of the morning trying to telephone you just for the fun of it, do you?"

"Of course not," Anne said drearily. "Garrett—" she hated herself for asking "—what does he want?"

"Darned if I know. Despite what you seem to think, he hasn't started to consult me about every personnel matter at the *Chronicle*. He's in the greenhouse, around back."

He rubbed the top layer of grease off his hands with a grimy towel, killed the Pierce-Arrow's engine and went off toward the house, whistling as if he didn't have a care in the world.

CHAPTER FIVE

A PERSONNEL MATTER.

He had given himself away with that comment, Anne thought. The *Chronicle*'s publisher might not be consulting his son about every decision, but Garrett was certainly under no illusion that this was an invitation to tea. It was business. And if it was important enough for Jim Garrett to summon her here, when he had only arrived home this morning . . .

Mixing up the man's name on a bunch of flowers is not a firing offense, she reminded herself rather desperately as she picked her way along the cobbled brick walkway that led from the carriage house around to the back of the house. *But if it's only a reprimand, he could have, should have, gone through the regular chain of command. Which means that I could be in big trouble. . . .*

She took a deep breath and tapped on the glass door of the tiny greenhouse that arched against the brick wall of the house, and went in.

When Garrett had said his father was in the greenhouse, she had had a vision of the man sitting weakly in a wheelchair in the sunshine. Instead, she found him perched on a high stool beside a gardener's bench, wearing a canvas apronlike affair. His sweater sleeves were pushed up and his elbows were propped on the edge of the table, and in front of him was a potted plant.

The plant's leaves looked a little limp, and she thought rather hysterically that it appeared to have just received a solid scolding and was looking properly penitent. *No, she told herself. You're letting your imagination run away with you. Just because you expect to get a raking down doesn't mean he's been practicing on the plants!*

"Do you know anything about orchids?" Jim Garrett asked.

She actually looked around to be sure she was the only one there, and it was with genuine regret that she said, "Not a thing, I'm afraid."

He answered with a sort of grunt and went back to staring at the plant. "Waterlogged," he announced finally. "That's the only thing I can figure out. No drinks for you for a week, my fine friend." He set the plant onto a shelf at the back of the gardener's bench and turned to face her. "Well, Anne McKenna, so you've finally turned up. Take your coat off."

It was not a promising beginning. She smothered the urge to tell him that her days off were her own, and began to untangle the silky scarf from under the collar of her jacket, saying, instead, "You're looking very well, Mr. Garrett. I didn't think that you'd be home yet."

He shrugged. "The miracles of modern medicine. What used to take weeks and leave foot-long scars now isn't much worse than having a cavity in a tooth filled, or at least they expect you to believe that. Of course the rest of the orders are still the same, watch your diet, exercise more and worry less. Which brings me to what I wanted to discuss with you, Miss McKenna."

Worry less. Well, she could put his mind to rest on a couple of points, and the sooner the better. She gulped, and said, "I'm awfully sorry, Mr. Garrett. I don't know what came over me Sunday, to accuse you of purposely discriminating against women at the *Chronicle*. And I'll never use another name without checking it, honestly. It was very careless of me—"

"Oh, it's a perfectly natural mistake," he said rather soberly. "I'll admit to some bewilderment about the phenomenon. The first half of my life I was known only as Matthew Garrett's son, and now suddenly I seem to be only Matt Garrett's father, but I suppose I'll adjust."

"You're making me feel like a worm, you know," she said frankly. "If you want to call me Jane, or Cassandra, or Hey-You in retaliation, I'll certainly understand."

He laughed, and his face lighted with a sudden boyish charm that made him look a great deal like his son.

It gave her the courage to go on. "And about the other thing," she said. "I really am sorry that I threatened—"

Jim Garrett interrupted firmly. "No, that was entirely my fault. You were quite right. I spoke before I'd had a chance to think over all the implications of asking you to take another assignment."

Then he didn't have a particular job in mind for me, she thought, *much less a better one than I've got now. Well, I knew that all along, so why should I feel disappointed?*

"I hope that you'll be gracious enough to forget an old man's reaction altogether, Anne."

"You're not old," she protested automatically.

He shook his head in disagreement. "You see, in my day, if there was any question of a young lady being in danger—"

"You protected her." Anne nodded. "You've taken care of that, you know. The new guards in the parking garage are so zealous that they walk every one of us to her car and practically lock her in!''

"That was the order they were given. But at any rate, my dear—'' He stopped suddenly. "I am sorry. That slipped out.''

It sounded so natural that it took an instant for her to realize what he was apologizing for. "Oh, please! Garrett seems to think I'm some sort of radical feminist, ready to beat up any man who holds a door for me, but—''

There was a gasp of laughter, quickly smothered, from the French doors that led into the house, and Garrett said, "You? A radical feminist? That's only a veneer, Just Plain Anne. The truth is you're a hidebound conservative.''

It annoyed her. "And how would you know?''

"The needlepoint pillows and the hot chocolate,'' he said promptly.

"My grandmother makes the pillows,'' she said, a little more sharply than she intended. "And even you must have noticed the hot chocolate was a mix.''

"The whipped cream wasn't.'' He tossed her Rudy's book.

Amazingly enough, it didn't even have a whisper of engine grease on the cover. Garrett wasn't displaying any, either. He had changed the ragged old sweatshirt for a hand-knit ski sweater in brown and green; it made his eyes look even bigger, or was that just the wolfish enjoyment in them?

She was tucking the book into the side pocket of her handbag when Jim Garrett said, "I'm glad you're here, Matt. I was just getting to the favor I want Anne to do for me.''

Favor? Then he hadn't summoned her to scold her after all? In her relief at getting her apologies off her chest, Anne had hardly noticed that he dealt with both matters politely, but not as if they were particularly important.

"I've always had this idea in the back of my mind, you see," Jim Garrett was saying, "but now that the time seems to be right, I'm suddenly under orders not to take on any new projects or concerns. At first I thought my idea was doomed, since I can't fuss over it and Matt—" he shot a look at his son "—Matt hasn't the time to devote to all the details."

He doesn't have time? Anne thought in disbelief. *It's the middle of a lovely autumn morning, when most of the world is working, and he's tearing apart the engine of an antique car. It looks as if he's got all the time in the world, and I'd bet his father agrees! But of course, once he's publisher...*

"It will require quite a bit of time, I'm afraid," Jim Garrett went on. "But of course that won't continue indefinitely. Once everything is set up, it should—"

"Dad," Garrett interrupted. "Don't keep the poor girl in suspense. She's about to explode from curiosity."

It wasn't curiosity, she wanted to tell him, but he was right about the explosion part.

"Oh. Of course. I haven't told you what it's all about, have I?" Jim Garrett smiled a little. "I want to endow a scholarship program for the journalism school at Nicolet, in memory of my father. But as I'm sure you know, Anne, it's very tricky to set up the rules for such a program so that the right people benefit. In this case, I'm interested not only in the ones who truly need the financial help and can't get it anywhere else, but students who will be the leaders of the profession in a few years. I don't particularly want to fund educations for kids who think they want to be reporters but who end up selling computers instead at the first hint of—"

"Your blood pressure is going up again," Garrett observed.

Whose blood pressure? Anne wanted to ask him. Hers was certainly creeping upward.

Jim Garrett ignored his son. "Career difficulty. Ted Lehmann thinks I'm putting too many conditions on my help, and says that no one could possibly meet all my specifications. I can't seem to make him comprehend that I know what I want." He stopped talking and gave her a long look. "Do you understand what I'm looking for, Anne?"

She nodded. "I think so. But—"

"I thought you would," he said with satisfaction. "I expect that only someone in the business of daily news coverage could."

She couldn't help it; she glanced at Garrett, with a hint of I-told-you-so in her eyes.

"Congratulations," he murmured.

"So you see why I want you involved in this, Anne," Jim Garrett said. "Since I can't do it myself, I need someone who can set up all those rules, and get the word out to the people who qualify, and then judge the applications."

It was a wonderful idea, in principle, she thought. Jim Garrett was right; there were many good students who could not afford to attend Nicolet, but who had the potential. But setting up the system that could isolate those students from the mass, and then convincing Ted Lehmann of its value—

Why does it have to be me? she thought. *I'm not cut out to play political games. And I positively hate having my charitable causes chosen for me!*

But it was Jim Garrett who was asking, and it would take unquestionable logic to get out of this. One did not lightly say no to the boss.

"Then Matt suggested that you would be a perfect choice," Jim Garrett went on.

"Thank you, my friend," she said to Garrett under her breath. It was not polite.

He grinned at her lazily from his perch on the end of one of the slatted benches, next to a gloriously blooming red orchid. "Well," he said reasonably, "weren't you thinking a minute ago that you were perfect for the job?"

"Since you've had firsthand experience at the journalism school," Jim Garrett continued. "And then Dorie Lehmann told me just how devoted you are to Nicolet, teaching that class and donating your pay back to the existing scholarship fund."

She had told Dorie Lehmann a great many things over coffee in the library that evening, but they had not discussed Anne's financial arrangements with the school. *Obviously,* Anne thought irritably, *someone has been asking questions about me.*

She took a long breath, held it till she counted to ten and released it slowly. "I think it's a lovely idea, Mr. Garrett—"

"Oh, call me Jim."

"And I wouldn't mind helping, but I just don't think I have the experience to set up such a program."

"You don't need experience," he said airily. "You just figure out what kind of rules and application procedure would have found you, Anne, and I'll be perfectly satisfied. You're certainly a leader in the profession, just the sort I'm looking for."

Garrett shifted uneasily, pulled his foot up onto the edge of the bench and folded his arms around his knee, as if, Anne thought, he'd heard all he could take.

She took another deep breath and tried again. "And as for President Lehmann," she said, "I don't think he'll be likely to take my word for—"

Jim Garrett dismissed that concern with a wave of the hand. "Oh, that's no problem. Matt's agreed to be my representative on the thing. You come up with the plan, and he'll take care of convincing Ted Lehmann."

She glanced at Garrett, who shrugged as if to say, *But it had better be a good plan.*

"It's just that he doesn't have time for the detail work," Jim Garrett went on. "Of course, I don't expect you'll do all this on your own time, Anne. We can make some arrangements in the newsroom so your schedule will be more flexible."

She turned her head so fast to glare at Garrett that her neck snapped. Extra time, she thought suspiciously. Was that his idea, too? And what was next? All of her time free, because she'd be fired for not doing her job? "No, thank you," she said crisply. "I'll manage."

Garrett murmured, "Welcome aboard."

Anne bit her tongue hard. She hadn't quite intended to say it that way, as if she was committing herself.

Jim Garrett certainly interpreted it that way, too. "I'll be looking forward to seeing what you come up with, my dear." He pushed himself back from the gardener's bench with a delighted smile, and held out his hand.

She was defeated; she might as well admit it. She nodded, rather numbly, and thought dispiritedly, that if she couldn't manage an effective refusal, there seemed little hope for the scholarship.

And something told her the situation was not going to get better. Not as long as Garrett was around. ___

"TELL THE TRUTH," she challenged as the maître d' seated them at the best corner table in the Lakemont Grand's famous dining room. "You're giving me the rope to hang myself. You're hoping I make such a mess of your father's scholarship program that he has no choice but to fire me."

Garrett frowned. "No," he said thoughtfully. "But keep talking, you might be on to something here. You're definitely better at plot development than Rudy is. Have you ever considered writing fiction?"

"Stop changing the subject, Garrett!"

He sighed. "I don't know where you got the idea I'm trying to get you fired, Anne."

"From you," she muttered. "You keep asking things like whether I've considered moving on to another newspaper and why don't I write a book."

"Oh? And from that you've concluded that I want to get rid of you? No, dear. I'm just asking civil, friendly questions, that's all. You forget that you have a tremendous advantage on me." He sniffed thoughtfully at the delicately colored wine the steward had poured into his glass, then tasted it and nodded.

"What advantage?" she asked warily.

"You know lots of things about me just from reading the column. I have to ask questions to find out about you."

It was logical enough, but Anne was not entirely convinced of his innocence; she still felt there'd been all kinds of hidden agendas floating around that greenhouse this morning.

The steward filled her glass. Anne sipped cautiously. Champagne, she'd found, always required discretion; she wondered briefly if that was why Garrett had ordered it. She looked around. She didn't get to the Lakemont Grand often, and she intended to enjoy this, no matter the company.

Once, the old hotel had held debutante balls, society weddings and every important convention and banquet that Lakemont ever boasted. Then the dictates of fashion changed; the hotel's decor was deemed ostentatious, and its popularity began to sag. Eventually it had been abandoned altogether as commercially unprofitable. A good thing, too, Anne thought, for remodeling would have destroyed the Roaring Twenties elegance. As it was, the brilliant colors and gorgeous ornamentation had all been there, ravaged, chipped and dirty, of course, but still there, when the renovators began to work. Now it was fashionable once more to sit each afternoon in the Marble Court for cocktails, to gather in the biggest ballroom for Sunday brunch, to toast a bride under the brass and crystal chandeliers and cheer as she tossed her bouquet from the grand staircase....

"It's beautiful, isn't it?" Anne said. "I can almost believe that when the band starts playing again, someone will begin dancing the Charleston."

"It does come to life, doesn't it? It's a pity that Rudy couldn't capture that liveliness."

Anne smothered a sigh.

"He tried so hard," Garrett went on sadly, "and it just didn't work. Didn't he even come down here and look at the place before he used it as a setting? You did recognize his feeble attempt, didn't you?"

"Yes, I recognized it. Do we have to talk about Rudy right now?"

Garrett was refilling her champagne glass. His eyebrows arched and he almost spilled the wine. Then he set the bottle cautiously back in the silver cooler at his elbow and reached across the table. "Of course not," he murmured. He let his fingertips come to rest lightly on her wrist. "I beg your pardon. I certainly didn't mean to be so clumsy."

"Clumsy? I don't—" She moved her hand.

He recaptured it, raised it to his mouth and kissed each fingertip, slowly.

"*Now* you're being clumsy, Garrett," she said under her breath. "Would you mind telling me what you think you're doing?"

Unhurried, he finished his task before saying, "I misunderstood, you see. I didn't realize you intended this to be a date. I honestly thought that Rudy's book was the entire reason you proposed dinner." He was still holding her hand firmly. "I beg your pardon for not realizing that it was only an excuse to be with me."

She tried to tug her fingers out of his, and failed.

"Our first date," he said with quiet satisfaction. "Of course, I feel a little foolish that you had to hit me over the head with the idea. If you'd only spoken plainly..."

"All right," Anne said, with the feeling that she was humoring a maniac. "We'll talk about Rudy's book, then."

"Oh, no," Garrett murmured, sounding a bit self-righteous. "You said you don't want to discuss it, and I wouldn't dream of forcing you."

The waiter brought their soup. With a great show of reluctance, Garrett released her hand. Anne realized, as she picked up her spoon, that her fingers were trembling ever so slightly. *The man has gone completely over the brink,* she told herself.

No, she decided suddenly. Garrett had never been caught up short like that in his life. This was only another game to him, just another line, and the more annoyed she became, the more he would enjoy tormenting her. If, instead, she played along, the fun would soon go out of it for him.

So she dropped her gaze to the artistically swirled surface of her soup and said, in her best femme fatale voice, "Well, it *was* a little embarrassing, to have you be so dense, Garrett."

She thought she heard him say "Touché," but it was only a breath, and she couldn't be certain.

She reached across the table to lay her fingers in his, and did her best to sound breathlessly shy. "The truth is, I've been in love with you practically forever. I fell in love with your marvelous prose—" she slanted a look up at him through her lashes and delivered the coup de grace in a silky murmur "—when I was just a child. In fact I could hardly read at all then; it's been so many years—"

His hand closed convulsively on hers. Anne jerked back and scowled at him, and shook her injured fingers. "Now I know why they call it a *crush,*" she muttered. "And if you're going to maul me, I'm finished with the one-upmanship games. Garrett, at least be honest. You laid a trap and I fell into it. But the truth is you don't want to talk about Rudy's book, either, because you're afraid you might end up apologizing in print for what you said. Aren't you?"

"'Either'?" he murmured. "All right, what's your reason for not wanting to talk about it?"

She bit her tongue but it was too late to deny what she'd said. "I didn't much care for the book," she said. "I might as well be honest. It's probably good, but—"

"No, it's not," Garrett interrupted. "Bad plot, bad writing, bad character development—"

"But I still think you should apologize."

Garrett's eyebrows almost disappeared into his hair. "Why? To preserve peace for you? Not on your life. I understand why you're defending Rudy, of course, that kind of knee-jerk reaction is typical of you."

"I am not defending Rudy!" It was loud enough to draw attention from the neighboring diners. Anne felt like crawling under the table. She settled for staring at her soup.

A woman who had just finished her dinner nearby paused beside their table to say rather haughtily, "Mr. Garrett, about your column this morning..."

Garrett rose politely. "Yes, ma'am?"

"I suggest you stop making a fool of yourself by pretending to be a literary critic. It's quite apparent that you haven't any idea what you're talking about, and frankly you're a dead bore on the subject of modern literature."

Anne choked back a laugh. Garrett gave her a sidelong glance that clearly said he was hurt that she'd abandoned him. Then he pulled a handful of coins from his pocket and held out a couple to the woman.

She looked at the money, and her face turned slightly purple. "What is this?"

"I'm so sorry to have bored you that I'm refunding the price of this morning's *Chronicle*," he said earnestly.

IT'S FUN! IT'S FREE!
AND IT COULD MAKE YOU A
MILLIONAIRE

If you've ever played scratch-off lottery tickets, you should be familiar with how our games work. On each of the first four tickets (numbered 1 to 4 in the upper right) there are Pink Metallic Strips to scratch off.

Using a coin, do just that—carefully scratch the PINK strips to reveal how much each ticket could be worth if it is a winning ticket. Tickets could be worth from $10.00 to $1,000,000.00 in lifetime money.

Note, also, that each of your 4 tickets has a unique sweepstakes Lucky Number . . . and that's 4 chances for a **BIG WIN!**

FREE BOOKS!

At the same time you play your tickets for big prizes, you are invited to play ticket #5 for the chance to get one or more free books from Harlequin®. We give away free books to introduce readers to the benefits of the Harlequin Reader Service®.

Accepting the free book(s) places you under no obligation to buy anything! You may keep your free book(s) and return the accompanying statement marked ''cancel.'' But if we don't hear from you, then every month, we'll deliver 6 of the newest Harlequin Romance® novels right to your door. You'll pay the low subscriber price of just $2.49* each—a saving of 30¢ apiece off the cover price! And there's no charge for shipping and handling!

Of course, you may play ''THE BIG WIN''without requesting any free books by scratching tickets #1 through #4 only. But remember, that first shipment of one or more books is FREE!

PLUS A FREE GIFT!

One more thing; when you accept the free book(s) on ticket #5, you are also entitled to play ticket #6, which is GOOD FOR A GREAT GIFT! Like the book(s), this gift is totally free and yours to keep as thanks for giving our Reader Service a try!

So scratch off the PINK STRIPS on all your BIG WIN tickets and send for everything today! You've got nothing to lose and everything to gain!

The women flung her fur scarf around her throat. "Well!" she said as she stalked away. "I have never been so insulted!"

Garrett sat down with a shrug. "I don't understand," he said mournfully. "All I did was be agreeable and offer to give her money back."

"You shouldn't have done that, Garrett."

"For the whole newspaper, too, not just the page that had my column on it."

"Don't be dense. You can't keep on this way, you know. A publisher doesn't exactly have to be above controversy, but it doesn't help any if the readers hate him on sight!"

Garrett's brow cleared. "She was only one reader," he pointed out. "And she obviously read the whole column, which is more attention than she gave to Rudy's book, I'll bet, or she wouldn't have been so quick to call *me* a dead bore."

They wrangled over it through Chateaubriand, through a crisp endive salad and through a light and luscious lemon trifle. They were still wrangling when the last half cup of coffee was pushed aside and the bill came. Garrett glanced at it, lying innocuously on its little tray, and then speculatively at Anne.

"Don't think I'm going to pick it up," she said firmly. "You lost this round. I may not like Rudy's style, but—"

"Tell the truth, Anne. You think it's easily one of the fifty books the world could best get along without."

"Stop putting words in my mouth. It doesn't matter what I think about the book, because I still think you were out of line to write that column. And so did the woman who gave you the piece of her mind."

Garrett shook his head. "No, she said I was a dead bore. It's an entirely different thing."

"Nevertheless, you owe me dinner."

Garrett smiled and reached for the bill.

Anne could hardly believe her eyes. "And you owe Rudy an apology, too."

"Don't push your luck," he murmured. "I'm not buying because I lost the bet, I'm buying because it's our first date, and I want you always to remember what a gentleman I am."

AT THE TOWN HOUSE, he followed her into the hallway. "Oh, you're coming in?" she asked, in mock surprise.

"Of course. When a woman tells a man that she's been in love with him practically forever, it would be very rude of him to ignore it." He took her coat and hung it up. "If you hadn't chosen such a public place to tell me, I wouldn't have waited so long."

He followed her into the kitchen, and when she stood on her toes to get a half-gallon jug of apple cider from the top shelf of the cabinet, he lifted it down for her, put it onto her hands, turned her around to face him and kissed her. Short of dropping the jar of cider on his toes, or hitting him on the side of the head with it, both of which she considered, she was helpless.

He began pulling the pins from her hair, and once it was loose and disheveled around her face his fingers slid into the blue black mass of it, moving and stroking and toying with the silky strands in an achingly slow sensuality. His mouth left hers after a while and began to wander, exploring her face, her throat, her ear. When he discovered the delicate spot just under her chin and his tongue flicked against it, the sensation inside her was like a slow explosion deep underwater, a combustion that took time to surface, and that grew in intensity as it rose. It was even more powerful than the last time he had kissed her—that lovers' embrace on the front steps that had held the cold at bay. "Anne," he said huskily, and smothered the word against her lips. She stopped breathing, and her muscles began to slacken and go limp.

Garrett caught the cider jug as it slid from her hands. "You're dangerous," he murmured and set it safely back on the kitchen counter. "Damned dangerous—"

"Garrett," she managed to say, under her breath. Her hands fluttered up to rest against his dinner jacket, caressing the strength of his broad shoulders.

He said, against her lips, "Don't you think you should start calling me Matt? Making love seems to call for first names—"

"Making...what?" Panic slammed her heart against her diaphragm and seemed to stop its beating. "Let's get one thing clear, Garrett. You're going home tonight. One kiss doesn't mean I'm interested in anything else."

His smile held a trace of amusement. "Oh, you're plenty interested."

She moved away from him and opened the cider, measuring it into a small pan and dumping in cinnamon sticks more liberally than she would have had her hands not been shaking so much.

He kissed the nape of her neck casually, and said, "But don't worry about it, Anne. I told you I knew you were a hidebound conservative."

That didn't make her feel any better. His voice had been matter-of-fact, but underneath it was a hint of almost breathless laughter.

Of course, she told herself wearily. *It's only a game for him. Oh, he might have stayed if you hadn't protested,*

*and no doubt he would have enjoyed sleeping with you,
as he would enjoy any casual fling. But it wouldn't have
mattered to him. So don't forget it, Anne McKenna.*

"Besides, I haven't forgotten that steam-whistle
scream of yours," he said. "And I'd hate to have you
wake all the neighbors with it. I'll see you this weekend."

"Weekend? What—" She followed him to the front
door.

"Oh, didn't I tell you? I arranged with Ted and Dorie
Lehmann to work on the scholarship details this weekend. We're going up to their cabin in Door County to
hash it all out."

"I thought you didn't have time for the details," she
said rather breathlessly.

"It seems more reasonable to me to come up with
something we all can agree on, and then present it to Dad
as a finished plan, rather than having him contemplate
all the infinite variations." He shrugged into his coat.
"A much better use of time."

He may be right, she thought. *But a weekend in a
Door County cabin with Garrett? I don't care if Ted and
Dorie Lehmann are there,* she told herself. It wouldn't
matter if the entire cast and crew of the world's largest
circus were there; it still wouldn't be enough company.

She cast about wildly for a suitable excuse. Before she
found one, Garrett had gone out the door.

Anne followed him, hugging herself against the wind.
"I have to work on Saturday!"

"I hadn't forgotten. So does Ted. So do I, as a matter of fact."

She couldn't help it. "You actually work?"

"I'll pick you up after you've finished your shift. It
only takes an hour to get up there."

"But I can't go. I have plans," Anne said. It sounded rather desperate.

Garrett came back to the door. "Liar," he said softly. "You told Rudy the other night that you were saving his masterpiece because you had nothing else to do all weekend. And since you read it today instead, that leaves you absolutely free. Doesn't it?"

He dropped a kiss on the end of her nose and left her standing there, half-frozen in the wind.

CHAPTER SIX

BY THE TIME she collected herself and returned to the kitchen, the cider had been merrily boiling over the edge of the pan for some time, and all that was left in the bottom was a brownish sludge. She put the syrupy mess to soak and began to mop up the top of the stove.

A cabin in Door County, she thought. The narrow peninsula between Lake Michigan and Green Bay was beautiful at any season, but it was not exactly her first choice of resorts for this time of year, when autumn could give way to winter with terrifying suddenness. She could imagine a cabin in Door County with the mercury plunging and the snow drifting and the icy spray storm-driven against the rocky coastline.

Don't be such a wimp, she told herself. *It isn't the weather you're frightened of. Anyway, it's only October.*

She gave up on cleaning the stove top, covered it with damp towels in the faint hope that by tomorrow the gluey mess might soak itself loose, and retreated to the living room.

Look on the bright side of it, she instructed herself. As long as she had to carry through with this project, it was far better to get it over with as soon as possible. The cabin would certainly provide all the peace and quiet Garrett could hope for, and with any luck by the end of the weekend they'd have hammered out the details. The worst of the work would be over, everybody would be satisfied, and Anne could go happily back to her own normal routine.

Of course, she thought, she could call up Jim Garrett in the morning instead, and tell him she couldn't take on the project after all. There were a dozen ways to say no, even to the boss, and make it stick.

The damnable part of it, though, was that when it came right down to it she didn't want to refuse. It wasn't the risk to her job that gave her second thoughts, either; it was the fact that Jim Garrett's scholarship fund was not only a very good cause, but one she happened to believe in. It was a cause that she would have been enthusiastic about, if not for the fact she'd been practically shanghaied into it.

And if Anne didn't take care of it, well, she couldn't quite see Garrett enthusiastically stepping up his participation. He'd made it rather plain his main interest in the entire affair was keeping his father contented while putting forth the minimum effort. So, either the project wouldn't be done at all, and the entire idea would die, or it would be thrown together by someone who didn't care, someone who didn't recognize the special nature of the people Jim Garrett was trying to help. It would end up as just one more academic fund like any other, earnestly awarding money for all the wrong reasons, and only by chance helping those who might someday make a real difference.

Time to go to bed, she told herself. *You're beginning to sound like a crusader yourself.* She flipped out the lights and for the first time saw the blinking red light on her answering machine.

The first message was from Rudy. He sounded penitent, he said that of course he didn't really think that she was to blame for the views of that arrogant columnist, and he asked her to call him.

The second message was also from Rudy, obviously much later in the evening, pointedly announcing that he had come to pick her up for their date and found the town house empty, and wondering how she could possibly be holding a grudge, because he had, after all, apologized.

A date, she thought irritably. After that tantrum this morning, he couldn't possibly think she would be sitting here waiting for him like a dutiful little girl! Or had he been so far out of control that he didn't even remember calling off the evening? And if he thought talking to her answering machine would take care of this problem...

She could have called him, but instead she erased the tape and climbed the stairs to her bedroom. He'd get the message, sooner or later.

Just on the edge of sleep, she found herself wondering what Rudy would have done at the Lakemont Grand tonight if the woman with the fur scarf had told him his book was a dead bore. He wouldn't have politely refunded her money, that was certain.

She started to giggle at the memory of the expression on the woman's face. One thing about Garrett, she reflected, he didn't suffer any haunting doubts, not about himself, not about his work, not about his views. That self-assurance didn't make him right, of course....

"Calling himself a gentleman," she said with a yawn. "What a fairy tale that is!"

EVERY TIME Anne shifted her feet under her desk, her toes connected with the overnight case she had stashed there. It made perfect sense for Garrett to pick her up at the *Chronicle* building rather than wait for her at the town house, she had to admit that; they would be getting a late enough start as it was. Still, there was a nagging feeling, almost a guilty twinge, about the presence of that moss green leather bag under her desk.

As if she were off on a weekend assignation with a married lover! she gibed at herself. *Just stop it, McKenna.*

Holly Andrews came in from the chamber of commerce awards dinner at the Lakemont Grand, looking like a million in a tailored wool suit. "Have you forgiven me yet, Anne?" she asked slyly as she slid a folded sheaf of paper across the desk. "I've finished my assigned punishment."

Anne glanced at the top sheet. Neatly typed in the unmistakable print produced by the *Chronicle*'s newsroom computers was one sentence repeated over and over: *I will always tell my editor the entire truth, no matter what.*

Anne riffled through the pages and said, "This doesn't count, you know. You were supposed to write it five hundred times, not just once and then hold the repeat key down!"

"For all you know, I've been at it for two days," Holly said reasonably. "Your friend Garrett was the hit of the evening, by the way. The chamber of commerce loved him."

So that was what he'd meant when he said he had to work on Saturday. "After-dinner speaking would be his field," Anne muttered. "Also stand-up comedy, improvisational playacting, and ringmastering a circus—"

"I thought you were beginning to like the guy. From what Dominique said . . ."

Anne eyed her suspiciously. "Since when have you been on a first-name basis with Dominique Delacourt?"

"I'm not, actually. It's the grapevine. One of the national-desk editors ran into her at the Lakemont Grand a couple of days ago, and Dominique was livid. Something about seeing Matt Garrett kissing you in the dining room."

Anne closed her eyes in sheer frustration.

"So was he, McKenna? Is that what you were doing on Thursday when you were too busy to go out with me?"

"He was not kissing me," Anne said firmly, and then conscience made her add, "Not exactly. It was only my fingers."

Holly gave her a sideways look and said under her breath, "Isn't that just like the grapevine? Always getting everything wrong! He was kissing your *fingers?*"

"It's not obscene, Holly. Oh, dammit, why didn't I have the sense to insist on going back to the Red Dragon instead?" In her irritation, she kicked at the wastebasket under her desk, and forgot the overnight case. It slid neatly out from its hiding place and stopped against the toe of Holly's high-heeled pump.

Holly looked at it for ten endless seconds, and then raised innocent eyes to meet Anne's gaze. "And I suppose you're sleeping over with a girlfriend tonight?" she asked gently.

Anne sighed. "As a matter of fact, no. I'm working this weekend."

"Don't be antique, Anne. The modern girl gets by with a toothbrush when she goes to spend the night with her guy."

"If I were doing something like that, would I advertise it?" Anne asked crisply. "And if you don't have a story to write, I'll find you one."

It was inevitable, she supposed, that Garrett would have chosen that precise moment to walk in.

"Right," Holly said in an undertone. "A working weekend. You know, Anne, the really up-to-date girls buy reversible skirts and jackets so they don't even have to go home in the morning to change clothes...."

Garrett's hands were in the pockets of a wool-and-canvas hunting jacket that was obviously as comfortable as it was old. He sauntered up to Anne's desk and perched on the corner of it, where he could see the clock on the newsroom wall. "Am I late?" he asked, his tone implying that he would rather believe the clock was wrong. "Sorry. Are you ready to go, Anne?"

"Not quite," she said, trying to sound very professional. "By the way, I should warn you that the managing editor had a few harsh things to say about your column for Monday. I don't think it was his favorite."

Garrett shrugged. *Obviously it doesn't bother him,* Anne thought. *The managing editor only terrifies those of us who don't have the publisher's power squarely in our pockets.*

"Which column is your personal favorite, Garrett?" Holly asked. "I've always wanted to know that."

"Whichever one I've just finished writing."

Holly turned that one over, and said blandly, "That's as diplomatic as saying that your favorite girl is the one you last kissed."

Garrett grinned. "And it's just as true."

Anne said firmly, "Your telephone is ringing, Holly."

"You don't mind if I answer it here, do you?" Holly said, and without waiting for a reply she punched in the code that summoned her call to Anne's desk. "*Chronicle* newsroom."

Anne said very softly, "Being late is the least of the things you're going to be sorry for, Garrett."

Holly's body tensed. She turned toward Anne, cupped her hand over the mouthpiece and said quietly, "The Sheboygan Building is on fire."

The Sheboygan Building. Anne's brain began to click out facts. Barely five years old, it was the tallest building in Lakemont's downtown section, a proud tower containing shops and offices and expensive apartments, which at this hour, would be full of people settling down for the night. . . .

"This isn't a gag, is it?" she said, but she didn't have to wait for an answer. The expression in Holly's eyes was the same she'd seen in hundreds of reporters over the years: the mingling of dread at a potential tragedy and excitement at having a big story to chase. No, Holly was telling the truth.

Anne reached for the telephone. "Go," she said briefly. "Grab a photographer on your way out the door, and call me the instant you see whether it's major."

Holly didn't wait for more.

"Has the paper gone to bed?" Garrett asked quietly.

"No, but it's close." Anne gathered what information she could from Holly's caller and put the phone down. "It's an office floor, could be anything from a blaze in a wastebasket to the classic nightmare. The fire department didn't want them to build that tower, you know. The chief said it was too tall to fight fires in—"

She glanced at her watch and punched the intercom button. Her mind was icily cool as she mentally ticked off the things that must be done. It was coming up on eleven o'clock; the press was ready to roll at the stroke of the hour, and the crew running it must be told to delay everything for a few vital minutes until Holly called. The composing room, where the work of organizing the pages was done, was shutting down by now, its night's work finished; she must catch the crew foreman and tell him not to send everyone home just yet....

The man in charge of the composing room didn't want to cooperate. "The truth is somebody probably smelled a cigarette in a no-smoking area and called the fire department," he complained. "Big deal! You want me to hold my people here for that? It's Saturday night—"

"You'll get overtime," Anne said crisply. "And if you don't want to keep them, let me remind you that I can put together a front page by myself if I have to."

"No, you can't. It's union rules."

"So file a complaint with the national union office on Monday morning. I assure you that's what I'll be doing, if you don't hold those people!" she said and hung up on him.

Garrett was looking at her rather oddly. *I suppose he thinks I set the damned fire myself,* she thought, *just to get out of going to Door County!* "Bad luck, this happening just now," she said briefly. "I can't leave till it's settled one way or the other, you know."

He nodded. "Bad luck for lots of people if it's really on fire." His voice was somber. "Can I help?"

She blinked at him once in surprise, and then waved a hand toward the long row of filing cabinets on the far wall of the newsroom. "You've used the morgue. There was a fuss about the sprinkler system when they were building that tower, but I was in Chicago at the time, and I don't remember the details. It's probably wasted effort, but—"

It was not wasted effort; the Sheboygan tower was on fire. Holly's voice, when she called a few minutes later, was grim. "It's hard to tell how bad it really is," she said, "but I'm across the street at the deli and I can see flames licking out the windows about ten floors up. Gary's already shooting pictures."

"Tell him I'll send someone down for the film. Get me a story as soon as you can, Holly." Anne put the telephone down and sat thoughtfully silent for a full minute while she plotted her course.

The Sunday edition was bigger and heavier than the average daily *Chronicle,* and it went out to subscribers across the state, instead of just in Lakemont itself. Much of the paper—the society section, the comics, the weekend magazine—was already printed, but those sections still had to be mechanically inserted into the yet-to-be-printed news sections, then trucked out to the delivery areas. All of that took time, and the sheer size of the edition meant holding back the press on Saturday night was a bigger risk than on any other day of the week. Anne would have to balance the time required to produce a clear and accurate story about the fire with the time needed for production and delivery of the finished product. If she closed the issue too quickly and the story was inaccurate, or if she waited too long and the subscribers did not get their papers promptly by six in the morning, there would be trouble.

She said to no one in particular, "I'm calling the managing editor."

Garrett looked up from a manila folder full of clippings spread out on the desk he had commandeered next to hers. He frowned a little. "Why?"

"For permission to hold up the press a little longer, of course," Anne snapped. "What did you think, that I want to ask him for a date?"

He turned back to the clippings. "You don't have to call anyone, Anne. Hold it as long as you need to."

It took a couple of seconds for the message to sink in. *Of course,* she thought finally. *I don't need the managing editor's permission if I have the publisher's. And obviously it makes little difference anymore which Garrett is occupying that office.*

"Thanks," she said gruffly and went back to work.

It was nearly one in the morning when the press began to roll, with a huge photograph of the leaping flames taking up almost half the front page, and Holly's story, phoned in to Anne, in the lead position, next to Garrett's thorough summary of the building's controversial history. The edition had the same professional polish as if they had worked on it for days.

"You look happy," Garrett observed as they walked out to the parking ramp.

"Shouldn't I be? I'm not pleased about the fire, of course, but it's under control and no one was badly injured. So it's not heartless to be happy that the story looks good."

"And we scooped the radio and television stations, which is no small feat anymore," he added.

The hint of comradeship in the "we" warmed her heart.

"That reminds me," Garrett went on. "As long as we're speaking of feet, when Holly called last time she said her next expense account was going to include a bill for a pair of alligator shoes that got drenched by a fire hose."

Anne winced. "Oh, well," she said. "We no doubt owe it to her. At least she waited till the fire was under control."

A car came up the ramp a little faster than was quite safe and pulled into a parking space right by the entrance. It was a spot that had been reserved for the handicapped, though Anne noted that none of the four people who got out of the car appeared less than ablebodied. Then she recognized a fur-trimmed cape, and had a sudden and almost overwhelming urge to crawl under the nearest car.

Dominique Delacourt stopped in the center of the walkway and stared at the green overnight case Garrett was carrying. "What on earth are you doing here at this hour, Matt? Running away from home?"

"Helping out with a story."

"I see," Dominique said sweetly. "Did you bring your sleeping bag, too? We stopped between parties to pick up a paper. Did you get the Sheboygan fire in, then?"

"Yes, *we* did," Anne said under her breath.

Only Garrett heard her, and he gave her a half smile, took her arm and drew her down the length of the ramp away from the small party at the door.

"Why," she asked, in a low voice that was incredibly level, "couldn't Dominique just buy the damned paper from the newsstand for once instead of trailing into the office to get a free copy? Of all the days to be so blasted cheap—"

Garrett seemed undisturbed. "She couldn't. The paper hasn't reached the newsstand yet, because you held up the press."

Anne gave a snarl that was worthy of a mother tiger protecting her cubs.

She saw the direction he was taking in the ramp and added a little sarcastically, "I see you're parking in out-of-the-way corners these days. Aren't you afraid of muggers?" It made her feel a little better. Then she saw the Pierce-Arrow gleaming in the darkness, its convertible top in place, and stopped short. "We're taking *that* to Door County?"

"Why not? I promised you a ride in it. Though I must admit if I'd known it was going to be the wee hours before we started out, I might have had second thoughts."

"Are you certain we should do this?" she said, looking doubtfully at the car, its elaborately curved fenders gleaming dully in the dim light.

"Don't you think we'll make it? It may be old, but I assure you it's reliable."

"It's not just the car. It will be awfully late by the time we get there," she said. "Dorie's not going to be pleased when we arrive in the middle of the night."

"I called her. They're not going to wait up for us."

He was holding the door open. She hesitated for an instant longer. "I just hope you got the heater fixed," she said with resignation, and climbed into the passenger seat. "Take me to Door County, James."

"My name," he said smoothly, "is Matt. I realize that you went to great lengths last night to avoid calling me that, but still, I think by now you ought to know it."

She was glad of the darkness inside the car; it helped, at least, to hide the warm color that had sprung into her cheeks. And she kept her voice carefully innocent. "What on earth are you talking about? Aren't all chauffeurs called James?"

The old car was not only roomy, but surprisingly quiet, and smooth-riding and warm. Garrett took the freeway north from Lakemont, and people in the few other cars out at that hour slowed and stared and honked and waved. Anne finally sat up and started waving back with enthusiasm. "It's probably the only chance I'll ever get to feel like a celebrity," she told Garrett.

But as they went farther north there were fewer and fewer cars, so she settled back and stared at the moon. It was gloriously full, a frozen pale disk floating on black velvet among the spangled stars. Here and there a jet blinked its silent way across the night.

She turned to rest her cheek against the mohair upholstery, and yawned. It was awfully pleasant here, she thought. The moonlight, and the old car, and the quiet night. If it wasn't for the slightly dusty smell of the wool under her cheek . . .

"Anne." He sounded almost plaintive.

She struggled briefly to figure out why, and then decided it didn't matter.

"Anne, my arm is asleep. I know that's nothing compared to your whole body, but it makes it very difficult to shift gears."

The wool didn't smell of dust anymore, she thought a little hazily. It smelled like Garrett. She opened her eyes a fraction and realized she was no longer leaning against the seat but was curled up against him, with her head pressed against his shoulder and her nose buried in his jacket.

"Oh, don't move the rest of you," he said hastily. "If you'd just lean your head somewhere else."

She realized belatedly that her fingertips were resting intimately on his thigh. She pulled back as if she'd been scorched, and wanted to choke him when he started to laugh.

"I was asleep," she said with all the dignity she could muster. "I am hardly responsible for what happens when I'm asleep!"

Garrett grinned. "Then why pull away as if you'd committed a crime? Believe me, I'm not going to complain. If you want, I'll give you my full attention, and we'll find out what happens when you're awake."

She turned her back on him and stared out the window into the night. "Don't let me take your concentration off your driving."

"Oh, I'd be happy to pull off the road." He began to whistle, his good nature obviously restored. A couple of minutes later the Pierce-Arrow turned into a smooth concrete driveway and glided to a quiet stop. Anne looked up at the silhouette of the clapboard building and said, "This is a cabin? It looks like a full-scale hotel."

Inside, most of the first floor was one huge room, dimly lit, its high ceiling left in shadow. In a massive, freestanding fieldstone fireplace in the center of the room, a fire had burned down to whispering embers. Beside it, on a low table made from a cross-section slice of an ancient tree, was a tray holding a vacuum bottle, two cups and a napkin-covered plate.

"Bless Dorie," Garrett said contentedly. "Sandwiches and hot chocolate, and a fire. She certainly knows the way to a man's heart." He began laying sticks of kindling carefully onto the hot coals, and before long a cheerful little blaze leaped up.

Anne sat down cross-legged on the flagstone hearth facing the fireplace and reached for a sandwich. It was chicken salad, she discovered happily, piled high on sourdough bread, and she was starving. It must be the stress from that last couple of hours' work. She broke the sandwich in two, took a big bite and said rather indistinctly, "Are you some kind of pyromaniac? You're always building a fire."

"One of the primitive instincts left over from tribal days, no doubt." He sat down beside her and very gently shifted her weight until she was leaning against his chest, almost cradled in the curve of his body. She was off balance, and both her hands were still full; she couldn't have pulled away from him if she had tried.

He kissed her temple, and then her cheek, and then her lips, and his hand wandered from her waist to the swell of her breast.

"Another primitive instinct?" she said. Her voice trembled a little.

"No, it's the same one, I expect. The intrigue of playing with dangerous things. Matches, dynamite, uranium waste...you."

She tried to sit up, and failed. "I thought you said you were hungry. If the way to a man's heart is really through his stomach—"

"Once in a while it's nice to take a detour." His teeth gleamed in the firelight as he snapped a bite out of her sandwich, savored it, then turned his attention back to her mouth. His tongue darted gently along the soft outline of her lips, tracking down a stray crumb of sourdough bread. "Anne," he whispered, and she waited, almost breathlessly. But he didn't go on, just pulled her closer and kissed her hard.

The flagstones were warm, and he lowered her gently onto them, cushioning her with his arm behind her neck and stretching her out in the fire's glow. His gaze swept the length of her, once.

Ted and Dorie are upstairs somewhere, she reminded herself. *But Garrett knows that, too, and so this cannot possibly get out of hand. There is not one reason on earth why I shouldn't enjoy this.*

And so she slowly unclenched the knot of self-control that lay deep inside her. There was sudden recklessness in her eyes, those huge, dark, soft blue eyes, and he saw it there and drew one short, sharp breath of wonder before he bent his head to take her mouth once more.

His fingertips began to roam, dissolving the barricades of sweater and bra that lay between his flesh and hers, stirring an aching gladness in her. She closed her eyes and allowed herself to drift away upon a sea of pleasure, without a thought for how she might ultimately get back to shore.

When, a good deal later, his hand slipped quietly away from her breast, she was confused for a moment by the sensation of loss and cold, and almost automatically she reached for him, wanting only to feel that sweet sensual touch once more.

"You've never done this before, have you?" he whispered. The palm of his hand brushed, very softly, against the firm tip of her breast.

She shivered and blinked, a little confused. "I wouldn't exactly say that."

He persisted. "Oh, cuddling by the fire, perhaps. But you're a virgin, aren't you?"

Anne let go of his hand. Her breath seemed to have stuck in her chest. "Why should it matter?" It was a hoarse little gasp; it was all she could manage.

Garrett's hand slid very slowly away from her breast. With one fingertip he stroked the soft hair at her temple and said cryptically, "Perhaps it shouldn't. But it does." His voice was rough around the edges, and it was a different thing altogether when he kissed her again. Tentative, that was it, as if he were suddenly afraid.

She braced herself against his chest and pushed herself up from the flagstones. "I think . . . that you're mistaken," she said tightly. "It wouldn't have gone any further. I'm awfully tired. If Dorie told you which room—"

"The first one on the right, at the top of the stairs." It was absentminded; he was brushing at a long stain of mayonnaise on the front of his shirt.

She looked down at the rest of her sandwich—chicken salad and tomato and mayonnaise and sourdough, mashed and smeared across the flagstone floor, a casualty of that blind and breathless embrace that had led so close to the brink.

Or, more accurately, just another casualty, she thought. *I feel a bit damaged myself.*

Garrett had seen the remains of the sandwich, too, that was apparent. Anne braced herself for the acerbic comment that he was certain to make, but he only said, "I'll take care of the mess. Don't worry about it."

Which mess, she wondered. Did he mean just the sandwich, or her, too? Or the whole idea of the scholarship, and the working weekend?

She was almost at the foot of the stairs when he said, "Anne."

She wheeled around. It hadn't been much more than a breath, as if he hadn't intended to say anything at all, and when she faced him, he ducked his head a little and said, "You were wonderful tonight."

For a half second she wondered what he was talking about, and then she knew. And with that painful clarity that sometimes accompanies great stress, she watched the moment when Garrett heard the double meaning in what he had said. He looked as if a hammer had come down across his ear.

He almost stammered, "The way you handled that story, I mean. The fire—"

She couldn't stand to let it go on another instant. "What else could you possibly have meant?" she asked, and turned and went up the stairs very quietly.

She didn't sleep, of course; she watched the moonlight creep along the pine boards of the floor, and she told herself she was a fool.

She had savored and enjoyed that sensual play, and wondered idly at the simmering emotions that seemed to lie just under the surface of her brain, of her body. She'd been just like a marshmallow being broiled over a fire, slightly gooey on the outside, pleasantly warm in the middle and just seconds away from bursting into flames that would consume her.

No wonder Garrett realized she had never had a lover; he had recognized that potential for explosion, and he knew, too, that she didn't understand what was happening to her. He, on the other hand, had not only known it for what it was, but had wanted to forestall it.

Because Ted and Dorie were upstairs, she thought, and things were getting out of hand. Or had it been more than that?

You're a virgin, aren't you? Yes, it matters....

He had not been afraid, she thought, so much as simply cautious, wary of what she might demand, and apprehensive about the promises she might expect. She couldn't blame him for protecting himself, and yet...

She lay awake and listened to the unfamiliar creaking of the house as it adjusted to the dropping temperature of the small, dark hours of the morning. At a little after three o'clock, she went to get herself a drink of water from the bathroom, and stopped absolutely dead in the doorway at the sight of Garrett, magnificently attired in royal blue sweat pants, and nothing else, brushing his teeth.

He grinned uncertainly at her in the mirror, through a mouthful of toothpaste foam, and his eyes widened just a bit at the sight of her emerald green nightshirt. Then he shrugged his shoulders. "Dorie is very discreet," he said. "She obviously didn't like to ask if we were sleeping together, so she just put us in adjoining rooms—"

"With only a bathroom between," Anne supplied. Beyond him, an open door showed the corner of another bedroom. She hadn't bothered to check that extra door earlier; she'd thought it was only a linen closet. "It could be worse, I suppose."

He seemed relieved by her matter-of-fact attitude. "I'll knock," he promised. "And I'll be very quiet."

Anne gritted her teeth and said politely, "Likewise." She went back to bed without her glass of water but with one eye on the door.

Not that she anticipated any more trouble from Garrett. On the contrary; he had seemed faintly worried that she might barge in and throw herself at him!

"You were wonderful tonight."

The fool, she thought rather viciously. *As if I could have been stupid enough to think he was talking about what happened downstairs!*

But I wish that was what he meant, she thought. *Oh, how I wish it was. . . .*

CHAPTER SEVEN

SUNDAY MORNING brought a golden glow to Anne's room and cast playful sunbeams across the brass bed with its yellow star-burst quilt. She puttered about for a long time, painstakingly making the bed and slowly gathering up her few possessions, wishing that she didn't have to go downstairs at all.

When she finally couldn't delay any longer, she found the great room empty, and she stood for a long moment by the crackling fire. It was pleasant there, with the warmth of the blaze in front of her and the late-autumn sunshine pouring through the big south windows and warming her back. She was looking thoughtfully at the trophy displayed on the wall over the mantel. Ted and Dorie Lehmann had not seemed the sort to want the majestic head of a moose or an elk staring down at them from above the fireplace, and sure enough, it was a different sort of animal hanging there, staring with glassy eyes into infinity. It was the biggest teddy bear Anne had ever seen, professionally mounted on what looked like a mahogany trophy board, with a big red bow around his neck.

How did she miss that last night, she wondered, and answered her own question. The same way she'd missed all the other obvious stuff that was going on, by being very, very wrapped up in herself.

From the kitchen corner, Dorie Lehmann called, "Good morning! But my dear, you should have slept longer. Matt told us what a night you had."

Anne stifled a shudder. The Sheboygan Building, she reminded herself. The fire. That was what he was talking about.

"I couldn't sleep on such a glorious morning as this." She took the coffee mug Dorie handed her and perched on a stool beside the half wall that pretended to isolate the kitchen from the rest of the great room.

"That's exactly what Matt said, so he and Ted went out for a swim."

This time the shudder could not be held back.

Dorie saw it and laughed. "At the gym, of course, not in the bay." She scattered a crumbly topping over a pan of batter and put it in the oven. "They'll be back in time for brunch. If you don't mind, Anne, while you and Matt and Ted are working out your plans, I'm going to stay right here in the kitchen."

Anne sniffed the air appreciatively. "No objections from me!"

"All our children and grandchildren will be coming for the holidays, and I want to get some of the work done early. It's like running a bed-and-breakfast with all of them here."

"This is a lovely house," Anne said. "When Garrett called it a cabin, I must admit I thought of a log shack in the woods."

"Oh, we've always called it that." Dorie began breaking eggs into a china bowl. "Or sometimes the second-honeymoon cottage, because we're going to retire here. In the meantime, though, keeping two houses going is a challenge. I hope you were comfortable last night, warm enough and everything."

Anne willed herself not to turn pink. *Dorie is not asking for the details,* she reminded herself. *It's only polite to inquire about a houseguest's comfort. And why should you be embarrassed, anyway? Because she put the two of you in adjoining rooms and you didn't sleep together? What an idiot you are, Anne McKenna!*

Anne was setting the table when the men returned, and Dorie sent Garrett in to help. His very presence made Anne nervous, and she almost dropped a hand-made pottery plate. Garrett, following her around the table to lay out the flatware, nearly stepped on her heel, and Anne jerked away.

He said something under his breath that sounded like a curse, and then muttered, "Look, Anne, last night was obviously a mistake all the way around, and I'm sorry."

She looked through him. "It certainly was a mistake," she said quietly. "All of us seemed to have wrong ideas—you, me, Dorie. Though I can't help but wonder, Garrett. Were the adjoining bedrooms really Dorie's idea? Or did you ask her for that convenient arrangement to make it easier to get around my hide-bound conservatism? That was what you called it, wasn't it?"

A little muscle right beside his mouth twitched slightly. "Damn it, Anne."

"And what changed your mind?" Anne went on smoothly. "A sudden attack of conscience? Or were you afraid that a woman my age who's never had an affair must have something wrong with her, and so you just weren't interested anymore?"

His eyes had gone almost black. "Damn it, at least be honest! You wouldn't have liked me any better this morning if I had taken you up on that invitation last night."

"Invitation?" she spat the word. "How dare you say I invited that—" She was too infuriated to finish.

"Well, you certainly weren't trying to cool off the situation. And you can't have it both ways, you know. You can be offended at me because I started to make love to you in the first place, or offended because I didn't finish, but not both."

Her mouth was open in shock.

"So let me know which it is, whenever you make up your mind," he said roughly, and walked around the table to fling down the rest of the flatware.

Dorie brought in a chafing dish of scrambled eggs just then, and Ted followed with a tray loaded with coffee cake and sausages, but the argument was already finished. There was certainly nothing left to say.

After brunch she curled up on the long couch; the Lehmanns had the kind of furniture that encouraged putting one's feet up. She watched in impatient disbelief as Ted began to lay out an enormous jigsaw puzzle on the low table by the fire. "Come on," he urged her. "You'll like this one. It's challenging but not impossible."

"I thought we were going to get this scholarship thing out of the way," she protested.

Garrett murmured, "Anxious to get back on the road, Anne?"

"Not particularly. And I'm no more compulsive about work than anyone else. But that is what we came up here for—" she looked up at him through her lashes and added sweetly "—isn't it?"

She thought his jaw might crack, it was so tight.

Ted snapped two pieces together. "I've found this works extremely well for creative brainstorming. It occupies the logical half of the brain, you see, and lets the visionary half be free to roam.''

It sounded to Anne as if a great deal more than half of his brain was roaming, but she found to her astonishment that it worked. Long minutes would go by with no sound but the occasional rustle of the puzzle pieces in the box, and then one of them would throw out an idea and the others would turn it over and examine it as if it were just another jigsaw piece, and either fit it in or toss it away. Gradually, as the photograph of a mountainside in autumn took shape, so did Jim Garrett's scholarship fund.

It was Ted who said, ''I'd suggest a fairly high academic standard. Jim's looking for intelligent young people, so we might as well eliminate the barely average students.''

Anne shook her head. She snapped the final piece into the flame red bush that formed a lower corner of the puzzle and said, ''If you do that, you'll turn it into a vanilla-flavored scholarship that benefits only vanilla-flavored people, instead of the licorice-and-raspberry-ripple sort that Jim is looking for.''

Garrett tapped the palm of his hand against the side of his head, as if to check his hearing. ''Licorice?'' he repeated. ''Raspberry ripple?''

The cynical twist in his voice made her want to throw something at him. ''I just mean that he's looking for people who aren't afraid to shake things up.''

''Then why didn't you say that?'' Garrett said wearily. ''It must be Rudy's book. Reading that sort of trashy descriptive language takes its toll on the best of brains.''

''Thank you for the compliment,'' Anne said politely. ''However, it happens to be true that the best journalists are not first-rate students.''

Ted said, "That's quite a sweeping generality."

"I'm serious. All-around honors students get that ranking by accepting what they're told, learning it by rote and spewing it back upon demand. Give them a reporter's notebook and they take notes."

"That is the way it's done—" Garrett began.

"Will you let me finish, Garrett? It's the average kids who want to know why things are, and who drive teachers to the brink by taking apart the objects that interest them. Those are the kids who want to know what the politicians are up to when they're not holding news conferences, and who don't mind slogging around in the mud to find out."

Ted sat back in his chair, fingering a piece of sky blue cardboard. "You know, I think you're right," he said. He seemed to be addressing the bear above the mantel. "As long as you're not eliminating honors students altogether, Anne."

"I'm not. I just don't want to give them a boost they haven't earned."

Garrett gave her a long and appraising look, and stayed silent.

Ted prompted, "Then you suggest basing the choice on—"

"Written applications, including an essay—"

"Five hundred words on 'Why I want to be a journalist when I grow up,' I suppose?" Garrett muttered.

Anne ignored him. "Followed by personal interviews."

"Who do you suggest should conduct all the interviews?" Garrett asked. "Dad certainly isn't up to it."

That stopped her for a moment. Then she shrugged her shoulders. "I'll volunteer, for the first run-through, at least. Do you have any better suggestions?"

"Draw the names out of a hat," he said brutally. "You'll have about the same odds of success. I'll bet that as soon as the diplomas are awarded, half of the Garrett Scholars, and all of your raspberry-ripple types, will write a thank-you note for the free education and then go off and do something else entirely. Join the Foreign Legion, probably, or start a knitting shop in Upper Sandusky. Anything but go to work for a newspaper."

Anne tossed her head. "While the other half—"

"Won't bother to write the thank-you note first!" Garrett finished triumphantly.

She glared at him, but he only smiled, reached for the puzzle piece she'd been holding for the past five minutes and fitted it smugly into a snowcapped tree on the peak of the mountain. In the sudden silence, the telephone began to ring, and Ted Lehmann went to answer it. Anne would have sworn he was trying not to laugh.

"And it's not like the Army, you know," Garrett went on. "You can't make them promise six years out of their lives in repayment."

She colored a little; it seemed as if he had read her mind. "You don't want him to do this at all, do you, Garrett?" she challenged. "I'm surprised you haven't talked him out of the whole idea."

"I never said he shouldn't do it."

"Well, you certainly sound as if you think it's a monstrous waste. Perhaps I should advise Jim to set up some sort of nonprofit institution to take care of it all—the scholarships and whatever other charitable brainstorms he might have in the future. He could fund it by assigning part of his stock in the newspaper, and then he'd be guaranteed that things would go on the way he wants them, because no one person could reverse his decisions."

"By 'no one person' you mean me, of course?" Garrett replied smoothly.

"Or perhaps he should hand over all his stock to a trust," Anne went on speculatively. "You couldn't be tempted to sell the *Chronicle* to some chain if you didn't own the controlling interest in it—"

His eyes hardened, and she stopped abruptly, certain she had gone too far this time.

"You wouldn't do that, would you, Garrett?" she asked uncertainly.

Garrett said mildly, "Stick to the scholarship, McKenna, that's all you were asked to do. How do you plan to make these people keep their promises?"

Obviously the other subject was closed. "I can't, exactly," she admitted. "But I can improve the odds, and save Jim some money at the same time, or more accurately, get him some immediate value for what he's spending."

Ted came back just then, rubbing his hands. "Matt, my boy, how would you like to get all togged up in fancy academic robes on the second Saturday in December and give my graduating seniors the benefit of your wisdom?"

"In return for an honorary degree, of course," Anne said under her breath. "Too bad there isn't such a thing as a Doctor of Arrogance—"

She thought Garrett gritted his teeth, but he said civilly enough, "That's awfully short notice, Ted."

"Yes, it is," Ted said cheerfully. "But I just found out my scheduled commencement speaker has been indicted for fraud."

"What a shame," Anne murmured, and made a mental note; that was a story the *Chronicle* should pursue. "To be only second choice..."

Garrett eyed her and said, "I have an alternate suggestion, Ted. Ask Anne to do it. She's the one who's got all the brilliant ideas today. Now what's this latest one you mentioned? I can't wait to hear it."

THEY STAYED FOR DINNER, because Dorie insisted, and they lingered over coffee and a sampling of the glorious array of cookies that had been scenting the cabin all afternoon. They drove back to Lakemont in the late evening in almost total silence.

Anne watched the moon rise, and wondered how the same highway, the same car, the same moon, the same man could fit together into such a prosaic pattern now, when just last night . . .

She stopped herself from pursuing that line of thought, since it was obviously not a constructive one, and said almost at random, "When are you and Ted going to present this plan to your father?"

"Ted's not going to be there."

She was startled. "Why not?"

"Because if he was, it would invite Dad to start the negotiations all over again. So a delegation of two will give him the findings of the committee. It's much less likely to be a free-for-all that way."

She said carefully, "A delegation of two?"

"Yes, you and me. You do want to be there, don't you, Anne? Just to be certain I present everything properly?"

He sounded a little sarcastic, but there was some validity to that point of view, Anne thought. Still, she hesitated. "Well, I hadn't exactly—"

"Besides, it's mostly your plan."

"That's true." She stopped suddenly, because she could feel his gaze on her, and she suspected it wasn't a flattering one.

"And if Dad hates it," Garrett went on gravely, "I'd rather he tell you directly instead of sending messages through me."

"Thanks a lot!"

"How about lunch tomorrow?"

"I have to be at work at two."

Garrett shrugged. "Then we'll make it an early lunch. Noon, at the house."

She let the silence grow, and finally said softly, "Do you really think he'll hate it?"

"I didn't say that. I expect he'll have a few refinements to suggest, such as, if one interview is good, two would be better."

She had to think about that for a minute. "You mean he'd drag you into it, too?"

"Well, he seems to be having no trouble delegating the work so far."

It would serve Garrett right, she thought. Of course, she wouldn't like it one bit!

"I've already told him that this is getting out of hand, and if he doesn't stop it he'll have only his orchids left to fret about."

Anne nodded. "And a criminally overworked son. I'm sure you remembered to warn him about that."

"Yes." Garrett sounded plaintive. "He didn't seem to mind, though. Why is it that nobody seems to think writing a column is really work?"

"Perhaps because you make it look so easy, and because no one ever sees you doing it."

"What am I supposed to do, set up a desk in the display window of a department store downtown so people can gather round and watch?"

"Not a bad idea," Anne applauded. "I'll suggest it to the promotional department, if you like. Or perhaps they could put you in the gondola of the hot-air balloon next time."

He winced at that, and they drove on in silence. She was still congratulating herself for having the last word when they reached the outskirts of Lakemont.

But as Garrett threaded the Pierce-Arrow down the residential streets toward Sherwood Forest, he said, "Look, Anne, I'm really sorry for what I said."

"Which time?" she asked crisply. "Last night, when you implied that there was something criminally suspicious about me still being a virgin, or this morning when you practically called me a blithering idiot?"

"Both. I didn't mean to imply your being a virgin was bad—"

"That's good to know. Let me assure you that my inexperience hasn't been for lack of opportunity."

"I never doubted that for a minute. Frankly, that's why I was so—" He stopped, and then said, "Anne, well, would you mind telling me why?"

She had to count to twenty before she could trust her voice, and even then it was slightly shrill. "You've got the nerve to want an explanation of why I don't hop in the sack with every man I date? It is none of your business, Garrett!"

"It certainly is my business," he countered. "You came damn close to the point of no return with me last night, and I think that gives me every right to know what's going on."

But she had stopped listening as the Pierce-Arrow slid to a smooth halt in front of her town house. "Oh, Lord," she muttered. "That's Rudy's car across the street."

Garrett sounded surprised. "Is he still hanging around?"

"I don't suppose you could just steal quietly away and let me deal with him? No, he couldn't miss this ocean liner." She opened the door of the Pierce-Arrow with a frustrated shove.

"I thought you liked my car," he complained.

Anne ignored him and climbed out. Garrett followed, a thoughtful frown between his brows.

Rudy came across the street at a jog. "Anne, I've been trying to find you all day. I could see your car in the garage, but there was no answer to the doorbell, and I didn't know if I should call the police or your parents."

"Rudy, old chap," Garrett said kindly, "it's awfully nice of you to be concerned, but there was really no need."

"I can see that," Rudy said. His voice hardened. "Here you are with this clown and a suitcase, obviously just back from a weekend of fun...."

If I had an ax, Anne thought, *there would be a body on my front lawn. How dare he accuse me!*

Beside her, Garrett started to whistle tunelessly under his breath. "Shall I just leave your suitcase on the porch, or take it inside?" he asked. He didn't wait for an answer before sauntering off across the lawn.

Make that two bodies, Anne told herself. *He's agitating Rudy for the fun of it!*

Rudy was glaring at her. "What the hell is going on, Anne?"

Anne said tightly, "I don't owe you any explanations. We're not engaged anymore." She was watching Garrett from the corner of her eye. If he'd had a key, she thought, he would probably have carried her overnight case upstairs and unpacked it, just so Rudy could see the lights in her bedroom and jump to a few more conclusions. But instead he left it on the porch and came back across the lawn, his step unhurried.

"Maybe not," Rudy said. "But I hardly think our disagreement was good enough reason to go off with a man for the weekend."

"Rudy, old chap," Garrett said, "she was working. Take my word for it."

"Why don't you get out of here and let us settle this?"

Garrett turned to Anne, one eyebrow lifted in a silent question.

"Please, Garrett," she whispered.

He looked down at her for ten long seconds, and then he turned to Rudy. "All right," he said levelly. "I'm going. But I have a couple of things to say first."

Anne shivered despite herself. She was not quite sure what she expected, but she knew it was going to be devastating.

Garrett glanced at her and said simply, "I doubt you've got enough sense to believe me, Rudy, but here's the truth. We were working, and Anne didn't sleep with me this weekend ... any more than she ever has with you." He turned on his heel, and a moment later the Pierce-Arrow's engine roared into life.

Anne stared in astonishment. *Maybe he is a gentleman after all!* She watched the car out of sight, and turned to see suspicion still flaring in Rudy's eyes. "You don't believe him, do you?" she asked.

"Why should I? Anne, just because I got a little upset with you on Thursday is no reason to behave this way."

"A little upset? You were screaming at me on a public sidewalk. You behaved like a child in a tantrum. You canceled a date and then expected me to be waiting for you anyway—?"

"All right, so the man got under my skin. If you're going to give me a scene from a daytime television drama every time we have a quarrel, Anne—"

She was shaking her head. "We aren't going to have any more quarrels, Rudy." It was very quiet. "No more discussions. No more excuses. No more bluster. And no more second chances. I'm finished."

It was obvious that he knew she meant it this time, and his shoulders sagged as he turned away. She didn't watch him go; she went inside instead, and sank into the rocking chair in the living room in a trembling heap, with her overnight case at her feet. She was too worn out even to carry it upstairs.

Too worn out, and in too much pain. Why, she wondered, should it hurt so much to say this final goodbye? She had loved Rudy once, yes, but that had been over long ago. Breaking their engagement had not been easy, but it hadn't caused her this kind of pain. So why was she feeling like this now, as if she had torn off an arm and thrown it away?

GARRETT HAD NOT announced whether he intended to pick her up for lunch, or if she was expected to find her own way across town, but Anne decided she wasn't going to sit at home and wait for him to turn up; it would be too horribly embarrassing if he didn't. So, precisely at noon on Monday, she rang the bell at the Tudor Revival house, and Jim Garrett's butler took her down a hallway she hadn't seen before and showed her into a small sunny room at the end of the house.

Garrett was there. He jumped up belatedly when she came in.

The odd little feeling in the pit of her stomach wouldn't let her look directly at him, so she focused on the room instead. It was filled with graceful, almost-feminine furniture, arranged on a delicately colored Oriental carpet. A stream of sunlight poured through tall windows opposite the fireplace, obscuring the face of the portrait that hung above the pale gray marble mantel. Below the portrait, in a crystal vase, was a single pink rose.

Garrett had been sitting on a chintz-flowered love seat in front of the fire, with his elbow propped on the delicate arm. It looked like a very comfortable love seat, she thought, despite the formal elegance of its curves. Indeed, it looked like a very comfortable room, as if someone had devoted many hours of time and thought to the selection of each detail.

But you weren't asked to study the furniture, she reminded herself, and with an effort she turned to Garrett. Her eyes fastened on a stripe on his tie. He was actually wearing a button-down shirt today, and a sport jacket, too.

"Come and sit down," he said, and reached for a decanter on the marble-topped tea table by the love seat. "Would you like sherry?"

Anne shook her head. "Not before I go to work, thanks. Is that tomato juice?"

He nodded. "That's all Dad's drinking these days." He handed her a glass, then poured an identical one for himself and sat down beside her. "Dad will be down in a couple of minutes."

She nodded.

"Don't be nervous about it," he said. "You stood up to him before, over the discrimination issue. You can do it again."

"I don't exactly want to stand up to him, you know. I'd rather he like the plan for itself."

"Then, here's to the plan," he said, and raised his glass. But she didn't think he sounded very enthusiastic, and she began to wonder; if he had any intention of sabotaging her, this was the best chance he'd ever have.

No, she told herself. *He wouldn't do that, because it would throw us right back to the beginning. And he doesn't want to devote any more time to this thing than he has to.*

There didn't seem to be anything to say after that. She sipped her tomato juice and studied the painting above the mantel. From her place on the love seat, the sunlight no longer interfered, and she could see the canvas clearly. The portrait was of a woman in her mid forties, perhaps, in a lacy evening gown, with an amethyst necklace at her throat, her blond hair upswept, her dark eyes wide and frank and curious.

There was no resemblance between the portrait and the man beside her, unless it was the eyes; and then it was less the color, Anne thought, than the expression, a sort of eagerness to embrace whatever was to come.

"You'll do fine," Garrett said. "He's always liked strong-minded women."

"Like her," Anne said.

Garrett looked surprised. "My mother? How did you know that? She never looked it."

"She's beautiful."

"Yes, she was. I don't think I ever heard her raise her voice to anyone, certainly not to my father. But she generally got her way, regardless."

"What happened to her?"

He was still staring at the portrait, and for a moment she thought he hadn't heard her. "She died when I was in college. She was the most incredible soul I've ever known. I've never met a woman like her."

And obviously he had looked. There was a lump in Anne's throat. "Garrett, thank you for telling me that."

He turned to look at her, a curious little frown between his brows.

It made her just a little nervous, and she said quickly, "And thank you for being...well, sensitive...last night."

He drained his glass and set it aside. "By leaving you and Rudy alone to settle your differences?" he asked dryly. "I hope you worked it out."

She nodded. It was casual conversation, no more, she thought, so there was no reason to go into the details. Obviously he didn't care whether she and Rudy had worked out their disagreements or not.

But she wanted him to care. She wanted it to be as desperately important to him as he was to her.

That was the instant when she knew why she had been in such pain last night. It hadn't been because Rudy was gone forever from her life, but because Garrett had walked away as if none of it mattered to him.

Not Anne herself, and certainly not the fact that she had fallen in love with him.

CHAPTER EIGHT

THE SHOCK OF IT hit her with such force that it seemed to have vaporized the center of her being. *It's not possible,* she tried to tell herself. *I can't have fallen in love with him!* But this sudden flash of understanding explained so much that it was impossible to deny the truth of it.

This was why she had felt that smothering sense of obligation when Rudy had asked her to give him a second chance. It had not, after all, been an abnormal request, and yet she had felt trapped and troubled at the idea. Only now did the feeling make sense, for it had not been Rudy who had made her hesitate, but the fact that in the hidden corners of her brain, she had known even then that he had been replaced in her heart.

This explained her own mixed-up feelings. Garrett was right; she had been behaving ridiculously yesterday in Door County, furious at him for thinking she was the kind of woman who would be an eager bed partner, and at the same time hurt and resentful that he had not found her desirable after all. He had pointed out that she could not have it both ways, and yet that was exactly how she had felt—baffled by contradictory emotions, torn between the insult to her character and the wound to her pride.

This flash of insight even explained the way she had reacted to Dominique Delacourt. Jealousy, she thought incredulously. She had been jealous of the way Dominique would walk up to Garrett with confidence, expecting a kiss, expecting his attention, jealous that Dominique was free to behave that way, and she was not.

The night of Jim Garrett's dinner party, when Dominique had come in and Anne had started to wonder just what the woman meant to Garrett, even then it had been jealousy at work.

How, she wondered, could it have happened so quickly?

But had it really been such a sudden thing? It seemed to Anne that she had known him forever. Had she unconsciously been telling the simple truth that night at the Lakemont Grand when she said she had fallen in love with him long ago, through the column?

Theirs had certainly not been a normal getting-to-know-each-other pattern; they had not seemed to need it. He had obviously felt from the beginning that he knew her, too; she had, after all, introduced herself quite forcibly through the *Chronicle*'s editorial page, long before they met in person.

And then, of course, there had been the mugger. When two people were drawn close in an episode of violence, she thought, there was ever after a special sort of trust between them, the knowledge that in a time of need there was someone to lean on. He'd been tender and gentle and very careful of her—rescuing, protecting, staying beside her until he was certain she was all right again, whether she wanted him or not.

And now she knew that she wanted him for always. How horribly much she wanted him!

Jim Garrett came in just then, vibrant and bubbly, apologizing for his lateness. It took every ounce of

Anne's self-control to drag her thoughts away from this carousel of confusion and concentrate on Jim.

He looked younger, better, than she had ever seen him before. A few days' rest and the relief of knowing Garrett would take care of things; it was amazing what good medicine that could be.

He took her arm and guided her to a sun porch where a table was informally set for three. Garrett followed lazily, almost reluctantly, Anne thought, as if he'd rather be anywhere else in the world.

Jim held her chair and gave her an enthusiastic report on his recuperating orchid as the butler served grapefruit, still sizzling from the broiler.

How could I ever have thought Jim Garrett was terrifying? she wondered. *He's uncomfortably astute sometimes, that's certain, and incredibly fast at finding the flaw in a line of reasoning and shooting it down. But he's also funny and charming and perceptive.*

She was nearly silent through the first course, eating her grapefruit, half listening to the two of them and trying at the same time not to think of how much she would have enjoyed getting to know Jim Garrett on something other than a professional level. Even this scholarship program, as distant from the *Chronicle* as it was, wasn't really personal.

She found herself watching Garrett across the table, and wondering what he was thinking. That was another fruitless pastime, she concluded finally. There appeared to be nothing important on his mind at all, not even a tinge of anxiety at how his father might react. The man must be truly gifted at poker, she told herself irritably.

That was the exact moment he kicked her ankle under the table, and she was so absorbed in her own thoughts that she glared at him for a full ten seconds

before she realized that she had better start to pay attention to the conversation, and fast. These men were not
blind, and it would be downright embarrassing if either
of them was to read her mind.

"So what have you come up with for me?" Jim Garrett asked genially as the butler began to clear the first
course and replace it with delicately poached salmon and
a colorful mix of vegetables.

She had the impression it wasn't the first time he'd
said it, and that of course would explain the kick under
the table.

She looked at Garrett, who raised his eyebrows a
fraction and stayed completely silent, as if to remind her
of what he had said earlier: this was largely her plan, and
therefore her responsibility. "If Dad hates it, I'd rather
he tell you directly." No wonder he didn't look concerned.

Well, she thought, *he's not the only one who can play
poker!*

It was bravado, though. She toyed with her salmon as
she talked, and she knew that despite her best efforts her
voice tightened when she saw Jim's forehead wrinkle
with concentration, or was it distaste?

He heard her out about the application essays and the
interviews, and said, "That's all very interesting...."

But you don't like it, Anne thought with a feeling of
foreboding. She took a deep breath and forced herself to
go on. "That's not quite all, Mr. Garrett—"

"It's Jim, please." He leaned forward. "Go on,
Anne. Matt told me you'd come up with some very interesting innovations."

He had? Anne's gaze flew to meet Garrett's. Discreet
silence was the most she had expected from him in the

way of cooperation; actual endorsement of her proposals was too much of a shock!

She gave him a slow, soft, grateful smile, and then caught herself up short when the only reaction was a lifted eyebrow. It figured, she thought. Jim seemed to be taking it seriously, but Garrett could have given the phrase *interesting innovations* any sort of sarcastic twist at all.

"I'm not sure it's such an innovation," she began warily. "Just an extension, perhaps, of an idea lots of people have had before. I started thinking about it when you said you intended this to be a full scholarship, Jim, tuition, room and board, fees, books, everything, so that the students could concentrate completely on their studies."

"Do you think it's a crazy idea, too?" Jim Garrett asked with a sigh. "Matt does."

"I know. He's told me. And—" she took a deep breath "—he's partially right."

"I am touched by your agreement," Garrett said. "What Anne's really saying is that despite all the elaborate applications and essays and interviews she's set up, and all the feminine intuition she's faithfully promised to apply, a person could fool her. He could take the education and run—"

"Or more likely," Anne interrupted firmly, "he could honestly change his mind, and decide that journalism isn't the right field for him after all. It does happen, you know—not everyone who makes a mistake is a crook, Garrett. So my innovation, if you want to call it that, is this: put the half-dozen Garrett scholars to work at the *Chronicle* every summer. We can find work for them— it may not be glamorous work, but believe me, by the end of the first summer, we'll all know if they are serious about a career in news.''

Jim Garrett was still frowning.

Anne swallowed hard and went on. ''Lots of professions offer on-the-job training, but most wait till the student is almost finished with his or her formal education. I never have understand the delay. Why not start early? That way if we, or the student, have made a mistake, we can cut our losses early, too. If not, the student is getting valuable experience that will give him or her a head start on a career, and we're getting an employee whose usefulness will increase over the four-year period.''

''Pay them, I suppose?'' Jim Garrett said.

''Yes, but it wouldn't cost any more, really. This lets them earn the money for their books and fees, at least.'' She pushed a bite of salmon around on her plate. ''Sometimes when you give people too much, they don't appreciate it.''

''You received a free education,'' Jim Garrett mused.

''Tuition, yes. But to pay the rest of my expenses, I worked in the ice cream shop across from the campus.''

Jim Garrett smiled. ''The ice cream shop? Well, it obviously didn't hurt you. But you'd rather have had a newspaper job, right? All right, you've sold me.''

She sank back in her chair, intercepted a sardonic smile from Garrett and instantly regretted letting her relief show. She sat up straight again.

''Anything else?'' Jim Garrett asked.

''No, I think we've covered everything.''

Garrett said promptly, ''If we've got all the details settled, then...'' He sounded thoroughly bored, and yet, was it watchfulness in his eyes?

Just a second too late, Anne remembered the exchange they'd had about setting up some kind of trust or institution to protect the *Chronicle*. Was that why he was in such a hurry to wind up this discussion, before she could suggest it to Jim?

Well, I wouldn't, she told herself. *I don't really think Garrett is scheming to sell the place...and even if he were, it's not my business.*

"And just in time, too," Jim murmured. "The applications will have to be distributed by the first of the year if we're to get applicants screened in time for next fall's classes."

Anne had forgotten for a moment about the work that still lay ahead. "I'll start to rough something out," she said and glanced at her wristwatch. "Meanwhile, I'd better get down to the *Chronicle* before someone reports me as a missing person."

"But you haven't had dessert yet," Jim protested. "And I haven't had a chance to tell you what wonderful coverage that was of the fire, Anne. It was in the best tradition of the old school of journalism, as Matt says—"

"Well, I'm glad to hear that you both approve." It warmed her heart a little, to know that Garrett had talked to his father about that. Professionally, at least, she had earned his respect, and that was something. "But much as I'd like to talk it over, Jim, I have to go. The weekly news conference starts in half an hour."

If she expected Garrett to add his persuasion to his father's, she was doomed to disappointment. He walked her out to her car, however, and she said, "When do you want to start work on the applications?"

He said carelessly, "I'll check Ted's schedule and get back to you."

"Do we need to bother him?"

Garrett looked startled, and Anne realized, too late, that it must have sounded as if she was desperate for his company. Very quickly she added, "I just thought we could get it out of the way and save him the trouble."

"It would double the trouble, more likely. He'll have to be consulted, sooner or later."

"Of course," she said acidly. "I beg your pardon."

"Don't take it personally, Just Plain Anne."

The nickname was the final straw. *He doesn't have to make it so obvious that I don't measure up to his standards*, she thought icily. "Oh, I'm not taking it personally, Garrett. I certainly understand that your one desire is to keep the peace with the least effort on your part!" She climbed into her car and slammed the door.

But she couldn't stop herself from glancing over her shoulder as she turned the corner. He hadn't gone back to the house; he was strolling down the sidewalk instead, his hands in his pockets, his head bent against the wind.

She was halfway downtown before she realized that Garrett obviously wasn't planning to attend the weekly news conference himself.

"Either he's got bigger fish to fry this afternoon," she muttered, "or the new job is already starting to pall. And neither sounds promising for the *Chronicle*, that's sure." She mulled that one over all the way to the newsroom, and finally decided that there was nothing she could do about it. It wasn't her problem, after all. But perhaps she should have warned Jim. . . .

Dominique Delacourt was just coming out of the managing editor's office when Anne reached the newsroom floor.

At least Garrett wasn't going to visit Dominique, Anne thought, and then lectured herself a bit. *It's time for a little self-control, my girl. You'll just make the pain worse if you don't stop this.*

Dominique paused beside Anne's desk and murmured, ''Are you applying for a job with the television station as an anchorwoman? That outfit should certainly get their attention.''

Anne wasn't quite sure whether to take offense at the slur on her best red wool suit, or be upset that Dominique, too, seemed to take it as a matter of course that she was looking for another job.

Slightly self-conscious, she tugged the cuffs of her black silk blouse into place, and Dominique smiled and moved off with lazy grace to her own desk.

Anne checked her calendar and the list of staff working the shift, but her mind wouldn't stay on tomorrow's newspaper. It kept flitting back to that quiet little room in the Tudor Revival house, and the fact that she had fallen in love with Garrett.

But what had been such a stunning bombshell only a couple of hours ago had now settled deeply into her heart and mind and body. It was no wonder she had lost interest in Holly's impromptu dating service; she simply hadn't recognized what was happening to her, that was all.

It was not, she had to admit, the kind of sensation she would have expected it to be. There was not a grand rush of well-being surging through her body, or an expansive wish to hug the whole world, or an overwhelming desire to stand on top of the city's tallest building and sing. It felt, to tell the truth, more like a bad case of butterflies in the stomach. Or like falling out of a tree. She'd done that once, and knocked all the breath out of her lungs—

"Miss McKenna." The managing editor was leaning on the corner of her desk, and he sounded as if it wasn't the first time he'd called her name. "I need to talk to you before the news conference."

She swallowed hard. *Time to get your mind back on business, McKenna,* she told herself as she gathered up her calendar and her notes for the week's news events and followed him across the newsroom to his office in the corner. "Hold up the conference for fifteen minutes," he instructed his secretary.

Anne was shocked. The hour of the weekly news conference was almost sacred.

"Sit down, Miss McKenna," he ordered, and closed the door. "Now tell me just what the hell you were thinking of Saturday night, when you held up the press for two full hours without bothering to let me know what was going on."

She looked down at the notes in her lap. It was obvious she wasn't going to need them. She had not considered the possibility that he might be calling her on the carpet for anything at all, and the sheer unexpectedness of this attack, coming so soon after Jim Garrett's compliments on how she had handled the situation, was stunning.

"It wasn't two full hours," she said faintly, trying to buy a little time to think. Should she tell him Jim Garrett had seemed to think she'd done well? Or would bringing up the publisher's name only make things worse?

"It was near enough." It was uncompromising. He sat down on the corner of his desk. "What made you take that kind of responsibility without even making a telephone call?"

"I had the authority, sir. Garrett was right here."

"Jim, you mean?" he barked.

"No." She swallowed hard. "Matt."

The managing editor laughed. It was not humorous. "Yes, I understand you have a lot of influence on Matt Garrett these days. Or think you do."

There was a snide twist in his voice, and a cold shiver trickled down Anne's spine.

"There is a chain of command here," the managing editor said flatly. "You should have followed it."

"I would have," she said, "if Garrett hadn't told me it wasn't necessary. Since he was here, I assumed—"

"You *assumed?* Well, let me fill you in, Miss McKenna. Matt Garrett has no authority at this newspaper. He's a loudmouthed columnist and that's all he is."

She was furious, or she never would have said it, but the words seemed to slip out. "Is that so? Why don't you discuss it with his father and see if he agrees?"

He watched her long and thoughtfully. "Don't worry. I shall. And I shall discuss your lapse into insolence, too, Miss McKenna. That comment makes it obvious that you don't consider yourself subject to orders from people like me."

Anne bit her tongue at the heavy sarcasm.

The managing editor rose. "You can consider yourself lucky if you don't lose your job over this."

Anne remained seated, stubbornly. "For doing good work? Jim Garrett seemed very pleased with the results—"

"Does he know you didn't bother to call your superiors before taking matters into your own hands?"

She didn't answer, because the question had never occurred to her. Until that moment, it hadn't seemed to matter whether Jim had known the whole story when he paid her that compliment. If all he knew was what Garrett had told him...would Garrett have thought that fact important enough to mention? *Probably not,* she told herself. *I certainly didn't. I assumed Garrett knew what he was doing, that he was within his authority. He must have thought that, too. But then, who was wrong? Garrett? Me? The managing editor?*

Her head was starting to swim with the possibilities.

"At least it turned out all right," she said drearily. "Can't you give me credit for that, at least?"

"You're lucky it didn't explode in your face. All hell could have broken loose over this."

"Isn't that what's happening right now?" she asked with faint irony.

"It would be, if it was up to me. But since you got lucky, we'll have to see what Jim Garrett has to say about the slipshod way you seem to want to run a newspaper. And just in case he doesn't fire you this time, Miss McKenna, let me warn you—if there's one more slip, I'll throw you out myself." He opened the door.

Anne reluctantly pulled herself out of her chair. Her heart was pounding at double speed, and she was so light-headed she wasn't certain she could walk across the newsroom to her desk, much less make it to the elevators and upstairs to the news conference. She had to pass Dominique's desk to do so, and when the woman looked up from the current issue of *Vogue* with a smirk, it stiffened Anne's spine and brought her back to earth.

So that was what Dominique was doing in Jack's office. Planting seeds. And what an early and bountiful harvest she'd achieved.

What Jim Garrett had to say was yet to be discovered, she told herself, and there was no sense in dreading the outcome until she knew if there was really something to panic about. If he already knew the whole story, he might well be amused by the managing editor's misunderstanding of the way things were going to operate from now on at the *Chronicle*. Or, if he hadn't actually given Garrett that much authority yet, surely he wouldn't blame Anne when he found out that she had acted in good faith, since she had honestly believed that Garrett had the power to override the rules. And if none of that worked . . .

Then I may be on my way out, she thought. *And if I find out that Garrett set me up . . .*

ON TUESDAY, Holly received a letter of commendation for her personnel file, signed by Jim Garrett, praising her devotion to duty and complimenting her on the quality of her work under the pressured conditions presented by the fire in the Sheboygan Building.

She waved the sheet of hot-pressed letterhead under Anne's nose. "It almost makes ruining my favorite pair of shoes worthwhile," she crowed. "Of course, if he'd included a couple of paragraphs about a raise in salary, that would have been a nicer compliment yet. You should ask him about it, Anne. Strike while the iron is hot, you know. There's no reason both of us shouldn't come out of this with an attractive little bonus."

Anne's heart twisted a little. Holly deserved the compliment, she told herself. She had done a marvelous job with that story.

But Anne couldn't help being a bit envious. She had done a marvelous job, too, but there was no letter of compliment for her. Even the electronic message center in her computer terminal remained stubbornly empty, and her telephone didn't ring, either. The fact that Jim Garrett had told her in person that he appreciated her work didn't fill the gap.

Editors never got credit, she told herself, but it didn't help.

The only consolation she could find was that the managing editor had not called her in for another chat; either he hadn't yet had an opportunity to talk to Jim Garrett, or he'd been firmly put in his place and wasn't about to apologize for his mistake.

That there was a third possibility didn't even occur to her.

She had hardly walked into the newsroom on Wednesday afternoon when Garrett called. "Ted Lehmann suggested another Sunday session at the cabin to finish up the scholarship application."

Anne's heart sank. *Please,* she thought. *This is just too cruel.* "We can't just meet for lunch or something?" she asked, and added lamely, "I'm awfully busy—"

Garrett's voice was crisp. "So's Ted. That's the problem. I think you're right, though, that we can do it fairly quickly. So let's plan to drive up on Sunday morning this time."

That made it all too horribly plain, she thought, that he didn't want to risk a repetition, any more than she did. She agreed, mechanically.

"Is nine too early? I know you'll be working till late on Saturday."

"Maybe," she said, "Maybe not."

"What does that mean?"

She sighed. "Nothing, just that you're not the only one who has trouble with the managing editor these days. He wasn't impressed that you gave me the authority to hold the press last Saturday, and if he has his say I'll probably never be in charge of an edition again."

There was a tiny silence. "But I didn't, Anne." It was very quiet.

She closed her eyes tightly, but she could still see the chasm that loomed in front of her, and the brink of it crumbling away beneath her feet. "You most certainly did!" she gasped, and then a terrible stillness descended on her. What difference did it make? she thought. If it came down to his word against hers, she could not possibly prevail.

"Thanks a lot, Garrett," she said. "That's just what I needed, for you to duck the responsibility." She slammed down the telephone and put her face into her hands.

He did it on purpose, she thought. And that means nothing matters anymore.

She was still sitting there when Jim Garrett's secretary called and asked her to report immediately to the publisher's office, that Mr. Garrett wished to speak with her.

My God, she thought. *If he thinks it's so important that he interrupted his peaceful recovery and came back to the office to handle it himself...*

"You can consider yourself lucky if you don't lose your job over this," the managing editor had warned. "One more slip and I will throw you out myself."

Well, it looked as if she wasn't going to get the chance for one more slip.

CHAPTER NINE

SHE SPENT the all-too-brief time in the elevator inspecting herself in the polished brass doors, straightening her narrow gray skirt, tucking her paisley blouse in more tightly, wishing that she had thought to pick up her makeup kit. She looked like a terrified child instead of the cool and professional woman who had stood up to Jim Garrett before, and, she had been told, been admired for it. Garrett had said his father liked strongminded women; that fact alone might help her now.

And there was no reason to be paranoid, she told herself. Any of a thousand things could have brought Jim Garrett to his office today. "Mr. Garrett wants to talk to you," the secretary had said. That was all. There was no sense in jumping to conclusions because of those few words, or the crisp tone of voice. The secretary wouldn't know what it was about, that was certain. Perhaps he had some further ideas about the scholarship, though they had dealt with that issue very thoroughly just two days ago, the tiny voice of warning in the back of her brain reminded her. If it was only that, he would have telephoned, even asked her to stop by the house....

The elevator door opened and Anne took a deep breath and stepped off onto the executive floor. The secretary at the desk just outside the publisher's office looked up and waved a hand. "Go right in, Miss McKenna. He's waiting for you."

But the voice of doom began to whisper again in the back of her mind as Jim Garrett turned from the window, with its glorious, almost-sunset view of Lakemont, to greet her. There wasn't so much as a letter on his desk, she noted with foreboding. He had come in just for this talk, after all.

He ushered her over to the corner of the office, where two couches faced each other, with a low carved wooden table between them. Anne sat stiffly upright on the edge of the upholstered seat.

He made every effort to put her at ease; she gave him credit for that. He even offered her coffee from the carafe on the conference table. Anne accepted a cup and sat toying with it, thinking that the man was charming beyond all belief; he could keep up a stream of small talk for as long as he chose. No wonder Garrett had such a way with words; he had come by the talent honestly.

But finally she couldn't stand it anymore, and she said abruptly, "It's about the Sheboygan Building fire, isn't it?"

Jim Garrett's eyebrows almost disappeared into his sandy hair, as if he was astonished that she had brought it up herself.

She took a deep breath. *I might as well face it head-on,* she thought. "The managing editor has told you then, that I didn't call him that night before I held the press. Or anyone else, either."

Jim Garrett nodded. "Yes, he told me," he said slowly. "I must say, Anne, I was surprised to hear you had taken that decision upon yourself."

Her last unreasoning hope that it might be all right died away, like the final tenacious flickering of a bed of embers, and a thread of anger rose in its place. *You,* Jim Garrett had said. Not a word about his precious son, who had pushed her into it. He, of course, was above reproach; this was all Anne's fault!

But she swallowed her frustration and said, "I'm sorry, sir. You see, I thought—

Jim Garrett was frowning.

Anne stopped herself there, feeling miserable. The fact that she had honestly believed Garrett had that authority, when in truth he had none, did not let her escape her own responsibility. And if she tried to put the blame on him, she would only end up making herself look worse.

It wasn't really Garrett's place to make that decision, she told herself, and she'd known it at the time. Whether he actually had the power was really not the issue. She could have, should have, thanked him for his advice and gone straight ahead with her call for help. And if she had, she wouldn't have been in this mess today.

So she said quietly, "I have no excuses, sir."

Jim Garrett shifted restlessly in his chair. "I thought we had agreed you were going to call me Jim."

For an instant she thought she was hallucinating.

"Oh, Anne, surely you don't believe I called you up here to scold you about how you handled that fire?" He saw the shock in her eyes, and went on more gently, "Yes, I can see that you do. Well, I haven't. The managing editor stormed out to the house to tell me that you hadn't called your supervisors, and I told him that it didn't make any damned difference."

She gulped, and told herself fiercely that professional women didn't cry.

"It would have taken precious time to get hold of someone in authority, time you didn't have that night. You did exactly the right thing. You made the right decisions under tremendous pressure, and I am very pleased with both you and Matt.''

She stammered, ''Th-thank you, sir. Jim.''

''You for doing what you knew was right despite the newsroom policies, and him for pointing out that you were capable of making that decision on your own.''

It staggered her. Was it possible she had misunderstood Garrett that night, that she had acted blindly on her own, despite her belief that he had given her permission? She couldn't remember now exactly what he had said. There had been too much confusion, and it was too long ago. Had she wronged him this afternoon when she had so quickly assumed that he'd laid a trap for her in an effort to make trouble?

She clenched her hands in a feeble effort to keep them from trembling, and said, ''What if it hadn't turned out all right?'' She knew she shouldn't be saying it; only a fool pointed out to the boss that she had, after all, been very lucky. ''If the paper had been late, or—''

''It would still have been the right decision,'' he said firmly. ''You got the story, and that's the thing that matters most at the *Chronicle*.''

''Then . . . but the managing editor told me—''

''Yes,'' Jim said wryly. ''He told me the same things, I imagine. Jack's a good man, but he occasionally has attacks of thinking that he's completely indispensable and therefore every decision must have his stamp of approval. I'm afraid there's only enough room at the *Chronicle* for one man with that sort of egotistical attitude, and you're having coffee with him.''

Anne laughed shakily. It was such a relief to be able to, now that the anxiety was over. Now that her job was safe.

A small wrinkle formed between her brows, and she asked, "Jim, if you didn't call me up here to scold me about the fire, then why?"

He stood. "Let me get you some fresh coffee," he said. "You've allowed it to get cold, I'm afraid."

She didn't want the coffee, but he so obviously didn't care to answer the question just then that she had no choice but to be patient. Jim dumped out the cold liquid and replaced it, and fussed around his desk for a little while, and finally he came back and sat down. "It did have to do with the fire," he said. "And even more than that, with the scholarship and the wonderful work you've done with it. I wanted to say thank you, you see, with something that will last as long as the good work you've done." He opened a drawer in the side of the table, and laid a package before her. "It took a little while to get just what I wanted."

It was thin and flat, about the size and weight of an awards plaque. *Precisely what I need,* she mocked herself. *Something else to hang on my wall, especially since here at the office I don't even have a wall to hang it on!*

The wrapping paper was heavy foil in a random design of gold and silver swirls, and it stubbornly resisted her efforts to tear it off. Finally she used her nails to slit the tape.

It was not an engraved award, but a lightweight black leather box with a tiny gold latch on one of the long sides. She stared at the box for a full thirty seconds as if it was likely to explode in her hands if she opened it, and then she stole a look at Jim.

He was watching her, with interest but no particular anxiety or excitement, she thought. He was merely drinking his coffee and waiting for her to get on with it.

So she caught her lower lip between her teeth and lifted the lid, and gasped.

The box was lined with dark blue satin, and against that luxurious surface a double strand of pearls glowed; glorious, perfectly matched pearls, each the size of a pea and the color of heavy cream.

She stared down at the necklace, her hands frozen on the sides of the box. The gems seemed to glow from within, as if they were pulsing with life.

"Jim," she said faintly. "Please tell me these are fake."

He looked at her thoughtfully. "Well, they're cultured—"

"That does not make me feel better. We ran a story not long ago on cultured pearls." She looked at the gems, and then up at him. "I can't, Jim. I can't accept this." She held the box out to him, still open.

He didn't take it. "You would have been insulted, I believe, if I had offered to pay you for all the work you've done on the scholarship."

"Of course I'd be insulted. I wouldn't have done it at all if I didn't believe in it, and so I volunteered."

"A simple gift of your time, I suppose," he said smoothly.

Anne bit her lip. The box was still in midair, and her arm was getting tired, so she set it down and gave it a little push across the table toward him. "If you're going to try to convince me that this is the same sort of simple gift . . . well, it isn't."

"Perhaps you're right. I could give you shares of *Chronicle* stock instead, if you like," he offered.

"No!" It was harsher than she had intended, and she tried to soften the blow. "If you'd like to put a letter in my personnel file, though, as you did for Holly, so whenever I have trouble with the managing editor I can tell him to go read it—''

Jim laughed at that. "Actually, I had a different method in mind for taking care of that problem," he confided. He picked up the box, closed it with a firm little snap and set it down at his elbow. Anne would not have been quite human if she hadn't watched the necklace disappear with more than a twinge of regret. That was absolutely the most perfect piece of jewelry she would ever have the chance to own.

"Quite a challenge, of course," Jim said, and she realized that he had gone on talking while she was dreaming over the necklace. "It's obvious that I can't do everything that I used to do, and so things are going to change here at the *Chronicle*. Someday soon there will be a new publisher...." He hesitated. "Well, the important thing for right now is that I've decided to create a new administrative position—Assistant to the Publisher. Quite a title, don't you think?"

She nodded. Garrett might be disappointed at being a mere assistant, she thought idly, but at least he'd get some on-the-job training before he took over completely, and that should be a bit of relief for everyone at the *Chronicle*.

Jim Garrett leaned back in his chair and tented his fingertips together judiciously. "How about it, Anne? Would you like to have the job?"

LIKE IT? It was the sort of opportunity that she had never even allowed herself to dream of, because a job like that only came along once in a lifetime, if then. This kind of break came so seldom that she hadn't even considered the possibility that he might be offering it to her instead of Garrett.

What about Garrett? she thought. A little voice in the back of her mind promptly answered, *Don't be such a fool. Garrett will go straight to the top as the new publisher. Jim just said so.*

"You'd have to work days," Jim added, absolutely straight-faced. "But I think the discrimination people would consider this a legitimate change of jobs, don't you?"

Anne couldn't help it; it might have been only nerves, but she started to laugh. "I think so," she managed to say.

He sounded completely serious, however, as he went on. "You would not be some sort of glorified secretary—I want to make that very clear. I mean a real assistant, an executive officer, for want of a better word for it, with the power to act in the publisher's name."

A glorified secretary? The possibility hadn't even occurred to her, so why had he mentioned it? Then, slowly, things began to come clear in her mind.

Now I see, she thought. He knew that Garrett would want to continue his column. And he surely knew, too, that even if Garrett had all the time in the world to devote to the job, he wasn't exactly excited about the responsibility. He certainly would never work at it as his father always had. So Jim was taking steps to circumvent that, before it became a problem.

She could almost hear the reasoning: make the boy the publisher because he had the name, and put in an assistant who would do the real work. *What I'm really being offered,* she thought, *is the job of following Garrett around and picking up the pieces. Tying up the loose ends. Keeping things on track.*

Not really, she told herself. He'd just told her that she wouldn't be a secretary. He'd said she'd have the power to act in the publisher's name—that was power of a sort, though what it really meant was anyone's guess.

"It won't be an easy adjustment, of course," Jim said. "You have all the experience I could want at the news-gathering end, but the *Chronicle* is a business, too—and you'll have a great deal to learn about managing that end of things—everything from advertising rates to negoti-ating with the unions." He got up to refill his cup and motioned with the carafe toward Anne's; she shook her head absently. "I understand you already do rather well with the unions."

Anne frowned. She hadn't the slightest idea what he meant.

Jim went on, "And then there's a good deal of public relations. You can't publish a newspaper unless you can convince readers to pick it up."

"It sounds like a very big job."

"I'd be lying to you if I said it wasn't. Still, if I didn't think you were capable, Anne, I wouldn't be talking to you now." He drank half his coffee while she turned that over in her mind, then he set the cup aside. "You'd like some time to think about it, I suppose?"

She looked him straight in the eyes. "Actually, I feel as if I should be able to give you an answer this minute, but—"

Jim shook his head, smiling. "I don't want an an-swer right now. I want you to think it over, because I want to be certain that you won't regret it next year when you're having a headache over the budget, or the mayor is threatening to drag the *Chronicle* into court for li-bel."

"You're certain I'll take it." It was not a question. Jim nodded.

"I suppose I am, too. How could I turn down a chance like this? But surely if I was truly ready to be an executive, I could make a fast decision on this!" She clenched her fists in frustration.

"Good executives only make snap decisions after they've looked at every side. You take your time and think it over. Then—" there was the faintest possible twinkle of mischief in his eyes "—let me know when you'll be ready to start."

"Thank you," she whispered.

"Oh, Anne, about this necklace," he said, when she had almost reached the door. "Are you certain you won't take it with you?"

Once more, she fought the battle with temptation. It was a good thing, she thought, that she couldn't see the pearls now, and that she had never touched them. But the opportunity he had offered was worth more to her than any number of pearls could ever be. "I'm certain. But I do appreciate the gesture."

"What in hell do you suggest I do with it then?" he asked plaintively, and she only smiled and went back down to the newsroom, to her neglected duties.

It was apparent that the entire staff knew where she had been; when she came in heads turned, keyboards fell silent and conversations died. Anne ostentatiously checked her wristwatch and the staff went back to work—all but Holly, who made it a point to come across to Anne's desk a few minutes later to check out a detail.

"And what have you and Jim Garrett been up to this afternoon?" she asked pertly.

Anne smiled. "Having a coffee break."

"And here I thought it was the younger one you were interested in," Holly said under her breath. "Coffee with the father, finger kissing with the son. Saints preserve us, Anne. Where is it going to end?"

With the promotion you told me I'd never get, Anne almost said. But discretion was, after all, one of an executive's most desirable traits.

An executive. It was safe now to think about it, and to admit to herself how much she had always wanted this opportunity. Holly had been right; two years on the city desk, without chance of advancement, and Anne had been beginning to feel restive and unchallenged. She had been starting to wonder if this was all there would ever be.

That was why this new job was so appealing. It stretched out before her in a glorious rainbow of opportunity, like a wide meadow full of flowers to sniff, animals to watch, fruits to taste—the possibilities were endless!

Well, perhaps not endless, she warned herself. Of course there would be limits. The key word in the job title was "assistant." She would still have to answer to Garrett.

Or, when it came right down to it, would she?

She twirled a pencil between her fingers, and thought about it.

If Garrett didn't like the publisher's job—and she would bet any amount of money that he wouldn't like the majority of it—was it possible that she might end up as a sort of stand-in for him altogether? If that was the case, all the challenges would be hers, all the opportunity, all the responsibility, everything about the job. Except, probably, any credit that was due.

Not getting credit for what she did would be an annoyance, she admitted, but if that was the price, she could bear to pay it. And as for the responsibility...

She waited patiently for the weight of it to strike her, and drag down this burst of enthusiasm. She sat there at her desk and contemplated having to face the entire load of the *Chronicle*—its employees, its legal problems, its place in the community, and all the additional concerns that hadn't even occurred to her yet. This was why she was so certain Garrett would hate the job, she thought. And yet it did not discourage her. Compared to the chance to build the *Chronicle* into an even better newspaper, it was nothing.

As long as she had Jim for a mentor, she thought, she wouldn't be afraid. So long as she could go to him with her concerns and her problems. The things she could learn from that man!

But perhaps she should not count on that. It would not be Jim who was her boss, not for long. He had said as much himself. It would be Garrett. She might not have the option of consulting Jim.

Face it squarely, she told herself. *And be honest with yourself as you've never been honest before. You've been dancing all the way around the question here, and you've never once looked at it straight on. Can you work for Garrett? Can you work with him?*

Jim must have asked him about it, she told herself, before he offered her the job. He wouldn't have hired a specific person without Garrett's agreement. And that must mean that Garrett thought it would work.

But honesty forced her to admit there was one factor Garrett could not have considered, because there was no way he could know it. He didn't know that Anne was in love with him.

And he must never know that.

Could she hold her secret close, and nurse the joy of being near him? Or, in time, would the pleasure be eaten away by the inevitable frustrations?

She thought rebelliously, *Who knows what time might do?*

She had plunged headlong into love with him, that was true, faster than she would have believed possible. But the sort of love that scorched at first encounter was not the only sort there was. Was it even possible that, with time, he might come to care for her as well?

Don't push your luck, she told herself dryly. *For right now, let's just worry about the job.*

SHE WAS WALKING out to her car at ten minutes past eleven, thinking rather vaguely that she had no idea what they had put in the lead position on page one that night, and hoping that Holly had not taken advantage of her preoccupation to take a swipe at the mayor. *No,* she told herself. *Holly's too good a reporter to do that. But if she ever catches him, Jim's right. I may someday be hauled into court to fight a libel case.*

The ramp was frigid; deep inside it, the sunlight never reached, and the concrete would grow steadily colder from now until spring returned. She shivered and hurried toward her car, not noticing that the security guard who greeted her so cheerfully each night was nowhere to be seen.

A hand came to rest on her shoulder. In one searing blast of memory, Anne relived the night when the mugger had tried to take her purse, and the next split second she released every molecule of air in her lungs in one tormented scream that bounced and echoed off the concrete walls.

"My God!" Garrett said behind her. "I thought you heard me. I called your name—"

It took her last ounce of willpower to turn and face him, eyes dilated, forearms crossed and hands spread to protect her face. She had recognized his voice and she knew she was safe, but still the waves of horror racked her, and she was unable to pull herself out of the hysteria.

"Anne," he said in a sort of choked gasp. "Oh, God, I am most everlastingly sorry—"

She clenched her fists and held them to her mouth and began to cry, great choking dry sobs that she could not control. She was shaking violently, but not so badly that she couldn't hold him off when he tried to put his arms around her. "Don't touch me," she managed. "I can't stand to have you touch me."

After that he stood there helplessly, shifting from one foot to the other, until the uniformed security guard came pounding up. "What the hell, Mr. Garrett! What happened?" His narrowed eyes expertly searched the shadows.

"No mugger," Garrett said briefly. "Only me. I startled her."

"I should say," the guard agreed. "Never had quite that much effect on a woman, myself. Sorry, Miss McKenna. I was walking a lady down to three—"

"It's all right," she managed. "And when I get...my breath back...I'm going to flay you alive...Garrett."

The hysteria passed, eventually, and left her with all the composure of a mildewed towel. She let Garrett put his arm around her then, but only because she didn't think her knees would hold up any longer without support.

"I think a brandy might help," he said, and without waiting for an answer he led her back to the building, into the elevator, then marched her around the corner and into the restaurant.

The bar was still open, and she sank down at a tiny table overlooking the atrium lobby. She was still shaky, and the brandy he brought her splashed in the snifter as she tried to sip it. He waited till she'd downed half of it, then asked somberly, "How do you feel?"

She closed her eyes and released a whoosh of air through parted lips. "Worse than when it was for real, thank you very much. It was like I was back there again, and it was all happening in slow motion this time, only I knew it was going to be worse."

He got rather white around the mouth. "I thought you must have heard me, Anne. What on earth did you have on your mind, anyway?"

"That's right. Blame me."

"Well, I never expected... What happened to the strong-minded lady who fought off the purse snatcher?"

She shook her head in disbelief. "I thought I was all right. I haven't even dreamed about it lately."

"Dreamed...?" But he didn't finish. Instead he sipped his brandy and said, "You'll still be able to hear that scream echoing come morning."

She managed to smile. "If I thought for one minute you'd done that on purpose, Garrett, I'd—" She stopped; there was no threat horrible enough to fit.

He said wryly, "Let me know when you decide. I'll take my punishment."

She had stopped shaking, and for the first time it occurred to her to wonder why he had been in the ramp at all. "I've certainly interfered with your plans, haven't I,

Garrett? I'm all right now, really, you don't need to nursemaid me.''

"I was coming to see you," he said. "We seemed to have a misunderstanding today, and I thought perhaps it should be sorted out."

"Oh, that." She twisted her snifter in her hands. "I'm awfully sorry about that, for snapping at you and hanging up on you. I wasn't thinking very clearly, you see. For a bit there I really thought that you'd done it on purpose. Trying to get me fired, you know. I didn't know until I talked to your father this afternoon how silly that was."

He merely looked at her, and then down into his brandy.

The silence made the goose bumps start to come back out on her arms.

"You do know that he offered me a job," she said uncertainly. "Don't you?"

Garrett looked at her as if she was suddenly speaking Swahili. "Anne, what's the matter with you?"

She stared at him, while bits of knowledge settled into a new, uncomfortable pattern in her mind. This was the question that had been nagging at her subconscious mind all afternoon, even while she sat there in Jim's office. Why would Jim Garrett offer this opportunity to a second-level employee plucked out of obscurity? There were other people who had far more experience—and seniority.

And the only possible answer was that he would not have considered it, if it hadn't been for Garrett, pulling strings behind the scenes to get her something she was not entitled to. Why? she wondered. What was it he wanted in return?

"Damn you," she said harshly. "Why, Garrett? Just tell me why."

He looked astonished. "What in hell have you got to be angry about? I didn't bend the facts, Anne, I just brought you to my father's attention a little. You weren't going to have much of a chance otherwise."

Something inside her snapped. It was true then, this cold suspicion that was rising from the pit of her stomach. This was not an opportunity she had earned; she was not good enough to have achieved this on her own. She had been insane to think that she could make that leap from newsroom to boardroom. Things just didn't work that way in a business the size of the *Chronicle*. This job was being handed to her simply because Garrett thought she might as well have the job as anybody.

"That's just part of your style, isn't it?" she said sharply. "Anybody could do the job. It's no big deal, so it doesn't matter who gets it. It might as well be someone you'd like to have owing you a favor. Is that it?"

His jaw tightened, but he didn't dispute it.

She pushed away her brandy. "Thanks, Garrett," she said, sarcastically. "But no thanks."

"Don't be such an idiot, Anne. You're cutting off your nose to spite your face. There's nothing wrong with using your contacts."

As if you were only that, she thought drearily. *But I could never work with you now. Not without that hope for a different future . . .*

But she couldn't tell him that, of course. "Garrett, I wouldn't want a job that depended on my knowing you. Now, will you just leave me alone?" She stumbled toward the door.

"Haven't you forgotten something?" he called after her. "We have a date for Sunday morning."

She thought about telling him what to do with his father's precious scholarship fund, but she could not leave unfinished something that had been so important to her. "I'll be ready."

And that will be the end of it, she thought. *I'll go to Door County on Sunday, and it will be over. Then my heart can break, and no one will be the wiser.*

CHAPTER TEN

ANNE WENT BACK to the town house, but she didn't bother to go to bed; she paced the floor instead in an agony of fury and confusion. To have her life's dream dangled so enticingly overhead, and then just as she had persuaded herself that she had only to stretch out her hand and take it, to have it snatched cruelly from her...

But had it been wrenched away? The offer was still good. She could call up Jim Garrett tomorrow—tonight!—and tell him that she would start to work on Monday morning.

It might not be that easy though. Garrett would object, she told herself. After that exchange tonight, he would most certainly have changed his mind. Or was it barely possible that he would not?

What was it he had said? She was cutting off her nose to spite her face if she turned the job down, that was it.

Was he right? Would it actually make any difference to him at all, whether she seized this chance or let it pass by? Or was she simply hurting herself if she turned down this opportunity of a lifetime?

He wouldn't want to work with her after that, she thought. And yet he hadn't said so.

She could still take the job. Regardless of what he thought of her abilities, she knew she was capable. *I could do that job, and I could do it well.* She could surprise him with how good she was, and force him to admit it.

She stopped herself there. Then he'd automatically fall in love with her, she finished brutally. *Well, grow up, McKenna, things don't happen like that. If the only reason you want to take that job is to impress Garrett, you'd better not bother!*

SHE DIDN'T SEE HIM again till Sunday morning. It had been peaceful around the *Chronicle* in the meantime. No disasters or public scandals had pushed their way onto the front page. The curiosity of the newsroom crew about Anne's visit to the executive floor had not abated, but it was quieter, though even the managing editor seemed to be watching Anne with cautious speculation.

That was one of her chief regrets; she would have liked calling him in, once she was settled and comfortable in her new position, and rewriting a few of those awkward newsroom administrative rules.

For she had decided, for the sake of her sanity, not to accept the job. If she was meant to hold that sort of power someday, she concluded, it would have to be somewhere besides Lakemont, and at some newspaper other than the *Chronicle*. Somewhere that she would not have Garrett to deal with.

And after long and thoughtful consideration, she had decided that even if she was not going to be working directly with him, it would be too difficult for her to stay in Lakemont at all. In order to preserve what little peace of mind she had managed to hang on to, she must start looking elsewhere very soon. As soon as she had told Jim of her decision.

She hadn't done that yet. There had not been an opportunity, for he didn't put in another appearance at the

Chronicle, and he didn't get in touch with her. She couldn't bring herself to contact him, for that might mean going to the house, and she didn't want Garrett to be involved in this last discussion. She could not bear to have it all hashed out with him looking on, or sarcastically commenting. Better to wait until the work on the scholarship was completed, and then tell Jim.

But tell him what? She hadn't quite made up her mind if it should be the truth—at least the portion of it that she could tell, that she didn't think she and Garrett would be comfortable co-workers—or if she should simply say that she did not feel up to the job, after all.

She was still debating the question on Sunday morning, when she picked up the *Chronicle* from her doorstep, opened the opinion section and discovered that Garrett had, for the first time in her memory, made an apology in print. An apology to Rudy Balfour.

She read it with her mouth ajar, dumbfounded. It was hardly an abject confession of fault, she concluded. "Restrained repentance" was the best she could say for it. Still, he admitted, seriously and with dignity, that he had gone overboard in his zeal against the modern novel, and for Garrett, that was incredible.

"I wonder if he's seen a doctor lately," she muttered. But just then the doorbell rang, so she scrambled the sections back together and pushed the paper under the coffee table and went to answer the door.

His sports car was a low, sleek silhouette in front of the town house. *It's much faster,* she thought. *We can get there, get done, get back. That's why he brought it instead of the Pierce-Arrow, with its suggestion of a leisurely drive in the country with a picnic lunch and a blanket in the back.*

He had suggested that once. The knowledge that now that lovely day could never happen would have wrenched her heart, if there had been enough left of it to hurt.

He looked impatient, she thought, and no wonder; it must look as if she was staring across the street in a daze! "I'll get my things," she said, and quickly stepped back out of his way to let him come into the small foyer.

"Have you gotten over your fit of pique?" he asked.

She had her back to him, getting her coat from the hall closet, and her hands stilled for a moment on the gray tweed. If he hadn't put it that way, she thought irritably, as if she were no more than a child throwing a tantrum, she might have actually apologized!

He took her coat out of her hands; rather stiffly, she let him help her into it. "I can't think it matters to you."

"Probably not. I just wondered what sort of day I'm in for."

She decided that it would be altogether better to ignore him. "I left my briefcase in the kitchen. I'll just be a minute."

She came back with briefcase and handbag and had stopped to retrieve a couple of sections of the *Chronicle*—if he was going to act like the neighborhood bully, she told herself, she could always hold up the newspaper between them and pretend to read—when the telephone rang.

She might have dismissed it and left the machine to answer, if he hadn't muttered something. It was inaudible, but he sounded disgusted.

"I'll just be a minute," she said mulishly, and went back to the living room to pick it up.

"Anne." It was breathless. "It's Dorie. I'm so glad I caught you in time!"

So am I, I think, Anne mused. She glanced over her shoulder at Garrett.

He intercepted the glance. "If that worried look means this is going to take a while, do you mind if I sit down?" he muttered, and did so.

"We've had a crisis," Dorie went on. "Or the university has, rather, and Ted's tied up with an emergency meeting of the board of trustees. He got a call and went straight out the door without even giving me the details."

"So our conference is off?"

Garrett seemed to perk up.

"That's what I don't know," Dorie said distractedly. "I've got no idea if he'll be gone an hour or all day, so I hardly know what to tell you. I'm just glad I caught you. It would have been awful if you and Matt drove all the way to Door County and found an empty cabin!"

"Yes," Anne said dryly. "You could say it would have been a shock."

"I'll call you back in half an hour or so. I think Ted will let me know by then whether he'll be able to get away, or if we'll have to reschedule."

Anne put the telephone down with a twinge of foreboding that she couldn't quite identify, and told Garrett what had happened.

"That's just great," Garrett said. "So what do we do now?"

Anne sighed. "We wait. Look, I'm not pleased about the delay, either, but at least she called. We could have gotten clear to Door County. As it is, we've got a half hour to kill."

"So what do you suggest we do?" It was almost a challenge. "It hardly makes sense for me to go home. I'd just get there and have to drive straight back to get you, if we're going."

He couldn't have made it plainer, she thought, that he did not care to spend any extra time with her. "You don't have to write it on the wall, Garrett," she said wryly. "I'm reasonably bright. Have a cup of coffee and read the newspaper, and the half hour will be gone before you know it. And you don't have to talk to me, either." She flung her coat across the back of the rocking chair and went to the kitchen to start the coffee. Whether he wanted any or not, she could certainly use another cup.

He followed. "I didn't mean to sound like a bear," he offered.

She bit her tongue. He was obviously making some effort; surely she could do the same. She didn't look at him, but she offered halfheartedly, "I can do bacon and eggs, if you'd like."

He shook his head. "Just coffee, thanks." He settled himself on a stool at the breakfast bar.

She had left dirty dishes in the sink; now she was glad, for it gave her something to do while the coffee was brewing, and let her keep her back almost completely to him. As soon as the coffee was done, she decided, she'd make an excuse and escape upstairs until Dorie called back.

"Have you thought any more about the job, Anne?"

It surprised her that he had brought it up. She waited until the coffeepot was done and pushed an earthenware mug across to him before she said, "I'm not going to take it."

"Why not?"

She ran through a dozen answers in her head while she stirred her coffee, and finally said, without looking at him, "I don't think I'm particularly well suited for it."

He didn't answer.

The unspoken agreement annoyed her, and she went on a bit perversely. "It's all right. You don't have to protect my feelings by denying it. Take last week, for instance. I wasn't very professional, was I?"

"You'd had a shock." He sounded as if the words were being forced from him.

"Yes. Still, it wasn't a very promising recommendation for any job in an executive capacity, where one is apt to get shocks regularly. It must be a relief to you to know you won't have to work with me—" She looked up finally, knowing she would have to face him sometime, and was astounded to see the expression in his eyes, for it was not agreement. It was not satisfaction or relief. It was plain, blank surprise.

But what on earth did Garrett have to be surprised about?

He set down his mug. "We wouldn't be working together, Anne."

"What do you mean? How could we possibly escape it, if you're the publisher, and I'm assistant to—" He shook his head, and Anne stammered to a halt, feeling as if she had run entirely out of breath.

"Didn't my father tell you that I'm not going to be the publisher?"

Anne swallowed hard and said rather wildly, "But he said there would be a new one, soon."

Garrett's eyes dropped to the dark liquid in his cup, and then rose to her face again. "He meant you, Anne," he said quietly. "If things work out, and if you want the job."

She had to lean rather hard against the breakfast bar to keep her feet from sliding out from under her.

"He probably didn't come straight out with it because he didn't want to raise your hopes too high just yet, until he was certain it would work out. But that's what he intends."

She edged around the end of the breakfast bar and fumbled for a stool.

"Give me some credit, Anne," he said. "I might not want the job myself, but I have plenty of respect for it. It's not something just anyone could do." He looked at her closely and shook his head in astonishment. "Anne, you can't have actually believed that I'd propose you for this job just because I wanted to blackmail you into bed with me or something?"

No, she almost said. *I never thought that . . . quite.*

"I thought you said all those wild things because you were so upset that night we talked about it, and because you didn't want to feel you owed me anything. I never dreamed you were serious."

"I *was* upset," she said. "And uncertain of myself. And, no, I don't want to owe you anything. Dammit, Garrett, I'm a city editor and not even the only one the *Chronicle* has. It was insane to think I could just jump all the way to the top of the corporation. Things don't happen that way!"

"Sometimes they do. Oh, you're not ready yet, that's certain. You said yourself there needs to be a long training and transition period. But then Dad isn't ready to let go of things for a while, either. He's found out this week, sitting around the house, that orchids aren't very challenging. He prefers things that talk back."

She was hardly listening. "Garrett, why did you tell me I could hold the press that night?"

He shook his head. "I was thinking that in a few weeks they'd be calling you for permission instead of the other way around, so why waste the time? I probably shouldn't have said anything at all." He tipped up his mug thoughtfully. After a full minute, when she still hadn't spoken, he added very quietly, "Is that why you turned it down, Anne? Because you couldn't bear to work with me?"

It was such a tidy answer, she thought. And it encompassed such a tiny fraction of the truth.

"Take it, Anne," he whispered. "It's what I want for you more than anything in the world. You won't have to worry about me. You don't owe me anything."

She shivered a little. As if it was so easy, she thought.

He added quickly, "I didn't do anything, anyway, except suggest that Dad ask you about the scholarship. It was only a way to bring you to his attention. Eventually he'd have decided to retire, and started to look around, and I don't think he'd have missed you. But, well, I'd like to think it's better this way. Please, Anne, take it. I give you my word, I'll stay out of your way."

The promise chilled her heart. She slid off the stool and went to get another cup of coffee. She didn't want it, but it was something to do with her hands.

He squared his shoulders a little and went on. "You wouldn't like to leave Lakemont now, surely. I understand Rudy's going to be offered tenure next year, on the strength of his book."

She slipped and poured coffee over her fingers. "Damn! That's nice. For Rudy, I mean. Where do you find out all these things, Garrett? Was there a list in the *Chronicle* or something?"

There was a half second of silence. "Do you mean you didn't know about it?"

"I haven't seen him."

"But—" he said slowly, as if he was thinking very hard. "When he was waiting for you here when we came back from Door County, and you so clearly wanted to get rid of me...it was to send him away?"

She nodded. There was nothing else she could do.

"But the next day when I asked if you'd patched it up, and you got silent and went all pink and lovely while you thought about him, well, it was obvious that Rudy was the one who mattered." It was almost a challenge.

She remembered. It had been in that little room of his mother's, and it had been Garrett she was thinking about just then. Garrett, and how much she loved him. "No." It was all she could manage; her tongue seemed suddenly unmanageable.

"Then it wasn't Rudy that you were busy with, too busy for this trip today?"

"No." *Stop it,* she wanted to say. *Stop stripping my pride away.* And yet, underneath, there was a whisper of hope.

"Anne," he said huskily. "Words have always been my business—my best talent. And now that I need them, the right ones just aren't there. I shouldn't even be trying to say this. It's too soon. But if you're not in love with Rudy, please, let me start again. We haven't had a chance."

She closed her eyes. *It can't be real,* she thought. *I'm making it up.* But the whisper, that nagging little voice of hope, was growing steadily louder.

"Just when I was beginning to think we might have something very special," he went on, "I messed it up. I was very clumsy. I rushed you and then I insulted you. My God, Anne, how could you think I was offended because you've never slept with anyone?"

"Offended?" she managed. "You were terrified."

"Yes, I was. I was afraid that if I lost control, your first experience would not be what I wanted it to be. I didn't want it to be hurried and embarrassed and sordid somehow. I can't think of anything worse than a flagstone floor with a chicken salad sandwich smashed all over it. That's not very romantic even to think about, is it? I'm sorry." He paused and said in almost a whisper, "I still wish you'd tell me, you know, why you've waited."

She looked down at her hands, clamped together on her cup as if it were a lifeline.

He pushed aside his mug and slid off the stool. "I'm sorry, I'm embarrassing you. I'll get out of your way. Let me know if Dorie calls."

She was too stunned to move. *I can't let him go now,* she thought. *Not now.* "Garrett!"

"You will think again about taking the job?"

She nodded. "Garrett—" It was only a whisper; it was all she could manage. She looked down at her hands and said, "I've never slept with anyone because making love is not just a physical act for me. It's everything, body and heart and soul, and I've never found any man I trust enough to let him have... all of me... like that."

It was scarcely audible at the end, and her lashes dropped; she knew he had moved slowly closer in order to hear. His index finger brushed her cheek softly, and he said, "Anne, may I try, someday, to be that man?"

Wide-eyed, she stared up at him.

"I'll be patient," he said dryly, and added almost under his breath, "at least, I'll learn to be."

Her breath was coming quick and shallow, and she was almost light-headed. If he didn't understand what she was telling him, what on earth else could she do? And then she remembered.

"That night at the cabin, by the fire," she said. "You told me the next day to let you know whenever I decided whether I was angry at you for trying to make love to me, or for not doing it."

"I did? I have no idea what I said that day. I was so frustrated with myself—"

"Matt," she said softly. "Shut up."

He stopped abruptly.

"I know now. It was because I thought you didn't want all of me."

Garrett exhaled as if something very solid had hit him right beneath the breastbone. And then, before she knew quite what had happened, he was holding her so tightly that she thought she would never be able to breathe again, and he was kissing her lips, her eyelids, her temples, her ears, her chin, and he was whispering things that she had never dreamed he would say, things that she thought she could never grow tired of hearing.

But finally he held her a little away from him and said firmly, "I love you, you know."

"That's positively the nicest line I've ever heard you use."

"Beginner's luck," he said contentedly. "But I'll practice. Now, answers please. Will you marry me, and argue happily ever after?"

She frowned a little. "It's so sudden, Garrett. What if it's wrong? What if it's not love after all?"

His arms tightened around her. "Does it feel wrong?"

"No, but—"

"We could wait years, and it wouldn't make a difference to me. What about you?"

"No," she whispered.

"Then why waste the time?"

She smiled, but she said, "There are a couple of things I still don't understand, you know."

"Such as?"

"Well, you kept saying you'd be too busy to take on obligations, like teaching a class, or administering the scholarship. So I thought surely you must mean that taking over your father's job was going to absorb too much time to let you do those other things."

He tweaked the end of her nose gently. "And now you're wondering if I intend to be a slothful husband and a drain on my hardworking wife?"

She colored a little. "Not quite, but what on earth did you mean?"

"There are people who should be teachers, and there are people who shouldn't, and I'm in the second group. All right?"

She nodded. "I suppose so, but—"

"As for the scholarship, I'll admit that I twisted the truth a little there. I have every intention of keeping my fingers on that scholarship fund. As a matter of fact, I'm to be officially appointed as chairman of the Garrett Institute, as soon as it's officially set up."

"What?" she gasped.

"Don't get bigheaded, it wasn't entirely your idea. I'm just as determined as my father is that the *Chronicle* remain independent, and this seemed the best way to ensure it. The institute will own a controlling interest in the newspaper, and use the profits for charitable purposes. I expect it to keep me as busy as I ever want to be." He grinned down at her, and his arms tightened. "Look at it this way, Anne. You'll be in charge of making the family money, and I'll take care of spending it."

"So you do have some management instincts after all," she mused. "Are you certain that you don't want to try being publisher?"

He shuddered. "Absolutely. I'm far too much of an iconoclast to ever be successful at the job."

"But that's not really you," she said absently. "You only do that to get people's attention." *Now I understand what he meant when he said I didn't really know him, only the columnist,* she thought. *There is a great deal of difference between Garrett the columnist and Matt the man. And I will have all my life to figure them both out. . . .* The realization sent a little shiver of pure happiness through every nerve.

"I thought I'd convinced my father years ago that I didn't want his job," Garrett went on. "I didn't know he had resurrected that old hope until you dropped the news on me, you know—and bless you for the warning."

"So you got busy right away working yourself out of it."

"You could say that. And just in case you're still worried about what I'm going to do with what's left of my time," he added, "there will be a book next year, a collection of my favorite columns. If it sells well, there will be others. And if you're going to be out making the world safe for journalists, somebody will have to stay home and supervise baths and bedtimes for a couple of little Garretts, I hope."

She turned a very delicate shell pink. "Several of them."

"Several?" He sounded a bit surprised, but not displeased. "Well, that will let us check out your theory on whether the urge to run a newspaper carries through the genetic code— There's the phone. I don't wish problems for Ted, but I really don't want to go up to Door

County today." He shifted his grip on Anne and reached for the telephone.

She could hear a masculine voice, not Ted's, though, surely. Then Garrett winked at her and said deliberately, "Yes, Dad, Dorie caught us. But thanks for passing on the message. By the way, Anne's going to take the job. And me, too." A moment later he abruptly put the telephone to her ear. "He wants to talk to you."

There wasn't time to think, or even panic. "Hello, Jim. I hope—"

"Welcome to the family," Jim said heartily. "It's a good thing I held on to those pearls, wouldn't you say? They'll go nicely with white satin on your wedding day." He added blandly, "I thought they might."

For an instant, the suspicion, the doubts that had caused her such trouble in the past few days tugged at her again. "Jim," she said, "you wouldn't do this just because I'm going to be family, would you?"

"Hell, no. Perhaps you haven't noticed, but I haven't promoted Matt!"

"Only because he didn't want the job."

"Well, that did discourage me, yes. But seriously, Anne, it's not only your work that impresses me, it's the way you think."

"That's terrifying."

Garrett, who was kissing the nape of her neck, stopped at that and raised his eyebrows. She shook her head at him; he went back to toying with the hair at the back of her neck.

"Take your arrangements for the scholarship, for instance," Jim said. "There were a hundred ways to do that, but the ones you chose were so close to what I would have done that I could almost believe I did it myself. And the Garrett Institute, that was sheer genius."

Oh? Not entirely my idea, was it? Anne thought with satisfaction.

"I think you'll make the same decisions in my name that I'd have made. And if someday you feel ready for the top job—"

Garrett took back the telephone. "This is not a business conference, Dad. She isn't working for you just yet."

Anne heard Jim laugh and then say, "All right, Matt. Let me know when to start forcing my white orchids to bloom for the wedding bouquet."

"Go give them their orders right now," Garrett said firmly. "Though if it takes long, I'm not going to promise we'll wait for them. And now we've got an awful lot to talk about, Dad, so if you don't mind..." He broke the connection and left the receiver on the countertop so no more calls could come through.

"You know," Anne said demurely, "I've been thinking. I didn't say I was waiting for my wedding, just for—"

"You didn't?" He reached for her again, and his kiss left her breathless and aching.

"Rudy had me scared, you know," he whispered. "As soon as it was too late to withdraw that damned column, I began to think I'd gone too far, that you'd have to defend him. And sure enough, you did."

"You apologized very nicely, though," she murmured. "I was impressed. You'll have to start doing that more often."

He held her off a little. "Don't get ideas," he warned. "I don't take orders from any publisher, even if she's my wife."

"Oh, I wasn't thinking of ordering you to do anything. I have great faith in my powers of persuasion."

Garrett grinned. "I'm not bad at that sort of thing myself."

"Really? I don't suppose you'd like to prove it."

HE WAS RIGHT, she decided contentedly, much later. He was very good at persuasion...and all that sort of thing.

my VALENTINE 1992

Celebrate the most romantic day of the year with
MY VALENTINE 1992—a sexy new collection of four
romantic stories written by our famous Temptation
authors:

GINA WILKINS
KRISTINE ROLOFSON
JOANN ROSS
VICKI LEWIS THOMPSON

My Valentine 1992—an exquisite escape into a romantic
and sensuous world.

 Harlequin Books

VAL-92-R

HARLEQUIN
PROUDLY PRESENTS
A DAZZLING NEW CONCEPT IN ROMANCE FICTION

One small town—twelve terrific love stories

Welcome to Tyler, Wisconsin—a town full of people
you'll enjoy getting to know, memorable friends and
unforgettable lovers, and a long-buried secret that
lurks beneath its serene surface....

JOIN US FOR A YEAR IN THE LIFE OF TYLER

Each book set in Tyler is a self-contained love story;
together, the twelve novels stitch the fabric of a
community.

LOSE YOUR HEART TO TYLER!

The excitement begins in March 1992, with
WHIRLWIND, by Nancy Martin. When lively, brash
Liza Baron arrives home unexpectedly, she moves
into the old family lodge, where the silent and
mysterious Cliff Forrester has been living in seclusion
for years....

WATCH FOR ALL TWELVE BOOKS
OF THE TYLER SERIES
Available wherever Harlequin books are sold

Back by Popular Demand

Janet Dailey
Americana

A romantic tour of America through fifty favorite
Harlequin Presents, each set in a different state
researched by Janet and her husband, Bill. A journey
of a lifetime in one cherished collection.

In January, don't miss the exciting states featured in:

Title #23 MINNESOTA
Giant of Mesabi

#24 MISSISSIPPI
A Tradition of Pride

Available wherever
Harlequin books are sold.

HARLEQUIN'S "BIG WIN"
SWEEPSTAKES RULES & REGULATIONS

NO PURCHASE NECESSARY TO ENTER OR RECEIVE A PRIZE

1. Alternate means of entry: Print your name and address on a 3″ ×5″ piece of plain paper and send to the appropriate address below:

In the U.S.	In Canada
Harlequin's "BIG WIN" Sweepstakes	Harlequin's "BIG WIN" Sweepstakes
P.O. Box 1867	P.O. Box 609
3010 Walden Ave.	Fort Erie, Ontario
Buffalo, NY 14269-1867	L2A 5X3

2. To enter the Sweepstakes and join the Reader Service, scratch off the metallic strips on all of your BIG WIN tickets #1-#6. This will reveal the values for each Sweepstakes entry number, the number of free books you will receive and your free bonus gift as part of our Reader Service. If you do not wish to take advantage of our Reader Service but wish to enter the Sweepstakes only, scratch off the metallic strips on your BIG WIN tickets #1-#4. Return your entire sheet of tickets intact. Incomplete and/or inaccurate entries are ineligible for that section or sections of prizes. Torstar Corp. and its affiliates are not responsible for mutilated or unreadable entries or inadvertent printing errors. Mechanically reproduced entries are null and void.

3. Whether you take advantage of this offer or not, on or about April 30, 1992, at the offices of D. L. Blair, Inc., Blair, NE, your Sweepstakes numbers will be compared against the list of winning numbers generated at random by the computer. However, prizes will only be awarded to individuals who have entered the Sweepstakes. In the event that all prizes are not claimed, a random drawing will be held from all qualified entries received from March 30, 1990 to March 31, 1992, to award all unclaimed prizes. All cash prizes (Grand to Sixth) will be mailed to the winners and are payable by check in U.S. funds. Seventh Prize will be shipped to winners via third-class mail. These prizes are in addition to any free, surprise or mystery gifts that might be offered. Versions of this Sweepstakes with different prizes of approximate equal value may appear at retail outlets or in other mailings by Torstar Corp. and its affiliates.

4. Prizes: (1) ★ Grand Prize $1,000,000.00 Annuity; (1)First Prize $25,000.00; (1)Second Prize $10,000.00; (5)Third Prize $5,000.00; (10)Fourth Prize $1,000.00; (100)Fifth Prize $250.00; (2,500)Sixth Prize $10.00; (6,000) ★ ★ Seventh Prize $12.95 ARV.

   ★ This presentation offers a Grand Prize of a $1,000,000.00 annuity. Winner will receive $33,333.33 a year for 30 years without interest totalling $1,000,000.00.

   ★ ★ Seventh Prize: A fully illustrated hardcover book published by Torstar Corp. Approximate Retail Value of the book is $12.95.

   Entrants may cancel the Reader Service at any time without cost or obligation (see details in Center Insert Card).

5. This Sweepstakes is being conducted under the supervision of D. L. Blair, Inc. By entering this Sweepstakes, each entrant accepts and agrees to be bound by these rules and the decisions of the judges, which shall be final and binding. Odds of winning in the random drawing are dependent upon the number of entries received. Taxes, if any, are the sole responsibility of the winners. Prizes are nontransferable. All entries must be received at the address on the detachable Business Reply Card and must be postmarked no later than 12:00 MIDNIGHT on March 31, 1992. The drawing for all unclaimed Sweepstakes prizes will take place on May 30, 1992, at 12:00 NOON, at the offices of D. L. Blair, Inc., Blair, NE.

6. This offer is open to residents of the U.S., the United Kingdom, France, Germany and Canada, 18 years or older, except employees and immediate family members of Torstar Corp., its affiliates, subsidiaries, and all the other agencies, entities and persons connected with the use, marketing or conduct of this Sweepstakes. All Federal, State, Provincial, Municipal and local laws apply. Void wherever prohibited or restricted by law. Any litigation within the Province of Quebec respecting the conduct and awarding of a prize in this publicity contest must be submitted to the Régie des loteries et courses du Québec.

7. Winners will be notified by mail and may be required to execute an affidavit of eligibility and release, which must be returned within 14 days after notification or an alternate winner will be selected. Canadian winners will be required to correctly answer an arithmetical, skill-testing question administered by mail, which must be returned within a limited time. Winners consent to the use of their name, photograph and/or likeness for advertising and publicity in conjunction with this and similar promotions without additional compensation.

8. For a list of our major prize winners, send a stamped, self-addressed ENVELOPE to: WINNERS LIST, P.O. Box 4510, Blair, NE 68009. Winners Lists will be supplied after the May 30, 1992 drawing date.

Offer limited to one per household.

© 1991 Harlequin Enterprises Limited   Printed in the U.S.A.

BWH192

HARLEQUIN Temptation

Rebels & Rogues

All men are not created equal. Some are rough around the edges. Tough-minded but tenderhearted. Incredibly sexy. The tempting fulfillment of every woman's fantasy.

When it's time to fight for what they believe in, to win that special woman, our Rebels and Rogues are heroes at heart.

Josh: He swore never to play the hero . . . unless the price was right.

THE PRIVATE EYE by Jayne Ann Krentz. Temptation #377, January 1992.

Matt: A hard man to forget . . . and an even harder man not to love.

THE HOOD by Carin Rafferty. Temptation #381, February 1992.

At Temptation, 1992 is the Year of Rebels and Rogues. Look for twelve exciting stories about bold and courageous men, one each month. Don't miss upcoming books from your favorite authors, including Candace Schuler, JoAnn Ross and Janice Kaiser.

Available wherever Harlequin books are sold. RR-1